THE LONEY

ANDREW MICHAEL HURLEY

LARGE
PRINT

First published in Great Britain 2016
by
John Murray (Publishers)

First Isis Edition
published 2017
by arrangement with
John Murray (Publishers)
An Hachette UK Company

A catalogue record for this book is available from the British Library.

ISBN 978–1–78541–307–0 (hb)
ISBN 978–1–78541–313–1 (pb)

Published by
F. A. Thorpe (Publishing)
Anstey, Leicestershire

Set by Words & Graphics Ltd.
Anstey, Leicestershire
Printed and bound in Great Britain by
T. J. International Ltd., Padstow, Cornwall

This book is printed on acid-free paper

THE LONEY

When a flood exposes the remains of a long-dead baby on the Loney — a desolate stretch of Lancastrian coastline raked by treacherous tides — Smith is catapulted back to his youth and an Easter Catholic pilgrimage to a shrine there. His brother Hanny was mute as a child, and his devout parents hoped for a miracle that would enable him to talk. But the mournful, rain-soaked Loney is full of enigmas for the boys: Miracles. Death. Superstition. Hidden rooms. Their sinister accommodation — a taxidermist's house. The new, younger priest leading the pilgrimage in place of the zealous, ritual-obsessed Father Wilfred, who died in mysterious circumstances. Something terrible is about to happen — something that will stay with Smith forever, no matter how hard he tries to forget . . .

SPECIAL MESSAGE TO READERS

THE ULVERSCROFT FOUNDATION
(registered UK charity number 264873)
was established in 1972 to provide funds for
research, diagnosis and treatment of eye diseases.
Examples of major projects funded by
the Ulverscroft Foundation are:-

- The Children's Eye Unit at Moorfields Eye Hospital, London
- The Ulverscroft Children's Eye Unit at Great Ormond Street Hospital for Sick Children
- Funding research into eye diseases and treatment at the Department of Ophthalmology, University of Leicester
- The Ulverscroft Vision Research Group, Institute of Child Health
- Twin operating theatres at the Western Ophthalmic Hospital, London
- The Chair of Ophthalmology at the Royal Australian College of Ophthalmologists

You can help further the work of the Foundation
by making a donation or leaving a legacy.
Every contribution is gratefully received. If you
would like to help support the Foundation or
require further information, please contact:

THE ULVERSCROFT FOUNDATION
**The Green, Bradgate Road, Anstey
Leicester LE7 7FU, England
Tel: (0116) 236 4325**

website: www.foundation.ulverscroft.com

For Ray and Rosalie

While they were going out, a man who was demon-possessed and could not talk was brought to Jesus. And when the demon was driven out, the man who had been mute spoke. The crowd was amazed and said, "Nothing like this has ever been seen in Israel." But the Pharisees said, "It is by the prince of demons that he drives out demons."

Matthew 9:32–34

And what rough beast, its hour come round at last,
Slouches towards Bethlehem to be born?

W. B. Yeats, "The Second Coming"

CHAPTER
ONE

It had certainly been a wild end to the autumn. On the Heath a gale stripped the glorious blaze of colour from Kenwood to Parliament Hill in a matter of hours, leaving several old oaks and beeches dead. Mist and silence followed and then, after a few days, there was only the smell of rotting and bonfires.

I spent so long there with my notebook one afternoon noting down all that had fallen that I missed my session with Doctor Baxter. He told me not to worry. About the appointment or the trees. Both he and Nature would recover. Things were never as bad as they seemed.

I suppose he was right in a way. We'd been let off lightly. In the north, train lines had been submerged and whole villages swamped by brown river water. There had been pictures of folk bailing out their living rooms, dead cattle floating down an A road. Then, latterly, the news about the sudden landslide on Coldbarrow, and the baby they'd found tumbled down with the old house at the foot of the cliffs.

Coldbarrow. There was a name I hadn't heard for a long time. Not for thirty years. No one I knew mentioned it any more and I'd tried very hard to forget it myself. But I suppose I always knew that what happened there wouldn't stay hidden forever, no matter how much I wanted it to.

I lay down on my bed and thought about calling Hanny, wondering if he too had seen the news and whether it meant anything to him. I'd never really asked him what he remembered about the place. But what I would say, where I would begin, I didn't know. And in any case he was a difficult man to get hold of. The church kept him so busy that he was always out ministering to the old and infirm or fulfilling his duties to one committee or another. I could hardly leave a message, not about this.

His book was on the shelf with the old paperbacks I'd been meaning to donate to the charity shop for years. I took it down and ran my finger over the embossed lettering of the title and then looked at the back cover. Hanny and Caroline in matching white shirts and the two boys, Michael and Peter, grinning and freckled, enclosed in their parents' arms. The happy family of Pastor Andrew Smith.

The book had been published almost a decade ago now and the boys had grown up — Michael was starting in the upper sixth at Cardinal Hume and Peter was in his final year at Corpus Christi — but Hanny and Caroline looked much the same then as they did now. Youthful, settled, in love.

I went to put the book back on the shelf and noticed that there were some newspaper cuttings inside the dust jacket. Hanny visiting a hospice in Guildford. A review of his book in the *Evening Standard*. The

2

Guardian interview that had really thrust him into the limelight. And the clipping from an American evangelical magazine when he'd gone over to do the Southern university circuit.

The success of *My Second Life with God* had taken everyone by surprise, not least Hanny himself. It was one of those books that — how did they put it in the paper? — captured the imagination, summed up the Zeitgeist. That kind of thing. I suppose there must have been something in it that people liked. It had bounced around the top twenty of the bestsellers list for months and made his publisher a small fortune.

Everyone had heard of Pastor Smith even if they hadn't read his book. And now, with the news from Coldbarrow, it seemed likely that they would be hearing of him again unless I got everything down on paper and struck the first blow, so to speak.

CHAPTER
TWO

If it had another name, I never knew, but the locals called it the Loney — that strange nowhere between the Wyre and the Lune where Hanny and I went every Easter time with Mummer, Farther, Mr and Mrs Belderboss and Father Wilfred, the parish priest. It was our week of penitence and prayer in which we would make our confessions, visit Saint Anne's shrine, and look for God in the emerging springtime, that, when it came, was hardly a spring at all; nothing so vibrant and effusive. It was more the soggy afterbirth of winter.

Dull and featureless it may have looked, but the Loney was a dangerous place. A wild and useless length of English coastline. A dead mouth of a bay that filled and emptied twice a day and made Coldbarrow — a desolate spit of land a mile off the coast into an island. The tides could come in quicker than a horse could run and every year a few people drowned. Unlucky fishermen were blown off course and ran aground. Opportunist cocklepickers, ignorant of what they were dealing with, drove their trucks onto the sands at low tide and washed up weeks later with green faces and skin like lint.

Sometimes these tragedies made the news, but there was such an inevitability about the Loney's cruelty that more often than not these souls went unremembered to join the countless others that had perished there over the centuries in trying to tame the place. The evidence of old industry was everywhere: breakwaters had been mashed to gravel by storms, jetties abandoned in the sludge and all that remained of the old causeway to Coldbarrow was a line of rotten black posts that gradually disappeared under the mud. And there were other, more mysterious structures — remnants of jerry-built shacks where they had once gutted mackerel for the markets inland, beacons with rusting fire-braces, the stump of a wooden lighthouse on the headland that had guided sailors and shepherds through the fickle shift of the sands.

But it was impossible to truly know the Loney. It changed with each influx and retreat of water and the neap tides would reveal the skeletons of those who thought they had read the place well enough to escape its insidious currents. There were animals, people sometimes, the remains of both once — a drover and his sheep cut off and drowned on the old crossing from Cumbria. And now, since their death, for a century or more, the Loney had been pushing their bones back inland, as if it were proving a point.

No one with any knowledge of the place ever went near the water. No one apart from us and Billy Tapper that is.

★ ★ ★

Billy was a local drunk. Everyone knew him. His fall from grace to failure was fixed like the weather into the mythology of the place, and he was nothing short of a gift to people like Mummer and Father Wilfred who used him as shorthand for what drink could do to a man. Billy Tapper wasn't a person, but a punishment.

Legend had it that he had been a music teacher at a boys' grammar school, or the head of a girls' school in Scotland, or down south, or in Hull, somewhere, anywhere. His history varied from person to person, but that the drink had sent him mad was universally accepted and there were any number of stories about his eccentricities. He lived in a cave. He had killed someone in Whitehaven with a hammer. He had a daughter somewhere. He thought that collecting certain combinations of stones and shells made him invisible and would often stagger into the Bell and Anchor in Little Hagby, his pockets chinking with shingle, and try to drink from other people's glasses, thinking that they couldn't see him. Hence the dented nose.

I wasn't sure how much of it was true, but it didn't matter. Once you'd seen Billy Tapper, anything they said about him seemed possible.

We first met him in the pebble-dashed concrete bus stop on the one road that skirted the coastline from Morecambe down to Knott End. It would have been 1973, when I was twelve and Hanny sixteen. Farther wasn't with us. He had gone out early with Father Wilfred and Mr and Mrs Belderboss to look at the stained glass in a village church twenty miles away where there was apparently a magnificent Gothic Revival window of Jesus calming the waters. And so Mummer had decided to take Hanny and me to Lancaster to stock up on food and visit an exhibition of old Psalters at the library — for Mummer never missed an opportunity to instruct us on the history of our faith. It looked like Billy was going the same way from the piece of cardboard strung around his neck — one of the several dozen that made it easy for the bus drivers to know where he was supposed to be going.

The other places he'd either been to or might need to visit revealed themselves as he stirred in his sleep. Kendal. Preston. Manchester. Hull. The last being where his sister lived, according to the square of bright red card that was attached to a separate shoestring necklace and contained information that might prove invaluable in an emergency, with his name, his sister's telephone number and a note in block capitals that he was allergic to penicillin.

This particular fact intrigued me as a child, and I wondered what would happen if he *was* given penicillin, whether it could possibly damage him any more than he had damaged himself already. I'd never seen a man be so unkind to his own body. His fingers and his palms were shattered with filth. Every crease and line was brown. Either side of his broken nose his eyes were twisted deep down into his skull. His hair crawled past his ears and down his neck which had turned sea-coloured with dozens of tattoos. There was something faintly heroic about his refusal to wash, I thought, when Hanny and I were so regularly scrubbed and towelled by Mummer.

He slumped on the bench, with an empty bottle of something evil lying on its side on the floor and a small, mouldy-looking potato in his lap that comforted me in a strange way. It seemed right that he should only have a raw potato. It was the kind of thing I assumed down-and-outs ate, nibbling at it bit by bit over weeks as they roamed the highways and byways looking for the next. Hitching lifts. Stealing what they could. Stowing away on trains. As I say, vagrancy wasn't entirely without its romance to me at that age.

He talked to himself in his sleep, scrunching his pockets — which, like everyone said, sounded as if they were full of stones — complaining bitterly about someone called O'Leary who owed him money and had never given it back to him, even though he owned a horse. When he woke up and noticed we were there he tried his best to be courteous and sober, offering a grin of three or four twisted black teeth and doffing his beret at Mummer, who smiled briefly but, as she managed to do with all strangers, got the measure of him instantly, and sat in a half-revolted, half-fearful silence, willing the bus to come by staring down the empty road.

Like most drunks, Billy bypassed the small talk and slapped his bleeding, broken heart into my palm like a lump of raw beef.

"Don't get taken in by the demon drink, lads. I've lost everything 'cause of this stuff," he said as he held up the bottle and swilled the dregs. "See that scar?"

He raised his hand and shook his sleeve down. A red seam ran from his wrist to his elbow, threading its way through tattoos of daggers and melon-chested girls.

"D'you know how I got that?"

I shook my head. Hanny stared.

"Fell off a roof. Bone ripped right through it," he said and used his finger to demonstrate the angle at which his ulna had protruded.

"Have you got a spare fag?"

I shook my head again and he sighed.

"Bollocks. I knew I should have stayed at Catterick," came another non-sequitur.

It was difficult to tell — and he looked nothing like the ruggedly handsome veterans that popped up in my *Commando* comics all the time — but I guessed that he must have been of an age to have fought in the war. And sure enough, when he doubled up in a coughing fit and took off his beret to wipe his mouth, it had some cockeyed metal, military insignia on the front.

I wondered if that was what had set him onto the booze, the war. It had done strange things to some people, so Farther said. Knocked their compasses out of whack, as it were.

Whatever the reason, Hanny and I couldn't take our eyes off him. We gorged ourselves on his dirtiness, on his brutal, alien smell. It was the same fearful excitement we felt when we happened to drive through what Mummer considered a *bad* part of London and found ourselves lost in a maze of terraces that sat shoulder to shoulder with industrial plants and scrapyards. We would turn in our seats and gawp out of the windows at the scruffy, staring children who had no toys but the bits of wood and metal torn off the broken furniture in their front yards where aproned women stood and screeched obscenities at the men stumbling out of corner pubs. It was a safari park of degradation. What a world without God looked like.

Billy glanced at Mummer and, keeping his eyes on her, he reached down into the plastic bag by his feet and brought out a few tatty bits of paper, which he pressed into my hand. They had been ripped out of a dirty magazine.

He winked at me and settled himself back against the wall. The bus appeared and Mummer stood up and held out her hand to stop it and I quickly stuffed the pictures away.

"What are you doing?" said Mummer.

"Nothing."

"Well, stop messing about and get Andrew ready."

I started trying to coax Hanny into standing so that we could get on the bus, but he wouldn't move. He was smiling and looking past me at Billy, who by this time had fallen asleep again.

"What is it, Hanny?"

He looked at me and then back at Billy. Then I understood what he was staring at: Billy wasn't holding a potato, but his penis.

The bus stopped and we got on. The driver looked past us and whistled at Billy but he didn't wake up. After another go, the driver shook his head and pressed the button which drew the door closed. We sat down and watched the front of Billy's trousers darken.

Mummer tutted and peeled our faces away from the window to look at her instead.

"Be warned," she said, as the bus pulled away. "That man is already inside you. It won't take more than a few wrong choices to bring him out, believe me."

She held her handbag on her lap and looked straight ahead. I clutched the dirty pictures tight in one hand and slipped the other inside my coat and pressed my stomach hard with my fingertips, trying to find the kernel of badness that only needed the right conditions of Godlessness and depravity for it to germinate and spread like a weed.

It happened so easily. Drink quickly possessed a man and made him its servant. Father Wilfred always said so.

When Mummer told him about Billy later that evening, he simply shook his head and sighed.

"What can one expect of a man like that, Mrs Smith? Someone so removed from God."

"I said to the boys that they ought to take note," said Mummer.

"And rightly so," he said, taking off his glasses and looking at Hanny and me as he polished them on his sleeve. "They should make it their business to know all the poisons that Satan peddles."

"I feel rather sorry for him," said Mrs Belderboss.

"So do I," said Farther.

Father Wilfred put his glasses back on and raised a brief, condescending smile.

"Then you'll be adding to his already brimming store. Pity is the only thing a drunk has in abundance."

"Still, he must have had an awfully hard life to have got himself into such a state," Mrs Belderboss said.

Father Wilfred scoffed. "I don't think he knows the meaning of a hard life. I'm sure my brother could tell you as many tales as I could about real poverty, real struggle, couldn't you, Reginald?"

Mr Belderboss nodded. "Everyone had it tough in Whitechapel," he said. "No work. Kiddies starving."

Mrs Belderboss touched her husband's arm in sympathy. Father Wilfred sat back and wiped his mouth with a napkin.

"No, a man like that is the worst kind of fool," he said. "He's thrown everything away. All his privileges and opportunities. He was a professional, I believe. A teacher. What a terrible waste."

It's odd, but when I was a child there were certain things that were so clear to me and their outcomes so inevitable that I thought I had a kind of sixth sense. A gift of foresight, like that of Elijah or Ezekiel, who had predicted drought and destruction with such unsettling accuracy.

I remember Hanny once swinging over a pond on the Heath and knowing, *knowing*, that the rope would break, which it did; like I knew that the stray cat he brought back from the park would end up minced on the tube line, and that he would drop the bowl of goldfish he'd won at the fair on the kitchen floor as soon as we got home.

In the same way, I knew after that conversation around the dinner table that Billy was going to die soon. The thought came to me as an established fact; as though it had already come to pass. No one could live like that for long. Being that filthy took so much effort that I was sure that the same merciful God who sent a whale to save Jonah and gave Noah a nod about the weather, would put him out of his misery.

CHAPTER
THREE

That Easter was the last time we went to the Loney for several years.

After the evening when he'd set us straight about Billy Tapper over supper, Father Wilfred changed in a way that no one could quite explain or understand. They put it down to him getting too old for the whole thing — after all it was a long journey up from London and the pressure of being shepherd to his flock during such an intense week of prayer and reflection was enough to wear out a man half his age. He was tired. That was all.

But as I had the uncanny knack of sensing the truth about things, I knew that it was something far more than that. There was something very wrong.

After the conversation about Billy had petered out and everyone had settled in the living room, he'd walked down to the beach and come back a different man. Distracted. Rattled by something. He complained rather unconvincingly of a stomach upset and went to lie down, locking his door with an emphatic swipe of the bolt. A little while later I heard noises coming from his room, and I realised he was crying. I'd never heard a man cry before, except for one of the mentally disadvantaged lot that came to do crafts at the parish hall once a fortnight with Mummer and some of the other ladies. It was a noise of fear and despair.

The next morning when he finally rose, dishevelled and still agitated, he muttered something about the sea and went out with his camera before anyone could ask him what was wrong. It wasn't like him to be so offhand. Nor for him to sleep in so late. He wasn't himself at all.

Everyone watched him walking down the lane and decided it was best to leave as soon as possible, convinced that once he was back at Saint Jude's he would quickly recover.

But when we returned home, his mood of fretfulness barely altered. In his sermons he seemed more worked up than ever about the ubiquitous evils of the world and any mention of the pilgrimage cast a shadow over his face and sent him into a kind of anxious daydream. After a while no one talked about going there any more. It was just something that we used to do.

Life pulled us along and we forgot about the Loney until 1976 when Father Wilfred died suddenly in the new year and Father Bernard McGill was relocated from some violent parish in New Cross to take on Saint Jude's in his stead.

After his inaugural Mass, at which the bishop presented him to the congregation, we had tea and cakes on the presbytery lawn so that Father Bernard could meet his parishioners in a less formal setting.

He ingratiated himself straight away and seemed at ease with everyone. He had that way about him. An easy charm that made the old boys laugh and the women unconsciously preen themselves.

As he went from group to group, the bishop wandered over to Mummer and me, trying to eat a large piece of Dundee cake in as dignified a manner as possible. He had taken off his robes and his surplice but kept on his plum-coloured cassock, so that he stood out amongst the browns and greys of the civilians as a man of importance.

"He seems nice, your Grace," said Mummer.

"Indeed," the bishop replied in his Midlothian accent that for some reason always made me think of wet moss.

He watched Father Bernard send Mr Belderboss into fits of laughter.

"He performed wonders to behold in his last parish."

"Oh, really?" said Mummer.

"Very good at encouraging the young folk to attend," the bishop said, looking at me with the specious grin of a teacher who wishes to punish and befriend in equal measure and ends up doing neither.

"Oh my lad's an altar boy, your Grace," Mummer replied.

"Is he?" said the bishop. "Well, good show. Father Bernard's quite at home with the teens as well as the more mature members of the congregation."

"Well, if he comes on your recommendation, your Grace, I'm sure he'll do well," said Mummer.

"Oh, I don't doubt it," the bishop replied, brushing crumbs off his stomach with the back of his hand. "He'll be able to steer you all through safe waters, make good around the capes, as it were. In fact my sailing analogy is quite apt," he said, looking into the middle distance and awarding himself a smile. "You see, I'm rather keen on Father Bernard taking the congregation out into the wider world. I don't know about you but I'm of the opinion that if one is cosseted by the familiar, faith becomes stagnant."

"Well, if you think so, your Grace," said Mummer.

The bishop turned to Mummer and smiled in that self-satisfied way again.

"Do I detect that there may be some resistance to the idea, Mrs . . .?"

"Smith," she said, then, seeing that the bishop was waiting for her to answer, she went on. "Perhaps there might be, your Grace, among the older members. They're not keen on things changing."

"Nor should they be, Mrs Smith. Nor should they be," he said. "Rest assured, I rather like to think of the appointment of a new incumbent as an organic process; a new shoot off the old vine, if you like; a continuum rather than a revolution. And in any case I wasn't suggesting that you went off to the far flung corners of the earth. I was thinking of Father Bernard taking a group away on a retreat at Easter time. It was a tradition that I know was very dear to Wilfred's heart, and one that I always thought worthwhile myself.

"It'd be a nice way to remember him," he added. "And a chance to look forward to the future. A continuum, Mrs Smith, as I say."

The sound of someone knocking a knife against a glass started to rise over the babble in the garden.

"Ah, you'll have to excuse me, I'm afraid," said the bishop, dabbing crumbs from his lips. "Duty calls."

He went off towards the trestle table that had been set up by the rose bushes, his cassock flapping around his ankles and getting wet.

When he had gone, Mrs Belderboss appeared at Mummer's side.

"You were having a long chat with the bishop," she said, nudging Mummer playfully in the arm. "What were you talking about?"

Mummer smiled. "I have some wonderful news," she said.

A few weeks later, Mummer organised a meeting of interested parties so as to get the ball rolling before the bishop could change his mind, as he was wont to do. She suggested that everyone come to our house to discuss where they might go, although Mummer had only one place in mind.

On the night she had set aside, they came in out of the rain, smelling of the damp and their dinners: Mr and Mrs Belderboss, and Miss Bunce, the presbytery housekeeper, and her fiancé, David Hobbs. They hung up their coats in the little porch with its cracked tiles and its intractable odour of feet and gathered in our front room anxiously watching the clock on the mantelpiece, with the tea things all set out, unable to relax until Father Bernard arrived.

Eventually, the bell went and everyone got to their feet as Mummer opened the door. Father Bernard stood there with his shoulders hunched in the rain.

"Come in, come in," said Mummer.

"Thank you, Mrs Smith."

"Are you well, Father?" she said. "You're not too wet I hope."

"No, no, Mrs Smith," said Father Bernard, his feet squelching inside his shoes. "I like the rain."

Unsure if he was being sarcastic, Mummer's smile wavered a little. It wasn't a trait she knew in priests. Father Wilfred had never been anything other than deadly serious.

"Good for the flowers," was all she could offer.

"Aye," said Father Bernard.

He looked back at his car.

"I wonder, Mrs Smith, how you'd feel about me bringing in Monro. He doesn't like being on his own and the rain on the roof sends him a wee bit crackers, you know."

"Monro?" said Mummer, peering past him.

"After Matt."

"Matt?"

"Matt Monro," said Father Bernard. "My one and only vice, Mrs Smith, I can assure you. I've had long consultations with the Lord about it, but I think He's given me up as a lost cause."

"I'm sorry," said Mummer. "Who are you talking about?"

"The daft feller mooning at the window there."

"Your dog?"

"Aye."

"Yes," said Mummer. "Well, I suppose that'll be all right. He won't, you know, will he?"

"Ah no, Mrs Smith, he's well house trained. He'll just doze off."

"It'll be fine, Esther," said Farther and Father Bernard went out to the car and came back with a black Labrador that sneezed on the doormat and shivered and stretched out in front of the fire as if he had always lived at our house.

Mummer offered Father Bernard the single armchair next to the television, a threadbare thing somewhere between olive and beige that Mummer had tried to pretty up with a lace-edged antimacassar, aligned using Farther's spirit level when she thought no one was looking.

He thanked her and wiped his brow with a handkerchief and sat down. Only when he was settled did everyone else do the same. Mummer clicked her fingers and shot me a look that was the equivalent of a kick up the backside. As with all social occasions at our house, it was my job to distribute the opening round of tea and biscuits, and so I knelt by the table and poured Father Bernard a cup, setting it down on top of the television which had been covered with a starched cloth — the way all the crucifixes and statues were at church now that it was Lent.

"Thank you, Tonto," Father Bernard said, smiling at me conspiratorially.

It was the nickname he'd given to me when he arrived at Saint Jude's. He was the Lone Ranger and I was Tonto. It was childish, I know, but I suppose I liked the idea of the two of us fighting side by side, like the pals did in the *Commando* stories. Though fighting what, I wasn't sure. The Devil, maybe. Heathens. Gluttons. Prodigals. The kinds of people Father Wilfred had trained us to despise.

Listening to the armchair groaning under him as he tried to make himself comfortable, I was struck once again by how enormous Father Bernard was. A farmer's son from Antrim, he was no more than thirty or so, though he looked middle-aged from years of hard graft. He had a solid, heavy face, with a nose that had been bashed flat and a roll of flesh that bulged at the back of his collar. His hair was always well groomed and oiled over his head to form a solid helmet. But it was his hands that seemed so out of place with the chalice and the pyx. They were large and red and toughened to leather from an adolescence spent building drystone walls and pinning down bullocks to have their ears notched. If not for the dog collar and his wool-soft voice, he could easily have passed for a doorman or a bank robber.

But, as I say, everyone at Saint Jude's liked him straight away. He was that sort of person. Uncomplicated, honest, easy to be with. A man to other men, fatherly to women twice his age. But I could tell that Mummer was reserving judgement. She respected him because he was a priest, of course, but only as far as he more or less replicated Father Wilfred. When he slipped up, Mummer would smile sweetly and touch him lightly on the arm.

"Father Wilfred would normally have led the Creed in Latin, Father, but it doesn't matter," she said after his first solo Mass at Saint Jude's. And, "Father Wilfred would normally have said grace himself," when he offered the slot to me over a Sunday lunch which it seemed Mummer had arranged merely to test him on such details.

We altar boys thought Father Bernard was fun — the way he gave us all nicknames and would invite us to the presbytery after Mass. We had, of course, never been asked there by Father Wilfred, and even to most of the adults in the parish it was a place of mystery almost as sacrosanct as the tabernacle. But Father Bernard seemed glad of the company, and once the silverware had been cleaned and put away and our vestments hung in the closet, he would take us across to his home and sit us around the dining table for tea and biscuits, and we'd swap stories and jokes to the sound of Matt Monro. Well, I didn't. I let the other boys do that. I preferred to listen. Or pretend to listen at least and let my eyes wander around the room and try to imagine Father Bernard's life, what he did when no one else was around, when no one was expecting him to be a priest. I didn't know if priests could ever knock off. I mean, Farther didn't spend his free time checking the mortar on the chimney stack or setting up a theodolite in the back garden, so it seemed unfair that a priest should have to be holy all the time. But perhaps it didn't work like that. Perhaps being a priest was like being a fish. Immersion for life.

Now that Father Bernard had been served, everyone else could have their tea. I poured out a cup for each person — finishing one pot and starting on the next —

until there was one mug left. Hanny's mug. The one with a London bus on the side. He always got a cup, even when he was away at Pinelands.

"How is Andrew?" Father Bernard asked, as he watched me.

"Fine, Father," Mummer said.

Father Bernard nodded and pulled his face into a smile that acknowledged what she was really saying, beneath the words.

"He'll be back at Easter, won't he?" said Father Bernard.

"Yes," said Mummer.

"You'll be glad to have him home, I'm sure."

"Yes," said Mummer. "Very glad."

There was an awkward pause. Father Bernard realised that he had strayed into private territory and changed the subject by raising his cup.

"That's a lovely brew, Mrs Smith," he said and Mummer smiled.

It wasn't that Mummer didn't want Hanny at home — she loved him with an intensity that made Farther and I seem like we were merely her acquaintances sometimes — but he reminded her of the test that she still hadn't passed. And while she delighted in any little advancement Hanny seemed to have made — he might be able to write the first letter of his name, or tie a bootlace, say — they were such small progressions that it still pained her to think of the long road ahead.

"And it will be a long road," Father Wilfred had once told her. "It will be full of disappointments and obstacles. But you should rejoice that God has chosen you to walk along it, that He has sent you Andrew as both a test and guide of your soul. He will remind you of your own muteness before God. And when at last he is able to speak, you will be able to speak, and ask of the Lord what you will. Not everyone receives such a chance, Mrs Smith. Be mindful of that."

The cup of tea that we poured for Hanny that went cold and grew a wrinkled skin of milk was proof that she hadn't forgotten. It was, strangely, a kind of prayer.

"So," Father Bernard said, putting down his half-empty tea cup and declining Mummer's offer of more. "Does anyone have any suggestions about where we ought to go at Easter?"

"Well," said Miss Bunce quickly, glancing at David who nodded encouragement. "There's a place called Glasfynydd."

"Where?" said Mummer, giving the others a sceptical look that Mr and Mrs Belderboss returned with a grin. They had never heard of the place either. It was just Miss Bunce trying to be different. She was young. It wasn't her fault.

"Glasfynydd. It's a retreat on the edge of the Brecon Beacons," she said. "It's beautiful. I've been lots of times. They have an outdoor church in the wood. Everyone sits on logs."

No one responded apart from David, who said, "That sounds nice," and sipped his tea.

"All right," said Father Bernard after a moment. "That's one idea. Any others?"

"Well, it's obvious," said Mummer. "We should go back to Moorings and visit the shrine." And buoyed on by Mr and Mrs Belderboss's murmurs of excitement in remembering the place, she added, "We know how to get there and where everything is and it's quiet. We can go at Holy Week and take Andrew to the shrine and stay on until Rogationtide to watch the beating of the bounds, like we used to do. It'll be lovely. The old gang back together."

"*I've* never been before," said Miss Bunce. "And neither has David."

"Well, you know what I mean," said Mummer.

Father Bernard looked round the room.

"Any other suggestions?" he said, and while he waited for a response he picked up a custard cream and bit it in half.

No one said anything.

"In that case," he said. "I think we ought to be democratic about it. All those who want to go to South Wales . . ."

Miss Bunce and her fiancé raised their hands.

"All those who want to go back to Moorings . . ."

Everyone else responded with much more vigour.

"That's that then," said Father Bernard. "Moorings it is."

"But you didn't vote, Father," said Miss Bunce.

Father Bernard smiled. "I've given myself the right to abstain this time, Miss Bunce. I'm happy to go wherever I'm led."

He grinned again and ate the remainder of his biscuit. Miss Bunce looked disappointed and shot glances at David, wanting his sympathy. But he shrugged and went over to the table for another cup of tea, which

Mummer poured with a flourish, as she relished the prospect of going back to the Loney.

Mr and Mrs Belderboss were already describing the place in minute detail to Father Bernard who nodded and picked another biscuit from his plate.

"And the shrine, Father," said Mrs Belderboss. "It's just beautiful, isn't it, Reg?"

"Oh, yes," said Mr Belderboss. "Quite a little paradise."

"So many flowers," Mrs Belderboss chipped in.

"And the water's so clean," said Mr Belderboss. "Isn't it, Esther?"

"Like crystal," said Mummer, as she passed the sofa.

She smiled at Father Bernard and went to offer Miss Bunce a biscuit, which she took with a *thank you* that could have drawn blood. Mummer nodded and moved on. At Moorings, she knew she could beat Miss Bunce and her Glasfynydd hands down, being on home turf as it were.

She had grown up on the north-west coast, within spitting distance of the Loney and the place still buttered the edges of her accent even though she had long since left and had lived in London for twenty years or more. She still called sparrows spaddies, starlings sheppies, and when we were young she would sing us rhymes that no one outside her village had ever heard.

She made us eat hotpot and tripe salads and longed to find the same curd tarts she had eaten as a girl; artery-clogging fancies made from the first milk a cow gave after calving.

It seemed that where she grew up almost every other day had been the feast of some saint or other. And even though hardly any of them were upheld any more, even by the most ardent at Saint Jude's, Mummer remembered every one and all the various accompanying rituals, which she insisted on performing at home.

On Saint John's day a metal cross was passed through a candle flame three times to symbolise the holy protection John had received when he went back into his burning house to rescue the lepers and the cripples staying there.

In October, on the feast of Saint Francis of Assisi, we would go to the park and collect autumn leaves and twigs and fashion them into crosses for the altar at Saint Jude's.

And on the first Sunday in May — as the people of Mummer's village had done since time immemorial — we would go out into the garden before Mass and wash our faces in the dew.

There was something special about the Loney. To Mummer, Saint Anne's shrine was second only to Lourdes; the two-mile walk across the fields from Moorings was her Camino de Santiago. She was convinced that there and only there would Hanny stand any chance of being cured.

CHAPTER
FOUR

Hanny came home from Pinelands at the start of the Easter holidays, bristling with excitement.

Even before Farther had turned off the car engine, he was running down the drive to show me the new watch Mummer had given him. I had seen it in the window of the shop where she worked. A heavy, golden-coloured thing with a picture of Golgotha on the face and an inscription from Matthew on the back: *Therefore, be aware. Because you do not know the day or the hour*.

"That's nice, Hanny," I said and gave it back to him.

He snatched it off me and slipped it on his wrist before handing over a term's worth of drawings and paintings. They were all for me. They always were. Never for Mummer or Farther.

"He's very glad to be home, aren't you, Andrew?" said Mummer, holding the door open for Farther to bundle Hanny's suitcase through the porch.

She tidied Hanny's hair with her fingers and held him by the shoulders.

"We've told him that we're going back to Moorings," she said. "He's looking forward to it already, aren't you?"

But Hanny was more interested in measuring me. He put his palm on the top of my head and slid his hand back towards his Adam's apple. He had grown again.

Satisfied that he was still the bigger of the two of us, he went up the stairs as noisily as he always did, the banister creaking as he hauled himself from step to step.

I went into the kitchen to make him a cup of tea in his London bus mug and when I found him in his room he still had on the old raincoat of Farthers that he had taken a shine to years before and insisted on wearing whatever the weather. He was standing by the window with his back to me looking at the houses on the other side of the street and the traffic going by.

"Are you all right, Hanny?"

He didn't move.

"Give me your coat," I said. "I'll hang it up for you."

He turned and looked at me.

"Your coat, Hanny," I said, shaking his sleeve.

He watched me as I undid the buttons for him and hung it on the peg on the back of the door. It weighed a ton with all the things he kept in the pockets to communicate with me. A rabbit's tooth meant he was hungry. A jar of nails was one of his headaches. He apologised with a plastic dinosaur and put on a rubber gorilla mask when he was frightened. He used combinations of these things sometimes and although Mummer and Farther pretended they knew what it all meant, only I really understood him. We had our world and Mummer and Farther had theirs. It wasn't their fault. Nor was it ours. That's just the way it was. And still is. We're closer than people can imagine. No one, not even Doctor Baxter, really understands that.

Hanny patted the bed and I sat down while he went through his paintings of animals and flowers and houses. His teachers. Other residents.

The last painting was different, though. It was of two stick figures standing on a beach littered with starfish and shells. The sea behind them was a bright blue wall that rose like a tsunami. To the left were yellow mountains topped with mohicans of green grass.

"This is the Loney, isn't it?" I said, surprised that he remembered it at all. It had been years since we'd been there and Hanny rarely drew anything that he couldn't see right in front of him.

He touched the water and then moved his finger to the camel-hump dunes, over which hung a great flock of birds. Hanny loved the birds. I taught him all about them. How you could tell if a gull was in its first, second or third winter by the mottle of its plumage and the differences between the calls of the hawks and terns and warblers. How, if you were very still, you could sit by the water and the knots would move around you in a swarm so close that you could feel the breeze from their wings on your skin.

I'd copy the cries of the curlews and the redshanks and the herring gulls for him, and we'd lie on our backs and watch the geese high up in a chevron and wonder what it would be like to part the air a mile above the earth with a beak as hard as bone.

Hanny smiled and tapped the figures on the painting.

"That's you," I said. "That's Hanny."

Hanny nodded and touched himself on the chest.

"That's me?" I said, pointing to the smaller of the two and Hanny gripped my shoulder.

"I'm glad you're home," I said, and I meant it.

Pinelands didn't do him much good. They didn't know him. They didn't care for him like I did. They never asked him what he needed. He was just the big lad in the TV lounge with his paints and crayons.

He held me close to his chest and stroked my hair. He was getting stronger. Every time I saw him he looked different. The puppy fat that had been there at Christmas had slipped from his face and he had no need to fake a moustache with a piece of burnt cork any more like we used to do as children. It seemed unimaginable, but Hanny was becoming an adult.

I think he sensed the strangeness of it too, albeit dimly. The way one might feel there was something different about a room but not be able to say what. Was there a missing picture, say, or a book shelved in a different place?

Sometimes I caught him looking at the span of his hands, the nest of black hairs on his breastbone, his hard, oval biceps, as though he couldn't quite understand what he was doing inside this man's body.

As we had always done in the past, we left for Moorings at first light on the Tuesday of Holy Week.

Once everyone had gathered at Saint Jude's and stowed their bags on the minibus, Father Bernard went to get into the driver's seat. But before he could start the engine, Mummer touched him on the arm.

"Father Wilfred usually led us in prayer before we left," she said.

"Yes, of course," said Father Bernard and he got down and started on the sign of the cross.

"We tended to go around the corner, Father," said Mummer. "And pray with Our Lady."

"Oh, right," said Father Bernard. "Yes, of course."

We gathered at the foot of the little Alpine rockery on which the Virgin stood and bowed our heads as Father Bernard made an impromptu prayer of intercession, asking her for a safe journey and a successful pilgrimage. After the Amen, we took it in turns to go to the railings, lean forward and kiss Mary's feet.

Father Bernard made way for Mrs Belderboss, who lowered herself slowly to her knees and had Mr Belderboss hold her by the shoulders as she leant over. Once she had kissed the Holy Mother's toes, she closed her eyes and began a whispered prayer that went on so long that Father Bernard began to look at his watch.

I was to be the last to go up, but Father Bernard said, "Leave it, Tonto. Otherwise we'll be sitting on the North Circular all day."

He looked up at Mary with her expression of vacancy and grief. "I'm sure She won't mind."

"If you say so, Father."

"I do," he said and jogged back to the minibus, making everyone laugh with a quip that I didn't catch as he climbed up the steps to the driver's seat.

32

I hadn't seen them all so happy for months. I knew what they were thinking. That this time it would be different. That Hanny would be cured. That they were on the cusp of a wonderful victory.

We drove out of London, heading north through the East Midlands and across Yorkshire to Lancashire. I sat in the back with Monro wedged under my seat and slept on and off as a dozen counties went by. Every so often I woke up with the feeling that I was repeating parts of the journey. But then England is much the same all over, I suppose. A duplication of old farms, new estates, church spires, cooling towers, sewage works, railway lines, bridges, canals, and towns that are identical but for a few small differences in architecture and stone.

The sunlight that, as we left, had begun to creep over the London suburbs, disappeared the further north we went, returning only momentarily on the shoulder of a yellow hill miles away or picking out a distant reservoir in a second or two of magnesium brilliance.

The temperature dropped and the clouds darkened. The road steamed in driving rain. Shreds of mist hung over the cold lakes and woods. Moorland turned the colour of mould and becks coursed in spate down the peaty slopes, white and solid-looking from a distance, like seams of quartz.

No one had mentioned it — hoping presumably that it would go away of its own accord — but for the last few miles the minibus had been making an awful racket, as though something was loose in the engine.

Every time Father Bernard changed gear there was a loud shuddering and grinding and eventually it refused to shift at all and he pulled in to the side of the road.

"What is it, Father?" said Mr Belderboss.

"The clutch, I think," Father Bernard replied.

"Oh, it'll be the damp, it gets into everything up here," said Mr Belderboss and sat back satisfied with his assessment.

"Can you fix it, Father?" Mrs Belderboss said.

"I certainly hope so, Mrs Belderboss," Father Bernard replied. "I get the impression that you have to rely on your own ingenuity out here."

He smiled and got out. He was right, of course. In every direction there was nothing but deserted, muddy fields where seabirds were blown like old rags.

The rain battered onto the windscreen and ran down in waves as Father Bernard lifted the bonnet and propped it open.

"Go and help him," Mummer said to Farther.

"What do I know about cars?" he replied, glancing up from the map he was studying.

"You could still give him a hand."

"He knows what he's doing, Esther. Too many cooks and all that."

"Well, I hope he does manage to get us going again," said Mummer, looking out of the window. "It's only going to get colder."

"I'm sure we'll survive," said Farther.

"I was thinking of Mr and Mrs Belderboss," Mummer replied.

"Oh, don't worry about us," said Mr Belderboss. "We've known cold, haven't we, Mary?"

"I should say so."

They started to harp on about the war and having heard it all before I turned to Hanny who had been tugging at my sleeve for the last five minutes, desperate for me to share his View-Master.

Hanny grinned and handed me the red binoculars that he'd had stuck to his face for most of the journey, clicking through the various reels he took out of his school satchel. It had been *Mountains of the World* until we stopped at Kettering for a toilet break, then *Strange Creatures of the Ocean*, and *Space Exploration* until Mummer had finally persuaded him onto *Scenes from The Old Testament*, which he now urged me to look through again. Eve with her private parts delicately blotted with foliage, Abraham's knife poised over Isaac's heart, Pharaoh's charioteers tumbling in the Red Sea.

When I had finished I noticed that he had his hands jammed between his legs.

"Do you need to go?" I said.

Hanny rocked back and forth, kicking the side of his boot against the door.

"Come on then."

While Father Bernard was poking about in the engine, I took him outside and walked down the lane a little so no one else would see. He went over to a fence and unzipped his jeans while I waited in the rain and listened to it tapping on the hood of the parka Mummer had insisted I bring.

I looked back at the minibus and thought I could hear raised voices. Mummer. Farther. They had tried their best to hold onto the cheerfulness that had been there when we left Saint Jude's, but it had been difficult not to feel despondent once the rain began pounding the roads and everything had been obscured by mist.

A stiff wind blew in across the fields bringing the smell of brine and rot as strong as an onion. It seemed that all our past pilgrimages were contained in that smell and I felt a tension start to grow in my stomach. We had been coming here for as long as I could remember, yet I'd never felt completely comfortable in this place. It was rather like my grandfather's house. Glum, lifeless, mildly threatening. Not somewhere you wanted to linger for very long. I was always glad to see the back of it once our Easter pilgrimage was over, and I'd breathed a private sigh of relief when we stopped going altogether.

The rest of them kept up their spirits with hymns and prayers but at times it seemed as though they were, without knowing it, warding things off, rather than inviting God in.

Hanny finished and waved me over to where he was standing.

"What is it?" I said.

He pointed at the fence in front of him. A hare had been shot and skinned and its hide splayed on the barbed wire, along with several dozen rats. Trophies or deterrents, I suppose they were both.

"Leave it alone, Hanny," I said. "Don't touch it."

He looked at me pleadingly.

"We can't save it now," I said.

He went to stroke it but withdrew his hand when I shook my head. The hare stared at us through a glassy brown eye.

We were starting to cross the road back to the minibus when I heard the sound of a car approaching. I grabbed Hanny's sleeve and held him tightly as an expensive-looking Daimler went past us, throwing water into the ditches on either side. There was a young girl asleep in the back, her face against the window. The driver slowed at the corner where we were standing and turned his head briefly to look at me before he rounded the bend and was gone. I had never seen a car like that here before. There was little in the way of traffic at all around the Loney. Mostly hay trucks and farm wagons and not always motorised either.

When Hanny and I got back to the minibus Father Bernard still had his hands deep in amongst the pipes and wires.

"What's wrong with it, Father?" I asked.

"I don't know, Tonto," he said and wiped the rain out of his eyes with his sleeve. "It might be the fly wheel, but I'd have to take the whole thing apart to be sure."

He closed the bonnet with some reluctance and followed me back on board.

"Any luck?" said Mr Belderboss.

"Not so far," Father Bernard replied, smoothing his sopping hair back over his head. "I think it'll be a garage job to be honest."

"Oh dear," said Mrs Belderboss. "What a start."

"Well at least it got us this far," said Farther.

"Aye, there's that," said Father Bernard.

Monro was whining. Father Bernard shushed him and he shrank into a white-eyed nervousness.

"I think the best thing to do," he said, "will be for me to walk on to the village and see if there's anyone there who can help us."

"In this weather, Father?" said Mrs Belderboss. "You'll catch your death."

"To be honest, the walk will do me good, Mrs Belderboss," he said. "I don't do well sitting for so long."

"It's a fair way, Father," said Mr Belderboss. "It must be a good three or four miles."

Father Bernard smiled dismissively and started to wind his scarf around his neck.

"You'll go with him, won't you?" Mummer said to me.

"Ah, don't worry yourself, Mrs Smith," said Father Bernard. "There's no sense in two of us getting soaked."

"It's no trouble, is it?" Mummer nudged me.

"No," I said.

The wind buffed around the minibus. Monro piped up again and Father Bernard leant down and scrubbed his neck to comfort him.

"What's the matter with him, Father?" said Mr Belderboss.

"I don't know," said Father Bernard. "Maybe it was that car going past."

"Perhaps you're right," said Mr Belderboss. "He was going at a fair gallop. I didn't think he was going to slow down for the bend."

"The girl was a pretty little thing, though, wasn't she?" said Mrs Belderboss.

Mr Belderboss frowned. "What girl?"

"The girl in the back."

"I didn't see a girl."

"Well then you missed out, Reg."

"Oh come on now, Mary," he said. "You know I only have eyes for you."

Mrs Belderboss leant over to Miss Bunce.

"Make the most of David's sincerity while it lasts," she said, but Miss Bunce was looking past her at Monro, who had crawled back under my seat and was shaking.

"Come on, old feller," said Father Bernard. "You're showing me up. What's the matter?"

Three men were coming across the field towards us. They were dressed in filthy green wax jackets and rubber boots. None of them wore hats or had umbrellas. They were local men, either hardened to the weather or possessed of the knowledge that it would pass over in a few moments.

One of them carried a shotgun over his arm. Another had a white terrier on a chain. One of those ones with a long face and wide-set eyes. A dog drawn by a child. The third man was older than the other two and walked several yards behind, coughing into his fist. They stopped and looked at us for a few moments before carrying on towards the road.

"Should we ask them for some help, Father?" said Mr Belderboss.

"I'd rather we didn't," said Miss Bunce, looking at David, who reassured her by taking her hand.

"Well, it's either that or we spend the rest of the week sitting here," said Mummer.

Father Bernard got out and looked along the road before crossing. The men climbed over the stile and waited when Father Bernard called to them. The tallest of them, who was bald and had the build of a Charolais bull, held his shotgun over the crook of his arm and looked at Father Bernard while he explained about the clutch. The one with the dog held its snout tightly closed and alternated his interest between what Father Bernard was saying and the strangers on the minibus. His left arm seemed to hang more loosely and on that hand he wore a black mitten tied at the wrist with some string. The elder man coughed again and sat down on a broken bit of wall. He was a strange colour. The colour of nicotine or dried daffodils. The same colour my grandfather went when his liver packed in.

"Oh dear," said Mrs Belderboss. "He doesn't look at all well, does he, Reg?"

"Toxoplasmosis, most likely," said Mr Belderboss.

"Toxo what?"

"They get it from cats," he said. "It's very common with farmers. Their cats pick up all sorts of things."

"What are you on about?"

"I read it in the paper," he said. "You have a look at their hands. They don't wash them properly. All they have to do is swallow a bit of cat's doings and that's that. I'm right, aren't I?"

"I think so," said Farther.

Mrs Belderboss shook her head.

"I'm telling you, it's toxoplasmosis," said Mr Belderboss. "Look at him. Poor bugger."

Outside, Father Bernard patted the bull man on the shoulder and brought him over to the minibus. The bull man handed the shotgun to his friend with the dog and leant over the engine when Father Bernard lifted the bonnet.

I could hear them talking, or rather Father Bernard talking and the other man listening or giving the occasional *aye*. After a few moments the man with the dog came over and put in his two penn'orth, and, eventually, Father Bernard dropped the bonnet and got back into the driver's seat.

"I think Mr Parkinson may well have saved the day," he said, responding to the bull man's gesture that he should start the engine.

"Mr who?" said Miss Bunce.

"Parkinson," said Father Bernard. "And the feller with the dog is called Collier."

"How do you know that?" said Miss Bunce.

"I asked them," he replied. "It's a wee habit I picked up in the Ardoyne. Ask a feller's name and shake his hand and more often than not he'll help you out whoever he is."

"I thought you'd come from New Cross," said Farther.

"Aye I did, but I was two years in the Ardoyne after I left seminary."

"No one told us that," said Mummer.

"Ah, you see, Mrs Smith, there's more to me than meets the eye."

The minibus slid smoothly into gear and Father Bernard gave a thumbs up which Parkinson returned with a slight nod of the head. We edged forward, the wheels spinning momentarily in the sludge by the side of the road and set off towards Moorings.

The men stood and watched us all the way down the lane, the dog straining on its leash, desperate to tear something to pieces.

A while later, familiar landmarks appeared — a pub with an unusual name, a monument on a very green hill, a crown of standing stones in a field. It only remained for the road to bore through a thickness of overhanging oak trees and then the coastline of the Loney was suddenly flung out to our left.

I remember how my eye used to leap instinctively to the horizon, how looking suddenly across that immense distance of grey seemed to produce the same feeling as looking down from the spire of Saint Jude's or the top floor of Farthers office block. A kind of vertigo.

"Lovely view, isn't it, Joan?" said Mrs Belderboss.

Miss Bunce looked past me at the grim plain of the sea and the gulls turning on the wind, frowned uncertainly and went back to the half sleep she'd been in since we'd set off again after the breakdown.

"Lovely view," Mrs Belderboss said again, verifying it to herself this time as fact.

Over the water, the cloud thinned and fingers of sunlight touched the bare bulge of Coldbarrow, lighting up its brown tundra and catching the windows of Thessaly, the old house sitting at its northern tip. They flared and then faded again, as if the place had been woken for a moment out of a long sleep.

I'd never liked the look of Thessaly and even though in the past we had always been under strict instructions never to cross the sands to Coldbarrow, we wouldn't have gone there anyway.

There were stories, naturally, of it being haunted. A witch had once lived there, they said; a beautiful woman called Elizabeth Percy who lured sailors onto the rocks, and who remained there in some form or other even though they'd hanged her in the old bell tower next to the house. In fact, all around the Loney people still clung to old superstitions out of conviction, it seemed, rather than nostalgia, and it wasn't unusual to come across farms where the occupants hadn't quite the courage to take down the horseshoes nailed to barn doors to keep boggarts from spoiling the hay or for people to leave an acorn in their window to turn lightning away from the house.

It's easy to scoff, I suppose, but there was so little of the modern world there that it was difficult not to think of the place being at a sort of standstill and — how shall I put it? — *primed* in some way.

A sudden mist, a mumble of thunder over the sea, the wind scurrying along the beach with its crop of old bones and litter, was sometimes all it took to make you feel as though something was about to happen. Though quite what, I didn't know.

I often thought there was too much time there. That the place was sick with it. Haunted by it. Time didn't leak away as it should. There was nowhere for it to go and no modernity to hurry it along. It collected as the black water did on the marshes and remained and stagnated in the same way.

Father Bernard drove at a snail's pace, hunched over the steering wheel, looking through the gaps he had rubbed out of the condensation with his sleeve. The track was strewn with potholes and everyone hung on as the minibus bounced in and out of the ruts.

It went on this way for half a mile or more, the suspension groaning, until we rounded a sharp bend at the top of the lane.

"Look," said Mummer suddenly, pointing up the hillside to our right. "There it is."

Moorings stood alone in a field of iron-coloured weeds and limestone boulders on the gentle rise of land that began at the seashore a mile away and continued to the foot of the steeper hills behind the house, where a spread of ashes, yews and oaks called Brownslack Wood marched over the top of the hill and down into the moorland of the next valley.

With its bowed roof, the house looked like a ship that had been washed far inland on a storm tide. A huge wisteria vine was its rigging. A crumbling chimney its crow's nest.

It had been the home of a taxidermist who retired there with his third wife in the late 1950s. She died within a year of them moving in and he didn't stick around for much longer than that himself, leaving the property to his son, a banker who lived in Hong Kong. Unable to sell the place, the son rented it out, and as far as I knew we were the only people who ever stayed there.

Going up the lane, I turned Hanny's face towards the large limestone boulder over to the left. We'd christened it the Panzer. Or at least I had. And when Mummer hadn't been watching us we'd thrown pebble grenades at it. Launched stick rockets at its tracks. Crawled on our bellies through the grass to do in the scar-faced Kapitän like the Tommies did in *Commando*.

I wondered if Hanny remembered any of that. He had remembered the beach, after all, and we were always very good at picking up our games where we left off, no matter how long it had been since we'd played them. Perhaps he would want to play soldiers again when we got to the shore. He never seemed to tire of it. Though what it meant to him, I don't know. I mean, he can't have had any conception of war or of the bravery and sacrifice we pretended to experience. It was the excitement of it all, I suppose. Charging down the dunes with driftwood machine guns and winning, always winning.

As we approached Moorings, there was a Land Rover parked up on a grass verge. It was dented and filthy and had crude white crosses painted on the doors like something that might have ferried men out of the Somme.

"Oh, there he is," said Mrs Belderboss, pointing out of the window. "Still the same as ever."

"Who?" said Miss Bunce, craning around her seat to see. "Clement," said Mrs Belderboss.

Miss Bunce peered at the large man standing by the front door with a woman half his size. Mrs Belderboss caught the look of concern on her face.

"Oh, he'll not bother you," she said. "He's just a bit, you know. Smile at him. That seems to do the trick."

"Who's the lady?"

Mrs Belderboss turned to her. "That's his mother," she said. "She's blind as a bat, poor thing."

"But she's wearing glasses," said Miss Bunce.

Mrs Belderboss laughed. "I know. She's a funny old bird."

Clement watched us as we pulled up in front of the house. Father Bernard waved to him, but he just stared like his mother.

There were unkind whispers about him, as there always are in such places about quiet, lonely men, but the general consensus was that he was harmless. And although the pig farm he kept with his mother was a desolate and ramshackle place thrown way out on the windswept fields south of Moorings, I got the impression that it wasn't in such poor repair from wilful neglect. By all accounts his mother took as much looking after as the swine.

Poor Clement. I always thought of him as something akin to a shire horse; in build and temperament. Clumping. Plodding. Head down in deference. Dependable to a fault.

The taxidermist's son could hardly have checked up on him all the way from Kowloon but he paid him to look after Moorings all the same, safe in the knowledge that Clement didn't have the brains to rip him off.

Everyone got out of the minibus and stretched. Miss Bunce buttoned up her coat and wrapped her arms around herself, pacing back and forth to keep warm, while David fetched her bags. Mr Belderboss struggled down the metal step with Farther taking his weight and Mrs Belderboss fussing around him like a moth.

Father Bernard put on his jacket, zipped it up to the neck and went over to Clement, bidding us to follow him.

As we got closer, Clement started to look confused.

"Where's t'other feller?" he said.

"Sorry?"

"The priest."

"Father Wilfred? Didn't anyone tell you? He passed away."

"Died, did he?"

"I'm afraid so."

"How?"

Father Bernard looked at us and then said, "I'm Father McGill, if that's any good."

"You're a priest an all?" said Clement.

47

"For my sins, aye." Father Bernard smiled and Clement shook his hand with relief.

Father Bernard paused and looked at Clement's mother, waiting to be introduced.

"Mother," said Clement, and the old lady jerked into life and held out her hand.

Father Bernard took it and said, "Good to meet you."

The old lady said nothing.

"Go and wait in the van," said Clement.

She remained expressionless.

"I said wait in the van." Clement nudged her and she set off with her stick, driving a wedge through the crowd of us standing there.

As she went past, she lifted up her glasses and looked at me with her grey milky eyes that were slick and glossy like the underside of a slug.

"Do you want to come inside?" said Clement.

"Aye, 'tis a bit raw," said Father Bernard.

"Rooks say we'll have a good summer, though."

"How's that?"

Clement pointed past the house to the woods where several dozen of the birds were going in and out of their nests.

"Building them right high up this year," he said.

"That's good," said Father Bernard.

"Aye, but it's not normal," Clement mumbled.

He turned up the path to the front door along the miniature boulevard of apple trees that were still winter-naked, their branches speckled with blight like the putrefying windfallen fruit that lay underneath them. There was always something rather sad about those trees, I thought. The way they dutifully grew their produce every summer only for it to blacken and fall off uncollected.

Every movement of Clement's was slow and heavy and it took an age for him to find the right key. Once the house was open, Mummer muscled her way through to the front and led everyone along the hall that, as it had always done in the past, smelled of cigars and spent matches and the air had a hard, porcelain coldness to it.

"Sitting room, drawing room, lavatory," she said as she turned the handle of each door.

Mr and Mrs Belderboss followed her down the hall and back, delighted at finding things in exactly the same place as they had always been and having new people to show around, although Miss Bunce seemed reluctant to go much further than the dead grandfather clock by the front door. She looked up anxiously as the bare bulb that illuminated the hallway faded and then came back on, brighter than it had been before.

"It's only the wind," said Mummer.

"It catches on the wires," said Clement, who was still lingering at the threshold.

I noticed for the first time that he was wearing a wooden crucifix around his neck. One he had made himself by the look of it. Two chunks of split wood bound with string.

"There you are," said Mummer. "It catches on the wires."

Clement adjusted his cap and turned to go.

"I'll bring thee some more firewood in a day or two," he said, nodding to the bags lined up in the hallway.

"Are you sure you need to, Clement? It looks like there's enough there for a month," said Father Bernard.

Clement frowned and looked very serious. "Quite sure, Father. When the wind gets down the chimney it draws the heart out of the fire in no time," he said.

"Is there bad weather on the way?" asked Father Bernard.

"There usually is," Clement replied.

Miss Bunce smiled thinly as he looked at us all one last time and closed the door.

"Now, come on, Joan," said Mr Belderboss, once Clement had left. "There's nothing to worry about."

And he took her arm and led her past the peeling wallpaper and the oil paintings of wild seascapes into the sitting room to show her the amount of expensive objects that had been left by the taxidermist. Something that charmed him and bewildered him in equal measure.

At his bidding, everyone else followed and listened as he pointed out the delicate knick-knacks worth hundreds apiece.

"Ah, now then," he said, plucking out a small clay pipe from a wooden box lying on the window ledge. "This is interesting. You can still see the teeth marks on the stem. Look."

He offered it to Mummer but she frowned and he put it back where he found it, making a beeline for Miss Bunce, whose attention had been taken by the books on the rosewood Davenport by the window.

Among them was a first edition of *The Island of Doctor Moreau*, one bound in leather that looked to have been signed by Longfellow, and a children's pop-up book of *Goldilocks and the Three Bears*, which Miss Bunce began to read, turning the fragile pages slowly. Late Victorian, Mr Belderboss reckoned, about the same time Moorings was finished.

"Chap called Gregson built it," said Mr Belderboss. "Cotton mill owner. That's what they were round here, wasn't it, Esther? Cotton men?"

"Yes," said Mummer. "Cotton or linen."

"There's a photograph of him and his missus somewhere," said Mr Belderboss, looking around the room. "Was it seven children they had, Mary? It might have been more. I don't think many of them saw their fifth birthday, mind you. TB and all that. That's why they built these sorts of places. To keep their little 'uns alive. They thought the sea air would do them good."

"They built them to last, as well," said Farther, smoothing his hand over the plaster. "They must be a yard thick these walls."

Miss Bunce looked around her and then out of the window, clearly unconvinced that anyone who stayed here would leave the place healthier than when they came in.

It came as no surprise to her when Mr Belderboss explained how the house had changed hands many times since it had been built and carefully renamed by each successive occupant in an attempt to make it deliver what it seemed to promise sometimes, sitting there quietly under the gentle ruffling of the wood and the flour-soft clouds.

Gregson had christened it Sunny Vale; then it was Rose Cottage, Softsands, Sea Breezes, and lastly Moorings by the taxidermist.

"It must have been lovely, though, in its heyday," said Mrs Belderboss, pushing aside the curtains a little more. "What with that view and everything."

"Clever landscapers, the Victorians," said Farther.

"Oh, yes," said Mr Belderboss. "The view was all part of the prophylactic, wasn't it?"

"There's something timeless about it," said Mrs Belderboss, looking out at the sea. "Don't you think?"

"Well, it's a very old part of the country," said Mr Belderboss.

Mrs Belderboss rolled her eyes. "It must be the same age as everywhere else, you fool."

"Oh, you know what I mean," he replied. "Untrodden, then. Some of the yew trees up in the woods must have been ancient in the time of Bede. And they do say there are places around here that haven't been set foot in since the Vikings came."

Mrs Belderboss scoffed again.

"It's true," Mr Belderboss replied. "A century in this place is nothing. I mean, it's quite easy to imagine that that book", he said, nodding to Miss Bunce's hands, "could have been read by some poor little consumptive only yesterday."

Miss Bunce put the book down and wiped her hands on her duffle coat, as Mr Belderboss went over to the other side of the room, enthusing over the seascapes of

52

tiny ships under colossal stormclouds that the taxidermist had spent his last years painting. His brushes were still there in a jamjar. His palette had a dry crust of dark oils. And under the dust a rag, a chewed pencil, some loose, pre-decimal change all contributed to the uneasy feeling I always had when I stayed at Moorings, that the taxidermist had merely stepped out to smoke one of his expensive cigars and that he might return at any moment and pop through a door like one of the three bears in the old book, to find a Goldilocks sleeping in every room.

CHAPTER
FIVE

The room Hanny and I shared was at the top of the house where the rooks scrabbled across the slates for the insects in the moss. Every so often, one of the more daring would come to the window ledge, quite unperturbed that we were watching it, and rake its pencil-sharp beak down the glass with a horrible squeal to nibble out the things living in the decaying woodwork of the frame.

Only when I banged on the window did it finally disappear, flapping away in a peal of grating laughter and sailing in a smooth scoop back up to the others in the woods. Hanny was sad to see it go, but I couldn't let it stay there. Mummer didn't care much for those kinds of birds. Crows, ravens, jackdaws and the like. She would even shoo the jays and magpies out of the back garden in London. There was an old saying in her village that they prevented the sick from getting better, and that when they gathered in numbers a death was imminent.

"Sorry, Hanny," I said. "We can go and look at them later if you like."

He took his face away from the window, leaving a little oval of condensation.

"We ought to unpack," I said and nodded to the duffle-bag at his feet. He bent down and handed it to me, looking over my shoulder, his face suddenly brightening at the abundance of interesting junk in the room.

I suppose it was like looking at it anew for him, but to my eyes nothing much had changed. Only the water stains on the ceiling had grown. The dark patches had assumed the shapes of foreign countries, and a succession of tide lines showed how the empire of dampness had expanded year on year since we'd last been.

I put Hanny's clothes away for him, hung up his coat on the back of the door and set his *Lives of the Saints* book down on the bedside table. At Pinelands they encouraged them to do these sorts of things for themselves, but Hanny was too excited by what was in the room to care about anything else and took the various objects down one by one to look at them: all the colourful stones and shells, the splints of driftwood, the bottles, cuttlebone, hornwrack, dried twists of coral, mermaids' purses. There was a whole shelf of scrimshaw: whale teeth polished to the delicacy of bone china and engraved with intricately detailed pictures of schooners and battleships. Against one wall was a chest of drawers that contained specimens of birds' eggs, each one labelled with common and Latin name and the date it had been found. Some were decades old.

On the floor and on top of the long wardrobes were Victorian curios under dusty glass domes that had always frightened me to death when I was a child. Exotic butterflies, horribly bright, impaled to a stump of silver birch, two squirrels playing cricket in caps and pads, a spider monkey wearing a fez and smoking a pipe.

There were music boxes and broken wind-up toys, grinning marionettes and tin humming tops, and between our beds sat a clock on which the hours were indicated by little paintings of the apostles. Mummer thought it wonderful, of course, and when we were children she told us the story of each of them: how Andrew had elected to be crucified on a saltire; how James was chosen to be with Jesus during the transfiguration and how he was beheaded by Herod Agrippa on his return to Judea; how Matthias had replaced the treacherous Judas and converted the cannibals of Ethiopia.

They had all suffered and toiled so that we could do the same. For God's work should never be easy.

I touched Hanny lightly on the shoulder and he turned around.

"Mummer says I've to give you a bath," I said.

I mimed washing under my armpits and Hanny smiled and went over to a shelf where there was a stuffed mallard.

"You can't take that in the bath," I said.

He frowned and held onto it tightly.

"You'll ruin it, Hanny."

I fetched some towels and he followed me down the landing to the bathroom. He insisted on bringing the duck with him and sat it on the rim of the bath while he lay there in the foam listening to the wind playing in the pipework and the drains. He nodded and listened and then nodded again.

"It's just the wind, Hanny," I said. "It's not talking to you."

He smiled at me and slipped under the water, sending a mushroom of bubbles to the surface. He stayed there for a moment longer than I was comfortable with, and then, just as I was about to reach in and pull him out, he resurfaced open-mouthed and blinking, his mop slapped down over his ears.

I got him out after half an hour. The water was cold and the suds had all dissolved. I dried him slowly in a ritual drummed into me by Mummer. One of the many she insisted Hanny and I follow for the sake of our health, like cleaning our teeth with hot water and cutting our fingernails every other day.

Once he was completely dry, I helped him on with his pyjamas. But he had stopped smiling. His whole body was stiff and uncooperative, making it difficult to get his arms down the sleeves and the buttons done up. I noticed that he was staring past me at the darkening sky outside and then I understood what was wrong. He had realised that we were staying here and he didn't like it. He wanted to go home.

I settled him into bed and let him pet a stuffed hare that he'd taken a fancy to, hoping it might send him off to sleep. He held it close to him and stroked its ears as I went and sat by the window and tried to look beyond my reflection to the sea, which was rapidly fading in the dusk.

The room went suddenly silent. The rooks had stopped croaking. A stillness settled around the house and over the fields, and everything seemed watchful and timorous.

The night crept in at the Loney, in a way that I've never known anywhere else. At home in London, it kept its distance from us, skulking behind the streetlights and the office blocks and could be easily knocked aside in a second by the rush of light and metal from the Metropolitan Line trains that flashed past the end of our garden. But here it was different. There was nothing to keep it away. The moon was cold and distant and the stars were as feeble as the tiny specks of light from the fishing boats way out at sea.

Like the shadow of a huge predatory bird, darkness moved slowly down the hillside, past Moorings, across the marshes, across the beach, across the sea, until all that was left was a muddy orange on the horizon as the last of England's light ebbed away.

I was about to draw the curtains when I saw someone cross the lane that led up to the house and make their way through the fields where the Panzer lay. A moment later someone else followed carrying a large haversack and once he had caught up with the first, I saw them both head over to the hedgerow on the far side. Farmers, I thought, taking a short cut home. I looked to see where they were going, but it was too dark and the rain was teeming down again.

Behind me, I heard Hanny getting out of bed and scratting about on the floor, rubbing his hands over the bare wood and knocking here and there with his knuckles.

"What are you doing?" I said. "You should be in bed. Mummer will be cross if you don't go to sleep."

He pointed to the floor.

"What?"

He pointed again.

"No, you can't go downstairs, Hanny."

He smiled and pulled me by the sleeve so that I knelt like him next to the grubby pink rug in the centre of the room. He turned it back and underneath there was a floorboard with a knothole pushed through. It was where we used to hide things we didn't want Mummer to see. I'd forgotten all about it.

"Can you open it?" I said and Hanny jammed his finger into the hole and lifted up the board. It creaked against the others but came out easily enough and Hanny shuffled forward and peered into the darkness.

"Reach in, Hanny," I said and mimed with my hand and Hanny stuck his arm into the cavity and felt around. A penknife came out, mottled with rust and blunt as a brick. The pornographic photographs Billy Tapper had pressed into my hand that day we saw him in the bus shelter. One, two, three, half a dozen stuffed rats that Hanny took out and threw into a pile without so much as flinching.

Reaching further than he'd been able to do the last time we came, he brought out a leather strap. He pulled it and something large banged against the underside of the floorboards.

It was an M1 Garand. I remembered from *Commando* that all the Yanks had them in the war. Bullets came in a metal clip that slotted into the top and jumped out with a loud ping when all the rounds had been used up — an unfortunate signal to the enemy that you were out of ammunition, but the rifle's only fault. It could put a bullet through an oak tree.

Protected by the bedsheet in which it had been wrapped, its wooden stock was still polished to a chestnut gloss and made of solid, sural curves like a muscle extracted from the leg of a racehorse. The sight mounted on top looked as if it would pull in a thousand yards or more.

God knows where the taxidermist had got it from.

I dusted down the barrel with my sleeve and we took it in turns to hold it. Then, uncertain what else there was to do, we laid it on the bed and looked at it.

"This is ours now," I said. "It belongs to you and me. But you mustn't touch it without me. All right?"

Hanny looked at me and smiled.

There was a knock at the door. I quickly covered the rifle with a blanket and sat down on top of it.

It was Father Bernard.

"How are you boys?" he said, looking around the door. "Have you settled in all right?"

"Yes, Father."

"Do you mind if I come in?"

"No, Father."

He stepped into the room and closed the door behind him. He wasn't wearing his dog collar and had his shirt sleeves rolled up over his ham-hock forearms that were surprisingly bare.

60

"Can I tempt you to half an hour of gin rummy?" he said.

I shifted uncomfortably, feeling the rifle digging into my backside. I realised that I had no idea if it was loaded or not, or if it was possible that by sitting on it I might inadvertently pull the trigger and blow Father Bernard's kneecaps off.

"I don't know about you boys," he said, fetching a stool from the side of the washbasin. "But I'm not tired at all."

He sat down and produced a pack of cards from his shirt pocket and handed them to me, moving the *Lives of the Saints* book off the bedside table to make room.

"You deal, Tonto," he said.

"Yes, Father."

He rubbed his hand over his mouth and we started playing, silently at first, though it didn't take long before he was on to the stories about the farm where he grew up, and then I could relax a little.

It was by all accounts a fairly miserable hovel on Rathlin Island, some barren speck of rock I'd never heard of between the Antrim coast and the Mull of Kintyre full of guillemots and storm petrels and razorbills. Mist and bog. Endless grey sea. It's easy to imagine the sort of place.

The only thing of note about it was that it was where the spider supposedly egged on Robert the Bruce to clobber the English, and there that the English replied by massacring the McDonnells. Even the children. Apparently you could still find bloodstains on the rocks that the sea refused to wash away.

So little happened on the island that memories were as long as the savage winters that were the starting point of most of Father Bernard's stories.

"Would you listen to that rain?" he said, looking towards the window. "It reminds me of the winter our stores were flooded out."

"When was that, Father?"

"Oh, I was only a wee boy. I can't have been any more than eight or nine."

"What happened, Father?"

"My daddy, God love him, was a good farmer but he was a lousy roofer. He'd patched up the storehouse with old bits of wood, you see, and they just rotted away like everything else on the island. One night the whole thing went in and nigh on every scrap of food we had was ruined. I remember my mammy chasing a whole load of carrots and turnips that were floating out of the yard.

"I shouldn't laugh," he said. "It wasn't funny. We weren't that far from starving."

"Didn't you have animals, Father?"

"Aye."

"Couldn't you eat them?"

"If we'd done that we'd have been poor as well as hungry come the New Year market in Ballycasde. The animals were why we nearly starved. We had to feed them first, you know?"

"Couldn't you have got some food from somewhere else?"

"Oh aye," he said. "The O'Connells from the farm over the way came around with potatoes and meat, but my daddy was too proud to take anything off them. He'd rather we all wasted away than rely on charity.

"When my mammy found out, she was furious. It was the only time she ever raised her voice to him, and when the O'Connells came around again she took everything they'd brought.

"You know, Tonto, it sounds daft, but I don't think my daddy was quite the same from then on. I think it half killed him, sacrificing his pride like that."

I stopped dealing and put the pack of cards in the middle of the table.

"Anyway," he said. "I'm going on. How's school at the moment? Almost done now, aren't you?"

"Yes, Father."

"Exams soon, is it?"

"Yes."

"Well make sure you work hard. Otherwise you might end up with a career in the priesthood."

He smiled and pulled his cards together, tapping them on the table.

"Are you a good lad at school?"

"Yes, Father."

"I was a wee terror," he said. "When they could get me to go, that is."

He fanned the cards in his hand and laid one down.

"Mind you, if you'd seen the place, Tonto, you wouldn't have gone either."

"Why's that, Father?"

"There were fifty of us in one room. Half of us hadn't any boots to wear. And it was so cold in the winter that the ink iced over in the wells. Can you imagine?"

"No, Father."

He frowned at my expression and then laughed.

"Ah, I'm just pulling your leg," he said. "It wasn't that bad. Apart from O'Flannery."

He threw a card down onto the pile, before picking up another.

"You'll not have anyone like O'Flannery where you are, I'm sure. He was a very old fashioned sort of teacher. You know what I mean? A real hardliner."

"Yes, Father."

"Some of the other lads said he wore a cilice. And I wouldn't have put it past him, the face he had on him sometimes. You know what a cilice is, right, Tonto?"

"Yes, Father."

He tapped his fingers on his cards and took his turn and then smiled to himself.

"I laugh hearty at it now," he said. "But O'Flannery was an out and out bullyman. Even the mammies and daddies were frightened of him. He made sure he put the fear of God into you from day one."

"How?"

"Well, whenever anyone new joined the class, he'd always ask them the same question."

"What was that?"

"It was to translate *dura lex, sed lex*."

He looked at me.

"Aye, that was the face they pulled too. Right before he'd give them a whack on the arse with his cane."

He pursed his lips and shook his head.

64

"You know, I can still feel it now. He'd hit you so hard with the old birch that all he had to do after that to stop us silly wee cubs in our tracks was to go to the desk and touch it. We shut up pretty quickly then, I can tell you."

"Didn't you have other teachers though, Father?" I said.

"Aye, we did in the end."

"How do you mean?"

He laughed drily to himself.

"Mr O'Flannery's career was cut short let's say."

"Why, what happened?"

"The silly sod fell off the cliffs at Rue Point, photographing the puffins. When they told us on the Monday morning, all the lads cheered, and to my eternal shame so did I.

"We were still cheering when the headmaster came in. I thought we were done for, you know. But he didn't scold us at all. He knew what O'Flannery was like. What people thought of him. He just sat on the edge of the desk asking us questions about geography and science and mathematics. And do you know what? Between us we answered every single one. He must have been there for an hour and then he said something that I've never forgotten to this day."

"What was that, Father?"

"He said, 'In time to come, each of you will thank the man who gave you your mind.' Then he got up and left. And he was right. I mean he was hard as nails, O'Flannery, and I hated him at the time, but I feel kind of grateful to him now, you know? There aren't many lessons of his that I don't remember."

"What did it mean, Father?"

"What did what mean?"

"The Latin."

He laughed. "The law is harsh, but it is the law. Then there was, let's see, *Ex fructu arbor agnoscitur* and *Veritas, vos liberabit.*"

"What does that one mean, Father?"

"The truth will set you free," he said and played his card.

"John," I said, automatically.

Father Bernard raised his eyebrows and then looked at me thoughtfully.

"Father Wilfred taught you a lot, didn't he?"

I nodded and was about to show Hanny which card to lay down when I realised that he had won.

"Show," I said and bent the cards towards Father Bernard.

Hanny pulled them back to his chest.

"It's all right, Hanny," I said. "You've won. You're the winner."

"Aye, he is that," said Father Bernard looking at Hanny's hand, and then throwing in his own cards.

He sat back and looked at me as I scooped the cards into a pile to deal them again.

"There was something I wanted to ask you actually, Tonto," he said.

"Yes, Father?"

"On behalf of Mr Belderboss."

"Yes, Father?"

66

"When Father Wilfred passed away," he said. "There was something of his that went missing. A book. You've not seen it knocking about have you?"

"A book?"

"Aye, you know, a diary, a notebook, that kind of thing. It was quite important. To the family. Mr Belderboss is pretty keen on getting it back."

"No, Father."

"Not in the vestry? Or the presbytery?"

"No, Father."

"Do you think any of the other lads might know?"

"I don't know, Father."

"Would it be worth me asking them?"

"I'm not sure, Father. Maybe."

He looked at me and I started dealing.

"You know, Tonto, confession is bound by a seal of secrecy. I can't tell a soul what you say to me," he said, pausing for a moment. "Even with a gun to my head."

I looked up at him sharply, thinking that he had somehow seen the rifle, but he was gathering his cards together and spreading them in his hands.

"But I'm not in confession, Father," I said.

He laughed and then outside on the landing I heard Mummer calling for him.

"You have a think about it, Tonto," he said and got up to open the door. "If anything comes to you, let me know."

Mummer came in. "Oh, there you are," she said. "I hope these two weren't keeping you up, Father."

"No, no, not at all, Mrs Smith," he said. "I just wanted to see if they'd got any better at cards."

"Oh," said Mummer, confused as to whether Father Bernard had set up some elaborate test to see if we were secret gamblers. "Have they?"

"No," he said, winking at me. "They're still terrible cheats."

"Oh," said Mummer. "Well, if I could borrow you for a moment, Father, there are a few things I wanted to speak to you about."

"By all means, Mrs Smith," he said.

He got up and went past Mummer who held the door open for him. When he had gone down the landing Mummer snapped at me.

"Why isn't Andrew asleep? You know he'll be no good if he's tired."

"I know."

"Well if you know, stop messing around up here and get him settled."

"Yes, Mother."

She looked at us both and then walked away. I waited for a moment and then went to the door and onto the landing.

"I don't know if you realised, Father," said Mummer as they went down the stairs. "But Father Wilfred made himself available for confession when we came here."

They had stopped in the hallway outside Father Bernard's room. Mummer had her arms folded in the way she had started doing since he had arrived at Saint Jude's.

"I see," said Father Bernard. He nodded at the door of the under-stairs cupboard. "Not in here, surely?"

Mummer gave him an indulgent smile.

"No, we used Father Wilfred's room. The room you're in. It has the little curtain around the wash stand you see."

"Ah."

"He was very accommodating."

"I'm sure."

Mummer moved closer to him. "I don't ask for myself particularly, Father," she said. "It's the others. Mr and Mrs Belderboss really. They find this place, this time of year, well it encourages an openness with God. A chance to cleanse the soul."

He held Mummer lightly by the shoulders. "Mrs Smith," he said, "rest assured that I will listen to whatever you wish to tell me."

"Thank you, Father," said Mummer. "Now about Andrew."

"Aye?"

"It's very important that he fasts like the rest of us over the weekend. I'm sure you'll agree that he must be properly prepared."

"Aye, of course."

"Then I'll need your help, Father."

"Naturally Mrs Smith."

"Now, when we get to the shrine itself . . ."

They moved off into the kitchen but I knew what Mummer was saying to him. What she wanted him to do. How they would get Hanny to drink the water. How the power of Jesus would cleanse his body and drive out the sickness that had kept him silent since the day he was born.

When they had closed the door, I went back to the bedroom. Hanny was standing by the window. He had taken the rifle out from under the blanket. He saluted me, fiddled with the firing pin, twisted the sight and before I could tell him to put it down, he pointed the rifle at me and pulled the trigger.

CHAPTER
SIX

For a moment I thought I was dead. I was dead and it was all right. I was strangely relieved that it was all over and that it had been as quick and painless as I'd always hoped it would be. But Hanny was still there, I was still in the room, we were still at Moorings. I realised that I'd been holding my breath and now I let it out and went over to him.

"Give," I said.

Hanny refused and turned away from me, clutching the rifle to his chest. They were forever taking his stuff off him at Pinelands and the bugger had learnt to fight his corner. I was proud of him for that but I couldn't have him thinking that he could parade around Moorings with a rifle. Mummer would have had a fit, I would have got the blame, and that would have been the end of that.

"I said give it to me."

I held out my hands and sensing that I was serious Hanny passed me the rifle. I wound the strap around the stock, slotted it under the floorboards and laid the rug back over the top.

Hanny sat down on his bed and then folded up his legs the way a child might do, grasping his ankles and

71

shuffling his feet under his backside. He picked up the book Father Bernard had removed from the bedside table and opened it. He wanted me to read to him.

"You need to go to sleep, Hanny," I said. "You heard Mummer. She'll only get cross."

He flipped through a few pages until he found the story that he wanted.

"All right, Hanny. But afterwards you've got to go to sleep or I'll get it in the neck."

We had barely got halfway through the story before Hanny was snoring. I turned off the lamp but I couldn't sleep at all and lay there in the darkness for a while before I fetched a torch out of my bag, took up the loose floorboard and brought out the rifle to look at it again. I felt around the metalwork and found the bolt that opened the receiver. It was empty of course. I closed it up again with a quiet click and then slipped it back under the floorboards.

I lay down on my bed once more and tried to sleep but I was too restless, and rather than staring at the dark, I went out to look at the photographs of the taxidermist and his wife that had been placed at intervals up the stairs.

He had been a diminutive man and looked to have owned only one shirt in the whole of his time at Moorings. He wore bottle-end glasses and slicked his hair back over his head. He looked a little like Charles Hawtrey, I thought. Or Himmler.

In each shot, he and his wife posed with a stuffed animal between them. A lioness. A beaver up on its back legs. A kangaroo wearing boxing gloves. The date neatly written in the corner.

The poor sod. Apparently he lost it when his wife died. Ended up sectioned in some hospital near Preston, where I always imagined him painting those seascapes over and over again. The boats getting a little smaller and the clouds a little bigger each time, until there was nothing but tempest.

As I was looking at the photographs, someone came out of the sitting room and knocked softly at Father Bernard's door. From the sniffing I knew it was Mrs Belderboss.

"Hello, Father," she said, when the door opened.

"Mrs Belderboss."

"Did Esther mention confession to you?"

"She did."

"Could I come in, Father?"

"Aye, of course," said Father Bernard. "But are you sure you want to? It's getting late."

Mrs Belderboss's voice went down to a whisper. "I know, but Reg is asleep on the sofa," she said. "And I thought while I've the opportunity. There's been something I've been wanting to get off my chest for a while now."

She went into Father Bernard's room and closed the door. I stayed very still to try and hear what was going on but there were only mumbles. Even at the foot of the stairs, their voices were muffled. I checked that no one else was around and slipped into the broom cupboard. Settling in next to the brushes and mops I could hear them both clearly. The wall between the cupboard and Father Bernard's room was only made out of plywood and where the damp had warped the wood there were gaps that let in little skewers of light.

I didn't mean to stay. As an ethical crime, it fell off the end of the scale. Listening to Mrs Belderboss's confession was like watching her take off her clothes. But now that I was ensconced, it would have been difficult to get out again without making a racket, and I reasoned that it was better to stay put and wait until they had finished. I couldn't imagine that Mrs Belderboss had very much to confess anyway.

I heard the chinking of the metal rings as Father Bernard yanked the curtain around the washbasin.

Mrs Belderboss rhymed off the Act of Contrition and Father Bernard said, "What is it you want to tell me?"

"It's Reg, Father," said Mrs Belderboss.

"Aye?"

"I'm worried about him."

"Why's that?"

"He won't sleep, Father. At home, I mean. He just lies there, staring at the ceiling until he gets up and goes out."

"Where does he go?"

"Well, this is it. I've asked him but he won't answer me, not properly. He just says he can't sleep and walks around to take his mind off things. Off what things? I ask him, but he just changes the subject, or gets cross with me."

"Is it his brother, do you think?"

"Father Wilfred? No. I don't think so. Reg would have said if that was bothering him. If anything, he's been remarkably philosophical since he passed away."

"You know, Mrs Belderboss," said Father Bernard. "It's often hard to explain how we feel when someone close to us dies. Even to those we love. People can put on a bit of a brave front. Wilfred did pass away very unexpectedly. Maybe Mr Belderboss hasn't quite come to terms with it yet. Grief is a peculiar business anyway and when it's compounded with shock, it can take a wee while longer to get over it."

"A month he's been at it now. Lord alone knows what the neighbours must think."

There was a pause and then Father Bernard said, "What is it you want to confess exactly, Mrs Belderboss?"

"Well," she said. "I was so worried about him, Father, wandering around at all hours, what with his heart and his hip. You hear such dreadful things, don't you? There are all sorts of odd folk about at night who wouldn't think twice about taking advantage of someone vulnerable like Reg."

"Aye, go on."

"Well, I went to the chemist to see if there was anything they could give me."

"I'm not sure I'm following you, Mrs Belderboss."

"For Reg. To take. To help him sleep."

"And did they?"

"Yes. Only he wouldn't take them, would he? You know what he's like."

"Aye."

"So I crushed up one of the pills and put it into his Horlicks."

Father Bernard cleared his throat.

"I feel awful, Father, but I couldn't stand it any more. I'm frightened he's going, you know. It happens, doesn't it? It always starts with little things like this. They say you've got to watch out for the warning signs, don't they?"

"And did it work?" Father Bernard asked. "The medicine?"

"It was the first decent night he'd had for weeks, but the guilt of it's been playing on my mind and now *I* can't sleep. It was wicked, wasn't it, Father?"

"I wouldn't call it that, Mrs Belderboss."

"But drugging my own husband."

"Mrs Belderboss," said Father Bernard. "When I look at you and your husband I see the love that God would wish us all to have if it were possible. There is no malice in your heart. The worst you're guilty of is a little desperation and that puts you in the company of a good many others, believe me. Go and say your rosary and pray for God's help to be patient with Reg. He'll tell you what's wrong in his own time."

"Are you sure that's all I need to do, Father?"

"Quite sure."

There was a pause and then Father Bernard spoke again.

"You seem a little disappointed, Mrs Belderboss."

"No, Father."

"Were you expecting me to say something else?"

"No."

There was a moment of silence and then Mrs Belderboss sighed.

"Oh, I don't know. Perhaps you're right about Wilfred, Father. It's only been a few months after all. And the way he went was, well, sudden, as you say."

"Aye."

"He'll get tired of all this gadding about, won't he, Father? Once he's stopped feeling so upset."

"I'm sure that'll be the case, Mrs Belderboss," said Father Bernard. "It's still raw in his mind. It's going to take time. I don't think you ever stop feeling for people that have died, but the feelings themselves do change if you give them time. I missed my mammy and daddy terrible when they went, so much that I didn't even want to think about them. It took a while but when I talk about them now it's a joy; it's when I feel closest to them and I know that they haven't really gone anywhere. It's not unlike our relationship with God, Mrs Belderboss. How's your Joshua?"

"Sorry, Father?"

"Joshua, verse one. 'Be strong and courageous. Do not be afraid; do not be discouraged, for the Lord, your God, will be with you wherever you go.'"

Father Bernard laughed quietly.

"Sorry," he said. "I can be an awful show-off with that one. They made me learn it by heart at school."

"And you're right, of course, Father," Mrs Belderboss said. "I know in my heart of hearts that Wilfred's looking down on us and keeping us safe, it's just he seems so — absent."

"And I think grief comes from that very contradiction," Father Bernard replied.

"Yes, perhaps it does, Father."

"Try and have a good night's sleep, Mrs Belderboss, and I'm sure in the morning things won't seem quite so bad."

"I'll try, Father. Goodnight."

I listened to her going past me and up the stairs. When it was quiet, I crept out and went back to my own room and held the rifle once more before I went to sleep.

CHAPTER
SEVEN

Late in the night, I heard far-off voices. Shouting. Whooping. Like a war dance. It only lasted for a few seconds and I wasn't sure if I was dreaming, but in the morning everyone was talking about it around the breakfast table where the smell of toast mingled with the stew Mummer had been making since first light.

"I didn't sleep a wink afterwards," said Mrs Belderboss.

"I wouldn't worry about it," said Father Bernard. "It was probably just farmers calling in their dogs, eh Monro?"

He reached down and rubbed at Monro's neck.

"At three in the morning?" Mrs Belderboss said.

"Farmers do keep odd hours, Mary," said Mummer.

"Well I wish they wouldn't."

"I thought it sounded as if it was coming up from the sea," said Mr Belderboss. "Didn't you?"

Everyone shrugged and finished drinking their tea. Only Miss Bunce passed any more comment.

"At Glasfynydd, it's totally silent at night," she said.

Mummer looked at her and took the dirty plates and bowls out to wash.

I didn't say anything, and I couldn't be certain that the wind blustering around the house in the early hours hadn't tricked my ears, but as I'd lain there in the dark, I had been convinced that the voices were coming from the woods.

I wondered if I ought to catch Father Bernard as everyone was leaving the dining room and tell him, but there was a crash from the kitchen and we could hear Mummer shouting.

When I went to see what had happened, she had Hanny tipped back over the sink, her fingers inside his mouth. Hanny was gripping the edge of the basin. The dish of stew that was to be eaten later that evening lay in pieces on the floor in a slick of beef and gravy.

"Spit it out," Mummer said. "Get rid of it."

Hanny swallowed whatever was in his mouth and Mummer gave a sigh of exasperation and let go of him.

Father Bernard appeared behind me. Then Farther.

"What's the matter, Mrs Smith?" said Father Bernard.

"Andrew's been at the stew," she said.

"Sure, he's not had all that much," he laughed.

"I told you, Father. He's got to fast, like the rest of us," said Mummer. "It's very important. He's got to be properly prepared."

"I don't think a mouthful of casserole will do much damage, Esther," said Farther.

"He's had half the lot," said Mummer, pointing to the brown puddle that Monro was sniffing with interest.

80

Father Bernard called him away but Mummer flicked her hand dismissively.

"No, let him eat it, Father. It's all it's good for now."

Hanny started to lick his fingers, and Mummer gasped and grabbed him by the arm and marched him over to the back door. She opened it to the hiss of rain and pushed Hanny's fingers further into his mouth until he emptied his stomach on the steps.

I cleaned him up at the kitchen sink and then took him to the bedroom to lie down.

I tried to get him to go back to sleep but he was still wound up and kept on wandering to the toilet. Each time he came back he looked paler than the last, his eyes red and sore. In the end he came and sat on the edge of my bed and rattled his jam jar of nails.

"Where does it hurt, Hanny?" I said, touching him on the temples, the forehead, the crown.

He put his hands over his head like a helmet. It hurt everywhere.

"Try and sleep, Hanny," I said. "You'll feel better."

He looked at me and then touched the mattress.

"Yes, all right," I said. "But only for a little while."

I lay next to him and after a few minutes he began snoring. I extracted myself as quietly as possible and went outside.

It had stopped raining and the last of the water was trickling down the old gutters that ran through the cobbles to a large iron drain in the middle of the yard.

Outside, as well as in, Moorings felt like a place that had been repeatedly abandoned. A place that had failed. The drystone walls that formed the yard were broken down to a puzzle of odd-sized rocks that no one had ever had the skill to rebuild, and so the gaps had been merely strung with wire. There was a small, tin-roofed outhouse in one corner, locked and chained, and plastered with bird muck. And beyond the yard stretched wide, empty fields that had been left fallow for so long that the rusting farm machinery that had been there since we'd first started coming here was now almost buried under the nettles and brambles.

The wind came rushing in off the sea, sweeping its comb through the scrubby grass and sending a shiver through the vast pools of standing water. I felt the wire moving forward and Father Bernard was standing next to me.

"Andrew all right now?"

"Yes, Father. He's sleeping."

"Good."

He smiled and then nodded towards the sea. "You used to come here every year, Tonto?"

"Yes."

He made a quick sound of disbelief with his lips.

"Can't have been much fun for a wee lad," he said.

"It was all right."

"It reminds me of the place I grew up," he said. "I couldn't wait to get away. I tell you, when they sent me to the Ardoyne, the place they gave me in the Bone was a paradise compared with Rathlin Island. It had an indoor toilet, for a start."

"What's it like? Belfast?" I said.

I'd seen it night after night on the news. Barricades and petrol bombs.

He looked at me, understood what I was getting at, and gazed across the field again. "You don't want to know, Tonto," he said. "Believe me."

"Please, Father."

"Why the sudden interest?"

I shrugged.

"Another time, eh? Suffice to say the Crumlin Road in July isn't much fun."

He nodded across the field.

"I was going to take a walk," he said. "Do you want to come?"

He parted the wire and I climbed through and did the same for him. Once through, he brushed down his jacket and we walked towards the Panzer, disturbing a pair of curlews that burst out of the grass and clapped away.

"She means well," Father Bernard said. "Your mother. She only wants to help Andrew."

"I know."

"She may not seem it, but she's frightened more than anything else."

"Yes."

"And fear can make people do funny things."

"Yes, Father. I know."

He patted me on the shoulder and then put his hands in his pockets.

"Will he get better?" I said. It slipped out before I could help it.

Father Bernard stopped walking and looked back at the house.

"What do you mean by better, Tonto?"

I hesitated and Father Bernard thought for a second before he rephrased the question.

"I mean, what would you change in him?" he said.

I hadn't thought about it before.

"I don't know, Father. That he could talk."

"Is that something you'd like? For him to talk?"

"Yes."

"You don't sound all that sure."

"I am sure, Father."

"Do you think it makes Andrew unhappy? Not being able to talk?"

"I don't know. It doesn't seem to."

He considered this with a deep breath and then spoke.

"Look," he said. "I don't know if Andrew will get better in the way you want him to. That's up to God to decide. All you can do is pray and put your trust in Him to make the right decisions about Andrew's happiness. You do still pray, don't you, Tonto?"

"Yes."

He gave me a wry smile. Even as he asked the question I think he knew that I didn't and hadn't for some time. Priests are like doctors. They know that people lie about the things they think will disappoint them.

We came to the Panzer and Father Bernard laid his hand against the rock and felt its texture. He ran his finger up a long crack and picked at a clod of moss, teasing the fibres of it between his fingers.

"God understands it's not all plain sailing, you know. He allows you to question your faith now and again," he said, looking closely at the fossils, the tiny bivalves and ammonites. "Come on now, mastermind, what does it say in Luke fifteen?"

"Something about lost sheep?"

"Aye. See, if you can remember that, sure you're not damned for all eternity just yet."

He moved around the rock, feeling for hand holds and pulled himself up onto the top. He put his hands on his hips as he surveyed the view, then something under his feet caught his attention.

"Hey, Tonto," he called down. "Come up here."

He was on his knees, paddling his fingers in a hole full of water. He looked at my puzzled expression.

"It's a bullaun," he said. "We had one on the farm when I was a wee boy."

He looked at me again and took hold of my hand, pressing my fingers to the edges of the hole.

"Feel that? How smooth it is? That's not been made by water. It was cut by a man."

"What's it for, Father?"

"They made them hundreds of years ago to collect rain. They thought the water was magical if it didn't touch the ground, you see."

He stood up and dried his hands on his coat.

"My granny used to make the cows drink out of the one in our field," he said. "And if I ever had a fever, she'd take me down there and wash me in it to make me better."

"Did it work?"

He looked at me and frowned and gave a little laugh. "No, Tonto, it didn't," he said.

He climbed down and I was about to do the same when I noticed the Land Rover parked on the road down below. I could tell it was Clement's by the cross painted on the door, though Clement wasn't inside.

The two men in the front had their faces turned towards me, though it was hard to tell whether they were staring at me or Moorings or the woods behind. Whatever they were looking at, it was clear even from this distance that it was the two men Father Bernard had asked for help the day before. The one built like a bull and the one with the dog. Parkinson and Collier.

"What do you think those noises were last night, Father?" I asked.

"Between you and me," he replied, "I didn't hear a thing."

"But you said it was farmers."

"It was a wee fib."

"You lied to them?"

"Ah come on, Tonto, I was just trying to reassure them that they weren't going to get murdered in their beds. Are you coming?"

"Yes, Father."

I looked back at the Land Rover and after a moment the driver set off in a plume of steel-coloured smoke.

Hanny was still asleep when I got back. Mummer hadn't yet forgiven him and the effort of rousing him and getting him dressed and nursing his headache was too much for her to cope with. So she allowed him to stay in bed while they went off to church for the Blessing of the Oils and the Washing of the Feet. It wasn't an integral part of his preparation for the shrine and he would only spoil it if he came.

"But don't let him lounge around all day," said Mummer, looking up the stairs as they were all leaving.

"Keep out of mischief," Farther added as he plucked his flat cap from the peg and helped Mr and Mrs Belderboss out.

I watched them go and when I closed the front door and turned around, Hanny was standing at the top of the stairs. He had been waiting for them to leave too. Now we could go down to the beach at last. We could leave their world and find ours.

CHAPTER
EIGHT

Since we had decided to come back to Moorings, I had rehearsed the journey down to the beach many times, trying to re-imagine the road and what I used to be able to see on either side. Now that I was here and walking across the marshes with Hanny it all seemed to unfold as it should. I remembered the single, twisted hawthorn tree overhanging the road, like the sole survivor of a shipwreck that had staggered inland, torn and cowed by the sea. I remembered the way the wind rasped through the reeds and shuddered across the black water. The way the sea hung between the valleys of the dunes.

This was the real world, the world as it should be, the one that was buried in London by concrete plazas and shopping parades of florists, chip shops and bookmakers; hidden under offices and schools and pubs and bingo halls.

Things lived at the Loney as they ought to live. The wind, the rain, the sea were all in their raw states, always freshly born and feral. Nature got on with itself. Its processes of death and replenishment happened without anyone noticing apart from Hanny and me.

When we came to the base of the dunes, we veered from the road and took off our boots to feel the cold sand under our feet.

I slung the rifle around so that it sat against my back and helped Hanny up. He had insisted on bringing the stuffed rats with him in his school satchel and kept slipping down, gouging deep scars into the sand with his feet.

At the top we could see the grey sea spreading out towards the horizon that was pressed flat by the huge block of sky. The tide was coming in quickly, washing over the mudflats.

Everything here was as it always had been, apart from the botched swastika someone had spraypainted on the side of the pillbox as a companion to the letters *NF*.

"How are you feeling now, Hanny?" I said and put my hand on his brow, the way Mummer did to check his temperature.

He smiled and shook his head. The headache had gone.

"Mummer means well," I said. "She's just worried that you won't get better. Fear can make people do funny things, you know."

We walked down onto the beach, following a ragged trail of debris. Seagulls had been strangled by the sea into sodden, twisted things of bones and feathers. Huge grey tree stumps, smoothed to a metallic finish had been washed up like abandoned war-time ordnance. All along the beach, in fact, the sea had left its offerings like a cat trying to curry favour with its owner. The

Loney had always been a dumping ground for the North's detritus, and tangled with the seaweed were shoes and bottles, milk crates and tyres. Yet all of it would be gone at the next high tide, raked back into the jumble of the sea.

With a difficulty that I didn't remember from the last time we'd come here, we climbed up onto the roof of the pillbox and stood either side of the hole. Inside it was deeply carpeted with sand. Pools of seawater sat in the gloom.

Hanny jumped down first and held me round the waist as I came down through the hole. Someone had been in here: the same person who had sprayed the outside wall, no doubt. It smelled of urine and spent matches. There was litter thrown up against one corner. Beer cans and chip wrappers. But despite all that, it remained more or less as sturdy as when it had first been built. There was never any bombing here and until we had claimed it for our own, I doubted that it had ever been manned at all. The Loney was just a place the Luftwaffe passed on their way to the Clyde. And the Third Reich never did come marauding up the Irish Sea in the end, of course.

We'd had to smash a hole in the roof to get inside — as the dunes had swallowed the back end where the door was — and the side facing the sea had begun to reveal its rusty skeleton, but it still felt as though it would last forever.

Using our hands we picked up and dumped the sand against the walls. Hanny worked like a machine, raking great clods of the stuff between his legs, checking his watch to see how long it was taking him.

Once there was space, Hanny opened the satchel and carefully arranged the rats on the floor and then his toy soldiers to face them. I took the rifle off my shoulder and positioned it through one of the gun slits, fitting my eye to the rubber cup at the end of the sight. It took time to get it right — for a few seconds there was only the magnification of my own eyelashes — but once I had the sea contained in the circle, it was brought to me sharp and silent.

The horizon I had seen with the naked eye from the top of the dunes was dragged closer and replaced by another much further out. A boat with a white sail that had been too far away to see before tracked slowly from one edge of my vision to the other, rising and falling, outrun by the terns and gulls scudding over the waves. There was another world out there that no one else but I could see.

I fancied myself as a naval captain on the lookout for U-boats, or a lone gunner charged with the defence of the coastline.

Those sorts of games only ever seemed real at the Loney. London was hard to convert into the kinds of places the men in *Commando* seemed to find themselves.

Although I had assassinated the park keeper — who morphed from one important Gestapo officer to another — several times from a hideout in the huge oak tree by the tennis courts and blown Mummer to pieces when she stepped on the land mine I'd buried in the vegetable patch, the parks, our garden, they were too prim and clean.

The cemetery up in Golders Green with its flat, white graves that looked as though they had been levelled by a bomb blast made for a half-decent blitzed town, but the groundsman had a dog that was supposed to be rabid. And anyway I could only play there on Saturdays, when the Jews weren't allowed to do anything, even visit the dead.

At the Loney, on the other hand, one could be at Sword Beach, Iwo Jima, Arnhem, El Alamein without much strain on the imagination. The pillbox was easily transformed into a cell in a German prisoner of war camp, which we'd fight our way out of with our bare hands, thwacking *Achtung!*-ing Nazis in freeze frames. Or it was a jungle hideout from which we watched a line of buck-toothed Japs come stalking through the marram and the sea holly and then we'd unzipper them with a burst of machine-gun fire before they had time to draw breath. The Japs were cruel and devious but screeched like girls when they died. They were always weaker than the Krauts and the Krauts were always more arrogant than the Brits, who naturally won every time.

"Here," I said and Hanny half crouching, took over, adjusting his grip, squinting into the sight. I moved to the slit next to Hanny's and watched the hordes of birds come in with the rushing tide, ransacking the foaming bore for the things dragged along in its thrust, or heading inland to the marshes with food for their young.

A flock of gulls came to land, squabbling over some dead thing from which they tore bits of fur and skin, the craftier ones making off with larger portions — a cluster of innards, or bones still jointed in the middle.

The sudden boom of the sea against the rocks close by scared them and they took off together, screeching and honking. All but one. A large gull thrashed about on the sand, trying to lift itself out of the incoming water. It beat one wing against the air, while the other stuck out from its body at an angle. It had been broken in the scrum.

It cawed, nuzzled at its leg and then resumed its strange dance, hopping one, two, three steps, lifting off and tumbling back onto the sand.

Hanny looked at me.

"We'll have to kill it," I said. "It's cruel to leave it in pain."

Hanny frowned. He didn't understand. I took the rifle off him and mimed stoving the bird in with the butt. He nodded and we climbed out of the pillbox and watched the seagull floundering on the sand. It stared back, wide-eyed.

"It's the right thing to do," I said, and gave Hanny the rifle.

He looked at me and smiled and then he turned his head sharply the other way, when he heard the sound of a car. I took the rifle back and ushered Hanny up onto the dunes, making for a natural trough in the grass, from where we could lie flat and observe the road across the marshes.

Once the car had passed the hawthorn tree, I could see through the crosshairs of the sight that it was the one that had passed us when we'd broken down on our way to Moorings.

This time there were three people in the car. Two in the front — a man and a woman — and one in the back, presumably the sleeping girl. The car slowed and as it came closer the tyres threw out waves of spray before passing through the gap in the dunes and coming to a halt on the fringes of the beach. Seeing that the sandflats were rapidly disappearing, the driver reversed. The engine idled for a moment, then shrivelled away to a rapid ticking as the mechanisms cooled under the bonnet. The birds that had been frightened away returned to what they were doing — the gulls coming down again to fight over the carcass on the beach, the curlews chunnering in the grass.

We moved carefully along the ridge and at the end where it sloped down to the road, we pressed ourselves into the sand. Parting the grass with the muzzle, I could see the front passenger more clearly now. Mummer would have thought her common for the way she was applying lipstick in the mirror of the sun visor, rolling her lips in and out. She was the kind of woman Mummer would have pointed out to Farther. The kind of woman she would have commented on.

Lifting her chin and turning her head, she began clearing up some imperfection in the corner of her open mouth with a folded arrowhead of tissue and then ran the tip of her little finger down her philtrum, giving it a flick at the end.

The driver distracted her for a moment and she turned to face him. There was evidently some kind of disagreement and the woman went back to her preening, impatiently dabbing powder across her cheeks and nose and pausing to shout something halfway through the process.

Inching to the right, I could see the girl sitting in the back. She leant forward and tried to intervene, but the adults in the front ignored her and she stared out of the window instead.

She looked straight at me, but didn't see me. I was careful to stay well hidden. I always was. When I played my games in London, I could be as silent as the dead in the Jewish cemetery. Deader than the dead.

Watching the girl, I didn't even hear my own breath, only sensed its warmth coming and going on my trigger finger.

Hanny was shaking my arm.

"What's the matter?"

He showed me his empty wrist, marked red from his watch strap.

"Did you drop it?" I said.

Hanny looked at his wrist again.

The driver finally got out and stood with the door open. He adjusted his tweed trilby, looked up at the seagulls and at the marshes through which they had just driven. I heard the clank of a lighter opening; a moment later the wind blew copper-blue smoke towards me, bringing the sweet dung smell of the man's cigar and the woman's voice.

"What are we going to do, Leonard?" she said, and the man ducked down to speak to her.

"The tide will be going out soon," he said.

"Before dark?"

"Of course."

"We can't have her sitting here in the cold for hours in her condition. We need to get her back across to the house."

"I know. Don't worry about it."

They argued quietly and I caught her name as he lifted his head again and tacked it contemptuously onto the end of his sentence. Laura.

Hanny was scuffling about in the sand looking for his watch. I nudged him to be quiet. Leonard slammed the car door, sending little birds flapping away, and stepped down off the road onto the sand. He walked away and stood watching the injured gull with an amused curiosity. He took off his hat, brushed it with the back of his hand and put it back on.

In his toffee-coloured jacket and his expensive shoes, he looked as out of place here as his Daimler. He was a lounge lizard, a spiv, a bent bookie with fingers full of sovereign rings and his blue shirt open two buttons at the collar. A smell of aftershave drifted up from him — a coniferous sap stirred with a fumigant like the stuff Farther sprayed over his roses to kill off the aphids.

Laura got out and fiddled with the boot of the car, eventually unlocking it and calling to Leonard. He sloped back up onto the tarmac and went over to her. They had a conversation that I couldn't hear properly, then Laura went to open the girl's door. Leonard

96

grappled with something in the boot, heaved, twisted and finally dragged out a wheelchair that by pressing some lever with his foot sprang open.

Laura held the door and Leonard parked the chair with its seat facing the girl. She inched slowly out, puffing and wincing as she held onto her belly. She was as pregnant as it was possible to be.

Leonard held her hand as she shuffled towards the open door and when she was close enough half fell into the chair, making it creak with her weight. She ran her fingers through her coppery hair and tucked it behind her ears and grimaced again. She was younger than me; thirteen or fourteen, I guessed. One of those girls that every school had. Even the Catholic comps. Girls that Mummer and the other ladies at Saint Jude's pretended they didn't like to talk about. They had probably brought her here to have the baby in this deserted place out of shame.

Leonard wheeled her to the edge of the road and carefully down onto the beach, where he headed towards the pillbox, leaving thin tyre tracks and scattering gulls from a pile of weed fizzing with flies. In her heels, Laura followed more slowly, coming to a standstill now and then as she decided how best to negotiate the swathes of wrack and litter.

She was dressed out of her time, somehow, like I imagined fashionable women might have dressed in the 1930s — a bottle-green coat with a stole made from an entire fox, a short haircut parted at the side.

Leonard set the wheelchair so that it faced the sea. Laura stayed with the girl and Leonard went off to investigate the pillbox. I put him in the sights and tracked him as he crossed the beach slowly and awkwardly with a gait that suggested a gammy knee. He came to the pillbox, looked at it, removed his shoes and took his hands out of his pockets so that he could swing his arms and get up the drift of sand. Rather satisfyingly he slipped a few times on his bad leg before he managed to put his fingers into one of the gun slits and pull himself up.

Making a visor with his hands, he peered inside and then suddenly jerked backwards, losing his footing and sliding ridiculously, one leg outstretched and the other crooked in such a way that it rolled him slowly but unavoidably onto his back. His shoes came out of his hand and tumbled away.

He got up, looked to see if anyone had witnessed his fall, and twisted to wipe the sand off his backside, before limping along the foot of the dunes in search of his brogues. He found one nestled in a pile of bladderwrack and stopped right underneath us to put it back on.

Having heard his involuntary cry, Laura made her way towards him.

"Are you all right?" she asked.

"Full of bloody rats." Leonard nodded to the pillbox.

Laura smiled to herself and took out a packet of cigarettes.

"Well, you will come to these sorts of places," she said, lighting up.

Leonard gave her a look. She walked away and picked up his other shoe, tipped it over, let a stream of sand come out and gave it back. Leonard slipped it on and then bent down to pick up something else — it was Hanny's watch. He thumbed away the sand, shook it, put it to his ear and then stuck it in his pocket.

I turned to tell Hanny, but he was staring past me over to where the girl was sitting in the wheelchair. The injured gull had stopped shrieking and was hopping tentatively over to her outstretched hand. When it was close to her, it angled its head and nipped at the weed she was holding, its damaged wing open like a fan. It came again for another feed and stayed this time. The girl stroked its neck and touched its feathers. The bird regarded her for a moment and then lifted off silently, rising, joining the others turning in a wheel under the clouds.

CHAPTER
NINE

Spring drowned the Loney.

Day after day the rain swept in off the sea in huge, vaporous curtains that licked Coldbarrow from view and then moved inland to drench the cattle fields. The beach turned to brown sludge and the dunes ruptured and sometimes crumbled altogether, so that the sea and the marsh water united in vast lakes, undulating with the carcasses of uprooted trees and bright red carrageen ripped from the sea bed.

Those were the worst days; the days of mist and driving rain, when Moorings dripped and leaked and the air was permanently damp. There was nowhere to go and nothing to do but wait for the weather to change. And sitting by the bay window of the front room watching the water flowing down the fields and the lanes, listening to the rooks barking in the cold woods, filled me with a sense of futility that I can remember even now.

I've not said anything to Doctor Baxter about Moorings or the Loney but he says he can tell that I'm harbouring a lot of negativity from the past — his words — and that I ought to try and let it go.

I told him that with me working in a museum the past was something of an occupational hazard and he laughed and wrote something down on his notepad. I can't seem to do or say anything without him making a note of it. I feel like a damn specimen.

With everyone stuck indoors, Moorings began to feel more and more cramped, and as we waited for a break in the weather people drifted away from the sitting room to find their own space. Mummer and Mr and Mrs Belderboss split off to different parts of the house to see if they could root out some decent cutlery to use instead of the huge, tarnished implements we'd made do with so far. Farther went to look at the rosemaling on the old furniture in the study. Miss Bunce and David sat at opposite ends of an ottoman reading. Hanny was upstairs drawing pictures of the girl he had seen at the Loney. The girl and the gull with the broken wing.

Only Father Bernard ventured out, taking Monro on a long walk that brought him back late in the afternoon.

I was in the kitchen, making Hanny some tea, when he came through the door saturated and dripping. He took off his cap and wrung it out on the doorstep. Monro sat beside him, blinking away rainwater and panting.

"And there's me thinking that the good Lord promised not to flood the world again," he said, hanging his coat on the back of the door. "I hope you've started work on the ark, Tonto."

He ruffled his hair with his fingertips and sent Monro off to the corner where there was an old blanket on the floor.

"Your mother's been hard at work, I see," he said, dusting his hands and going over to the stove where Mummer had something simmering. He lifted the lid and his face was swathed in vapours.

"God preserve us," he said. "It's a good job I have a will of iron. Otherwise I'd have a spoon in this before you could say jack rabbit."

Mummer appeared and closed the door behind her. Father Bernard put the lid back on the pot and smiled.

"God bless you, Mrs Smith," he said. "My old teacher in seminary always said that there was no better way to praise the Lord than feeding a priest. Mind you, I'm not sure whose side you're on, tempting me like this."

Mummer folded her arms.

"We were wondering, Father, if you knew about the arrangements for wet days," she said.

Father Bernard's smile wavered a little. "No, I don't think so."

"When it was too wet to go out anywhere," said Mummer, "Father Wilfred liked to gather everyone together for prayers at ten, noon and four. To give a structure to the day. Otherwise it's all too easy for people to get distracted. Hunger can do funny things to the mind. Pledges get broken. Father Wilfred always made sure that we stayed focused on our sacrifice so that we would remember the greater one."

"I see," said Father Bernard.

Mummer looked at her watch.

"It's almost four, Father," she said. "There's still time. As long as it won't keep you from whatever else you need to do."

He looked at her. "No, that's quite all right," he said and he went off to dry himself and to change his trousers, while Mummer gathered everyone in the sitting room to wait for him.

"Give him time," Mrs Belderboss was saying as I came in. "He's doing his best."

"I'm sure he didn't need to be out for quite so long," Mummer retorted.

"They need a lot of exercise those sorts of dogs," said Mrs Belderboss.

"Well, perhaps he ought not to have brought his dog with him," said Mummer.

"He couldn't very well have left it behind now could he? And anyway, I'm sure the boys are enjoying having a dog around, aren't you?"

She looked at me and smiled.

"Father Wilfred would never have kept a dog," said Mummer.

"Everyone's different, Esther."

"That's as may be," she replied. "But it's not the dog I'm concerned about."

"Oh?"

"I'm sure I smelled drink on him when he came in just now."

"On Father Bernard?"

"Yes."

"I don't think so."

"My father was a drunk, Mary," said Mummer. "I think I know the stench of ale well enough."

"But even so."

"I know what I smelled."

"All right, Esther," said Mrs Belderboss. "Don't get upset."

Mummer turned on me and frowned.

"Instead of earwigging," she said, "why don't you make yourself useful and see to the fire."

I got up and looked in the wicker basket for a chunk of wood that might last the rest of the afternoon. Mummer sat with her legs crossed, red-faced, her eyes fixed on the door the same way she had watched the road the day we'd met Billy Tapper in the bus shelter. Father Bernard couldn't come back quickly enough.

I'd learnt by now that my grandfather was a disgrace Mummer liked to keep under the carpet along with my uncle Ian who lived with another man in Hastings and a second cousin who had been twice divorced.

I'd asked her about him a number of times in the past, of course — as all boys are interested in their grandfathers — but I still knew little about him other than that he was an alcoholic and a layabout and had spent his short adult life carting his withering liver from one public house to the next until he died one Saturday afternoon in the tap room of the Red Lion, his head on a table of empties.

Eventually Father Bernard came in, his face red from scrubbing and his hair slicked back over his head. He had his thumb stuck inside his Bible, marking a particular passage that he perhaps thought might redeem him.

"You must be freezing, Father," said Mrs Belderboss, getting up. "You have my chair."

"No no, Mrs Belderboss, don't worry about me, I'm like rhubarb."

"Come again?"

"I don't mind the cold," he said.

"Well, if you're sure you're all right," Mrs Belderboss said and sat back down.

Mr Belderboss stared out of the window.

"Will you look at the weather?" he said.

The rain blustered about the yard and the fields, where mist lingered in stretches over the grass.

"Do you think we might be able to get out tomorrow, Father?" said Miss Bunce.

"I don't know," Father Bernard replied. "Perhaps we could listen to the forecast later."

Mr Belderboss chuckled as he looked at the ancient radio sitting on the sideboard — the sort of dark, wooden thing that would still be broadcasting Churchill's speeches if we were to turn it on.

"Oh, you'll not get a station here, Father," he said. "It's the hill, you see. Blocks the signal."

"Well," said Father Bernard. "We'll just have to take it as the Lord gives it. Is that everyone here?"

"No," said Mummer. "My husband seems to be dragging his heels somewhere." She looked at me and gestured at the door. "Go and see where he is."

I went to get up when Farther appeared, sorting through the huge bunch of keys Clement had left us.

"Oh, there you are," said Mummer. "We were about to send out the search party."

"Mm?" Farther said, distracted by a small brass key he had twisted off the ring.

"Where have you been?" said Mummer.

"In the study," he replied.

"All this time? What have you been doing?"

"I've found another room," he said.

"What are you talking about?" said Mummer.

"At the back of the study," Farther said. "There's a little room. I've never seen it before."

"Are you sure?" Mr Belderboss said.

"You know the old tapestry?" said Farther. "Between the paintings?"

"Yes?" replied Mr Belderboss.

"I knocked it aside by accident and there was a door behind it."

"Good Lord," said Mr Belderboss.

"I thought if I could find a key for it, we might be able to get inside and have a look."

"Well, it'll have to wait," said Mummer, gaining Farther's attention for the first time and indicating with her eyes that Father Bernard was poised to lead the prayers.

"Oh, sorry, Father," he said and sat down.

"We're still missing someone," said Mrs Belderboss. "Where's Andrew?"

"He's upstairs resting," I said.

"Well go and fetch him," said Mummer.

"Oh, leave him," said Mrs Belderboss.

"Leave him?" said Mummer. "He ought to be here if we're praying for him."

"He's tired," I said.

"What's that got to do with anything?" said Mummer. "We're all tired."

"I know," said Mrs Belderboss. "But with all that noise last night, I should think he slept less than any of us. If he's settled, it's probably best to leave him where he is."

"I agree with Mary," said Mr Belderboss.

Father Bernard cleared his throat. "Perhaps we should make a start, Mrs Smith?"

"Esther?" said Farther.

"Yes, all right," said Mummer sharply and she leant forward to light the candles set out on the table.

Mrs Belderboss sighed and looked out of the window.

"I do hope it improves for when we go to the shrine on Monday," she said. "It won't be the same if it's raining, will it, Reg?"

"No," said Mr Belderboss. "Not like last time, do you remember?"

Mrs Belderboss turned to Father Bernard. "It was a glorious day," she said. "The sun came out just as we arrived. And the flowers were just beautiful. All the magnolias and the azaleas."

Father Bernard smiled.

"Everyone was so happy, weren't they, Reg?" she went on. "Wilfred, especially."

"It must be nice to have that memory of your brother, Mr Belderboss," said Father Bernard.

Mr Belderboss nodded. "I suppose so. They do say that you ought to remember people at their happiest, don't they?"

"Aye," said Father Bernard. "I can't see that there's much to be gained by doing anything else."

Mr Belderboss looked at his hands. "It's the last time I remember him being so — certain — about everything. After that, I don't know. He just sort of seemed to . . ."

"Seemed to what?" Father Bernard asked.

Mr Belderboss looked around the room at everyone. Mummer narrowed her eyes at him, very slightly, but enough for him to notice and stop talking. There was a moment of silence. Mrs Belderboss touched her husband on the arm and he put his hand over hers. Mummer blew out the match she was holding.

"I thought we were going to begin?" she said.

Father Bernard looked at her and then at Mr Belderboss.

"Sorry, Reg," he said. "I didn't mean to upset you."

"Oh, don't worry about me," said Mr Belderboss, wiping his eyes with a handkerchief. "I'm all right. You carry on, Father."

Father Bernard opened his Bible and handed it to me.

"Would you read for us, Tonto?" he said.

I set the Bible on my knees and read Jesus' instructions to his disciples to prepare for the persecution that would most certainly be coming their way.

" 'Brother will betray brother to death, and a father his child; children will rebel against their parents and have them put to death. You will be hated by everyone because of me, but the one who stands firm to the end will be saved.' "

Mummer looked at Father Bernard and nodded her approval. The passage was her manifesto. Back at home, it was up in a frame in the kitchen, scribed in ornate calligraphy like the page of an illuminated Bible. Duty, or rather the active show of duty, was everything and to ignore the call to service was, in Mummer's eyes, possibly the most heinous sin of all. She was of the opinion that men should at least consider the priesthood and that all boys should serve on the altar. In some ways, she said, she was envious of me because I had the opportunity to be closer to God, to assist in the miracle of the transubstantiation, whereas she had to make do with organising fêtes and jumble sales.

It had been mooted a number of times since my Confirmation, but when we returned from Moorings the last time, it became Mummer's mission to get me into a cassock. It was time, she said, and it was obvious that Father Wilfred needed help.

"You ought to do it for your brother's sake, if anything," she said. "He'll never get the chance."

I think it came as something of a surprise to her when I agreed so readily. I wanted to be an altar boy. I wanted to be a servant to the Lord. I wanted, more than anything, to see the parts of the church that no one else did.

And so I see myself aged thirteen walking up the path to the presbytery one wet Saturday morning in an ill-fitting beige suit with Mummer's instructions on the etiquette of speaking to a priest fixed firmly in my head. Yes, Father Wilfred. No, Father Wilfred. Speak when you're spoken to. But look interested. Answer his questions like a boy who's been going to church since the day he was born. Don't drop your aitches.

Miss Bunce answered the door and I told her what I'd come for. She let me in and pointed at the row of chairs in the hallway. There was another boy there, suffering from the first fierce assault of acne and breathing loudly. He had been stuffed into an even worse suit than I had, the lapels of which were sprinkled with dandruff and stray hairs. He looked at me and smiled nervously as he put out his hand.

"Did your mother send you too?"

Plump, freckled, a little older than me, poor Henry McCullough with egg breath and spots was to become my opposite number on the altar, performing the parts that required little or no wit. He was a towel holder and a candle straightener. He opened the lid of the organ before Mass and brought out the stool for Miss Bunce to sit on.

"Yes," I said, to make him feel better. "She did."

Father Wilfred came out of the dining room, wiping away the remains of his breakfast from his lips with the corner of a handkerchief. He looked at us both sitting there and weighed us up from our polished shoes to our parted hair.

110

"Miss Bunce," he said, nodding to the door. "Would you be so kind?"

"Yes, Father."

Miss Bunce withdrew a black umbrella from the stand and handed it to Father Wilfred once he had buttoned his long raincoat. He gave her a rare smile and then clicked his fingers at us to follow him down the gravel path to the church, keeping the umbrella to himself.

It's gone now, demolished to make way for flats, and much lamented by those who remember it, but I always thought Saint Jude's was a monstrosity.

It was a large brown brick place, built towards the end of the nineteenth century when Catholicism became fashionable again with a people that didn't do things by halves. From the outside it was imposing and gloomy and the thick, hexagonal spire gave it the look of a mill or factory. Indeed, it seemed purpose-built in the same sort of way, with each architectural component carefully designed to churn out obedience, faith or hope in units per week according to demand. Even the way Miss Bunce played the organ made it seem as though she was operating a complicated loom.

As a token bit of mysticism, the mason had fixed an Eye of God way up on the steeple, above the clock — an oval shape carved into a block of stone that I'd noticed on the old country churches Farther dragged us round at weekends. Yet at Saint Jude's, it seemed more like a sharp-eyed overseer of the factory floor, looking out for the workshy and the seditious.

Inside, a bigger than life-sized crucified Christ was carefully suspended in front of a vast window so that when the sun shone his shadow fell among the congregation and touched them all. The pulpit was high up like a watchtower. Even the air felt as though it had been specially commissioned to be church-like; to be soup-thick with sound when Miss Bunce touched the organ keys, and when the nave was empty to be thin enough to let the slightest whisper flutter round the stonework.

"So," said Father Wilfred, indicating for us to sit on the front pew. "Let's start at the beginning. McCullough, tell me something about the Penitential Bate."

Father Wilfred put his hands behind his back and began a slow pacing alongside the altar rail, looking up into the vault like a teacher awaiting the answer to an impenetrable maths question.

Actually, I often thought he had missed his calling on that score. Mummer had cut a photograph of him out of the paper when he'd protested about a new horror film they were showing at the Curzon, and in it he looked every inch the Edwardian schoolmaster — thin and pale behind the round-rimmed glasses, the hair raked into a severe parting.

Henry looked down at his sweaty hands and shifted uncomfortably as though something unpleasant was passing through his gut. Father Wilfred suddenly stopped and turned to face him.

"Problem?"

"I don't know," said Henry.

"I don't know, Father."

"Eh?"

"You'll address me as Father."

"Yes, Father."

"Well?"

"I still don't know, Father."

"You don't know if there's a problem or you don't know what the Penitential Bite is?"

"Eh?" said Henry.

"Well at least tell me when it comes in the Introductory Rites, McCullough."

"I don't know, Father."

"You wish to be a servant of God and you can't even tell me the order of the Mass?"

Father Wilfred's raised voice echoed briefly around the church. Henry looked at his fingers again.

"You do want to become an altar boy, don't you, McCullough?" Father Wilfred said, more quietly this time.

"Yes, Father."

He looked at him and then resumed his pacing.

"The Penitential Rite comes at the start of the Mass, McCullough, once the priest has come to the altar. It enables us to confess our sins before God and to cleanse our souls ready for the reception of His holy word.

"Now, Smith," he said, stopping to buff the golden eagle lectern where Mr Belderboss struggled with the Old Testament names when it was his turn to read, "what comes after the Penitential Rite?"

"The Kyrie, Father."

"And then?"

"The Gloria, Father."

"And then?"

"The Liturgy, Father."

Suspecting I was being facetious, his eyes narrowed for a second, but he turned and walked back the way he had come.

"Right, McCullough," he said. "Let's see if you've been listening. Tell me the order of the Introductory Rites."

And so it went on until Henry could recite the structure of the Mass down to where people stood, sat or knelt.

While they spoke, I stared at the altar, wondering when we would be allowed up there, if it would *feel* holier beyond the invisible screen where only the privileged directors of the Mass were allowed to penetrate. If the air was different. Sweeter. If I might be allowed to open the tabernacle in the reredos, and look upon the very resting place of God. Whether there was some evidence of Him inside that golden box.

Having passed one test, I was sent away to complete another. I was to go into the office next to the vestry and bring back a pyx, a censer and a chaplet of the Divine Mercy. Father Wilfred handed me a key and then looked at me sternly.

"You are to go to the vestry office and nowhere else," he said. "Do you understand?"

"Yes, Father."

"You are to touch nothing other than the things I have asked for."

"Yes, Father."

"Good. On you go."

The office was cramped and smelled of old books and snuffed wicks. There was a desk and several bookshelves and locked cupboards. In the corner was a sink with a grimy mirror above it. A candle in a red jar guttered in the draught coming through the window frame. But the things which interested me the most, as they would any boy of thirteen, I suppose, were the two crossed swords fastened to the wall — long and slender and curving gently towards their tips — the kind Hanny's Napoleonic soldiers wore. I longed more than anything to hold one of them. To feel my chest tighten like it always did when we sang "O God of Earth and Altar".

I searched for the things Father Wilfred had asked me to fetch and found them easily, setting them down on the desk where a few books had been left open.

One had a painting of Jesus standing on the edge of a mountain in the desert being tempted by Satan, who flitted about him like a giant red bat. I didn't like that one at all. It was the Devil of my nightmares, all cloven hooves and horns, with a snake for a tail.

I turned the page and found Simeon Stylites standing on his tower. He was a popular figure in Father Wilfred's sermons. Along with the Rich Fool and the Prodigal Son, he was an example to us all of how we could change, how we could rid ourselves of temporal desire.

Surviving only on the Eucharist, he had lived on top of a stone pillar in the desert so that he could meditate on the Word untouched by the world of sin below him.

His devotion was absolute. He had stripped his life to the quick for God. And his reward was that he needed to look no further than heaven for all the things that the sinners beneath him pursued through selfish, lustful means and suffered for in the chase. Food, love, fulfilment, peace. They were all his.

In the painting he had his face turned to the sky and his arms outstretched as though he was letting something go or waiting for something to fall.

Next to it was a photograph album full of pictures of a place that I recognised. It was the Loney. Shots of the beach, our pillbox, the dunes, the marshes. Dozens of them. These were the photographs he had taken that last morning of the pilgrimage.

He had left a magnifying glass on top of a photograph of the mudflats at low tide, the sea far out, the way over to Coldbarrow clear and Coldbarrow itself a grey mound in the distance. I picked it up and moved it back and forth but couldn't find that there was anything much to see apart from the black sludge and the sea and the low sky. What he had been looking for, I couldn't tell.

"Smith." Father Wilfred was at the door, with Henry behind him.

"Yes, Father?"

"What are you doing?"

"Nothing, Father," I said and stood up.

"I trust that you've found what I asked you to find?"

"Yes, Father," I said and showed him the stuff on the table. He looked at me and came over and picked up each object, turning them in his hands as though he'd never seen them before. After a moment or two he realised that we were waiting for him to dismiss us and he turned sharply.

"On Sunday morning," he said. "I shall expect to see you both standing outside the vestry door at nine o'clock on the dot."

"Yes, Father Wilfred."

"Let me be absolutely clear," he said. "Lateness is not only a discourtesy to me, it is a discourtesy to God, and I will not tolerate it."

"Yes, Father Wilfred."

He said no more but drew back the chair I'd been sitting on and wedged himself under the desk to look at the books. He licked his finger and turned the page in the photograph album and squinted into the magnifying glass.

CHAPTER
TEN

Early on good Friday, just before the clock chimed for Saint Matthew, Mummer came into our room and drew back the curtains. Hanny rolled over and snuffled into his pillow.

"Ten minutes," she said. "Don't keep us waiting."

I watched her go and then got out of bed. Outside the sky was obscured by a low swirling cloud of moisture that was somewhere between fog and drizzle. Down in the front garden where the fruit trees dripped and bent in the wind, I saw Father Bernard setting a wooden crucifix against the gate — the last of the fourteen Mummer would have had him distributing round the outside of the house since the first washes of dawn.

Once this was done, he put his hands on the drystone wall and let his head tip forward before coming back inside. He was as tired as I was.

I rolled back the rug, took up the floorboard and checked the rifle. It was still there, of course. I touched the cold metal of the trigger, flicked the little safety catch on and off and tried to imagine what it would be like to fire it. To feel it punch my shoulder. The noise it would make.

The small hand of the clock found Matthew the tax collector and rang five times in soft dabs that seemed to come from deep inside the mechanisms. I put the rifle back and then shook Hanny until he was awake.

He immediately touched his wrist and looked at me expectantly.

"Yes, Hanny," I said. "I know. We'll get your watch back today."

When we got downstairs, everyone was already sitting around the kitchen table in their coats.

"Morning, lads," said Father Bernard. He had his hand inside a shoe and was scuffing off the dirt in quick movements. "Sleep well?"

"Yes, Father."

"Thank you for asking," Mummer said, looking at me and then to Father Bernard.

"Thank you for asking, Father," I said and he slowed his brushing for a moment, glancing up at Mummer and then me.

Hanny went over to one of the cupboards and started looking for cereal. Mummer snapped at him and then, remembering herself, she smiled at him instead and touched him gently on the arm.

"No, Andrew," she said. "We don't eat until it goes dark. And when we do, it will be fish, not cornflakes."

Hanny didn't understand. Mummer took the box off him and put it back in the cupboard.

Farther came in coughing and sat down, laying a single key on the table.

"I've got that door open," he said. "The one in the study."

Mummer rolled her eyes, but Mr Belderboss leant forward.

"What was inside?" he said.

"A bed," Farther replied.

Mr Belderboss frowned.

"And some toys," said Farther.

"Was it a playroom, do you think?" Mr Belderboss said.

"No," said Farther, barking into his fist again. "I've a feeling it was a quarantine."

"For the children with TB?"

Farther nodded. "There's a little barred window that's been bricked up from the outside. That's probably why we've never noticed it before."

He launched into a rasping cough.

"Oh, will you stop," said Mummer. "What is the matter with you?"

"I think it's that room," said Farther. "Full of dust."

"Funny place to keep the children, right next to the study," said Mr Belderboss.

"Perhaps it wasn't a study then," said Farther. "Or perhaps it was so Gregson could keep an eye on them while he worked. I don't know."

"It's a constant surprise this place," said Mr Belderboss. "I shall look forward to seeing it."

"Not now, Reg," said Mrs Belderboss. "Father's waiting to begin."

120

Father Bernard was standing by the back door in his coat and shoes.

"Only if everyone's ready," he said.

The rain came down harder as soon as we went outside and the back yard became a delta of little streams gushing through the cobbles. Father Bernard walked across to the middle and stopped.

"Here?" he said to Mummer.

"That's where Father Wilfred started, yes," said Mummer.

Father Bernard nodded and then began.

"In the name of the Father and of the Son and of the Holy Spirit. As it was in the beginning, is now, and ever shall be, world without end. Amen."

Everyone responded and then went to their knees, apart from Mr and Mrs Belderboss who wouldn't have got up again if they had. Hanny was looking around, more interested in the way the rain was pattering out of the broken gutter, until I pulled him down next to me.

Father Bernard closed his eyes and lifted up his hands.

"We ask our Lord Jesus Christ to forgive us our sins. And we pray especially for Andrew that he be filled with the Holy Spirit and find peace this Eastertide. Hail Mary, full of grace . . ."

Hanny watched as we all spoke the words together.

Once the prayer was over, everyone stood up and moved across the yard to the first station. There we got on our knees again and Father Bernard said, "We adore thee, O Christ, and we praise thee."

Everyone replied: "Because by Thy holy cross, Thou hast redeemed the world."

Father Bernard opened a small prayer book, shielding it from the rain with his hand.

Pilate condemned Jesus to death and he took up the cross that was given to him. He fell. His mother came to wipe away the blood and Simon picked him and his crucifix up off the floor. He fell again. And again.

And so it went on, until we had circled Moorings and Jesus was dead.

Once it was over, I was allowed to take Hanny out for a few hours before the Tenebrae service at Little Hagby.

We went down to the beach, chancing that the crossing to Coldbarrow would be clear and we could get his watch back. I didn't want to go at all. I'd have quite happily let Leonard keep the damn thing — Hanny would have forgotten about it in a day — but Mummer would notice it was missing and make me pay for a new one. It would be my fault that he had lost it.

We had no idea of the tides any more. We hadn't been here for so long that that kind of knowledge had been lost. But when we got there the sea was well out — a line of foam at the edge of the mud flats. A huge stillness had settled now that waters had retreated but the clouds on the horizon had the look of something building to attack. Darkening and darkening, turning the silent gulls that swooped before them an unnatural white.

Had it been like this for the farmers that had once grazed their cattle here? Had they always looked out to sea, wondering when it would come sweeping in again and with what ferocity? I suppose they must have done.

For half a mile, we followed the marker posts of the old causeway and then, when they gave out, the wandering tracks the Daimler had left in the sand were the only thing to guide us around the patches of sinking mud and the deep cuttings still eroding from the withdrawal of the tide. It was out here in the maw of the bay that one felt most exposed. The flatness of the sands made everything seem a long way away. There was nothing but the wind and the coming and going of light; and the gulls were bigger and unafraid. This was their territory, and we were nothing.

When we finally came to Coldbarrow itself there was a cobbled slipway leading onto a dirt road that ran around the perimeter. Rutted and claggy with sludge and sand it looked impassable, yet there were footprints and tyre grooves criss-crossing the lane all the way towards Thessaly, the house which sat away on the edge of the cliffs at the north end. Nevertheless, it was better to cut across the heather moor and save our boots. Mummer would only start asking questions if we came back up to our knees in mud.

I held open a barbed wire fence for Hanny to climb through and then showed him where to hold it so that I could do the same. The land rose a little and then we were on the peat moor where the heather had been ravaged to stubble by the wind.

It was easy to see why no one ever came here. What was there to come for? No livestock could survive for long on the stony ground and anything one tried to build would be knocked flat by the first storm to come barrelling across the Irish Sea. For there was nothing beyond Coldbarrow, only a yawning openness of grey water until one hit the coast of County Louth a hundred and fifty miles away.

Perhaps that was what made me stop and look across the sands at our footprints. To know that there was a place we could go back to.

The mainland was a thin strand of grey, the pillbox barely distinguishable in the range of dunes. Only Moorings stood out, white against the trees of Brownslack Wood that moved in the wind like the pelt of a huge, dozing animal.

Seeing it like that, so thickly heaped over the fell, I reckoned Mr Belderboss was right. Maybe no one had set foot in there for centuries. There must still have been places like that, even in England. Wild woods left to themselves.

Hanny tugged at my hand and we carried on through the heather. As we walked, I became aware of a faint ringing sound, like someone running a finger around the rim of a wine glass.

"Can you hear that?"

He stopped and I touched my ear.

"That sound," I said.

He shook his head.

The grass rustled and then a flash of white fur made us both turn at the same time. A slender, staring cat emerged and mewed with a tiny voice. Hanny put out his hand and it came to him. It had no collar and no

124

name tag, but it wasn't feral. The fur had been well looked after.

It was an albino, with eyes that looked as if they had been marinated in blood. It mewed again and sprayed its musk onto a rock, its tail erect and shivering. Again came that faint, high-pitched smoothing of the air. It seemed to be calling the cat. It licked its paw and then sprang off through the grass towards Thessaly.

Hanny got there before me and was standing at the end of a cutting that led to the house through the black stems of heather and the ferns that had yet to unfurl their little crosiers.

The ringing sound was stronger here and I realised that I had been hearing the wind moving the bell in the small brick tower that they said the Devil had built for Elizabeth Percy to entice poor foreign sailors onto the rocks.

The wind wasn't strong enough to swing it against the clapper and it shimmered over its surface instead, producing a delicate, liquid sound that floated on the damp air.

The girl we had seen at the Loney was sitting under the lopsided portico of the house in her wheelchair. After a moment she held up her hand and Hanny started to walk towards the house, following the albino cat.

Standing close to it for the first time, Thessaly was an ugly place. Built low and long to withstand the weather, it seemed to have emerged from the earth like a stunted fungus. Every window was black and stains ran from the sills down the grimy plasterwork as though the place was permanently weeping. The portico was an attempt at elegance that had failed in the most spectacular way and reminded me of the gateways to the vaults in the graveyard at Saint Jude's with their life-sized angels and broken gates.

Hanny stopped a few feet from the girl and was staring at her as she smoothed her hands over her swollen stomach. Perhaps it was the dry, russet hair and its attendant dribble of freckles across the bridge of her nose; perhaps it was pregnancy that had given her a fleshiness about the face, but she seemed even younger than I'd first thought. The prettiness that Mrs Belderboss had noticed came and went too quickly for it to be a constant quality and it disappeared altogether when she grimaced as the baby moved.

The door behind her was open and Laura's voice came from inside the house.

"Is that him back?" she said, and then looked disappointed as she came out and saw Hanny and me standing there.

She was smoking a cigarette and was dressed in a matching liver-coloured skirt and jacket. She had pearls around her neck and, like her husband, smelled strongly of fragrance.

"Can I help you?" she said, touching the edges of her painted mouth with her little finger.

I told her that we'd come for the watch.

"Watch?" she said.

"Your husband found a watch yesterday at the Loney. It belongs to us."

"The where?"

126

"The beach," I said. "He found it in the sand."

"I don't recall seeing you there," she said.

"Well, we were."

Laura took another drag and tapped the ash from the end with her forefinger.

"What's the matter with him?" she asked, gesturing towards Hanny.

"Nothing," I said.

"Why is he staring at me? Is he a bit slow?"

I nudged Hanny to stop and he looked at his feet instead.

"Do you live around here?" Laura said.

"No."

"On holiday?"

"Yes."

"Poor you," she said, as the rain started again.

She looked at us both and then turned back into the house.

"Come in," she said. "I'll see if he's left it lying around. Give Else a hand over the step."

The girl smiled at Hanny again, hoping that he would do the honours.

"He doesn't understand," I said.

But Hanny took hold of the handles and wheeled her backwards through the doorway and into a long corridor lined with empty coat hooks on which a smell of old, damp gabardine hung. There was room for little else other than a pair of Wellingtons and an umbrella.

There were no stairs, only doors either side and one at the end, next to which there was an upturned plant pot for a telephone to sit on.

The rain came down hard outside and the hallway darkened. I had been right to think of the place as a tomb. The plaster had been left unpainted, the woodwork without varnish, as though it had been built and immediately abandoned. Its walls had never contained a family. No one had ever laughed there. It had a kind of airlessness, a heavy silence, that made it immediately unsettling. I've never felt it anywhere else since, but there was definitely something that I picked up with a different sense. Not a ghost or anything ridiculous like that, but something nevertheless.

"Wait here," Laura said and went along the hallway to the door at the end where she paused to sort through the bunch of keys. She unlocked the door, there was a brief glimpse of a bare kitchen, and then she closed it behind her, locking it from the inside.

"What's his name?" Else said to me.

"Andrew," I said.

"That's a nice name," she said and smiled at Hanny.

Hanny smiled back and touched her hair.

"Don't do that," I said.

"No, it's all right," said Else, rearranging it back behind her ears.

She shifted in her chair and winced a little and breathed out.

"The baby's moving," she said to Hanny. "Do you want to feel it?"

She took Hanny's hand and placed it on her belly. He hesitated but Else put her hands over his and a grin spread across his face as he felt the baby kicking against his palm.

128

Laura came back out of the kitchen and then went to a different door, moving the keys around the ring until she came to the one she needed. She was about to go into the room when the telephone rang.

"Let them in here," said Laura.

Else looked at her.

"Don't worry," she said. "This room is all right for them to be in." And she went to pick up the phone.

Like the hallway, the room was bare and cold. There were no curtains, only yellow nets covering the windows that were thick with cold condensation. The fireplace was boarded up and there were footprints in the dust where someone had walked in and out of the room carrying the boxes that were stacked against the wall. A porcelain doll in a bonnet and pinafore sat on top of one of the boxes staring at us. Hanny went over and picked it up. He smiled and showed me how its eyes closed and opened when he tipped it back and forth.

"He might have put it there," said Else, pointing to the battered desk in the alcove of the chimney breast. "That's where he keeps the things he finds."

I went over and looked through the various shells and bits of glass and bone. There was a sheep's skull resting as a paperweight on a pile of brown envelopes and next to it was an old toothbrush in a mug. Leonard had evidently got halfway through cleaning off the green mould stuck between the sutures. I picked up the skull and looked into one of the eye sockets. The white worm of the optic nerve was still attached, though the eye and brain had long since been eaten or rotted away.

Hanny was sitting on a chair with the doll on his knee. The box next to him was open and he reached inside and took out an old encyclopaedia. I told him to leave it alone.

"It's all right," said Else.

Hanny nipped through the pages, stopping now and then to show Else a picture that he liked. A matador. A mandarin duck. A magician.

The albino cat wandered in and jumped up onto Hanny's lap. He stroked it gently and then picked it up and pressed it to his cheek. The cat licked his face and then hopped down to Else.

"Thank you for bringing her back," she said. "She goes off for days sometimes, don't you?"

She scolded the cat and then kissed Hanny, leaving a smudged half-moon of red on his lips.

It took me more by surprise than it did Hanny. He smiled and looked back at the book.

"Do you want to keep it?" she said to him.

"No, he doesn't," I said.

"It's all right," said Else. "They're just old books. He's got hundreds of them. He never looks at them, but he won't throw them out."

"Do you want the book?" I said to Hanny.

He looked at me and I went over and put it in his satchel.

"Take some more, if you like," said Else.

"One's enough."

"Please," she said. "I want him to have them."

"He'd rather just have his watch back."

"Well, it'll be here somewhere, if you're sure it was picked up."

"It was."

She frowned and cocked her head to one side.

"Are you really here on holiday?" she said.

"Yes," I replied.

"Why?"

"What do you mean?"

"I mean why come here? What is there to do?"

"There's the beach," I said.

"Is that it?"

I shrugged.

"It didn't look much fun to me," she said.

"Well it is."

"What do you do there, apart from hide in the grass?"

"You wouldn't understand."

"Wouldn't I?"

"No."

"Boys' stuff is it?"

I said nothing. Her smile suddenly faded again and she gave a sudden sharp intake of breath and put her hands on her stomach. Exhaling slowly, she caught the expression of concern on Hanny's face.

"Oh, don't worry, Andrew," she said, holding his hand. "It's nothing. I've done this before. It gets easier the more you have."

Hanny smiled and she touched his face and kissed him again. I reached into the box and took out a pile of other books and gave them to Hanny. He put them in his bag and went over to the desk to look at the sheep's skull.

I heard Laura put down the phone and then she came into the room.

"Well?" she said.

"It's not here."

"Then I'm afraid you've had a bit of a wasted journey."

"Is there nowhere else it might be?"

Laura lit another cigarette and shook her head. "If it's not in here, I wouldn't like to say."

"But it's my brother's. He wants it back."

"I'm sorry," she said, and then holding the cigarette in her lips, she dipped into her pocket and brought out a purse. She thumbed open the catches and took out a five pound note.

"Here. Buy him a new one," she said, holding the note out to me.

"He doesn't want a new one," I said.

Laura looked at me and then took out another note.

"Buy one for yourself as well," she said, folding the two notes together and pressing them into my hand. "All right?"

I held the notes back to her.

"Isn't your husband in?"

"No."

"When will he be back?"

"I'm afraid I don't know."

"Will he be here tomorrow?"

"Possibly. It's hard to say. He's very busy."

"We'll come back tomorrow."

"I wouldn't want you to waste your time again."

"It won't be a waste if Hanny gets his watch."

"It's all right," said Else, pulling aside the net curtains. "He's here."

The rain was coming down in needles now and battering the roof of Leonard's Daimler. Water washed under its tyres and seeped away into the bracken. He looked at us standing on the porch.

Laura flapped open an umbrella and went down the steps to the car. Leonard got out and said something to her that I couldn't hear for the rain. She spoke back to him and then they both looked at us. Leonard hitched up the collar of his jacket and came stiffly up the steps to the house while Laura took a wicker basket from the back seat.

"I'm told you've lost a watch," he said.

"Yes."

"And that you think I've got it."

"You found it at the beach yesterday."

"Did I now?"

He lit up a stump of a cigar in his cupped hands.

"What did it look like, this watch?" he said, blowing smoke out of the side of his mouth.

"Just give it back, Leonard," Laura said quietly as she passed him. "Before the tide comes in," she added.

He clamped the cigar in his teeth and withdrew a handkerchief from his breast pocket. He looked at us as he shook it loose and then refolded it into a square pad. Another long suck on the cigar and then he tossed it away and held the hankie to Hanny's face. Hanny drew back, but Leonard held him firmly by the shoulder.

"She's right, boys," he said, wiping the lipstick off Hanny's mouth. "The thing you have to remember about the tides here, is that no one can say they know them. Not really."

He took hold of Hanny's chin and moved his head left and right, inspecting it for any more traces of make-up.

"I mean," he said, spitting on the hankie and moving over to Else, "someone could tell you to set off now and before you know it you might be swimming home, or not swimming home, if you know what I mean."

Leonard dabbed at Else's lips, taking off the redness there, and then shoved the hankie into his pocket.

"They say it's the biggest graveyard in the north of England," he said, looking behind him at the sea and the sludge.

He took out a paper bag of mints and ate one. He noticed Hanny staring at them, and he smiled to himself and put them away. Laura banged on the window at him and after waving her away, Leonard looked at Hanny and me in turn and then pulled up his sleeve.

"Is this it?" he said, showing us the watch he was wearing.

"Yes."

He looked at us again and undid the buckle and handed it to me.

"I should stay well away from here if I were you," he said. "Dangerous place. It's very easy to misjudge

134

things. You could get well out of your depth and end up in all sorts of trouble."

Hanny put the watch back on his wrist.

"Listen," said Leonard. "Hear that?"

A steady hiss was coming as the sea began to wash up against the rocks at the bottom of the cliff behind the house.

"I should get a move on if I were you," he said. "I wouldn't want you to be stuck here all night."

He looked at us again and went behind Else, turned her chair around and pushed her into the house.

CHAPTER
ELEVEN

We left coldbarrow at the right time.

Looking back once we reached the pillbox, the sea was pounding the rocks by Thessaly, sending up spikes of foam that hung in the air before disintegrating back into the swell. The sands were gone.

Hanny was pleased to have his watch back and kept on showing it to me, wanting me to tell him the time.

"We're late, Hanny," I said. "That's all that matters."

When we got back to Moorings, Father Bernard was standing at the top of the lane, looking out for us.

"Come on, you two," he said as we passed him. "You'd better get a move on before your mother has an aneurysm."

Everyone was waiting on the bus with firm-set faces. Mummer pulled up her sleeve to reveal her watch and looked at me. That was all she needed to say.

I sat next to Hanny and he smiled at me and put his fingers on his lips where Else had kissed him. I took hold of his hand and moved it away.

"Leave it, Hanny," I said and gave him a look that made him lower his head. I didn't mean to scold him like that. It wasn't his fault after all. It was just that I didn't want Mummer to see.

136

That was what I told myself anyway. There was another feeling that I didn't want to recognise at the time but seems rather obvious now. I was jealous. But only in the way that I was jealous of the boys at school whose sexual exploits had elevated them above the playground proles.

It wasn't that I particularly wanted their experiences — my God, I would have been terrified — only to be in their club, where membership guaranteed that you didn't have your gym shoes rammed down a toilet pan full of muck and urine or your ribs blackened by discerning elbows in the corridors. The sex stuff didn't really matter. I didn't care about that.

I suppose I was jealous because that kiss had been wasted on Hanny. It didn't matter to him or to his peers at Pinelands. What I could have done with that experience back at school. To have had the ears of the changing room as I described it all in lurid detail, to have been thought of in another way, if only for the final term, might have made all the difference. I don't know.

Hanny touched his face again. There were still faint traces of lipstick on his chin that Leonard hadn't managed to get rid of. I wondered if Mummer might notice, as she noticed every small difference in Hanny's appearance, but she had her back to me and was watching silently out of the window like everyone else.

No one spoke at all, in fact, until a few miles further on when Mrs Belderboss patted the back of Father Bernard's seat.

"Stop, Father," she said and he pulled into the side of the road. "Look."

Everyone peered out of the windows as a swarm of bright red butterflies spun over the field in a flexuous shape, twisting and spiralling as one entity.

"Have you ever seen anything so beautiful?" said Mrs Belderboss.

"What are they doing out? It's too early in the year for them," said Mr Belderboss. "They'll die before the day's done."

"'Tis God's world, Mr Belderboss," said Father Bernard, smiling. "I'm sure He knows what He's doing."

"I think it's a sign," said Mrs Belderboss to Mummer and put her hand on hers. "That God will be with us when we go to the shrine."

"Yes," said Mummer. "Perhaps it is."

"I'm sure of it," Mrs Belderboss replied.

After all, signs and wonders were everywhere.

Father Wilfred had told us time and time again that it was our duty as Christians to see what our faith had taught us to see. And consequently Mummer used to come home from the shop with all kinds of stories about how God had seen fit to reward the good and justly punish the wicked.

The lady who worked at the bookmakers had developed warts on her fingers from handling dirty money all day long. The Wilkinson girl, who had visited the clinic on the Finchley Road that the women at Saint Jude's talked about in hushed tones, had been knocked down by a car not a week later and had her pelvis snapped beyond repair. Conversely an elderly lady who came into the shop every week for prayer cards and had spent much of the previous decade raising money for Cafod, won a trip to Fatima.

Mummer would tell us these tales over the dinner table without a flicker of doubt that God's hand was at work in the world, as it had been in the time of the saints and martyrs, the violent deaths of whom were regularly inflicted upon us as exempla of not only the unconditional oath we had to make to the service of the Lord, but of the necessity of suffering.

The worse the torment, the more God was able to make Himself known, Mummer said, invoking the same branch of esoteric mathematics Father Wilfred used in his sermons to explain why the world was full of war and murder — a formula by which cruelty could be shown to be inversely proportionate to mercy. The more inhumane the misery we could inflict upon one another, the more compassionate God seemed as a counterpoint to us. It was through pain that we would know how far we still had to go to be perfect in His eyes. And so, unless one suffered, Father Wilfred was wont to remind us, one could not be a true Christian.

In the vestry after Mass, if it wasn't chastisement over one thing or another, it was a lesson on a particular saint that he considered to be an encouragement for young boys to seek the opportunity of hardship, though it was hard to tell the difference between the two sometimes when he used the saints like a birch rod.

When Henry turned up late for Mass one Sunday, Father Wilfred thrashed him with the Blessed Alexandrina De Costa — the Portuguese mystic who had leapt from a window to escape being raped, had crippled herself in the fall, but still managed to come to Mass every Sunday on time. Even when she decided to devote her life to God, and ate nothing but the Eucharist, and each Friday had the blessed joy of experiencing the agony of Our Lord on the cross, she was still there at church before everyone else. It was the least Henry could do, even if his bicycle had developed a puncture on the Edgware Road.

"I'm sorry, Father," Henry said. "I'll pray to Saint Christopher," he added in a moment of inspiration.

"Idiot boy," Father Wilfred said. "We pray *with* the saints, not *to* them. The saints intercede on our behalf and petition God to help us."

"Oh, yes, Father."

"Will you remember that, McCullough?"

"Yes, Father."

"But how will you remember it, McCullough?"

"I don't know, Father."

Father Wilfred looked on the desk and picked up a metal ruler. He grabbed Henry by the wrist and before Henry could flinch he brought the edge of the ruler down on his knuckles, splitting them open.

"Will that help you to remember, McCullough?"

Henry gripped his bleeding hand tightly and moved backwards and sat down on a chair.

"Well?" said Father Wilfred.

"Yes, Father," said Henry. "I won't forget."

Father Wilfred looked at him and after a moment he went to the sink and handed Henry a paper towel with a look of contempt.

I suppose I took it for granted that Henry was one of those children that adults dislike — there are children like that — but quite why Father Wilfred despised Henry so much I didn't know. Perhaps it was because Henry was rich when he had been so poor. The Poor, after all, were Father Wilfred's favourite yardstick. They were the caste by which all things had to be measured and in doing so he made every small enjoyment an affront to their dignity. We were to think of the Poor when we reached for a second helping of cake. We were to think of the Poor when we wished for presents at Christmas, or when we coveted the new bicycle in the shop window. Father Wilfred had never had enough to eat. Never enough clothing to keep him warm in the Whitechapel slums. He had never possessed anything other than an old tyre which he used to knock along the road with a stick, trying to keep it from falling into the gutter.

It wasn't simply out of some obligatory moral stance demanded by scripture that he felt for the Poor so much, it was the core of his calling. Everyone was disappointed, but perhaps not surprised, that he chose in the end to give up his plot in Saint Jude's churchyard and requested that he be interred with his mother and father and his dead brothers and sisters in the Great Northern Cemetery instead.

But it seemed that there was more to it than that. We Smiths were better off than the McCulloughs by a long way and Father Wilfred never berated me the way he did Henry. Henry just seemed to rile him for some reason.

Father Wilfred had turned to me suddenly, aware that I was staring at them both.

"Carry on, Smith," he said.

I went back to winding the handle of the spirit bander that was copying the parish newsletters. It was something I did on the first Sunday of the month and always tried to hold my breath as much as possible to stop the methylated spirits from raking out the back of my throat.

"Why were you late, McCullough?" said Father Wilfred, folding his arms.

"I told you, Father," he said. "I got a puncture."

Father Wilfred nodded. "Yes, I know that's what you *said*."

He went to a bookshelf, pulled out a Bible and dropped it into Henry's lap.

"But I'm not convinced that it is necessarily the truth. Psalm one hundred and one, verse seven," he said.

"Sorry, Father?"

"Find it, McCullough."

"But I'll get blood on it, Father."

"You won't."

Henry carefully flipped through the book, trying not to bleed onto the pages.

"Well?" said Father Wilfred.

"I can't find it, Father."

"Psalms, McCullough. Between Job and Proverbs. It's not difficult."

At last Henry found the right place and started reading.

"'He that worketh deceit shall not dwell in my house; he that telleth lies shall not tarry in my sight.'"

Father Wilfred repeated what Henry had said in a slow, measured way, pacing up and down the office.

"God hates liars, McCullough," he said, nodding to the Bible on Henry's knee. "It's in there a thousand times over. Proverbs, Romans, Jeremiah. When you lie, McCullough, you are brethren with the serpent in the garden. You forfeit your place in heaven. God has no time for deceivers. I'll ask you again. Why were you so late?"

Henry looked down at his bleeding knuckles.

"You were too lazy to get out of bed, weren't you?"

"Yes, Father."

"And too overweight to make up the lost time."

"Yes, Father."

"Yes, Father," he repeated. "Psalm fifty-five, verse twenty-three. Quicker this time, McCullough."

Henry sped through the pages and traced his finger along the line.

"'But thou, O God, shalt bring them down into the pit of destruction; bloody and deceitful men shall not live out half their days.'"

Father Wilfred held out his hand for the Bible.

"Do you know what the most terrible torment of Hell is?" he said.

Henry passed it to him. "No, Father."

"The worst torment, McCullough," he said, "is not being able to repent of the sins you have committed."

"Yes, Father."

"In Hell, it is far too late."

"Yes, Father."

"You must come and see me in confession, McCullough."

"Yes, Father. I will."

"And then at least we may stand a chance of saving your soul."

CHAPTER
TWELVE

The butterflies dispersed as the rain returned and began the next washing of the land. Stone walls shone like iron. The trees bowed and dripped. The sullen countryside disappeared behind condensation and for a long time we could have been going anywhere until a low spire appeared on the other side of a cattle field, barely rising above the trees that surrounded it.

The Church of the Sacred Heart was an ancient place — dark and squat and glistening amphibiously in the rain. The large front door was green with moss and over the years long sinews of ivy had wormed their way around the tower.

We crowded under the lych-gate to wait for a particularly heavy burst of rain to pass. Water leaked through the canopy onto the stone seats that had been worn into scoops over the years by the backsides of countless pall-bearers or by people like us simply sheltering from the rain.

The churchyard itself was small but well stocked with the village dead — a second, more populous settlement bordering the first — all of them lying east-west as though the wind had combed them that way over the centuries. Gravestones listed against one another under the shade of several huge, dripping yew trees, one of which had been blasted by lightning at some point and had a new stem growing out of the blackened split.

"What do you think, Father?" said Mummer, nodding towards the church itself.

"Very atmospheric, Mrs Smith."

"Fifteenth-century," said Farther.

"Is that right?" Father Bernard replied.

"Some of it anyway. The stonework inside's all Saxon. They managed to escape the Reformation."

"How's that?"

"I don't think they could find it, Father."

The rain shower ended as suddenly as it had come. Water poured off the slate roof and along the lead flumes to spew from the mouths of gargoyles that had been weathered to lumps of stone. Father Bernard held open the gate and everyone went quickly up the path to the church before the rain came back, but Hanny stood looking up at the mangled grey demons, trying to pull his face to match theirs.

Inside, we took up a pew towards the back, shuffling along as quietly as possible so as not to disturb the silence. All around the church, the statues of saints had been covered up for Lent, like ghosts half hidden in the shadows of the alcoves. Now and then their drapes shivered in a draught. The wind was getting in somewhere and whistled like a seabird around the rafters.

Hanny held my hand.

"It's all right," I said as he glanced nervously at the nearest shrouded saint. "Just don't look at them."

Once everyone was settled, Farther inclined his head to Father Bernard.

"See the windows in the clerestory," he said, pointing at the tiny arches high up on the wall, each of them letting in a trickle of red light. "Look at the thickness of the mullions. And the glass, that's Romanesque."

"Is that good?" said Father Bernard.

"It's about seven hundred years old."

Father Bernard looked impressed.

"They should open this place for a museum," he whispered to Farther. "They must have kept everything they've ever owned."

It was true. Nothing, it seemed, had ever escaped the oak doors or the castle-thick walls. Any light that had entered, through the windows had been held captive and absorbed into the wood. Over the centuries the pews, pulpit and misericords had blackened to ebony like the beams which supported the roof — each one made from the fork of a huge oak tree, giving the congregation the sense of being inside an upturned boat.

The smells of benedictions and snuffed candles remained as steadfast as the gravestones that floored the central aisle. The doors to the aumbry opened on hinges that had been forged at a time when they still dunked witches and died of plague. It was a place where wafer ovens, alms boxes and rush-holders remained as working tools; where there was a sanctuary knocker, a parish chest carved out of a single trunk of walnut, and a Table of Consanguinity attached to the wall above the font as a ready-reckoner to prevent interbreeding amongst the ignorant poor. Though I suppose by the time the child was being dipped into the water, it was rather too late.

At the end of pews were effigies of the Seven Deadly Sins, smoothed almost to anonymity by the countless hands that had gripped them during genuflection. But one could just make out Sloth curled up like a dormouse, and Gluttony vomiting on his own beard and Wrath beating his brother-man with the jawbone of an ass.

Between the nave and the chancel, the church still had its rood screen with its painted melange of saints at the bottom and the crucifixion at the top. Above it was part of a Doom painting, and though much of it had flaked off it was still a considerable size and sprawled like dark rot across the stone.

"It's the only one I've ever seen north of Gloucester," said Farther, leaning close to Father Bernard again and pointing up to it. "I mean, it's got nothing on the ones at Patcham or Wenhaston, but still."

"I wouldn't have it on my wall," Father Bernard said.

"I don't know," said Farther. "It has a certain charm."

"Rather you than me."

When I was a child and I believed all that Father Wilfred said about Hell and damnation, the Doom gave me no end of sleepless nights at Moorings. I suppose because, in a sense, I already knew the place it depicted and that meant it might just be real.

It reminded me of the school playground with its casual despotism and the constant anxiety of never knowing which traits in a boy might be punishable with instant violence. Too tall, too small. No father, no mother. Wet trousers. Broken shoes. Wrong estate. Sluttish sister. Nits.

Hell was a place ruled by the logic of children. *Schadenfreude* that lasted for eternity.

In the painting, the damned were forced down through a narrow crack in the earth, crushed against one another, swimming headfirst through the soil, before they tumbled in a naked landslide towards the clutches of lascivious black-skinned demons who grasped their hair and drove red-hot knives into their flesh. Yet, this was only the initial punishment. They had merely fallen on the welcome mat, where some of the old lags of Hades had gathered to pray for the souls of these newcomers in the vain hope of their own redemption, their faces upturned, their mouths wide open and desperate, like blackbird chicks.

From here, the wicked were collected in enormous cauldrons to be cooked for Satan, who squatted like a sort of horned toad and dipped into the pots with a fondue fork, impaling the squirming human worms and swallowing them down whole, presumably to slither through his bowels and out the other end to begin the whole process once more.

In other parts of Hell were tortures so vile they bordered on being funny, which in turn worried me even more. The mockery of Hell, I thought, would result in an even worse punishment if I ever ended up there.

In one dark corner a demon had its arm down a man's throat so far that it came out of his backside to throttle the woman cowering beneath him. People had their limbs torn off and were hung upside down by hooks through their privates. Some had their tongues nailed to trees and their bellies slit to feed the slavering dogs that obediently attended the devils. Eyeballs were pecked out by things that looked like oversized starlings. Boiling lead was funnelled down throats. Severed heads were emptied of blood to irrigate the paddy fields of black weeds that grew up the sheer rock walls of Hell and broke through into the lush green pastures of the living to ensnare the sunflowers and the lilies growing there. It was all Father Wilfred had promised us it would be.

As we had always done when we'd come to the Tenebrae service in the past we doubled the congregation in one fell swoop. The few people kneeling with their faces in their hands were the same people that had always been there. And when they broke out of their prayers, they looked at us not as strangers but as people they half-recognised even though it had been years since we'd last come.

"Isn't that Clement?" said Mr Belderboss, pointing to someone sitting alone in one of the side pews.

"Yes, I think it is," Mrs Belderboss replied and she tried to attract his attention.

"His mother's not with him, though," said Mr Belderboss. "I wonder why?"

"Well, she's perhaps not up to church any more," Mrs Belderboss replied. "She is getting on, I suppose."

Mummer shushed them as the organist struck up a dirge and a miserable-looking altar boy, acned and gangly, brought out the hearse, placed it on a low table and lit the fifteen candles with a taper. He went away again and came back with a small, fat candle that he lit and placed down under the altar out of sight.

The priest came in and we all stood up. He gave a brief introduction — his voice thudding around the stone walls and gathering into a boom — and then the two-hour cycle of Matins and Lauds began — all in Latin of course — and after each a candle was extinguished by the altar boy until little by little the church darkened to match the encroaching gloom outside.

The wind continued to rise and fall. Whining and shrilling. It was as insistent as the priest, louder sometimes, preaching an older sermon, about the sand and the sea. Warning the faithful to stay away from the Loney.

Hanny fell asleep but no one bothered him, as Mr Belderboss had done the same, leaning his fluffy white head against my shoulder. In any case, Mummer was too engrossed in a contest with Miss Bunce as to who could be the most moved by the ceremony. At each increment of darkness, Mummer held her rosary tighter and prayed harder. Miss Bunce had tears in her eyes when Jesus called out to God and the candles on the hearse were snuffed out in quick succession. She even managed a small, anguished wail of her own when in the darkness the altar boy went down the aisle and slammed the heavy church doors shut to symbolise the earthquake that had buckled Golgotha at the moment Jesus' human heart stopped beating.

Mr Belderboss woke with a start and clutched at his chest.

Once the service was over and the single candle that had been secreted under the altar had been brought out to symbolise the promise of resurrection, we filed out into the rain. The altar boy held an umbrella over the priest as he quickly clamped each cold hand in his and passed on God's blessing. The regulars disappeared quickly, back to the sombre little houses hunkered down in the rain around the village green and as soon as the last person was out of the church, which was Mr Belderboss, rolling up and down on the cam of his bad hip, the priest went back inside and closed the door.

"Well," said Mummer, as we walked back to the minibus. "I thought that was a lovely service."

She was talking to Farther but he had stopped several paces behind and was running his hand over the carvings worked into the stone around a side door.

"I say it was a lovely service," she called over to him, but he either didn't hear her or he ignored her and moved his glasses to the end of his nose to better inspect the men and demons locked in mortal combat.

"It was," said Mr Belderboss. "It was."

"What do you know, you great lug," said Mrs Belderboss, batting his shoulder with the back of her hand. "You missed most of it."

"I did not," he said, rubbing his arm and smiling. "I was deep in prayer."

"Cobblers," said Mrs Belderboss.

"I think moving is probably the right word," said Miss Bunce. "It's meant to be quite a sombre service."

David nodded in solemn agreement.

"Oh, I didn't enjoy it, as such," said Mummer.

"I didn't say I didn't enjoy it," Miss Bunce said.

"So where's this fish feller?" Father Bernard said, leading Mummer back to the minibus.

Mummer sat in the front with Father Bernard and directed him to a wooden shack in the middle of nowhere where a man with a face full of scars sat behind plastic trays of skate and mackerel and vicious-looking eels freshly pulled out of the Irish Sea. It had been a tradition in the time of Father Wilfred to stop here on Good Friday and Mummer was delighted to see that the shop was still there and the same man was still taking the money using an old chum bucket for a till. The change came out greasy but Mummer didn't seem to mind.

We all waited in the minibus as Mummer and Farther chatted to the man while he wrapped up their fish in newspaper. A Land Rover went past us and pulled up next to the stall. It was Clement's. The same one that I had seen parked on the road down from Moorings. Parkinson, the bull man, got out first and looked at us, nodded at Father Bernard specifically and then wandered over to the stall, followed by Collier and his dog. Freed from the cab but still on its chain, it went off sniffing and barking and then squatted in the middle of the road.

"Aren't those the men we saw on the way here, Father?" said Miss Bunce.

"Aye," he said, with a look of irritation that Parkinson had singled him out.

"Where's Clement, I wonder?" said Mrs Belderboss.

"I don't know," Mr Belderboss replied. "Why?"

"That is his Land Rover, isn't it?"

"So?"

"Well, why have they got it?"

"How should I know?"

"Do you think he's lent it to them?"

"Don't be silly, Mary."

"I'm not being silly, I should think they all muck in together round here, don't they?"

"Hardly," said Mr Belderboss. "If they've got his Land Rover, then it's because he's sold it to them. Or it's an exchange for something. I mean they don't always deal in money out here, but they don't give things away either. It's a tough life being a farmer. You can't afford charity."

The elderly man got out last and, coughing violently into his sleeve, he leant against the side of the Land Rover watching us.

"Toxoplasmosis," said Mr Belderboss, nodding to him.

"Oh, give it a rest, Reg," Mrs Belderboss sighed.

154

Parkinson and Collier went and stood by the side of the fish stall smoking cigarettes. Mummer said hello to them, these were her people, after all. The men listened as she tried to start up a conversation, but they didn't talk back. Rather, they grinned, Collier winding the chain around his forearm to keep the dog obedient.

"Who *are* they?" said Miss Bunce as Mummer and Farther got back onto the bus.

"Who?" said Mummer.

"Them," said Miss Bunce, pointing out of the window. "They don't seem very friendly."

Mummer looked back at the men who were now selecting fish and laughing with the fishmonger, as the one with jaundice spluttered into his fist.

"Oh, Joan, you really have lived in London too long," she said. "They just have different ways. Here, hold this."

She handed the newspaper packet to Miss Bunce while she settled herself into her seat and we pulled away.

The men watched us leave, Parkinson nodding to Father Bernard and Collier saluting with his black mitten.

The smell of fish filled the bus and steadily bloomed as we ran along the lanes back to the house.

Miss Bunce held her hand over her nose. "I think I'm going to be sick," she said. David reached across and held her hand.

"Oh for goodness' sake, Joan," said Mummer. "Don't be so dramatic."

Miss Bunce wafted the smell away with her hand. "I thought that fish shouldn't smell at all if it was fresh."

"No, that's beef, isn't it?" said Mr Belderboss.

"Chicken," Mrs Belderboss replied. "Is it beef or chicken?"

"Look," said Mummer. "We've bought fish from that stall for years and it's never done us any harm, has it?"

She looked at Farther.

"No," he said. "It's always been very nice."

"Well, I'm not having any of it," Miss Bunce said.

"Well then you'll be hungry," said Mummer.

"And I'll be glad," said Miss Bunce. "We ought not to be eating at all today."

Mummer rolled her eyes. "That rule only applies to meat, Joan," she said. "Fish is fine, isn't it, Father?"

"I think we might risk it, aye," said Father Bernard as he changed gear and slowed down to take a hairpin bend in the road.

"That's just as well. I'm not sure I'd last until tomorrow with nothing inside me," Mr Belderboss laughed from the back seat.

Around the corner we came across someone walking on the edge of the ditch.

"That's Clement," said Mrs Belderboss. "Slow down, Father."

Father Bernard pulled in a few yards ahead and wound the window down. Clement stopped.

"Can I give you a lift?" Father Bernard called.

Clement looked around him and then came to the window, peering at us all and then at Father Bernard.

"Nay you're all right," he said.

"It's no bother to take you home."

"I've not far to go," Clement said.

"Well how about I at least take you as far as Moorings?"

Clement looked up into the rain. "Aye, all right," he said. "Take me to Moorings and I'll see me sen right from there."

Clement wedged himself between Hanny and me on the back seat. His wax jacket smelled of dried-up bodily excretions and damp straw. An astonishing, curdled smell that had subtle layers of foulness for the nose to explore.

He didn't say a word all the way back, but stared straight ahead and I got to know his profile intimately: a mangled ear stuck on the side of his head like a lump of bubble gum; a nose that had, like his cheeks, turned purulent with end-stage rosacea; a few stray wiry hairs around his lips that the razor had missed several times. When he went to scratch his nose, his sleeve slipped down and revealed a swallow tattooed on his forearm. He saw me staring at it and covered it up.

There was a rumour that he had done time at Haverigg, though whether it was true or what he was supposed to have done, I didn't know.

When we arrived back at Moorings, Clement waited until everyone had gone into the house and there was only Father Bernard and I coaxing Monro out from under the seat where he had been sleeping. Monro yawned and ambled down the steps and into the house. Father Bernard watched him go and then turned to Clement.

"Are you sure you won't let me take you back to the farm?"

Clement shook his head. "I'd rather walk from here."

"All right, well you take care of yourself."

Clement walked away and then stopped and came back.

"I don't know if I should say anything, Father," he said. "But I'd not forgive me sen if I didn't give thee a word of warning."

"Oh? About what?"

"Stay indoors as much as you can."

"With the weather, you mean?"

"No, I mean keep thaselves to thaselves."

"What makes you think we were going to do otherwise?" said Father Bernard with a small laugh.

"There are folk around here who aren't that happy that you've come."

"Like who?"

"I'd rather not say."

Father Bernard smiled faintly to himself. He knew who Clement was talking about.

"Well, I'm sure we won't do anything to upset them, Clement. And in any case, it didn't seem like that to me."

Clement frowned. "How do you mean, Father?"

Father Bernard glanced at me.

"Well, I stopped in the Bell and Anchor the other day to get out of the rain and someone very kindly bought me a drink."

Clement looked as though he had swallowed something nasty.

"Who was it?"

"Mr Parkinson, the butcher. Why?"

"And did you return the favour?"

Father Bernard shook his head. "I hadn't time to stay."

"I don't mean a drink, Father."

"I don't follow you, Clement."

"I mean, did you invite him up to Moorings?"

"I don't recall —"

"He has a way of making folk feel obliged to him, you see," Clement cut in.

"Well, I didn't feel like that," said Father Bernard. "Like I say, it was just a drink."

But Clement wasn't listening. He clutched Father Bernard's arm.

"Because if you were to invite him, he wouldn't just take it as a pleasantry. He'd come and bring them all with him."

"Who's all?"

"It's just better if tha keeps away from him."

"But there must be a reason, Clement."

"Aye, plenty."

"Such as what?"

"I can't say."

"Clement?"

"I'm sorry, Father. I must get back to Mother."

Clement looked at Father Bernard and then down at his feet, as though he had failed in some way. Then he walked to the lane, paused while he looked around him again, and then went off through a gate and over the fields.

CHAPTER
THIRTEEN

Clement's odd behaviour was all everyone talked about once he had gone.

"He's always been a little eccentric," said Mrs Belderboss.

"It's not surprising living out here," Mr Belderboss added. "Stuck with his mother day in, day out. It's enough to make anyone go a bit strange."

"I'm sure he doesn't think of her as a burden, Reg."

"Oh, I didn't mean that. I meant he focuses so much of his time on her that the rest of the world, the real world, sort of gets pushed to the sidelines."

Everyone seemed to agree, and perhaps it was this consent that made Father Bernard dismiss Clement's warnings as easily as he had obviously wanted to.

Perhaps they were right. Maybe Clement was just paranoid, but he had seemed so serious, so genuinely concerned.

Mummer and Mrs Belderboss went into the kitchen to prepare the fish while the rest of us waited. Miss Bunce and her fiancé sat together on the sofa. She was back with her Bible and he was reading a battered Dickens novel that had pages like tissue paper. Mr Belderboss snored in an armchair, Father Bernard went to his room to pray, and Farther sat at a table, looking at the nativity set he had found in the little room next to the study.

A new wave of rain swept in off the sea and made its fingertaps on the windows. Mummer came in from the kitchen and handed me a box of matches.

"Here, make yourself useful and light the candles," she said and shooed me off around the room, distracted by Farther's coughing.

It had got worse and there was a soft wheeze every time he breathed.

"You ought to stay out of that room," said Mummer. "It's not doing your chest any good."

"I'm fine," said Farther.

Mummer looked at the figures on the table. "I hope you've cleaned those," she said. "TB can live on for years."

"Of course I have," he said, setting a shepherd down next to a lamb.

"I really think you ought to have left them alone."

"Why?"

"I don't know," said Mummer. "It just doesn't seem right going through people's things."

Farther ignored her and rooted amongst the tissue paper that the little figurines had been wrapped in.

"Funny," he said. "There's no Jesus."

The meal was brought out and placed in the centre of the table among the tea lights Mummer had brought from the shop. On each jar was a portrait of a blond-haired Jesus blood-streaked from the crown of thorns and pointing to his huge blazing heart. We ate quietly, the rain hitting the windows and slithering down. Miss Bunce would only eat the vegetables. There was no dessert. Only water to drink.

Afterwards, Hanny was excused from the table and he went off to play in our bedroom, while the rest of us prayed again, thanking God for the meal.

"I thought I'd go for a walk up the field to the woods and back," said Miss Bunce, dabbing at her mouth with a napkin. "If anyone wishes to join me."

Mummer looked out at the dusk. The rain had stopped but the wind shuddered against the window.

"I'll give it a miss," she said. "It'll be bitter out there by now."

"I know," said Miss Bunce. "It's a penance."

Mummer looked at the window again. The wind got in through a gap in the frame and made a sound like cattle. She looked back at the table full of dirty plates and dishes.

"You go," she said. "I'll devote the washing up to God."

"Are you sure you don't want to come?" said Miss Bunce.

"It's not that I don't want to come, Joan," Mummer replied. "It's just that there's a more pressing need to clear the table. You go for your walk and I'll scrape the plates. I'm sure God is capable of receiving two offerings at once."

There was a pause and everyone looked at the table.

"I'll come with you," said David.

"Thank you," said Miss Bunce.

"Would you take Monro?" said Father Bernard. "The poor wee man hasn't been out for hours."

"Yes, all right, of course, Father," said Miss Bunce, looking at David who smiled to reassure her.

Hanny was in the bedroom, pitting his toy soldiers against the stuffed rats again. So far the soldiers were winning. One of the rats lay on its side surrounded by tanks.

He smiled at me as I came in and he showed me his watch for the millionth time.

"Yes, Hanny," I said. "I know. It's good that we got it back."

He ought to have been tired, but he seemed agitated and excited. I thought it was because he had found his watch or he had been so involved in the game he'd been playing, but he took me by the hand and led me to where his satchel was hanging on the back of the door. He opened the flap and took out the encyclopaedia he'd been looking at with Else.

He closed his eyes and touched his lips with his fingers.

"What does that mean, Hanny?"

He touched his lips again.

"You mean the girl at the house? I know, she gave you the book, didn't she?"

He sat on the bed and opened the book near the back. Inside was a brown envelope. One of the ones on which the sheep's skull had been sitting. He must have put it into his bag while I was talking to Laura. He took it out and opened it so that I could see. It was full of money.

"Give it to me, Hanny."

Seeing my outstretched hand, he gave his head a little shake, frowned and hid the book behind his folded arms.

"I said give it to me."

He shook his head more slowly this time, uncertain about what he should do. I held my foot over his soldiers.

"Give, Hanny," I said and he looked at me and then slowly brought it over, nudging me aside and kneeling down to resume his game.

I sat on the bed and looked inside the envelope. There were dozens and dozens of ten pound notes, and in amongst the money was a list of names

Hale. Parry. Parkinson. Collier.

"You shouldn't have taken this, Hanny," I said. "You got your watch back, didn't you? Why did you have to take this as well?"

He didn't respond.

"Christ, Hanny," I said, grasping him by the arm and showing him. "There must be thousands of pounds here."

He caught the tone of my voice and sat against the bed and put his head in his hands.

"Tomorrow," I said. "You're going to take this back. I'm not getting the blame. Whatever they want to do to you, I'll let them."

It was a cruel thing to say, I know, but Hanny deserved to feel as worried as I was, especially after

164

what Clement had said. He went to put on his gorilla mask and I let him. It would do him good to be frightened. He had to learn to deal with the consequences of the things he did. I wasn't going to be around to look after him forever. I mean, it was inevitable we would drift apart. University, career, marriage, mortgage, children. Even though they seemed unimaginable then, I was certain that, even without necessarily desiring them, I would receive these sacraments of adulthood sooner or later. They were as predictable as ageing. It was just what happened in life. Wasn't that so?

Hanny lay down and after glancing at me once or twice for some sympathy he went still and didn't wake even when the door banged open downstairs a while later.

Going out onto the landing, I heard someone sobbing and Monro's claws skittering on the tiles. People went rushing out to see what was going on. I quickly stuffed the money back into the book and shoved it under my pillow.

Miss Bunce was sitting on the bottom step, crying and gasping, several hands rubbing her back, trying to coax out of her what was wrong. Mummer stood with her arms folded. David was nowhere to be seen.

"It was horrible," Miss Bunce said.

"What was?" Mrs Belderboss asked.

Miss Bunce waved her hand towards the darkness and blubbed again.

"Where's David?" Mr Belderboss said, moving to the open door.

"I don't know," she said. "I just ran. I thought he was behind me."

"Did you get lost or something, dear?" Mrs Belderboss said.

"No."

"Did you and David fall out?"

"No, no," Miss Bunce snapped. "It wasn't that at all."

"Well, where is he then?"

"I told you, I don't know."

"I'm sure he won't be far away," said Father Bernard, gesturing for Farther and I to put on our coats. "We'll go and look for him."

We left the commotion in the house and walked up the lane to the field gate, where a smaller path cut through the grass to the wood. Monro charged off ahead and as we got further Father Bernard whistled for him and we heard him come bungling out of the darkness to appear on top of a pile of stones to our right, daft with the run, his tongue hanging over his teeth, sending out little puffs of breath.

"Good lad, Monro," said Father Bernard, ruffling his ears.

We stopped for a moment and then Father Bernard called David's name.

Nothing. Only the wind through the wood and a blackbird twittering in the darkness.

We climbed a little further and then stopped again at the tree line, our torch beams shaking and crossing, catching the eyes of animals just before they bolted. Father Bernard called out again and Monro went off, lumbering into the gloom. When we caught up with him, he was sniffing around David, who had heard Father Bernard and come to meet us.

"David?" said Father Bernard. "Is everything all right? Joan's in a terrible state."

"It's this way," he said. "In the trees over there."

"What is?" said Father Bernard.

"A man's hanged himself, I think."

"Jesus," said Farther, then apologised to Father Bernard.

"Show me where," said Father Bernard.

"I'm sorry, Father," said David. "Monro just slipped his lead and he was off before we could catch him. He obviously got the smell of it."

"Show me where, David," said Father Bernard again.

But David shook his head.

"I'd rather not," he said.

"All right," said Father Bernard. "You go back to the house and make sure Joan's all right."

"Should I call the police?" he asked.

"You can't. There's no phone," said Farther.

David looked distressed.

"Look," said Father Bernard. "I'll see what's what and if we need to fetch the police, I'll drive to Little Hagby all right? There's a pay phone in the pub."

David nodded and took the torch Farther offered him and went back down the field to Moorings.

Father Bernard watched him go, and then turned to look at the trees. "Come on, then," he said quietly. "And Tonto, you shut your eyes if I tell you to, is that clear?"

"Yes, Father."

The dark of the wood was absolute. Even with the torches we tripped over roots and caught our feet on brambles. Farther slipped and fell into a mire of foetid leaves and mud. We helped him out and went on, with one beam trained on the floor and the other scanning the trees, which moved to and fro in the wind and made a noise like rain. Some had been beaten down by storms and lay like the spines of dinosaurs, rotting into the ground or leaning heavily against the living. Others had fallen but not died and, searching for the daylight again, had grown serpently along the ground.

There was no easy way through. Every turn took us to a fresh tangle of branches that were impossible to part without being scratched and snagged.

In the dark, the place seemed boundless and every sound carried a long way, from our boots breaking down the branches that had fallen between the trees to the noise of something thrashing through the undergrowth deep in the wood.

"Deer," said Father Bernard when we stopped to listen.

"I hope so," said Farther.

The crashing came again, sending a wood pigeon blundering through the trees nearest to us.

"It must be," said Father Bernard. "They can be noisy buggers sometimes."

"Won't they bother about Monro?" said Farther.

"No," said Father Bernard.

"I thought deer didn't get on with dogs."

"They'd be long gone before that lummox got anywhere near them," Father Bernard replied.

168

"Where is he, anyway?" said Farther, roving his torch beam across the trees.

Monro's barks echoed around the wood and it was impossible to tell which way he had gone. Father Bernard whistled for him and there was a great deal of rustling and when Monro barked again it sounded as if he was much closer and directly over to our left. He, of course, could slip under the branches and nose through the bracken, but for us the way was blocked and we skirted around the limbs and briars until Farther spotted a gap where the undergrowth had been trodden down by David and Miss Bunce as they chased Monro earlier.

Yet they hadn't been the only ones to have come this way. There were beer cans in the undergrowth and the damp smell of an old fire hung about the place, stirred with the dungy odour of cooked meat.

We came to a clearing and there was indeed a pile of burnt logs, white with ash and heaped with the remains of some animal. At first I thought it might still be alive, as its skin seemed to be moving, but as I stepped closer I could see that it merely crawled with flies and beetles foraging in its belly.

Farther swallowed. "Where's that dog got to?" he said quietly.

"There," said Father Bernard and pointed to where Monro was jumping up at a long dark shape suspended from the bough of an oak tree, surely one of the oldest in the wood, swollen and contorted by its own weight.

We stopped short and Father Bernard called Monro to heel, which he complied with at the third, more irritable command.

169

"What have you found, old man?" he said and put the light on what Monro had been sniffing.

The beam illuminated a leering, bone face for a second before Father Bernard dropped the torch.

"Jesus," Farther said again, his breath shivering out of him. "What is it?"

"Well," said Father Bernard, with a little relieved laugh and knocking the torch back into life on the palm of his hand. "It's not a man, thank God."

He put the light back onto the face again and held it there. From inside a dark cowl, a sheep's skull rubbed with boot polish lolled against the pull of the rope by which it had been strung to the bough, its snooker ball eyes knocking against the bone. The rest of the body, as we discovered when Father Bernard poked at it with a branch, was made of sandbags and wood covered in a rough woollen blanket.

"Then what is it?" said Farther. "A scarecrow?"

"No, I think you were right first time, Mr Smith."

"Sorry?"

"I think 'tis meant to be Himself," said Father Bernard. "See the crown of thorns there."

He put the beam back on the head and lifted the cowl with the stick. Farther winced at the twisted band of barbed wire that had been hammered into the skull.

"Who'd do something like that?" Farther said.

"I couldn't say, Mr Smith," he said, moving closer and moving the folds of the cloak covering the torso. "But they've obviously spent some time on it."

Father Bernard glanced at me and I knew that he suspected, like me, that the effigy had been strung up here by the men Clement had warned us about. Parkinson and Collier. But, he kept it to himself and showed us how the chest had been made from what looked like an old rabbit hutch.

"There's something inside," said Father Bernard and he poked it with the stick.

"What is it?" asked Farther.

Monro was jumping up again, sniffing the air. Father Bernard popped the latch on the wire mesh door and it swung open and something landed at his feet. Monro leapt upon it immediately and took a chunk out of it before it slithered out of his jaws.

"Bloody hell," Farther said and backed away, taking me with him.

Father Bernard grabbed Monro's collar and hauled him off.

"Let's go," he said and we made our way quickly back through the trees, almost running by the time we got to the field above Moorings.

Back on the lane, we walked three abreast, Farther's boots squelching with mud. Monro padded along just ahead. No one spoke. Each of us was thinking how we might explain what we'd seen in the wood. We'd tell them that there was no man hanging there. It was a joke. There was nothing to worry about.

There was nothing else we could say. At the moment it had fallen from Jesus' chest and onto the ground we had agreed instantly and silently that we would tell no one about the pig's heart stuck through with nails.

CHAPTER
FOURTEEN

Everyone was waiting in the hallway, and as soon as we got through the door, they all broke off from their conversations and moved towards Father Bernard. What had happened? Had someone really hanged themselves? Should they fetch the police? Father Bernard sent Monro off to the kitchen, closed the door behind him and waved his hands to quieten everyone down.

"It was nothing," he said. "Someone's strung up an old blanket for a joke, that's all."

Farther nodded in assent and took off his coat.

"There, Joan, you see. It'll just be kids from the village messing about," said Mrs Belderboss, patting Miss Bunce on the shoulder.

She was still sitting at the foot of the stairs, biting the edges of her fingernails, puffy-eyed and cross with herself for being hysterical in front of everyone.

Mr Belderboss clicked his fingers. "That's probably what we heard the other night," he said. "The noises."

"Aye, well, there you go," Father Bernard replied.

"Honestly some people have got nothing better to do," said Mrs Belderboss.

"Not round here, they haven't," said Miss Bunce, directing her resentment at Mummer.

Mummer's face began to open with indignation and before anything could flare up Father Bernard took her by the shoulders and steered her away.

"In my room there is a bottle of brandy on the dresser. Would you be so kind as to go and fetch it for me?" he said.

"Brandy, Father? It's Lent," said Mummer.

"I brought it for Monro. The cold plays havoc with his chest. I thought a drop of it might do Miss Bunce some good," he said. "For the shock."

Mummer folded her arms and rolled her eyes.

"She's been sat there for half an hour, Father. I should think the shock will have subsided by now."

Father Bernard gave her a straight look. "Even so."

"Will you need to call the police, Father?" said Mr Belderboss.

Father Bernard looked at Mummer for a moment and then shook his head.

"To be honest, I can't see them taking it too seriously."

"Well, I'm not staying here, Father," said Miss Bunce.

"Oh, will you talk some sense into her," said Mrs Belderboss to Father Bernard. "She's sent poor David upstairs to pack her bags for her."

"I don't care," said Miss Bunce. "This is an awful place. I said we ought to have gone to Glasfynydd."

"But how will you get home, dear?" Mrs Belderboss said, sitting down next to her and taking her hand.

Miss Bunce looked up at Father Bernard.

"I was going to ask Father if he'd drive us to Little Hagby," she said. "We'll be able to phone for a taxi to take us to the station in Lancaster."

"Oh, for pity's sake, Joan. You can't expect Father to go out now," said Mummer. "It's gone nine. You'll have missed any trains to London."

Miss Bunce squared her face.

"There are rooms at the pub," she said. "We can stay there overnight and get a train in the morning."

"Don't be ridiculous," said Mummer.

"Mrs Smith," Father Bernard said abruptly. Then, calming his voice, "Would you please go and have a look for that brandy?"

"Go on, Esther," said Farther.

Mummer looked at Miss Bunce a second longer and then went off along the hallway. Everyone turned to Father Bernard. He regarded Miss Bunce and then took off his coat and hung it up on the rack by the door. He rubbed his eyes, kneading them with the heels of his palms.

"Miss Bunce," he said, sitting down on the chair next to the grandfather clock. "I know you've had a fright, but I should try and forget about what you've seen in the woods and make the most of the time we have here."

Mummer came back with a glass tumbler of brandy and handed it to Father Bernard, who in turn passed it to Miss Bunce.

"I don't want it, Father."

"Just take a sip and you'll feel better."

Miss Bunce wetted her lips with the brandy and screwed up her face.

"You may not agree at the moment," said Father Bernard, taking the glass from her as she held it out. "But, given what I know of your commitment to your faith, I think that in the cold light of day you would regret it very much if you went home so soon."

"Father's right," said Mrs Belderboss. "We haven't been to the shrine yet. You wouldn't want to miss that."

Miss Bunce nodded and wiped her eyes. David came down the stairs, alternately banging Miss Bunce's suitcase against the wall and the banisters.

"Are you ready, Joan?" he said.

"False alarm," said Mrs Belderboss and David hesitated for a moment, looked at Miss Bunce and then went back upstairs.

When everyone had dispersed, I went up to check on Hanny. He was sound asleep, an arm lolling out of the bed towards his soldiers, the stuffed rats and the envelope of money. He'd taken it out from under my pillow and rifled through the contents. There were bank notes all over the floor. I collected everything together and hid the money under the mattress so that Hanny wouldn't find it again before we had to take it back.

In his other hand were the pornographic pictures Billy Tapper had given me. I took them off him and screwed them into a ball. They needed to go on the fire whenever the opportunity arose. Why we'd kept them, I didn't know, and what Mummer would have done had she found him with them, I couldn't imagine. Though

I'd have naturally got the blame and been branded a deviant like poor Henry McCullough who had been caught in mid strike as he lay on his bed with his mother's underwear catalogues.

It had been around that time that a boy called Paul Peavey joined us as an altar server. He was younger than Henry and I, thin and pale, small for his age and keen as mustard to please Father Wilfred. He was the type that, given a different time and place, would have joined the Hitler Youth like a shot or been on the front row at a public hanging. His father was a regular fixture at the bar of the church social centre, where I helped collect the glasses on a Friday night. One of those loud individuals whose thinking is done for them by the tabloids. With him it was usually something about immigrants, or the unemployed or the Labour Party, or the nefarious connection between all three.

One Sunday after our cassocks had been inspected for dirt and creases and stowed in the vestry wardrobe, Father Wilfred went into his little office next door and came back with two pairs of gardening gloves. One for me and one for Paul. Henry held out his hands for his pair of gloves but Father Wilfred told him to sit down and guided Paul and I to the vestry door with instructions to go to the end of the graveyard and pick as many nettles as we could carry.

Not daring to question Father Wilfred, we duly hurried out, found a clump of nettles by the large Victorian vaults and came back with fistfuls of the things, which, despite the gloves, had still managed to sting our arms.

176

Henry looked up at us, his eyes widening when he saw what we'd brought back, knowing that they were destined for him in some way, his mind racing with terrible possibilities.

"Sit down," Father Wilfred said to us and we did so, trying not to let the nettles sting us any more.

Henry started to ask us what was going on, but then jumped back into a rigid shape when Father Wilfred slammed the door to the vestry. For a few moments, Father Wilfred stood against the wall looking at us, prolonging Henry's unease.

"I have a question for you, boys," he said at last, setting off on his routine of pacing back and forth across the stone flags, patting his Bible. "Come the Day of Judgement, who is to be cast down the deepest?"

Paul immediately raised his hand.

"Heathens?" he said.

"No," said Father Wilfred. "Even lower than the heathens."

"Protestants?" said Paul.

Father Wilfred stopped abruptly and stood in front of Henry.

"What do you think, McCullough?"

Henry looked up at him nervously.

"Murderers, Father?"

Father Wilfred shook his head.

"No, McCullough," he said. "The people I am talking about will look on with envy at the punishments of murderers."

"Fornicators," Paul said suddenly.

"Close, Peavey. Onanists," said Father Wilfred.

177

Henry looked down at his feet.

"Wicked little fellows who have too much time on their hands," he said. "McCullough, your mother tells me that you are an onanist."

"No, Father."

"She tells me that you keep vile magazines in your room."

"I don't, Father. They're hers."

"Are you calling your mother a liar?"

Henry said nothing.

"Fifth Commandment, Peavey."

"Honour thy father and thy mother," said Paul, watching Henry expectantly.

Father Wilfred put down his Bible on the table. "I'll ask you again, McCullough. Is your mother a liar?"

"No, Father."

"Then what she tells me is true?"

Henry put his head in his hands and Father Wilfred curled his top lip as though he had smelled something unpleasant.

"Sinful boy," he said. "I didn't have time for that kind of behaviour when I was your age. I was too busy begging for the scraps the butcher's dog wouldn't even eat, to feed my family and the family next door. Think of the Poor next time you're tempted; they don't have idle hands, lad. They're either working or praying for work."

"I'm sorry, Father," Henry sobbed.

Father Wilfred continued to glare at Henry, but held out his hands towards me and Paul, and after a moment where we looked at one another uncertainly, we passed him the nettles, which he took from us without flinching.

"Hands," he said to Henry.

"What?"

"Give me your hands."

Henry held out his hands and Father Wilfred put the nettles into his open palms.

"Squeeze them," he said.

"Please, Father," Henry said. "I won't do it again."

"Squeeze them, McCullough."

Henry gently closed his hands and Father Wilfred suddenly clamped them tight. Henry cried out, but Father Wilfred only crushed them harder until green juice seeped out from between his fingers and ran down his arms.

"Believe me, McCullough, this is nothing to the pain onanists receive in Hell."

After another minute of sobbing, Father Wilfred told Henry to put the nettles in the wastebin and sent him out into the church to pray for forgiveness.

"Not a word, boys," said Father Wilfred to me and Paul as we put on our coats. Paul had gone a shade of pink with the excitement of it all. "These lessons are for you and nobody else."

"Yes, Father Wilfred," we said in monotone chorus.

"Good," he said. "Kneel down now."

We knelt down before him on the stone flags of the vestry, and in turn he placed a cold hand on our heads, reciting one of his favourite passages from Proverbs.

"'Trust in the Lord with all your heart and do not lean on your own understanding. In all your ways acknowledge Him, and He will make your paths straight.'"

"Amen," we said and he smiled and went into his office and closed the door.

We were like that old bike tyre he used to roll down the streets of Whitechapel as a boy, giving it little corrective taps to stop it tumbling into the filth, something which poor Henry frequently seemed to do.

We found him in the lady chapel, kneeling in front of the Virgin, looking up into her doe-eyes, whispering and crying, his swollen hands shaking as he desperately tried to keep them together. Paul laughed and zipped up his coat and went outside.

CHAPTER
FIFTEEN

Even though Moorings had been built fortress-solid to withstand the weather, and Mummer, out of London habit, made a point of checking every door and window before she went to bed, I still had the rifle next to me that night.

I couldn't stop thinking about what we'd seen in the woods. It seemed clear that Monro had been lured up there on purpose by the smell of the meat. We were supposed to find the thing hanging from the oak bough. It was meant to frighten us into leaving. And if we didn't, what then?

I thought about the animal roasted on the fire; the flies crawling in and out of its face.

Every knock and creak of the house brought me back from the edge of sleep and I felt my hands tense around the rifle. Quite what I would do if anyone broke in, I didn't know. The sight of the rifle might be enough to make most people turn heel and run, but Parkinson and Collier were used to guns and they'd know immediately that it wasn't loaded.

It must have been around eleven o'clock when I heard someone knocking on Father Bernard's door. It was Mr

Belderboss. I stood at the head of the stairs and waited until he had gone in and then went down one step at a time, sticking to the edges where they didn't creak quite so much, and slotted myself into the darkness of the understairs cupboard.

I could hear the clink of glasses and Father Bernard said, "Do you want a drink, Reg?"

"Do you think we ought to, Father? Esther was right. It is Lent."

"I'm sure the Lord would permit us a small one, Reg. After all that's gone on this evening."

"Well, I will, Father, thank you," Mr Belderboss said. "Just don't tell Mary. You know what she's like. Anything stronger than Typhoo and she thinks I'm going to drop down dead."

Father Bernard laughed. "Is everyone all right now?"

"Oh, yes," said Mr Belderboss dismissively. "They don't half get into a two-and-eight about nothing sometimes. Like I say, it'll just have been kids from the village messing about."

"Aye," said Father Bernard.

They knocked their glasses together and there was a moment of silence while they presumably took back whatever it was they were drinking.

"Father," said Mr Belderboss.

"Yes?"

"I'd like you to hear confession."

"Of course, Reg," said Father Bernard. "If you're sure you want me to."

"I am, Father," he said.

"Well, finish your drink first," said Father Bernard. "Then we'll talk."

"All right."

Edging back a little, I found a box that would take my weight. Lower down there was a crack between the wooden boards and I could see a narrow slice of the room. Mr Belderboss was sitting on a chair in front of the grubby curtain that curved around the washbasin.

He crossed himself and said the Act of Contrition.

"What's on your mind?" Father Bernard asked.

"It's Wilfred," said Mr Belderboss.

"Ah look, Reg, I'm sorry if it seemed as though I was prying the other day."

"Oh, no no, Father," said Mr Belderboss. "That isn't why I came to speak to you. I'm not cross with you."

He hesitated and rubbed the back of his neck.

"Father, Mary doesn't know, but the police brought me home from the cemetery one night the other week," he said.

"Why what happened?" Father Bernard asked.

"Nothing happened, as such," said Mr Belderboss, shaking his head. "I think they were going to take me in, but I got the impression they thought I was a bit doolally, being out at that time of night, so I let them think it and they brought me home instead."

"What time was this?"

"Oh, I don't know. After midnight sometime. One. Two. Perhaps. I can't remember."

"What made you go and see Wilfred at that time of night?"

"I just wanted to make sure no one had pinched the flowers," said Mr Belderboss. "They were quite expensive, you see, but it wasn't the money really. I just couldn't sleep for worrying that he was lying there all alone and thinking no one cared."

"Wilfred's with God," said Father Bernard. "He knows how much you miss him. I'm not sure you need flowers to convince him of that."

"But someone had taken them," said Mr Belderboss.

"Oh," said Father Bernard. "So what did you do?"

"Well this is it, Father. I wandered around for a bit, trying to see if they'd been put on someone else's grave. People do that, don't they? If they forget to bring some or they can't afford them. Then I saw this woman. She was sitting in one of the little shelters they have there, you know the ones, Father?"

"Aye."

"She looked quite normal at first," said Mr Belderboss. "She was dressed up in a fancy hat and she had a fur round her neck and new shoes, like she was on her way home from a party or something. I was going to ask her if she'd seen anyone acting suspiciously, but when I got closer I could tell she was a drunk. You know how they smell of the stuff? And when she moved, her coat opened and she wasn't wearing anything on her lower half, if you know what I mean, apart from her shoes. She went on and on about someone called Nathaniel. I thought, who on earth is she talking to? But then I realised she thought I was him. She kept on thanking me for sending her these flowers. So I said — what flowers? — and she had Wilfred's next to her on the bench. Even the little card was still there with them."

"Go on."

"Well I tried to take them off her and she started screaming and next thing I knew there were two bobbies coming along the path with torches. She'd disappeared and I was there holding this bunch of hyacinths. I felt such a fool, Father. I mean, getting into trouble with the law at my time of life, can you imagine?"

"It's perfectly all right, Reg. To miss people that have died, I mean."

"But not normal to go to their graves in the middle of the night?"

"I'm not sure normal comes into it when you're grieving," said Father Bernard. "But it might be better to go and see your brother during the day. I'm not sure I'd want to be wandering round Great Northern in the dark."

Mr Belderboss looked up at the ceiling and sighed.

"I just feel ashamed that I've kept it from Mary," he said. "I ought to tell her what happened, just in case she gets to hear about it secondhand. They're a nosy bunch down our street. One flash of a blue light and the curtains are going."

"I'm sure she'd understand if you did tell her."

"So you think I ought to, Father?"

"I can't answer that. It's up to you. You know her best."

"So it wouldn't be a sin to keep something important from someone?"

Father Bernard paused.

"Reg," he said. "I'm struggling to see what sin you've committed exactly. I'm not just going to send you off like a child to say three Hail Marys for mouthing off to your mammy. I think you need time to think about what to do for the best."

"But what does God want me to do?"

"Whatever decision you make will be the right one, if you trust in Him."

Mr Belderboss rubbed the back of his neck and breathed out heavily.

"Look," said Father Bernard. "It seems to me that you need to be in a dialogue with God, not putting out your hands for a caning. Take some time, talk to Him, pray for guidance, not punishment. God will answer you, Reg."

"Yes, of course, I know."

"You need to think about what there is to be gained from telling Mary," Father Bernard went on. "Are you going to be happier for telling her, but make her worried in return? Or would it punish you too much to keep it to yourself?"

Mr Belderboss shook his head.

"I don't know," he said. "It all just seems wrong."

"Well, grief can often make you feel like that."

"No, I don't mean that, Father. I mean where Wilfred's buried seems wrong."

There was silence for a moment and then Father Bernard spoke.

"Why did he choose to be buried away from Saint Jude's, Reg?"

"So that he could be with the family."

"You don't sound so sure."

Mr Belderboss said nothing but stared at the floor in front of his feet.

"Tell me if I'm prying again," said Father Bernard. "But the other day you said that Wilfred seemed to change after you came here the last time."

"Yes, Father, he did."

"How?"

"I don't know. He just wasn't himself any more. He just seemed to give up."

"Give up what?"

"Honestly, Father?" said Mr Belderboss. "I think it was his faith."

"Why would that have happened?"

"I don't know, Father, but for all he said every Sunday at Mass, I wasn't convinced he believed any of it any more. It just seemed like lip service. Like he was trying too hard. You know how if you say something often enough you can get yourself to believe it? And then in the end, well, he just seemed to shut himself away from everyone. Wouldn't speak to me or Mary."

Mr Belderboss closed his eyes.

"Poor Wilfred," he said, shaking his head. "It's bad enough for anyone to stop believing, but it must be a terrible thing for a priest. It must have driven him out of his mind."

Father Bernard pulled back the curtain and poured Mr Belderboss another drink, but he didn't touch it. They sat for a while and didn't really talk other than to

187

eventually bid one another goodnight. They shook hands and Father Bernard patted Mr Belderboss on the shoulder.

"Peace be with you," he said.

"And also with you, Father," said Mr Belderboss.

When he had gone, Father Bernard stared at the door, deep in thought, then downed Mr Belderboss's brandy as well as his own and got up, disappearing from the splinter of the room I could see. I heard him talking to Monro, scolding him affectionately, then he returned with a book.

I made no sound, but he suddenly turned as though he had seen my eye in the crack. He looked directly at me, but then went back to reading, shivering a little as the wind lowed against the window and dimmed the bulb in the room.

CHAPTER
SIXTEEN

A gale battered Moorings all night long and I woke several times and clutched the rifle. Sometime in the small hours there was an almighty bang and in the morning I woke to find that the doors to one of the outhouses had been taken clean off and lay several feet away, scattered like playing cards.

Hanny was up and dressed already, standing at the window, stroking the stuffed hare. He set the hare down on the windowsill and put his fingers to his lips. He wanted to see Else.

"Yes, Hanny, we'll go back today," I said. "But you might not be able to see the girl. They might not let you."

He kissed his fingers again. And rubbed his belly slowly like Else had done to soothe the ache of the baby inside.

"I said, we'll go back."

This seemed to satisfy him and he picked up the hare again and looked out of the window at the outhouse.

"Do you want to go and see?" I said.

There was no one else around. Monro lifted his head when we came into the kitchen and I gave him some of the biscuits Father Bernard had left on the table to

189

quieten him down. I wanted to have the outhouse to ourselves first, before it became everyone's discovery.

We walked across the yard, trampling over the heavy wooden doors, and stood at the gap where they had once been.

Inside was an ark of stuffed animals — a hundred or more. These were the unsold, uncollected, unfinished works. Botched jobs. Seconds. The cold and damp had taken its toll and there were rows and rows of shrunken squirrels and rabbits. A poodle's head had sunk in on itself like an old balloon. In the far corner we found a tandem being ridden by two mangy chimps. Neither of us wanted to touch them, so we fetched a broom and pushed them off. They fell stiffly to the floor, still grinning, their hands like claws, as though they had been frozen solid.

Hanging from the ceiling were dozens of bird skeletons, hawks of some kind, trussed up by the feet and left to decompose. Why he hadn't stuffed them too, I didn't know. Perhaps he had died before he'd had time, but there were so many of them and the way they were hung they seemed more like the hare and the rats Hanny had found stretched out on the fence. Proof of a victory of some kind.

Although the floor was littered with their bones and feathers, the smell of rotting was strangely absent, as the air had been allowed to move freely through the gaps around the wooden doors and out of the barred window set just above head height on the far wall. There was a chest of drawers underneath it with bootprints on the top where the taxidermist had stood

190

to look out of the window. On the floor, almost obscured by dust and spiderwebs were spent bullet casings. This must have been a firing step, though what he was trying to shoot, I didn't know. The hawks, perhaps, as they came out of the woods.

"Look in the drawers, Hanny," I said and rattled the handles to show him.

He took hold of the top drawer and yanked it open. Spiders darted away, following the dark into the corners. Inside were dozens of old spanners wet with rust.

"Try the next one," I said.

And here we found what I'd hoped was there. Under a thin cotton sheet were boxes and boxes of bullets. Hanny went to touch them, but I held his sleeve.

"Let me get them," I said, and took out the nearest box and opened it. The bullets were set in a metal clip and were sharp and cold.

"You mustn't let anyone know that they're here, Hanny," I said. "This is a secret now. We'll take them down to the pillbox on our way to Coldbarrow."

He stared at the bullets and I closed the drawer tightly.

Eventually, everyone came to look and wandered between the animals with curiosity or revulsion.

Miss Bunce stood in the doorway and refused to come in.

"It's awful," she said. "Poor things."

David put his hands on her shoulders and steered her away.

"That's a decent-looking machine, mind you," said Father Bernard, nodding at the tandem that the chimps had been riding.

Hanny and I managed to haul it out and pushed it around the yard. The tyres had perished and the gears were clotted with rust but it didn't seem as though it would take much to be able to ride it again and Father Bernard only put up a mild protest about his clothes getting dirty before he fetched his tool box from the minibus.

Before long he had the tandem upside down in the kitchen on sheets of old newspaper and was taking apart the cogs and gears, his usually well-slicked hair flopping in front of his eyes. He seemed to be in his element as he knelt down with a spanner in his hand. More at home with nuts and screws and other pieces of greasy metal than giving out communion.

Mummer tutted and fussed until she finally stood over us with her arms folded.

"Boys," she said. "Will you please let Father have his breakfast now? There's too much to do to be spending the day messing about with that bit of junk."

"It's quite all right, Mrs Smith," said Father Bernard. "It's nice revisiting one of the few genuine pleasures of my youth."

She looked irritably at his black hands and the smudges on his face, as though she was, at any moment, going to spit on a handkerchief and start wiping.

"Well, everything's on the table, Father," she said. "We'll wait for you to say grace."

"Oh, don't let me stop you, Mrs Smith," he said. "I might be a wee while getting all this oil off my hands."

"All the same. I think we'd rather do things properly, Father, even if it means eating things cold."

"As you wish, Mrs Smith," he said, looking at her with a curious expression.

I've thought about that look quite often as I've been getting all this down. What it meant. What Father Bernard had let slip just at that moment. What he really thought of Mummer.

A line of dominos, spinning plates, a house of cards. Pick a cliché. He had realised what I'd known about Mummer for a long time — that if one thing gave way, if one ritual was missed or a method abridged for convenience, then her faith would collapse and shatter.

I think it was then that he began to pity her.

Father Bernard went off to clean himself and Hanny and I went into the dining room to wait for him. Everyone was sitting around the table watching Mr Belderboss. He seemed in a brighter mood than he'd been in the previous night with Father Bernard, though I got the impression he was deliberately distracting himself from thoughts of his brother with the object he was examining. It was a small, brown earthenware bottle with a cork stopper in the end and a gargoyle face crudely scratched on one side.

"It was on the window ledge, you say?" said Mr Belderboss.

"Yes," said Farther. "Stuck between the bars."

"Oh, put it down, Reg, it's absolutely hideous," said Mrs Belderboss. "No one wants to see that at the breakfast table."

He looked around at the others and then went back to studying the face on the jar.

"I don't see anyone complaining, Mary."

Mrs Belderboss made a noise of exasperation that Father Bernard caught as he came in through the door.

"My, my, Mrs Belderboss," he said. "That sounded like a soul in distress."

"Oh, you tell him, Father," she said. "He won't listen to me."

"About what?"

She gestured to the bottle Mr Belderboss was looking at.

"He's obsessing again."

"It was in the quarantine room, Father," said Mr Belderboss. "Between the bars on the window. There's definitely something inside it."

He shook the jar and handed it to Father Bernard.

"Sounds like liquid of some sort. What do you think?"

Father Bernard put it close to his ear and listened as he moved it from side to side.

"Aye," he said. "There's definitely something in there."

"Ugly thing, isn't it?" said Mr Belderboss.

"Aye, it is that."

"What do you think it is?" asked Farther.

Father Bernard passed it back to Mr Belderboss and laughed and shook his head.

"I'm afraid I've no idea."

"Father Wilfred would have known," said Mrs Belderboss. "Wouldn't he, Esther?"

Mummer handed Father Bernard a plate but didn't look at him.

"I'm sure he would," she said.

"He'd a doctorate from Oxford," said Mrs Belderboss, leaning towards Father Bernard, as he began buttering a slice of toast.

"Cambridge," said Mr Belderboss, without taking his eyes off the jar that he was now turning round and round in his hands.

"One of those places, anyway," said Mrs Belderboss. "He was a very clever man."

"And so well travelled," said Mr Belderboss, shaking the jar gently next to his ear.

"Oh, yes," said Mrs Belderboss. "I'd have given my eye-teeth to have gone to some of the places he did. You were very lucky, Joan."

Father Bernard looked confused. Mrs Belderboss leant towards him again and smiled at Miss Bunce across the table as she explained.

"Miss Bunce was lucky enough to accompany Father Wilfred on his trip to the Holy Land last summer. As his personal secretary no less."

"Really?" said Father Bernard, looking at Miss Bunce. "Well, well."

Miss Bunce flushed slightly and scraped off a clod of butter from the block in the middle of the table.

"Mrs Belderboss makes it sound grander than it was, Father, but it was a wonderful experience," she said.

Mummer suddenly remembered there was something she had to do and went out of the room.

It was still a bone of contention with her that Miss Bunce had been picked to go to Jerusalem with Father Wilfred. It wasn't because she hadn't been asked herself — she could hardly have accepted anyway, what with the shop to run — but because it was Miss Bunce who *had*.

She put on a front but had soon become utterly sick of the endless talk about the trip and had sat sour-faced through the slide show that had done the rounds of people's houses during the autumn of 1975: Father Wilfred coming out of the tomb of Lazarus. Father Wilfred standing outside the Church of the Holy Sepulchre. Father Wilfred walking along the Via Dolorosa. Father Wilfred in Al Bustan, waist deep in a crowd of poor, grinning Palestinian children wanting sweets as he tried to find the garden where King David set down the Psalms.

After a while, she came back in with a tray of tea cups, and during the silence as she set them out on the table, there was a knock at the front door. Everyone looked up. Father Bernard wiped his mouth and went to see who it was. We heard him speaking to someone in a tone of surprise and then the door to the dining room opened and Clement's mother appeared, dressed in a long coat — the hem of which met the tops of her Wellingtons — and carrying a sack of firewood. Everyone watched as she moved backwards across the room, dragging the sack towards the nook beside the fireplace.

196

"Don't you want some help, Mrs Parry?" said Mr Belderboss, looking towards Father Bernard, who shrugged in a way that suggested he had already asked her and she had declined.

"Nay," she said and looked up at us. She wasn't wearing her glasses any more and her eyes were a bright blue.

"Where's Clement?" asked Mrs Belderboss.

"He's out," she said, dusting off her hands.

"Oh," said Mrs Belderboss. "Well how did you get here?"

She lifted her Wellingtons in turn. "Shanks' Pony," she said.

"On your own?"

"Aye," she said.

"Oh."

Clement's mother put her hands in the pockets of her coat and looked at the wood she had brought in.

"That should be enough for now," she said. "As long as it dunt get any colder."

She went to the door and Father Bernard opened it for her.

"It's all right," she said. "I'll see me sen out."

Father Bernard watched her as she went down the hallway and out through the front door.

"I thought she was blind," Mrs Belderboss said quietly to her husband.

"Well, perhaps she had an operation," he replied. "They can sort out cataracts nowadays, can't they?"

"Is that what you think it was? Cataracts?"

"I don't know. Probably."

"That's astonishing," said Mrs Belderboss. "It was so quick. We only saw her the other day."

"You see what I mean about this place," said Mr Belderboss, looking around the table. "A constant surprise."

After breakfast, I went upstairs and fetched the envelope of money from under the mattress. Mummer was still annoyed about Mrs Belderboss bringing up the Jerusalem trip, and was so distracted by all the preparations she needed to make for the visit to the shrine that she agreed Hanny and I could go out for a few hours.

Hanny wanted to take the tandem. I told him it was broken and pinched the tyres until my fingers met, but he still didn't understand.

"Father Bernard said he would mend them," I said.

Hanny grasped the handlebars and rocked the bike back and forth, looking at me expectantly.

"No, Hanny. We can't ride it yet."

As a compromise, I let him push it from the kitchen out into the yard, but he was soon distracted by a hare running off down the lane and he left the bike against a stone wall and chased after it. I went into the outbuilding and took a box of bullets out of the drawer. The box was too big, so I took out one of the clips and pushed it deep down into an inside pocket. I would stow it away in the pillbox when I got a chance. And then I could fire the rifle. Send a bullet out over the sea. Practise my aim in case Parkinson and Collier came.

The mist had thinned a little and looking over the fields there was something different that I couldn't quite place until I got further down the lane.

Hanny had stopped running and held on to the wall, breathing hard and looking across the field at the hare. I stood next to him and watched as it cut a furrow through swathes of fresh green grass that seemed to have appeared overnight.

Down at the beach and over the sea, the fog had lingered in the cold air and was so thick that we couldn't see more than a few yards. We waited and tried to listen for the sound of the sea to gauge whether the tide was in or out. Hanny went and sat on a rock and picked off the dried seaweed. I moved a little further towards the water, but was reluctant to go too far in case I lost Hanny in the mist. I looked over at him and he stared back and kissed his fingers.

"I know, Hanny, I know," I said, and picked up a stone and pitched it into the fog. It landed with a single thud, and walking a little further I could see that there was only a thin wash of water. The tide was receding. The weed on the rocks was still wet.

"Come on, Hanny," I said. "We need to go now."

Hanny walked off quickly and I had to jog at times to keep up with him. When I finally called to him to wait, he stopped in the mist up ahead.

"Hold my hand tight," I said.

We had come to the last of the timber posts and there was half a mile of open sand that couldn't be crossed as quickly. The tide had scrubbed away any tracks Leonard's car might have made and even if I could have roughly remembered the route they had marked, a safe path yesterday could be quite the opposite now.

"Hold my hand," I said again, but Hanny was too distracted and so I took hold of his arm and led him around the standing water.

"You mustn't let her kiss you again," I said. "The man will be cross with you."

He smiled.

"I'll be cross with you too."

He touched his lips again.

"No, Hanny."

He stuck out his tongue and turned away.

"Listen," I said, holding him by the shoulders and nudging his chin with my knuckle so that he faced me. "There are men who don't want us to be here. Men who might hurt you. So we've got to be careful about what we do. We just need to give the money back and leave them alone."

He looked down at his feet.

"Hanny, I'm serious," I said, hitting him a little harder this time. "I won't be able to stop them if they want to hurt you."

He rubbed his chin and felt around in his coat pockets until he found the plastic dinosaur and handed it to me.

"You don't need to say sorry," I said. "Just don't do anything stupid."

He held my hand and we carried on. Not for the first time, I wished that I'd brought the rifle. The mist had turned the sands an ashen colour, and was so thick that all sense of space was lost. Oystercatchers and gulls would sound far off one moment and then suddenly loud as they flew by. And from time to time there was a steady rumble that I thought at first was thunder or an aeroplane but realised that it was the sea churning its way over the sands, drawing out to its limit, like a bowstring.

Leonard's car was parked outside Thessaly when we got there. The place was Sabbath quiet. I knocked on the door, waited, and then when no one had come after a minute, I knocked again.

Hanny had wandered away to look at the bell tower.

I called him back, but he ignored me. I shouted a little louder, but he was too intent on opening the door and so I went over to try and lead him back to the house.

It was impossible to tell from the mainland, and even from Thessaly one could miss it, but it seemed that there had once been another building there — a chapel, perhaps, by the fragments of stone archways half hidden in the bracken. What had happened to it, I didn't know. I'd never heard of any place of worship on Coldbarrow. Perhaps they had got it wrong, or the old stories had succumbed to Chinese whispers as old stories do. Perhaps the Devil hadn't built the tower at all, but knocked down the church around it. Perhaps he had built Thessaly from the remains. They were of the same stone after all.

Before I could stop him, Hanny put his shoulder to the door and it grated open enough for us to look inside. Water dripped and something fluttered up to the belfry where the wind murmured around the wooden scaffold that held the bell in place. I wondered if, long ago, they had crept in here to satisfy themselves that Elizabeth Percy was really dead and had stood as quietly as we did now, looking up, watching her turning on the end of the rope, her bare soles curled in rigor mortis.

A stronger gust came in off the sea and swung the bell into a soft tolling. Hanny looked suddenly frightened and started to back away, almost running into Leonard, who had come out of the house and was standing in the door watching us.

"I didn't expect to see you two here again so soon," he said.

He was dressed down from the last time we'd been here. No jacket or aftershave, just shirt sleeves and corduroys. The kind of thing Farther put on when he was creosoting the fence or touching up the gloss work on the skirting boards.

But Leonard's arms were spattered with dried blood. He saw me looking and rolled down his sleeves.

"What do you want?" he said.

I opened my coat and took out the envelope.

"I've brought this back," I said.

Leonard took it from me and frowned.

"Where did you get this?" he said, opening the envelope and looking inside.

202

"It was in the book your daughter gave Hanny to keep. I don't think she knew it was in there."

It was the lie that I thought the least damaging.

"Daughter?"

"Else."

"Oh," he said. "No, I dare say she didn't know."

"It's all there," I said.

"How do you know that?" Leonard smiled and looked inside the envelope again. "Had a quick count of it, did you?"

Hanny was tugging at my sleeve and stroking his stomach.

"What's the matter with him?" said Leonard.

"He wants to see Else."

"Does he now?"

"Yes."

"Well, I'm afraid that isn't possible."

From somewhere inside Thessaly there came the sound of a baby crying. Hanny stopped what he was doing and looked at the window at the far end of the house. He smiled. Leonard followed Hanny's gaze and then looked at me, considered something, and took out several notes from the envelope. He came closer to me, hobbling on his bad leg, and slipped them into the breast pocket of my parka. I went to remove the money but Leonard kept his hand on my chest.

"Please, it's the least I can do," he said. "Since you came all this way to bring it back."

"But I don't want it."

"That's us settled," he said. "I don't expect there's anything else you'll need to come back for now, is there?"

"No."

"Good lad," he said. "And those names on that list."

"What about them?"

"Can you remember any of them?"

"No."

"That's the way," he said.

The baby cried again and Leonard nodded towards the lane.

"On you go then."

I pulled Hanny away and Leonard watched us go before he went back inside the house. Hanny insisted on walking backwards so that he could keep looking for Else. He kept on stumbhng and fell over more than once, on the last occasion refusing point-blank to get up. I went to pull him to his feet, but he wrestled out of my grip and kept his eyes fixed on the house.

"You can't see her, Hanny," I said. "Didn't you hear what the man said?"

Suddenly he stood up and stared. A figure had appeared at the end window. It was Else. She waved at Hanny and after a moment Hanny raised his hand and waved back. They stood staring at each other until Else turned sharply as if called by someone and disappeared.

CHAPTER
SEVENTEEN

"Forgive me, Father, for I have sinned," said Miss Bunce. "It has been three months since my last confession."

"I see."

"It was with Father Wilfred, just before he passed away." Father Bernard sounded genuinely surprised. "Not that you have a multitude of sins to confess to, I'm sure, but it doesn't seem like you to distance yourself from God for so long, Miss Bunce. It's not me putting you off, I hope."

Miss Bunce sniffed.

"No, Father. It's not you. I did try to come and speak to you, several times. I even made it to the door of the confessional once, but I went home again."

"Well, confession isn't always easy."

"I thought that I might be able to forget about it, but I can't. The more you try and forget the more you remember. Sin's like that, isn't it? It haunts you. That's what Father Wilfred used to say."

Father Bernard paused. "Well, you're here now, Miss Bunce," he said. "That's all that matters. You take your time. I'm quite happy to sit here and wait until you're ready. I'm not on the tight schedule of absolutions I usually am at Saint Jude's."

Miss Bunce laughed joylessly, sniffed again, mumbled a bunged-up thank you and emptied her nose.

"I don't know how to begin, really," she said. "It was listening to Mrs Belderboss talking about that trip to Jerusalem that set me off again. I just feel so upset about Father Wilfred. It was me who found him, you know."

"So I believe," said Father Bernard. "It must have been a terrible shock."

"It was, Father. And we parted on such bad terms."

"Bad terms? Why, what happened?"

"Well, the last time I saw him at the presbytery before he died he was acting so strangely."

"In what way?"

"He was worried about something."

"About what?"

"I don't know. I didn't like to ask."

"But you could tell he was worried?"

"He was just so distracted, Father. Like there was something behind him all the time, you know?"

"Aye, go on."

"Well, he asked me to go back to Jerusalem with him. For a longer trip. He said that was where he felt safe."

"Safe?"

"That was the word he used, Father."

"All right."

"Well, I told him I couldn't. I didn't want to be away from David for so long, not with the wedding to organise and everything."

206

"And what happened?"

"Well, we had a row."

"I can't imagine you having a row with anybody," said Father Bernard. "Let alone Father Wilfred."

"Well, it wasn't a row so much as, well, it felt more like he was lecturing me. He didn't approve of David, he said. He said that I had to stop seeing him. I had to call off the engagement. I couldn't understand why. He's got a good job. He goes to church every Sunday. He's kind and considerate. What is there not to approve of?"

Father Bernard laughed quietly.

"I'm sure Father Wilfred had his reasons, but I must confess I can't for the life of me think of one. David's a fine feller."

"He said there was something about him that he didn't like. I asked him what, but he wouldn't tell me. I thought that perhaps he knew something about David that I didn't, but it seemed to be more the fact that I would be moving away after we got married that he wasn't happy with. David has this job lined up in Saint Albans, as you know."

"Aye, well, maybe that's it. He had a good cook and he didn't want to let you go. I know I'm reluctant myself."

Miss Bunce managed a little laugh but quickly went back to her concerns.

"Why do you think he was so angry with me, Father?"

"I think what you have to remember, Miss Bunce," he replied, "is that Father Wilfred was an old man. I'm not saying you have to excuse his bad temper, but a lifetime's service to the Church and you get stuck in your ways and it's hard to change. I'm sure that he didn't mean to upset you and he probably spent as much time kicking himself for it as you did worrying about it."

He paused and when Miss Bunce didn't say anything but sniffle into her handkerchief, he went on.

"You know," he said, "my daddy used to say that death has the timing of the world's worst comedian and I think he was right. When people die, it's natural to regret how we treated them when they were alive. Heaven knows, there are dozens of things I wished I'd asked my mammy and daddy when they were around; times I'd like to wipe clean away. Things I wish I had or hadn't said. It's the worst kind of guilt, because it's completely irreparable."

"Oh, I know," said Miss Bunce. "I'd just hate to think of him still angry with me."

"The blessed souls in heaven don't take anything like that with them. Father Wilfred is at peace now. He doesn't bear you any grudges. I'm sure that he only wishes you to be happy. And being unable to grant him that wish is the only sin you've committed, Miss Bunce."

Miss Bunce began to sob again. "No," she said. "There's more I haven't told you, Father. I don't think you'll be so kind to me when you hear it."

"Ah, I see. And this is what made you hesitate outside the confessional?"

"Yes, Father." Miss Bunce snivelled again.

208

"Well, it sounds to me like it's been bothering you, whatever it is, so it might be best just to tell me and have it out in the open."

"Yes," said Miss Bunce, sounding as though she was steeling herself. "You're right."

She took a deep breath and sighed.

"I got drunk, Father," she said. "There. That's it. I went home and I drank half a bottle of Mum's sherry."

"All right."

"I did it to spite Father Wilfred."

"I see. And there's me forcing brandy down your neck the other night."

"I don't know what came over me. It wasn't like me at all. I mean, Mum has a drink to calm herself down sometimes, so I suppose that was why I had a glass. But I just couldn't stop. It was so deliberate. I was so angry."

"With Father Wilfred?"

"With myself. I said nothing to defend David. Father Wilfred was so determined about it that for a moment I thought he was right and that I ought to call it all off."

"You didn't, did you?"

"No, of course not."

"Did you tell David?"

"I phoned him when I got home, but by the time he came round I was so drunk that I could hardly speak. I don't know what I said to him. I must have looked a complete idiot. It's a wonder that he still wants to marry me at all. But he was so kind. I don't remember getting there, but he put me to bed and stayed with me until Mum came home."

"See. He's a good man."

"Yes, he is." Miss Bunce blew her nose. "Father," she said. "Drunkenness is a terrible sin, isn't it? Father Wilfred always said so."

"I think," said Father Bernard, "that it depends on the person. I think it depends on what the drunkenness leads to. It's a venial sin at most perhaps but in your case I wouldn't call it a sin at all."

"But I knew what I was doing was wrong and I still went ahead and did it, Father. Doesn't that mean I'll end up in Purgatory? I mean, the drunkenness aside, wrath is one of the Seven Deadly Sins."

Father Bernard coughed and hesitated for a moment before he answered.

"There is a school of thought in the Catholic Church, Miss Bunce, that says it's possible to experience Purgatory here on earth, that guilt is a kind of purification in itself. It sounds to me like that's exactly what you've been through already and that being the case I can't see God wanting to make you go through it again. You've tormented yourself over what happened with Father Wilfred, you've burdened yourself with guilt and I should think the hangover alone was punishment enough."

"I've never been so sick in all my life."

"So I can assume that you won't be hitting the bottle anytime soon?"

"Oh, never again, Father."

"Well then, listen. God forgives you your anger and your moment of weakness. Don't dwell on it any more. Put Father Wilfred's feelings down to those of an old man afraid of being lonely, and marry David. You have my blessing, if you want it."

"Thank you, Father."

"All right now?"

"Yes, Father."

I heard Father Bernard draw back the curtain, then saw him stand next to Miss Bunce. He put his hand on her head and she crossed herself.

It made sense now why, after the carol service, Miss Bunce had come into the vestry from the presbytery, crying and agitated, looking for her umbrella.

"Have you seen it anywhere?" she asked.

All three of us, Henry, Paul and I, shook our heads and watched with interest as she upended the room and then went out into the rain without it, running down the path and out of the church grounds.

"She's very odd," said Paul. "Don't you think?"

Henry and I said nothing and continued stacking the hymn books on the shelf as we had been instructed to do by Father Wilfred.

Paul sat down on a bench and crossed his legs. Father Wilfred had asked him to supervise us and he thought himself quite the foreman.

"She's not a bad-looking woman, though," he said.

It was a phrase I'd often heard his father use in the social centre.

"Quite pretty in a certain light," he added. "Bet you like her, don't you, Henry?"

Henry said nothing, only looked up at me briefly as he straightened the books.

"I bet you've thought about what she looks like naked, haven't you?"

Paul got up and went to the door to check that Father Wilfred wasn't coming. He wasn't. The lights were still on in the presbytery and he always switched them off when he left the place, even for a minute.

"Go on," he said. "You can tell me. Do you think about her when you're at it?"

Henry turned and looked at him.

"You do, don't you?" said Paul.

He looked across to the presbytery.

"I suppose Father ought to know," he said.

"Don't," said Henry.

"Why not?"

"Don't," Henry said, though this time it wasn't a plea.

"He's coming now," said Paul.

We heard the presbytery door slam and then Father Wilfred's footsteps on the gravel path.

"Don't you say anything, you sod," Henry said.

"Oh dear, oh dear," said Paul shaking his head. "Foul language as well."

"I mean it," said Henry.

Paul smiled at him as Father Wilfred appeared at the open door.

"Are you still putting the books away?" he said. "I thought you were supervising, Peavey?"

"I am, Father, but they won't listen."

"Won't they?"

"No, Father. They're being impertinent," said Paul and waited eagerly to see Father Wilfred's reaction.

"I'm not interested in your excuses, Peavey," he said. "Did Miss Bunce happen to come here?"

"Yes, Father," said Paul, his smile fading.

"Where did she go?"

"I don't know, Father. She seemed a bit upset."

"Did she?"

"Yes, Father."

"Did she say anything to you?"

"No, Father. She just wanted her brolly."

Father Wilfred looked on the back of the door where a red umbrella was hanging. He took it down and then went out, looked for her on the street and then hurried back to the presbytery.

CHAPTER
EIGHTEEN

On Easter morning, it was still dark as we walked about the yard looking for stones. Ones about the size of a fist were the best, the shape as close to an egg as possible.

Mummer and Farther had already found some for Mr and Mrs Belderboss and were back at the foot of the dry-stone wall looking for more. Miss Bunce and David, who couldn't see the point in any of it, had satisfied themselves with the first pebbles they had laid their hands on and returned to the warmth of the kitchen, where Father Bernard, who had overslept, was hurriedly putting on his boots.

"Morning, Tonto," he said, coming out with his hair wild at one side and his face black with stubble. "Happy Easter."

"Happy Easter, Father."

Mummer came over. "I'd try over by the wall if I were you, Father."

"Right," he said.

He went off and kicked about in the rubble, eventually selecting a flat block of slate. He held it up to me for approval and I shrugged and he tossed it back and moved on.

With pockets weighed down with stones, we made our way up the lane to the woods. What we'd seen the other night still troubled me and it was obvious that Miss Bunce and David were reluctant to go back as well, but the sky was lightening moment by moment and the trees were coming out of the shadows. It seemed a different place altogether.

Mummer led the way through the field and up behind Moorings, bearing right and heading for Nick's Lane — the treeless stripe that cut through Brownslack Wood as cleanly as if someone had taken a razor and drawn it up the hill. No trees had ever grown there and Mr Belderboss thought that the land must have been poisoned in some way. Hadn't they used lime on their fields around here? Too much of it might have killed off the trees. Farther suggested that by some freak of nature the wind blasted that particular part of the ridge and knocked the trees flat, but neither of their theories seemed any more plausible than the old story about the Devil burning a path through the woods as he left the Loney in a fit of rage the night they strung up Elizabeth Percy.

Mr and Mrs Belderboss were left far behind and by the time they caught up with us on the ridge, the sky had started to lift in the east — the distant Pennines becoming noticeable moment by moment, pale and lavender-coloured in the dawn.

Mummer let her stone drop from her hand and it tumbled down the fellside as she whispered a prayer. Farther did the same and then everyone followed so

215

that there were several rocks bouncing through the ferns and knocking against the limestone shelves, rousing pheasants and curlews from their sleep.

Hanny was tugging at my sleeve and pointing.

"What is it?" I whispered.

He went down the hillside a little and beckoned me to follow him.

"What's the matter, Hanny?"

"What has he seen?" said Mummer.

Hanny went off, wading through the ferns. Mummer called him back but he didn't respond.

"Stay here," said Farther. "I'll fetch him."

Farther went after Hanny, following the trail he had cut through the undergrowth, calling to him. Hanny turned around once or twice, but was determined to get to whatever he had seen from the ridge.

Way down the hill, he stopped. Farther caught up with him a minute later and he looked at what Hanny had found. He waved and called for Father Bernard and me to come.

Before we got within twenty yards of Farther, he raised his hand to keep us quiet, never taking his eyes off the thing by his feet.

"What is it?" Father Bernard said.

"Look," said Farther.

A pregnant ewe was there in the ferns, her eyes yellow and wild, possessed by the ancient hormones that had driven her to hoof out a nest in the soil and lie down.

"Is she all right, Father?"

"Aye, I think so."

Father Bernard knelt down and put his hand on the ewe's belly, hushing her when she jerked suddenly and scuffled in the mud.

"There now," he said softly.

"Did you keep sheep, Father? On your farm?"

"We'd a few, aye."

The ewe raised her head a few times and then laid it down on the ground. In the cold of the early morning, her hot breath hung around her nose and mouth.

"She's breathing hard, isn't she?" said Farther.

"Aye, well look," said Father Bernard. "She's at her time."

He moved around to her rear end, where a hoof protruded, then another, before the lamb's nose appeared, opening and closing behind the water sac. He edged a little closer and put his hand on the ewe's side, stroking her fleece with his thumb.

"It won't be long now," he said.

The ewe looked at us with her black keyhole eyes and stiffened her legs as her stomach bulged. She gave a loud bray as her body shuddered in the final contractions that squeezed out the lamb in a steaming discharge.

It lay there, tarred and feathered by its mother's gunk and the dead ferns, shivering and convulsing as it tried to breathe.

Father Bernard ripped up a few leaves and scrubbed the lamb with them, breaking the caul that had been covering its face. It opened its mouth to cry and tried to stand and then lay down again, bleating feebly. Father Bernard took hold of the lamb and pulled it around so that it lay in front of its mother's face. The ewe lifted her head and began to lick.

Mummer and the rest of them had appeared by this time, having taken the path that wound down the hillside, and stood around watching. Miss Bunce held her nose and David's hand. Mr Belderboss crossed himself.

"God be praised," he said. "Is she all right?"

Father Bernard nodded.

The ewe had got up and wandered away from us into the bracken. After a few attempts, the lamb followed on its crumpled legs and began its first tottering steps, crying out with a little red spike of a tongue. The ewe called and the lamb went to her, ramming at her udders.

"Father Bernard saved its life," said Farther.

"I did nothing so heroic, Mr Smith. His mammy would have got rid of the caul herself right enough. I just didn't want to see the poor lad struggling."

"First those butterflies," said Mrs Belderboss. "And now this. God couldn't have sent us a more obvious sign. And Andrew finding it as well. Wonderful things are going to happen at the shrine, Esther."

"If only Wilfred were here," said Mr Belderboss. "He'd have had quite a take on all this, wouldn't he? He had that way about him, didn't he? Of knowing just what to say."

"He did," said Mrs Belderboss. "It's a rare gift, isn't it, Father?"

"Aye it is that," Father Bernard replied.

"Do you remember the outing we had to the Fens that weekend?" said Mr Belderboss.

Everyone nodded and exchanged knowing smiles. Mrs Belderboss touched her husband on the arm.

"There was that terrific thunderstorm, wasn't there, Reg?"

"Oh, Lord yes. Almost apocalyptic it was, Father," Mr Belderboss laughed.

"We were all stuck in that bird hide," said Mrs Belderboss. "Do you remember?"

"Golden Orioles," said Mr Belderboss.

"Sorry?" said Father Bernard.

"We were looking at the Golden Orioles."

"They have the most beautiful song," said Mrs Belderboss.

"Like someone playing a flute," Mr Belderboss added.

"Well," said Mrs Belderboss. "We hadn't seen one all day, had we? And then when the storm came, one started singing its heart out, didn't it? It never stopped, right through all the thunder and lightning. And Father Wilfred got us all to kneel down and pray. What was that bit from Saint John he read, Reg?"

"Oh, don't ask me," he said. "I've got no memory for that sort of thing."

"A voice of one calling in the wilderness?" Father Bernard suggested.

"Yes, that was it, Father," said Mrs Belderboss. "He said that we had to keep on singing like that little bird no matter what befell us in life."

★　★　★

The Christmas of 1975 came and went and Father Wilfred performed his duties at Mass but, as Mr Belderboss had said, he seemed to have retreated from the world. When the service was over he didn't lecture us any more. He barely spoke a word before he was off to the presbytery where he shut himself away until he was next required. Miss Bunce came and made him his meals but left immediately afterwards. He no longer went to visit the sick, or took communion to the housebound. If anyone called he wouldn't answer. People began to worry about him again as they had done at the Loney.

It was only when his diary went missing that we saw something of his former self.

The Sunday after Christmas Day was the Feast of the Holy Innocents. Mr Belderboss had read the lesson from Matthew and Father Wilfred had given a long sermon about the reasons why the children slaughtered by Herod had been martyred, though it drifted off into incoherent mumbles from time to time, and it sounded as if he was talking to himself rather than the congregation.

Afterwards, we were getting changed in the vestry, when Father Wilfred came out of the office in a foul temper.

"Where is it?" he said, looking from me to Henry to Paul.

"Where's what, Father?" said Paul.

"My book."

"Your book?" said Paul.

"You're starting to sound like a parrot, Peavey. Yes, my book. I left it in the office by mistake. Where has it gone?"

"What did it look like, Father?"

"Black," he said. "A black diary."

"I don't know, Father," said Paul. "Henry was the last one in the office."

"McCullough," said Father Wilfred.

"I haven't got it," Henry said, looking at Paul who smiled and hung up his cassock.

"But Peavey says you were in the office."

"I was cleaning the sink, like you told me to."

Father Wilfred grasped his elbow. "Do you know what a syllogism is, McCullough?"

"No, Father."

"It's a form of deductive analysis. A method of coming to a logical conclusion about something."

"Eh?"

"My book has gone missing from the office. You were the last person in the office. Therefore you have the book."

"But I don't, Father. I've never seen it before."

"I should check his coat pockets, Father," said Paul.

"Be quiet, Peavey," said Father Wilfred. "Of course I'll check his pockets. Where is your coat, McCullough?"

Henry pointed to the back of the door, but his coat was gone.

"I left it there," he said, his mouth quivering a little now, knowing that Paul had set him up.

"Well it isn't there now, is it, McCullough?"

"No, Father."

"So where is it?" he said, shaking Henry's arm.

"I don't know. It wasn't me, Father," Henry said, pointing at Paul. "It's him. He's trying to get me into trouble."

Father Wilfred suddenly gripped Henry by the collar and turned him to face me.

"Proverbs, Smith," said Father Wilfred.

"Sorry, Father?"

"Tell McCullough the things set out in Proverbs. The things that Our Lord hates above all others."

"Pride?"

"Yes."

"People that kill the innocent."

"Yes, yes. What else?"

"The devious, troublemakers."

"And?"

"Liars, Father."

"Yes," said Father Wilfred. "Slanderers, McCullough. Those who bear false witness. Those who blame others for their own failings. God orders us to cast them down with Satan."

Henry was twisting under Father Wilfred's grip, his puffy face bright red.

"Tell me where it is, McCullough," Father Wilfred said, trying to grasp Henry's flailing hands.

Henry got hold of Father Wilfred's wrist suddenly and pulled him to one side, making him stumble into the wall and fall to the floor.

"I'm sorry, Father," he said, immediately reaching out to see if he was all right.

Father Wilfred was breathing hard, the skin under his eye already swelling and reddening. He put his hands on his knees.

"Get out," he said quietly. "All of you get out."

"I'm sorry," said Henry again, looking to Paul and me for help.

"I said, out, McCullough."

"But are you hurt, Father?"

Father Wilfred looked up at Henry with a face like that of a child knocked flat by the school bully. Frightened, angry, but bewildered more than anything.

"Why must you torment me?" he said and went into the vestry office and closed the door.

The three of us stood there in silence for a moment, not sure whether we ought to wait for him to dismiss us. Then Paul made a noise of contempt and shook his head and went outside. Henry and I looked at one another.

"Do you think he'll be all right?" said Henry.

"Yes."

"I didn't mean to hurt him."

"I know."

Henry made a move towards the office door.

"Perhaps I should make sure," he said.

"Leave him," I said and Henry looked down at his feet and then followed me outside.

"I thought he was going to kill you, McCullough," said Paul, glancing over his shoulder as he unchained his bike from the drainpipe.

"Where is it?" said Henry.

Paul slung his leg over the saddle.

"Where's what?"

"You know what."

"Your coat?"

"Yes."

Paul looked over Henry's shoulder and nodded. His coat was wrapped around a branch of one of the beech trees next to the presbytery.

"And what about the book?" said Henry.

"I don't know," replied Paul. "Who cares?"

Paul tried to set off, but Henry held onto the handlebars.

"Where is it?" Henry asked him again.

"Let go, McCullough. Do you want me to call Father Wilfred?"

"Depends. Do you want me to smash your teeth in?"

"You wouldn't dare."

"Wouldn't I?"

"No, fatty, you wouldn't."

Henry looked down. "Just tell me if you took it," he said.

"You'd love that, wouldn't you?" said Paul. "Going off to grass me up."

Henry suddenly raised his voice. "Do you think I'm going to come back? I never want to set foot in this place ever again, so it doesn't really matter what you tell me."

This wrong-footed Paul, but he pretended to be bored with the whole thing.

"It's in the belfry," he said, then scowled at Henry. "You need to lighten up, McCullough. It was only a bloody joke."

Henry let go of the handlebars and Paul went off slowly so that he could give Henry a grin. We watched him go and then Henry sat down on the steps outside the vestry.

"It's all right," I said. "I'll tell Father Wilfred."

"Will you?"

"Yes."

"Thanks."

I looked at him.

"What will your mother say when you tell her you want to leave?"

"Make me come back."

"Can't you tell her what Father Wilfred's like?"

"No," he said. "She wouldn't believe me. She thinks the sun shines out of his arse. Help me get my coat down, will you?"

"All right."

We walked around the base of the tree trying to find a stick long enough to reach it. In the end, with some effort, I gave him a leg up and he managed to get his fingertips to the sleeve that was hanging down.

It was, I remember, an expensive-looking leather thing with wide lapels and a belt with a circular buckle. He turned it over to inspect the damage and then spat on his hand and rubbed away the moss stains with his fingertips.

"Do you believe in Hell?" he said.

"About as much as Father Christmas," I replied.

"Seriously, though. What if it does exist?" he said.

"It doesn't."

"Yeah, but what if it does?"

"It's just an idea," I said. "That's all."

"But where did the idea come from?"

"Someone's imagination."

"You can't imagine something like that," he said. "No one can have invented Hell. It's like saying someone invented air. It's just always been there."

"Look, don't worry about Father Wilfred," I said. "I'll make something up."

He smiled weakly and put on his coat and did up the belt as he went to fetch his bike from the holly bush where Paul had evidently thrown it.

"Thanks, Smith," he said.

He stood with one foot on the pedal, pushed himself along and once he was moving lifted his leg over and went out through the gate, the front wheel wobbling. The bike was much too big for him. Or he was much too big for the bike. One or the other.

I waited for a moment, wondering if I ought to go home too and just let the whole thing blow over. But if I knew Father Wilfred he wouldn't let up and in any case I felt sorry for Henry. If his mother did force him back, as he was convinced she would, then it wouldn't be fair for him to face Father Wilfred's fury when he'd done nothing wrong.

I make it sound so noble, but in truth I just didn't want Paul to have the satisfaction of making Henry the whipping boy any more.

I climbed back up the steps to the vestry and Father Wilfred was still turning the office upside down.

"Yes? What is it, Smith?"

"I know where your diary is, Father."

226

"Ah, McCullough owned up to stealing it, did he?"

"No, Father. Henry didn't take it."

"Then who did? Peavey?"

"No, Father."

"You?"

"Of course not, Father."

"Surely not Miss Bunce," he said.

"It wasn't Miss Bunce."

"She has been acting rather rashly these last few weeks. Talking about leaving Saint Jude's. Moving away."

"Father, it wasn't her."

He stopped and sat down on the wooden chair. He had one of his antique swords laid across the table.

"All that I do seems to go amiss," he said, picking it up and inspecting the blade. "Why won't McCullough change?"

"I don't know, Father."

"I punish him and still he sins. When will he see that I'm trying to save him?"

"I don't know, Father."

"I fear for his soul as I fear for my own."

"Yes, Father. I know you do."

He turned his attention to the portrait of Jesus hanging over the sink.

"When will he realise that I give these lessons out of love? Because I do love him. If I could only save one, it would be him."

"Father, your diary."

"What about it?"

"I told you, I know where it is."

"Who took it? McCullough?"

"No, Father."

"Where is it then?"

"In the belfry."

"The belfry? How did it get up there?"

"I don't know, Father. Perhaps you left it there by mistake."

"Yes, perhaps I did. I don't remember," he said, staring into space.

"Would you like me to get it for you, Father?"

He snapped out of his gaze and looked at me.

"I don't know what I would do if I lost my diary, Smith," he said. "It has everything in there, you see. Everything. It's how I keep control of my thoughts. It's how I can understand where a thought has come from. I can trace it back to its origin. I can pinpoint where things went wrong. It's a map. Do you see?"

"Where things went wrong, Father?"

"With McCullough."

"Shall I fetch it for you, Father?"

"No, no." He waved his hand irritably. "I shall go up to the belfry myself."

He went out and I followed him and watched him going down the central aisle of the church talking to himself. I don't think he realised that he still had the sword in his hand.

CHAPTER
NINETEEN

The newborn lamb caused so much excitement that breakfast went on too long and we set off late for Mass. But no one seemed to be worried, jubilant as they were about it being Easter Sunday and excited about visiting the shrine the following day.

On the minibus, Mr Belderboss got out his harmonica and had everyone singing "Come Let Us with Our Lord Arise" and "Jesus Lives and So Shall I". Miss Bunce smiled for the first time in days. Mummer sat with her eyes closed, enjoying the rare sunlight that was blessing the coast that morning and giving the sea a deep blue calmness that I'd never seen before. I felt the same sense of hope that I'd felt at Saint Jude's the morning we'd set off. There was nothing to worry about. Parkinson and Collier may have hung the gruesome thing in the wood to scare us, but that seemed to have been the extent of their menace. They were nothing more than oversized children playing knock-a-door-run.

I took everything that was offered that morning — the warm sunlight, the soft shadows on the fields, the spangle of a brook as it wound under some willows towards the sea — and managed to convince myself that nothing would harm us.

Such naivety makes me laugh now.

The small spire of the Sacred Heart appeared and everyone stopped singing so that they could hear the bells. But there was nothing. Only the bleating of the sheep in the field.

"That's odd," said Mr Belderboss. "They always ring the bells on Easter morning."

"I know," said Farther. "A full peal too."

"Why is everyone standing outside?" said Miss Bunce as we pulled up next to the church.

"What's going on, Father?" said Mrs Belderboss.

Father Bernard stopped the minibus and we all got out and joined the rest of the congregation as they milled about in front of the church doors.

The priest came over to meet us.

"I'm sorry, I'm afraid there'll be no Mass this morning," he said.

"Why? What's happened?" said Mummer.

"An act of vandalism," he said.

"Oh no," said Mrs Belderboss. "Is there much damage?"

The priest seemed lost for words. He could only look back at his flock, gathered around the main door. Clement was among them and when he saw us he waved us over to look.

There on the ground was the wooden Jesus that had hung over the altar smashed and splintered.

"Good Lord," said Mr Belderboss. "They've been at it with sledgehammers by the looks of it."

"Aye, you're not wrong," said Father Bernard, bending down to inspect the damage.

"Five hundred and ninety years," said the priest from behind us. "Five hundred and ninety years that's been hanging over the altar here. And now this. In five minutes of madness. I mean, why?"

"Oh, there is no reason for it with these people," said Mrs Belderboss. "They're just mindless thugs."

"It's their upbringing," Mr Belderboss said. "They don't teach them right from wrong at home any more."

"Will it be kids from the village?" said Mrs Belderboss.

"Yes," said the priest knowingly. "There's a few little hooligans that I wouldn't put it past to do something like this. I've seen them spraypainting and littering."

I saw Clement glance at Father Bernard. It was clear who he suspected, though he didn't say anything.

"Can't you take it inside?" said Farther. "See if there's any way of salvaging it?"

The priest said nothing but pushed past us and went to the main doors. A huge chain had been passed through the handles and padlocked together. He lifted it up and let it fall back against the doors by way of an answer.

"The side door's the same," he said.

"What about breaking a window?" Mr Belderboss suggested.

"Break a window?" the priest said. "The glass is priceless, man, don't be ridiculous."

"Have you called the police?" asked Mrs Belderboss.

"Yes, of course," the priest replied.

"It might have been better to have fetched the fire brigade," said Mr Belderboss.

"The fire brigade?" said the priest, trying to untangle the chain in the vain hope that it might only be an obstinate knot. "What good would that do?"

"Well, they have things which would cut through that like a knife through butter," said Mr Belderboss.

"I can't believe anyone would do something like this," said Mummer. "Locking people out of the church on Easter morning."

"What about saying Mass outdoors?" suggested Miss Bunce. "Like they do at Glasfynydd."

Mummer made a derisive noise and turned away, but the priest seemed to consider it a decent idea, given the circumstances, and asked the regulars if they agreed. They said little but nodded in supplication and the priest gathered us in front of one of the yew trees and began.

The police turned up halfway through and went around the church, inspecting the doors and windows. I noticed that Clement had stopped singing and was watching them anxiously as they squatted down on their haunches to look at the battered crucifix.

After the blessing, the priest seemed a little calmer for having got through the unusual Mass and that the police had arrived. He went around shaking hands and accepting condolences and finally went off to speak to the two policemen who had been standing patiently by, their helmets under their arms, as though they were at a funeral.

"What a disappointment," said Mummer.

"I thought it was quite nice, really, in the end," said Miss Bunce. "Quite liberating."

"Don't worry, Esther," said Mrs Belderboss, patting Mummer's arm. "It'll be all better when we go to the shrine tomorrow."

"Yes," said Mummer. "I know. I know."

"You can't let something like this get you down. It's not worth it. It's what these little villains want."

"I know," said Mummer. "You're right. I just wish we could have had a normal service and that Andrew could have taken communion."

"Come on, Esther," said Mrs Belderboss. "Don't be sad. There's nothing more you can do now but trust that the Lord will visit Andrew tomorrow. All the signs are there."

I saw Clement wave Father Bernard over to the shade of some cypress trees, where he had been lingering as the policemen went around taking statements. Father Bernard excused himself and went over to speak to him. They had a conversation that I couldn't hear. Father Bernard put his hand on Clement's shoulder. Clement nodded, and then Father Bernard came back to where we were standing.

"It's all right if Clement comes back for a bite to eat, isn't it?" he said. "His mother's out and it seems a shame for him to be on his own today."

Clement hung behind him, scratching the back of his neck, pretending to scrutinise the inscription on one of the gravestones.

"Well, I don't know," said Mummer. "I've not really catered for another mouth, Father."

She caught Miss Bunce's eye.

"But," she said. "I'm sure there'll be enough. It'll be nice to have another guest to celebrate with us."

We sat down at the dinner table as soon as we got back. If nothing else was going to go right, Mummer at least wanted to eat on time.

Clement had been persuaded to take off his filthy jacket and hang it up by the front door so the smell was at least confined to the hallway. Underneath, he wore a bulging tanktop of red, black and orange chevrons, a khaki shirt and tie that seemed to be strangling him.

Outside, the day had turned overcast and rain was starting to set in again. The room became gloomy enough for candles, which Father Bernard lit one by one.

Mummer, Miss Bunce and Mrs Belderboss came in and out with trays of steaming meat and vegetables, a loaf of bread, sauces in silver boats. A warm plate was set in front of each person and once everyone was sitting down, Father Bernard invited Clement to say grace, not noticing, or wilfully ignoring, the look of horror that Mummer tried to slide discreetly his way, as though on a folded piece of paper.

Without a moment's hesitation, Clement said, "Lord, we humbly thank Thee for the food Thou hast set before us and ask that Thou bestow on us Thy blessing on this glorious day. Amen."

234

There was complete silence as everyone looked at him. It was the most he had ever said in one go.

"Thank you," said Father Bernard, and Clement nodded and dug his fork into the mound of potatoes.

Everyone watched as he shovelled the food into his mouth and slopped gravy down his tie. Hanny was especially fascinated by him and barely touched his own food for watching Clement eat his.

"How are things on the farm?" Father Bernard asked. "It must be a busy time of year for you."

Clement looked up briefly and then went back to his potatoes.

"Not too good, Father."

"Oh, why's that?"

"We're going to have to sell up."

"I'm sorry to hear that," said Father Bernard. "What's happened?"

Clement looked around the table again and said nothing. Mr Belderboss tried a different tack.

"We were all wondering, Clement, if your mother had had an operation or something."

"Eh?"

"Well she came with firewood the other day."

"Oh, aye," he said. "Aye, she's had an operation."

"And now she can see all right?" said Mrs Belderboss.

"Aye."

"It's amazing what they can do nowadays, isn't it?" she said.

"Aye," said Clement, without looking up from his plate. "It is."

The main course over, Mummer brought out the simnel cake she had made the day before with its sugar paste face of Jesus in the middle and its twelve marzipan balls around the edge representing the disciples.

She placed the cake in the centre of the table and everyone, apart from Miss Bunce, made a fuss over it, praising the detail on Jesus' face, how intricate the thorns were, how the cochineal colouring had made the blood trickling down his cheek so vibrantly red. Hanny picked up the cake slice, but Mummer took it gently from him and went back into the kitchen, returning with a fistful of leaves left over from Palm Sunday.

"It seemed fitting," she said.

Everyone drew one from her hand. Clement was last and looked around the table before taking one for himself.

"Now," said Mummer, "let's see." And everyone placed their leaves down on the table.

Clement had drawn the shortest.

"What does that mean?" he said.

"It means," said Mummer, trying to hide her disappointment that he of all people had won. "That you get to throw Judas on the fire."

"Pardon?"

"Choose one of the balls on the cake," said Farther, leaning towards him. "And toss it into the fire."

Clement looked at the cake and then at the fire churning in the grate.

"It's all right," he said. "Someone else can do it."

"But you've won," said Mrs Belderboss.

"Aye," said Clement. "But I'd rather not."

"It's only a bit of fun," Father Bernard said.

"Go on, son," said Mr Belderboss, plucking one of the marzipan balls from the cake and handing it to him.

Clement looked at the thing in his hand and then, holding it as though it were a delicate glass marble, he edged his chair back across the stone floor, stood up and went over to the fire. He glanced back at the table and then tipped his hand and sent Judas into the flames. Everyone clapped and for the first time Clement managed a smile, albeit a self-conscious one that made him run his finger round the inside of his collar.

"What was that?" Miss Bunce said through the applause. She half stood up, holding onto the table. The clapping died away and we sat in silence listening to the rain pummelling the yard outside.

"What's the matter, dear?" Mrs Belderboss said.

"Shh," said Miss Bunce.

A screeching noise came from outside.

Hanny gripped my hand under the table. Everyone turned to look at the window. But there was nothing to see, only the rain beating down.

"Owls," said Mr Belderboss, picking up the cake slice and handing it to Mummer. "I'll just have a small piece."

"No, no, it's not," said Miss Bunce.

"It was owls," said Mr Belderboss. "Barn owls, if I know anything."

The noise came again, closer this time. The shriek of something in agony.

"You might be right, Reg," said Farther. "It certainly sounded like a barn owl."

Everyone apart from Clement got up and crowded at the window as we heard the sound of barking. In the field beyond the yard, a small white dog was edging backwards, dragging something in its mouth.

"Isn't that your friend's dog, Father?" said Mrs Belderboss.

"Which friend is that?"

"Your pal who helped fix the minibus."

"I wouldn't call him a pal, Mrs Belderboss."

"Heavens. What is it doing?" Mummer said.

"Has it caught a bird, Father?" said Mrs Belderboss.

"It's certainly got its teeth into something," said Father Bernard.

"I told you. It'll have got a barn owl," said Mr Belderboss. "They screech like stink when there are dogs about."

"Don't be silly, Reg," said Mrs Belderboss. "How on earth could a dog catch an owl?"

"It's not an owl," said Miss Bunce indignantly. "It's much bigger than that."

"What *is* it?" Mummer said again.

Far away someone whistled and the dog looked up and after a moment shot off across the grass, leaving whatever it had been chewing to die in the middle of the field.

Monro was pining to be let out, lifting himself up and pawing at the door.

"Hey, hey." Father Bernard went over and tried to calm him down.

238

"What's the matter with him?" said Mrs Belderboss.

Father Bernard struggled to get hold of Monro's collar.

"It'll be the dog outside," he said. "He's not good with other dogs."

"Oh, get him to stop that awful noise, Father," said Mrs Belderboss.

Clement was looking anxiously from one person to another.

"Come on, you silly wee beggar," Father Bernard said gently and put his arms around Monro's neck.

But Monro was still as white-eyed as Clement and jumped out of his grasp and knocked over the small table next to the door on which Mr Belderboss had left the earthenware jar.

It smashed on the floor and its contents spilled everywhere. A few small bones. A piece of leather cut into a crude heart shape. Iron nails pickled with rust. And there was the missing Christ from the nativity set stained the colour of malt whisky.

"Oh, my Lord," said Mrs Belderboss as her feet were soaked. "What on earth have you done, you great lump?"

"That smell," said Mummer, covering her nose with her hand. "I think your dog's been."

"It's not Monro," said Father Bernard. "It's what was inside."

A dark yellow fluid was leaking from the jar onto the stone floor.

"What's that?" said Miss Bunce, backing away.

In the puddle of urine there floated what looked like strands of human hair and nail clippings.

Through the commotion, Clement started to call out. Everyone turned back to the table and stared at him. He had left his dinner half finished and had, in the custom of the place, left his knife and fork crossed on the plate. He had his hands flat on the table and was staring at the remains of the jar on the floor.

"I'd like to go home now," he said.

Clement went out to fetch his jacket. Everyone watched him go and then Mummer swept up the pieces of the jar while Farther laid down some newspaper to soak up the spillage.

"I hope you're going to lock that room up for good," said Mummer.

"Of course I will," said Farther. "I'm sorry, everyone."

"It was hidden for a reason."

"I know, I know."

"You can't leave things alone, can you?"

"Oh, Esther, that's enough," he said. "I've apologised. What more do you want me to do?"

"All right," said Father Bernard. "Let's not dwell on it. What's done is done."

"Well I'm still none the wiser," said Mr Belderboss, "what that jar was for."

"I don't know, Reg," said Mrs Belderboss. "Perhaps it was a litter bin. Now give it a rest. There are more important things to worry about." She eyed the door through which Clement had just gone.

"I was only saying."

"And I was only thinking of poor Clement," said Mrs Belderboss.

"How do you mean, poor Clement?" said Mummer.

"Well it's obvious, isn't it?" replied Mrs Belderboss.

"What is?"

Mrs Belderboss lowered her voice, aware that Clement might be able to hear them from the hall.

"They've had to sell the farm to pay for his mother's operation, haven't they?"

"They do have the NHS up here, you know," said Mummer.

"Oh, they'll not have got that done on the National Health so quickly," said Mrs Belderboss. "Will they, Father?"

"I shouldn't think so."

"No, it'll have been some private place," said Mr Belderboss. "Very expensive."

"What a wonderful thing to do for someone though," said Mrs Belderboss. "Give everything up like that."

"Aye," said Father Bernard.

"I wonder what he's going to do now?" said Mrs Belderboss.

"Leave us alone to salvage what we can of the day, I hope," said Mummer.

"Esther," said Mrs Belderboss. "Don't be unkind. It's Easter Sunday after all."

"Well," said Mummer. "A grown man going all strange at the dinner table like that just over a broken old pot. It was so awkward."

"He didn't make as much fuss as you," said Farther, scrunching up the newspaper and feeding it to the fire.

Mummer gave him a look and went back to the conversation around the table.

"His nerves are probably bad," said Mrs Belderboss. "He has had to sell his farm."

"So he says," Mummer replied. "But you know what he's like."

"What do you mean?" said Mrs Belderboss.

"Aye, what is he *like* exactly?" said Father Bernard.

Mr Belderboss leant in towards him and Father Bernard listened, still with his eyes fixed on Mummer.

"He's one of these that tends to exaggerate things sometimes, Father. Doesn't quite live in the same world as you and I, if you know what I mean."

"But I don't think he's making it up this time," said Mrs Belderboss. "I mean his mother can see again. There's no disputing that. They must have got the money from somewhere."

"I must say, I'm inclined to agree with you, Mrs Belderboss," said Father Bernard. "I think we ought to make allowances for the poor man, and if he has had to sell everything then we should perhaps consider what we can do to help. Isn't that the reason we're here?"

"Well, if you think, Father," Mr Belderboss replied, with a hint of defensiveness.

Father Bernard lowered his voice. "I don't want to get on my high horse about it, but can you think of anything worse than losing your home? When I was in the Bone I saw people left with nothing. Good families who had their houses burned down in front of their eyes for no other reason than being Catholic or Protestant. Can you imagine what that does to people?"

"It's hardly the same thing," said Mummer.

"You must admit it was their choice to sell, Father," said Mr Belderboss. "Clement and his mother's. No one forced them."

"What do you think Wilfred would have done, Reg?" asked Father Bernard. "He wouldn't have just ignored it, would he?"

"Of course he wouldn't have ignored it, Father. But all the same, I don't think he would have liked us to have got involved. It's nothing to do with us."

"Isn't it?"

Miss Bunce hadn't said a word throughout, but now she put down her cup and said, "I think Father Bernard's right. Think of the Samaritan."

"Hear, hear," said Farther from the fireplace.

Mr Belderboss smiled at him sympathetically and then at Miss Bunce.

"The thing is, Joan, what you have to understand about these country folk is that they don't want help, and certainly not help from outsiders like us. They're a proud people. It'd be an insult to them. There are times, like Esther says, when the greatest kindness is to leave people be. Isn't that right, David?"

David put his arm around Miss Bunce.

"I think Mr Belderboss is right," he said.

Miss Bunce looked at him and then down at her tea cup. Mummer took up the reins and steered the conversation back to Father Bernard again.

"You see when Father Wilfred brought us here it felt as though he was able to draw a circle around us. To keep us focused on our own relationship with God, and allow him to guide us through the days with an attention that he wasn't always able to give us back at Saint Jude's. That was the whole point of being here. It wasn't just a pilgrimage, Father. It was a sanctuary too. It might be worth bearing that in mind."

Everyone was looking at Father Bernard. He stood up.

"I'll be taking Clement home now," he said.

"Yes, all right, Father," said Mr Belderboss.

"Do you want me to come with you?" said Farther. "Make sure you don't get lost."

"No, no, Mr Smith," he said. "It's kind of you to offer, but I'll be all right."

"If you're sure."

"I'd rather you got that fire going for when I get back. The weather looks fair brutal out there."

"I will, Father," he said, and began untying the bundles of firewood Clement's mother had brought.

"Mind how you go, Father," Mrs Belderboss called after him as he went out to get his coat. "Oh dear," she said once the door was closed. "I hope we haven't upset him."

"I think we did," said Miss Bunce.

"I was right, though, wasn't I?" said Mr Belderboss. "I mean no one's persecuting Clement, are they? It's not our fault."

Mrs Belderboss patted his hand.

"No, it's not," she said and then shook her head. "What a mess," she continued. "I don't remember it being so — difficult — when we came with Wilfred."

"He kept everything simple, that's why," said Mr Belderboss. "And he didn't go prying into other people's affairs."

"Still," said Mrs Belderboss. "Everything will be better tomorrow, when we go to the shrine. What's that bit from Isaiah? About not worrying about the days that have gone?"

"'Forget the former things; do not dwell in the past,'" said Miss Bunce and finished off her piece of cake.

"That's the one," said Mrs Belderboss. "Tomorrow's another day."

Clement was still waiting patiently on the little chair in the hallway, his walking stick balanced on his knees.

"Can I go home now?" he said.

"I think Father Bernard's just getting his coat," I replied.

He looked down at the floor.

"I told them not to ring that bell," he said.

When I didn't respond, he looked up again.

"The bell on Coldbarrow. You know the one up in the old tower next to the house?"

"Yes."

"It were boarded up for years. But they went out to it."

"Who did?"

Clement was about to answer but stopped short when a door opened along the hallway. Father Bernard appeared and frowned as he zipped up his coat.

"What's going on?" he said and Clement waved him over and made him sit on the stairs.

"Parkinson and Collier, Father. They went out to Coldbarrow on New Year's Eve just gone and took the boards off the tower and started ringing that bloody bell. And not a day or two later there were lights on at Thessaly and then all this business started."

Father Bernard looked at me and then back at Clement. "What business?"

"They told me not to come here any more," he said. "They said they'd get me sent back to Haverigg, like they did last time. But I had to come and warn you about what they've done. And now that your dog's broke that bottle, it might be the only opportunity I get."

"That old jar in the dining room? What's that to do with anything?"

"Don't you know what it is?"

"No."

"They're meant to keep witches away from the house," he said. "But you have to keep them sealed. And now it's been opened . . ."

"Clement," said Father Bernard. "Is there someone you want us to call? A doctor maybe. Will your mother be in when we get back? Maybe I ought to speak with her. See if we can get you some help with whatever it is that's bothering you."

Clement lowered his eyes.

"You don't understand, Father," he said. "You must keep away from Parkinson and Collier."

"Why? What is it that you think they've done?"

But Clement didn't have time to answer before someone knocked at the front door with a heavy, rhythmic thud.

Hanny came out of the dining room and grabbed my arm, wanting me to open the door. Gradually everyone was gathered in the hallway and we all listened to the singing coming from outside.

"Who on earth is it?" said Mummer, and she sidled through the throng to see.

CHAPTER
TWENTY

The Pace Eggers had always frightened me as a child, looking as they did like things that had crawled out of a nightmare. Each one a mishmash of fairy tale characters, grotesque as Punch and Judy puppets. Natives of some savage tribe as painted by the children of missionaries.

When we'd come here in the past we'd sometimes see them performing on the green at Little Hagby — half a dozen local men, blacked-up like chimney sweeps with only their eyes showing and armed with swords and staffs.

The stink of booze drifted from them as they sang old songs in bass voices; songs that didn't have the predictable, homely rise and fall of the hymns we'd been singing all week, but which tumbled through strange minor keys and moved across intervals that sounded like they might have once charmed the Devil to the surface of the world.

At the front of the pack was Saint George, dressed in a crusaders tabard and banging his wooden staff in time to the song. When it ended he removed his cardboard crown and bowed. Even under all the make-up I could see that it was Parkinson. Collier stood behind him dressed as the character called Brownbags, his dog chained to the gate post outside, straining and yelping.

"We've come as agreed," said Parkinson to Father Bernard and smiled. Father Bernard glanced at Mummer, who frowned at him.

"And is that Clement you've been entertaining?" Parkinson looked towards the back of the crowd, and everyone turned to see the colour drain from Clement's face. "Well well. Tha gets about, dunt tha, Clement?"

Mummer still had her hand on the door.

"I'm afraid you must have the wrong house," she said. "We weren't expecting you."

Parkinson looked at Father Bernard and smiled.

"We like to get around all the big houses on Easter Sunday," he said. "And we thought tha might appreciate some entertainment what with the weather being so foul."

"Well, perhaps we could come down to the village and watch you some other time?" said Mummer.

"Oh, we won't stop long," Parkinson replied.

He seemed to have somehow crossed the threshold without Mummer noticing and she had no choice but to step back and allow the men to enter. Each of them nodded their thanks and wiped their feet on the mat — Saint George, Brownbags, the Turkish Knight and the others, one of whom swept quickly past completely swaddled in a black cloak, leaving Old Ball, the horse, to come in last, wearing a brown smock and holding a real horse's skull on the end of a pole, a set of glass eyes clacking inside. It rolled about, grinning, like the thing we'd found in the woods.

Whoever was under the cloak stooped the nag's head so that it would fit through the doorway to the sitting room.

As it swung down, Miss Bunce stepped back and grabbed at Father Bernard's sleeve.

"Do you think this is a good idea?" she whispered to him when the men had all filed past. "I mean they could be anyone. Is it some pagan thing?"

"Oh, Joan, it's tradition," Mummer said. "We've always watched the Pace Egging."

"What, here?"

"Well no not here. But, look, it's just a bit of fun."

"Fun?"

"Yes," said Mummer, not quite convinced herself, as she followed the men and started to organise a space for them to perform.

She might have been doubtful about letting them in, or embarrassed that she had been doorstepped so easily, but now that the Pace Eggers were here Mummer quickly took charge. She would have them in and out quick sharp.

The room was cleared and Mrs Belderboss was dispatched with Miss Bunce to make sandwiches and tea, while Farther and David gathered up as many of the vulnerable ornaments as they could and took them out into the hall.

I helped Father Bernard shift a table out of the way, carrying it into the bay of the window. He kept his eye

250

on the Pace Eggers as they waited for us to get the room ready. Parkinson waved Clement over and handed him an old curtain, which he strung between two lampstands to form a makeshift wing from which they could enter and exit.

"I didn't think they'd really come," said Father Bernard.

"What do you mean, Father?"

"I didn't say anything to Clement the other day, but Mr Parkinson had already promised to bring the Pace Eggers up to Moorings. I thought it was just the ale talking. He'd had a fair few, like."

"Do you think we should have let them in, Father?"

He looked over to where the men were getting ready.

"Why? Because of what Clement said about them?"

"And what we saw in the woods."

"Look, we don't know that that had anything to do with them, Tonto. Not really."

He glanced at them again and laughed quietly at their costumes.

"I think they're harmless enough. And in any case how would it look if we asked them to leave now? I think it's best if we just let them get on with it. What are they going to do here?"

"I don't know."

"Exactly. Don't worry about what Clement said just now. That's between him and them. It's nothing to do with us. All right?"

"Yes, Father," I said, though I was less convinced than he was.

He smiled at Mummer, who came over with an expensive-looking floorlamp, and set it on the table out of harm's way. She looked at him and went away to help David shift a delicate crystal vase off the mantelpiece.

"What would Father Wilfred have made of these fellers, Tonto?" said Father Bernard.

"I don't know."

"You don't really talk about him all that much. Did you get along with him all right?" he said, dusting his hands.

"I suppose so."

"Only suppose so?"

"He did a lot for the poor," I said, and Father Bernard looked at me and smiled.

"Aye," he said. "I know he did, Tonto."

At Mummer's request, he started to close the curtains.

"I'm only asking, because I know nothing much about the man," he said. "I mean, I know he was well respected but was he happy in his work, would you say?"

"I think so."

"I mean, how did he seem before he died?"

"How did he seem?"

"Aye."

"I don't know."

"Would you say there was something on his mind?"

The sound of a bell came from behind the curtain and Mummer turned off the main light.

"I don't know, Father."

He knew I was being obtuse, but he smiled and turned his attention to the Pace Eggers instead, storing away what I'd said or hadn't said for later.

"Who's your man in the purple there?" he asked in a whisper, pointing to the player pressing his Zapata moustache back into place.

"That's the Turkish Knight," I said.

"Is he the villain? He looks like a villain."

"Yes."

First out of the shadows was Collier, dressed in a frayed kilt, a harlequin shirt and a top hat like a broken chimney-pot. He carried a wicker basket under his arm.

"Who's this?" Father Bernard said behind his hand.

"That's Brownbags," I said. "He collects the money."

"Money?"

"You're supposed to give them some money before they perform."

Brownbags walked from person to person, as they dug into their pockets for any loose change and threw it into the basket. At each clink of metal, he touched the brim of his hat with his finger and when he had passed along the row he began.

"Give as much as you can spare, we only come but once a year. Build up the fire and let the flames burn. Here are some jolly boys to give you a turn."

Mummer started clapping and gradually everyone else joined in.

Brownbags went off and was replaced by Saint George and his daughter, Mary.

"Isn't that your man from Little Hagby?" Father Bernard whispered.

I looked again. He was right. Mary was the gangly altar boy from the Tenebrae service, got up in a blonde wig and a white dress which was filthy with mud at the bottom.

Saint George drew his sword from its scabbard and clasped Mary to his side.

"In I come, old Saint George. The champion of Ingyland. My sword was made in God's own forge. A flash of lightning in my hand."

There was loud cackling from the dark and the Turkish Knight stepped into the circle and drew his sword. Into the spirit of the thing now, everyone booed and hissed on cue, even David, who had let go of Miss Bunce's hand and was watching the play with a face like a child at a pantomime.

The Turkish Knight twirled the end of his long moustache and stepped closer to us.

"I am Sullyman from Turkey Land. I seek to find Saint George the brave. I'll take his life and his daughter's hand. And toss his body in a cave."

Saint George pulled Mary behind him, shielding her from the Turkish Knight. Mary cowered on her knees, the back of her hand on her brow.

"I am George of Ingyland," he said. "My sword is sharp and keen as wind. I will fight you Sillyman. And God will judge you for your sins."

"Now, Saint George, I will have your life."

"No, sir, I will strike you dead."

"I'll take your Mary for my wife."

"And marry her without your head?"

The two men circled each other, then leapt forward and clashed their swords. Mary screamed, and everyone began to cheer for Saint George, who at last ran the Turkish Knight through, knocking him to the ground where he lay with the sword sticking upright, clamped in his armpit. Mary rushed to the dead knight's side and lay her head upon his chest, weeping.

"Oh, Father, you have killed my one true love."

Saint George knelt down and put his hand on her shoulder.

"Oh, my poor little turtle dove."

He turned to us and pleaded, "Is there a doctor in this town? One that can be quickly found?"

There was a knock at the door. All faces turned to where a small figure appeared, wearing a bowler hat and a coat that trailed on the floor. Everyone was a little startled that he had slipped out unnoticed during the performance.

"Here comes little Doctor Dog," he said, stopping on the way to pat the top of Hanny's head. "Best doctor in the county, sir."

"Can you cure this knight of Turkeyshire?" Saint George said, taking off the doctor's hat and speaking into it.

"Of what affliction?" said the doctor, removing Saint George's crown and doing likewise. "Tell me, sir. Confess."

"Of death, sir doctor, darkest death."

"Not for five pounds, sir," the doctor said.

"For ten pounds, sir?"

"For fifteen, sir."

"Twelve, sir."

"Yes, for twelve whole pounds and Spanish wine, it shall be done."

The doctor felt around in the pockets of his huge coat, making Father Bernard laugh louder with each scrap of junk he turned out and dropped onto the floor — toy cars, plastic animals, golf balls, seashells. Eventually, he found a small bottle and knelt down by the dead knight.

"Now, my sleeping Turkey knight, drink this brew of holy breath. Old Doctor Dog will cure you, sir, and call you back from blissful death."

The dead knight began to cough and then sat upright and clasped Mary to his chest. Saint George embraced the doctor and then flung out his arms to us.

"Rise up, rise up and sing and sing, a song of warm and merry things."

The knight stood up, touching the wound in his side.

"Once I was dead and now I am alive. God bless Doctor, George and wife. Bring me flesh and oranges and beer. A happy Easter to all our friends here."

They were about to go off, when a banging sound came from the far end of the room. All their smiles dropped as they sloped away one by one, leaving Saint George who said:

"Yet, there is one who will not sing, or dance about."

I felt Hanny grip my hand. He had obviously remembered who was coming next.

Another player, the one who had arrived completely swathed in a black cloak, came into the circle holding a single candle at chest height so that it lit up his face.

256

Once he was in the middle of the circle, he reached up and took down the hood. Unlike the others, his face was a postbox red and he had a pair of horns growing out of his bald head. Real buck antlers fastened by some device that was undetectable.

"Ah, now I know this feller," Father Bernard whispered and nudged me gently in the shoulder.

"In I come to say farewell. Devil Doubt shall take his bow. Come to take your souls to Hell. Where is God the Father now?"

And as he smiled and pinched out the candle I felt Hanny's hand slip out of mine.

I couldn't find him anywhere. He wasn't in the bedroom. Nor was he out in the yard, for it had gone dark now and he wouldn't have gone out on his own. I looked around, checking all the places Hanny liked to hide: behind the ancient upright piano, in the wide bay window on the other side of the curtains, under the tiger-skin rug.

Looking in the kitchen, thinking that he might have gone searching for food, I found Parkinson talking to one of the other Pace Eggers who was at the sink stripped to the waist and scrubbing his face vigorously with a flannel. The water in the bowl had turned to ink. His robes were on the table along with his false moustache and his sword. I put the tray on the table as he patted his face dry with a towel and went to put his shirt back on. I saw that it was the elderly companion of Parkinson and Collier who we had first seen wheezing across the field the day we came to Moorings.

Yet now his face was a healthy pink and he radiated the vitality of a much younger man.

"Isn't it wonderful?" he said, holding me briefly by the shoulders, as he went off to join the others. "Wonderful," he said to Parkinson, who smiled and nodded and watched him go.

"Dying from the drink, he was, Mr Hale," said Parkinson.

Hale. I remembered the name from the list in the envelope Hanny had brought back from Thessaly.

I turned to go, but Parkinson spoke again.

"I didn't think a good Catholic boy like thee would dismiss a miracle so readily."

He walked past me and closed the kitchen door on the laughter coming from the sitting room.

"I hear tha's been over to Thessaly quite a bit," he said. "You and your retard."

I looked at him.

"Oh, I know all about your retard," he said. "Your padre's quite a gasbag when he's had a drink."

"He's not a retard. Father wouldn't have called him that."

Parkinson smiled.

"How much did he give you?"

"Who?"

"My friend at Thessaly."

"I don't know what you mean."

"What was it? Five, ten quid?"

"I told you, I don't know anything about any money."

He looked at me.

"Twenty," I said.

"And is that going to be enough?"

"For what?"

"Come on, tha knows what he gave thee that money for."

I said nothing and Parkinson shook his head and sighed.

"I told him it wouldn't be enough. You see, my friend at Thessaly hasn't quite got the head for business I have. I know people much better than he does. I don't believe people always want money. Not when there's something more important to them. Money you can piss away like ale. What people really want is something that's going to last."

He put his hands in his pockets and went on.

"I said to him there were a better way of making sure that tha didn't misunderstand what were going on. I said to him that we ought to invite you and your retard to Thessaly, see if there's something we can do to help."

"Help?"

"Aye, make him better, I mean. Like Mr Hale."

"I need to go now," I said.

Parkinson looked at me and then opened the door. The Pace Eggers were singing again. He followed me as I went back to the sitting room.

"He looks after this place well, dunt he, Clement?" he said, patting the wall. "These old places are a bugger sometimes. Damp as hell. All the wiring shot. Dunt take much for a fire to start in them. You hear stories all the time around here. People burnt in their beds."

When we came to the sitting room door, he stood and looked in on the singing and dancing. The noise had grown louder.

"We'll be expecting thee then," he said. "Tha knows where to come. Or we can come and fetch thee, if tha likes."

He smiled and went off to join the other men who had linked arms in a circle and were stamping and singing as Hale swung Mummer round in a dance that she pretended to enjoy as much as she could. Father Bernard stood by and clapped along. Mr and Mrs Belderboss looked anxious for the antiques that had been too large to move. Miss Bunce clung to David's arm with a thin smile, as Collier tried to coax her into the circle. Only Clement sat apart, with a protective arm around Monro's neck. Two outcast dogs.

CHAPTER
TWENTY-ONE

I found Hanny asleep under his bed with his crayons and his sketch pad. Drawings of Else were everywhere, covering the mattress like a patchwork blanket. He was curled up and snoring softly, a crayon melting in his sweaty hand. I eased it out and, not really awake, he shuffled out from under the bed and put his arms around me.

He had drawn Else in the window at Thessaly, with the bell tower next to it and Leonard's car parked at the side. Else standing outside in the grass under a huge yellow flower of a sun, holding her albino cat. The one he had been working on as he had fallen asleep showed he and Else standing side by side holding hands with a grinning baby between them.

The silly sod thought the baby was his, that, when Else had let him feel it butting her stomach like the lamb had its mother, she was teasing him with a present that she would give to him one day. That was why he wanted to go back to Coldbarrow. He wanted his gift.

But I couldn't take him there. Not after what Parkinson had said.

I removed the pieces of paper and loose crayons from his bed and drew the candlewick over him. He didn't stir at all. He had no idea what was going to happen to him at the shrine tomorrow. He wouldn't remember anything about it until we got there. I watched him sleeping, and wished that his peace could last. I knew what they would make him do at the shrine but he wouldn't understand even if I tried to warn him. I thought about slipping away and taking him down to the Loney to hide when the time came, but there would be no point. Mummer wouldn't let up until she had made him go. I knew that I would be coerced into helping to get him there. Keep him happy and keep him ignorant of what we were really going for. I hated her for that.

Despite what Mrs Belderboss had said in her confession, Father Wilfred didn't seem all that absent to me. I still felt his hand at work, pushing Hanny towards his role as the touchstone that would prove God's love for the faithful.

I remembered their faces last time we'd been to the shrine. Half fearful, half rapturous that they were about to witness a miracle as Hanny took a mugful of holy water and started to choke. Mummer went to help him, but Father Wilfred held her back.

"Wait," he said. "Let the Lord do His work."

Hanny bent over and gasped for breath. When he stood up his mouth was opening and closing. Father Wilfred held his face tightly, stared into his wide, frightened eyes and began to repeat the Hail Mary until everyone joined in.

"Speak," said Father Wilfred.

Everyone became silent and listened to the frail note that came out of Hanny's mouth.

"Speak," Father Wilfred said again. "Speak."

He gripped Hanny's head tighter and shook it. Hanny opened his mouth wider but no other sound came out.

Although Father Wilfred looked down his throat with an expression of anguish, as though he could see the miracle disappearing like water down a drain, he still thanked God for sending His spirit down. For showing us His power and munificence. For showing us a taste of the bounty to be had if only we might pray longer and harder.

Now that Moorings was quiet, I could hear the ewe bleating in the field. She was standing alone in the dusk, nosing at the white pile by her feet. When I went outside, she moved away and lay down under a tree. I climbed through the wire and waded through the long grass, feeling my trousers wet and tight against my thighs. There was a strewing of white cotton and limbs, and then I found a small hoof, polished and black, like a mussel washed in on a surge tide. The lamb had been torn to pieces by Collier's dog. I couldn't even find the head.

When I got back to the house, Father Bernard was there, carefully rolling apples out of the bib he had made with the bottom of his coat onto the table. He looked up as I came in and underarmed one of them to me. I quickly took my hands out of my pockets and caught it.

"Where did you get these from?" I asked.

"Outside."

"Outside here?"

"Aye," he said. "Every tree's full of fruit."

"How can they be?"

"Perhaps they're a type that comes early, I don't know. Aren't you going to eat it?"

"I'm not hungry."

"Suit yourself," he said and took a bite from the one that he had been buffing on his sleeve. Juice ran down his chin and he made a cup with his other hand to catch it.

"Was Clement all right?" I asked.

"Aye, I think so," replied Father Bernard, flicking out a handkerchief. "He didn't say much, to be honest."

"Do you think he was telling the truth?" I said.

"What? About witches and lucky charms?" he replied, giving me a half smile as he wiped his chin. "Come on, Tonto."

"He seemed frightened all the same," I said.

"Look," he said. "I don't know what's going on with Clement and those other fellers. Probably nothing. I can't imagine why on earth they'd want to intimidate him, or us for that matter. But it's obvious that they're keeping a close eye on what we're doing and I think your mother and Mr Belderboss may be right. It's probably best if we don't get involved. If I were you, I'd stay away from them and from Coldbarrow."

"Maybe we ought to leave, Father," I said, taking the opportunity to plant the idea into his head, hoping it might germinate before Parkinson had a chance to pay us another visit. Once we were back in London, they could do what they liked to Moorings. Burn the place to the ground for all I cared.

"You know what, Tonto," said Father Bernard. "Between you and me, I'm so exhausted I'd be away back home tonight if I could, but I might very well find myself out of a job tomorrow. And anyway, don't you want to take Andrew to the shrine?"

"I suppose so."

"There you are then," he said. "We'll have to do the full stretch."

The door to the dining room opened and Mummer was there.

"Father," she said. "I'd like a word with you."

"All right."

"In private."

"Now?"

"If that's convenient."

"Is that all right with you, Tonto?" he said, catching Mummer's eye as he spoke and I nodded, feeling a little awkward that I was caught in the middle.

Father Bernard left with Mummer and they went down the hallway to his room. After a moment I took up my place in the understairs cupboard and waited for them to speak. Neither of them said anything until Father Bernard started to draw the curtain around the washbasin.

"There's no need for that, Father," said Mummer. "I've not come for confession."

"Oh, well would you like to sit down anyway?" I heard Father Bernard say.

"No, I'm fine as I am, Father."

"Are you sure?"

"Yes."

"What was it you wanted to talk to me about, Mrs Smith?"

Mummer paused and then said, "You've not told us much about your last parish, Father."

"I'm sorry?"

"Your last parish. What was it like?"

"The people or the place?"

"Both."

"The people were wonderful, the place was terrible."

"And Belfast, Father?"

"Much the same."

"Nevertheless, the bishop said you'd worked wonders in these places."

"I'm not sure anyone works wonders in the Ardoyne, Mrs Smith, but I'll take a pat on the back for trying."

"Come on, Father," said Mummer. "Don't do yourself a disservice. If the bishop said you'd worked wonders then I believe him. Tell me what you did."

"Look," he said, laughing quietly. "The bishopric goes hoopla about the tiniest victories over apathy these days. It doesn't take much to get a gold star. Kick a ball about the cinder fields with some wee rogues and get them to church the next Sunday and they'll consider you for the Vatican."

"There," said Mummer. "You hit the nail on the head, Father."

"Did I?"

"You said you'd played football with some deprived children."

"Aye."

"And they enjoyed it?"

"Aye. More than the Mass I swapped it for, I have to say, but one or two of them kept on coming back."

"What did they come back for though, Father?"

"Lots of reasons."

"Such as?"

"What, you want me to pick something out of a hat? They liked the other people there. The singing. The youth club of a Friday. It was better than being out on the street, throwing bricks at the Saracens. I don't know. Look, is this heading somewhere dark and confined, Mrs Smith? Because I feel like I'm being led into a corner."

"I just wanted to prove something to you, Father."

"Prove what?"

"That you were successful in those places because you knew exactly what the congregation needed, what they expected of you."

"Mrs Smith . . ."

"Wouldn't you say that was the mark of a good priest, Father? Knowing what your parishioners need?"

"Of course."

"And that a priest ought to respond to those needs?"

"Naturally."

"Rather than trying to change them?"

"Mrs Smith, if there's something you want to say to me, I'd rather you had it out. It's late and I'm very tired."

"I want to help you," she said. "I know it must be difficult to be thrown into a new parish, but what you need to understand, Father, is that there can only be success in a church when the priest and his congregation are in harmony. If one side wants something different than the other then it all unravels. Father Wilfred knew that."

Father Bernard sighed and Mummer raised her voice a little.

"He might have been different to you, Father, but he knew how to *be* with us. He knew exactly how to make us feel that God was present in our lives."

"You mean he told you what you wanted to hear?"

"Yes, Father. Exactly that. We wanted to hear that the road was going to be difficult. We wanted to be told to pray harder if we wished to be heard. And if we concealed our sins from him, then we wanted to hear that we would be punished. We're all going through a very difficult time, Father," she went on. "And I think it's best to keep things the way they were. The way they've always been. It's what everyone knows. We all need a rock to cling to in the storm."

"Mrs Smith, I'm not trying to change anything."

"I think you are, Father. Without realising it, perhaps."

"I'm not. I'm here to listen and guide you spiritually, if I can. That's all. That's the entirety of my remit. I think you must have misinterpreted my interest in

268

wanting to know what happened to Father Wilfred, Mrs Smith. It's not out of some lurid voyeurism. I'm of the opinion that talking about things is the best way to heal the wounds and move on."

"The wounds are beginning to heal by themselves, Father. All you're doing is opening them up again."

"Is that what you think I'm trying to do, Mrs Smith? That I'm somehow trying to sabotage everything?"

"Of course not, Father. I just think you can be a little — well — heavy-handed sometimes. It's your age, perhaps. Foisting your own views upon us. All that about Clement and his mother. It's not for us to deal with. Not when we have so many other things to consider. If you want to listen, then listen to what I'm telling you. Guide us by letting us go the way we know best. We know how to get through all this."

"By standing still?"

"By sheltering, Father. By being patient."

"And waiting for what?"

"For things to settle again."

"And if they don't?"

"Look, Mr Belderboss is vulnerable at the moment, Father. He's still confused by everything that's happened and liable to say things that aren't entirely accurate. I don't want you to go back to Saint Jude's with the wrong impression of Father Wilfred. I know you wouldn't mean to, but things can often slip out and rumours start to spread. It doesn't take much for a reputation to be dismantled."

"Do you want me to leave, Mrs Smith? Is that it?"

"No, Father. I want you to be our priest."

"So do I."

"Then hold onto the rock with us, Father. Until the waters retreat."

"Mrs Smith, I understand that Wilfred's death has been a significant blow to Saint Jude's, but I think you need to face facts if you want to recover from it. He isn't coming back. There's nothing to hold onto any more."

"There is, Father," she said. "We have Andrew."

"And what does Andrew think about that?"

There was silence and after a moment Mummer excused herself curtly and went out of the room. Father Bernard didn't stir for some time. Then I heard the sound of a bottle opening and its contents going into a glass.

CHAPTER
TWENTY-TWO

The day of the visit to the shrine came around and Hanny was the centre of attention from the moment we got downstairs, where everyone was drinking tea and helping themselves to the apples that Father Bernard had picked the day before. The men had adopted a strange kind of machismo and clapped Hanny on the shoulder and shook his hand, as though they were pages fitting their knight for battle.

Mummer had a basin of hot water ready and she and Mrs Belderboss washed Hanny's face and hands slowly and carefully.

"The Lord will come upon you today," said Mrs Belderboss. "I know He will. You're ready. It's your time."

Father Bernard packed a bag with the things that he would need. Some matches. His stole. A small silver chalice that he had brought from Saint Jude's.

When he had finished he sat at the table with Monro next to him. He said nothing but stroked the dog's head and watched them attending to Hanny, who lapped up the fuss and smiled as Mummer combed his hair and then took a pair of scissors to his nails. He caught my eyes and kissed his fingers. The poor sod thought all this was for Else. Perhaps he thought he was going to marry her. That this was the day she would give him the child and they would be together.

"What does that mean?" said Mummer. "Why is he doing that with his hand?"

"I don't know," I said.

"Why don't you tell him where we're going," she said, nodding at the chair next to her for me to sit down.

I did as I was told and touched Hanny on the arm.

"Hanny," I said. "We're going to see God."

At the mention of the name, Hanny looked upwards and pointed to the ceiling.

"That's it," said Mummer. "But we're not going to heaven. God is going to come down here. He's going to make a special visit just for you. Isn't that right, Mrs Belderboss?"

"Yes," she said. "We're going to go to a wonderful place, Andrew. It's a secret garden where God makes people better."

"Now," said Mummer, inspecting Hanny's nails and knocking his fringe about with her fingers until it was as neat as it was ever going to be. "I think it's time for Andrew's present. Where's my husband got to?"

"Oh, don't worry, I'll fetch it," said Mrs Belderboss and she went out and came back a moment later with a cardboard box tied together with an ivory ribbon. She laid it down on the table and everyone gathered around.

"Go on," said Mummer and gave Hanny the end of the ribbon so that all he needed to do was pull.

Hanny drew back his hand and the bow flopped apart. He opened the lid and put it aside. Inside there was a layer of mist-thin tissue paper. Hanny responded to the hush that had fallen on the room and unwrapped the parcel slowly and gently. Underneath was a new white shirt, the buttons bright and pearlescent, each one etched with a little cross.

"It's beautiful," said Mrs Belderboss.

"Just the business," Mr Belderboss added.

"I got it from the shop," said Mummer. "It was made in the Holy Land." And took it out of the box and held it up for everyone to see.

When they had all had a chance to admire it, Mummer gave it to me to hold and made Hanny lift his arms so that she could pull off his vest, taking care not to ruin his hair. Hanny stood and squeezed the fat on his belly between his thumb and forefinger, while Mummer brushed a few loose strands of cotton off the shirt.

"Here," she said and put Hanny's arm down one of the sleeves and then the other, working his big hands through the cuffs. She moved around the front and pulled it closed across his chest.

"Now when we get to God's special place," she said, fastening the buttons, "you mustn't be afraid. You mustn't get upset. Because if you do then God will disappear again. Do as I say and everything will be all right."

When she had finished doing up his shirt, she ran her hand down the buttons and stood back waiting for the reaction she knew would come. No one had spotted it before, but a large crucifix had been stitched into the front of the shirt, the pleat for the buttons forming the upright and the crossbeam devised out of some delicate embroidery that only showed itself now that Hanny was wearing the garment.

"We have something for you too," said Mrs Belderboss. "Reg?"

"Oh, yes," said Mr Belderboss and he went slowly over to the sideboard and came back with a long thin box, which he gave to his wife.

Mrs Belderboss opened the box and slid out a white candle.

"Here," she said, passing it to Hanny to hold. "It's been blessed by the bishop. You can take it with you."

She hugged him.

"He's like a crusader," she said, noting the way the candle was so long it looked like a sword.

"All he needs is a shield," Mr Belderboss said.

"He has one already," Mrs Belderboss replied, patting the cross on Hanny's chest.

The morning was damp and cold. Low grey clouds sat over the Loney and kept the woods and ditches full of shadow.

"Nice of you to join us," Mummer said to Farther, who had appeared at last, rather subdued and distracted.

"Not now, Esther," he said and cleared his throat.

"Where have you been anyway? Poking about in that room again, I'll bet."

Farther looked at her.

"It's important that Andrew has everyone with him today," said Mummer. "And I don't just mean physically."

"I know," he said.

She led the way across the fields with Hanny in tow, fuelling and enjoying his excitement by telling him about the place we were going to.

Quickly, the group stretched and fell apart. Miss Bunce and David negotiated the pools of mud and cow muck hand in hand, Farther followed them, deep in thought and Mr and Mrs Belderboss made up the rearguard, struggling already with the soft, rutted ground and the long detours we had to take around the floodwater.

"Don't let them get lost," Mummer called back over her shoulder, leaving me and Father Bernard to look after them.

Mr Belderboss leant on his stick, breathing like a dog every few steps. He was determined to walk all the way despite Mrs Belderboss fussing over him.

"Oh, look, woman," he said. "If Our Lord did forty days and nights in the desert. I'm sure I can manage a mile or two through a sheep field."

"I'm only thinking of your heart, Reg."

He waved her off and carried on.

I found myself walking next to Father Bernard, rather by design than accident. If Parkinson and Collier decided to follow us, as, lying awake in the night, I had convinced myself they would, then I felt safer next to him, no matter how distant he seemed that morning.

I looked at him and he smiled back. His argument with Mummer the night before was obviously still playing on his mind. He brought out a couple of apples from his bag but didn't say anything much until Moorings was out of sight and we stopped by a gate to wait for Mr and Mrs Belderboss.

"Andrew seems fair excited," he said, nodding up ahead where Hanny was straddling a fence and waving for everyone to hurry up.

"Yes," I said.

"So does everyone."

"Yes, Father."

"Apart from you."

I didn't reply. Father Bernard leant on the gate with his forearms and watched the Belderbosses coming at a snail's pace; a faint argument.

"If nothing happens today Tonto," he said. "You won't be too disappointed, will you?"

"No, Father."

"Because I'd hate for you to lose faith in what God can do."

"Yes, Father."

"You know, not all miracles are instantaneous. I've never seen one like that anyway. I think it takes a while for them to ripen. If all you look for are Damascus experiences, then you miss all the smaller things that are part of His plan. Do you know what I mean?"

"Yes, Father. I think so."

He turned and smiled and held the gate open for Mr and Mrs Belderboss, who went through still bickering.

★ ★ ★

The shrine seemed much further than everyone remembered, but eventually we arrived at a small gravel car park, deserted apart from a mattress and some old car tyres.

The little booth where an elderly attendant had once sold penny information leaflets was gone and there was only the wind and the sounds of sheep far away on the hills.

"You mean we could have come by road?" Miss Bunce said, looking at her muddied shoes.

"We could have come by road, Joan," said Mummer. "But I'm not sure arriving in a minibus shows quite the same sense of devotion."

"Where is everyone?" said Mrs Belderboss as she and her husband finally appeared.

Across the car park was a gate almost completely throttled by the branches of the trees next to it. The gate led to a weedy, gravel pathway that meandered through the trees and came eventually to the shrine itself after another half a mile. All along the path were little figurines half hidden in the undergrowth — Christs and saints and angels peeping around the sides of plastic urns like curious fairy folk.

Here and there were little clearings where grottoes had been set up in honour of various saints and holy men, the trees dressed with the rosaries and rags previous pilgrims had left behind with their transgressions.

Mummer caught up with Hanny who was ahead of us all and steered him well clear of the ribbons, making sure that he passed along the path as quickly as possible. Father Bernard stopped and ran his hand through them.

"Oh, mind they don't come away, Father," Mr Belderboss said. "You'll take the sins home with you."

We came to where Hanny was looking at a statue of Saint Francis that had fallen over and smashed. His head had cracked off and rolled into the undergrowth and wood lice swarmed in and out of his hollow body.

"Oh, Esther," said Mrs Belderboss. "It's such a shame."

"Well, perhaps the groundsman hasn't got round to it yet," said Mummer.

"I'm not sure there is a groundsman any more," said Mr Belderboss.

"There must be," said Mummer. "They wouldn't just let the place go to seed."

"But if there's no money, Esther," said Mrs Belderboss.

"Of course there's money," said Mummer. "There's always money. Someone's always got money."

"I don't think it's anything to do with money," said Farther. "It's just that no one comes to places like this any more."

"What about Lourdes?" said Mummer.

"That's different," said Farther. "And anyway, it's like Disneyland nowadays."

"Well God is still here," said Mummer. "Despite what it looks like."

"Yes," said Mrs Belderboss. "Of course He is."

We walked a little further through a tight kissing gate and then the path was flanked on either side by a tall hedge, as though we were in a maze. The hedge had gone wild and in places had almost met in the middle of the path so that we had to squeeze past the brambles and thorns in single file.

A hundred yards further on, the path ended. Mummer stopped and pulled away some of the branches and leaves to get at the handle of a small iron gate.

"Here we are," she said, and opened it inwards with one, two, three hard pushes, tearing aside more of the foliage that clung to the railings.

Everyone stopped talking and went through the tangle of rhododendrons until we came to a set of stone steps, damp and black with moss, which led down to where the spring itself bubbled to the surface and could be accessed by opening a small trapdoor in the ground.

Father Bernard helped the ladies down first and they negotiated the narrow, greasy slabs slowly and carefully. When they were safely at the bottom, Father Bernard went back up the steps to help Mr Belderboss. Everyone seemed to hold their breath when he was in the precarious moment between Father Bernard's hands letting go of him at the top and Mummer's hands reaching to him from the bottom.

"You go first, Hanny," I said, when it was our turn.

He stared down into the shrine and turned to look at me.

"It's all right," I said. "Go on."

Everyone was watching, waiting. He shook his head.

"There's nothing to worry about," I said. "I'll come with you."

I held Hanny's hand and step by step he went down and joined everyone else huddled in the damp.

"I can't believe what's happened here," said Mrs Belderboss, looking around. "I'm so sorry for you, Esther."

"It's all right," said Mummer.

"The well was always so beautifully dressed," Mrs Belderboss explained to Father Bernard, who had taken his gold-coloured stole from his bag and was looping it around his neck. "So many flowers and candles."

Now, it was an oubliette; cramped and dank and filled with permanent shadow by the yew trees twisting above us. Where the large stones that formed the sheer walls jutted out, there were stumps of wax, which no one could get to light, and so David was designated to hold up a match so that everyone could see the wooden board nailed to the wall on which a scene had been painted of Saint Anne shimmering in white and hovering above the startled peasant children that had first witnessed her apparition three centuries earlier.

Father Bernard knelt down and opened the little trap-door that was inches thick and braced with iron straps. Everyone gathered round. The holy water trickled past, black and silky-looking with a smell of autumn deadfall and eggs.

I could feel Hanny crushing my hand.

"It's all right," I said. "Don't be scared."

Miss Bunce went first as she was closest to Father Bernard. She took off her coat and handed it to David to hold. Accepting Father Bernard's hand, she knelt down in front of him and bent her head forward. Father

Bernard placed his hand gently on her crown, said a quiet prayer, and then reached down into the hole with the chalice to let it fill with water. He brought it up spattering onto the stone and handed it to Miss Bunce. She closed her eyes and drank from the cup and was replaced by David, and then the rest of us one by one.

When it came to Mummer's turn she remained standing. Father Bernard looked at her and then dipped the chalice into the water and stood up to face her.

"Drink this water, the healing balm of Christ," he said, giving her the invitation he had given to everyone.

"Amen," said Mummer and sipped until the chalice was empty.

There was only Hanny left. Farther lit the candle Mr and Mrs Belderboss had given him and Mummer took off his coat, so that she could rearrange the collar of his new shirt. Smiling at her son, she tidied his hair and with a kiss on his forehead, she turned him to face Father Bernard.

"He's ready now, Father."

Father Bernard held out his hand.

"Andrew," he said, over the sound of the water. "Come and kneel down here by me."

Hanny stood clutching his candle.

"Andrew?" Father Bernard said again. And this time Mummer nudged Hanny and pointed to where he should go. Hanny looked at me and I nodded.

Father Bernard held Hanny's hand as he went slowly to his knees.

"All right, Andrew," he said, pressing lightly on the back of Hanny's head to make him bow down. "Don't be afraid now. God is with you."

He kept one hand on Hanny's head and held out the other for the mug Mummer had brought. The one with the London bus on the side. He dipped the cup into the well and brought it out.

"Now, Andrew," he said, allowing Hanny to lift his head. "Would you drink this for me?"

Hanny looked at him. I could see his eyes widening. He turned round to find me, but Mummer snapped at him. "Andrew. Remember what I said."

"God wants to heal you, Andrew," Mrs Belderboss said.

"Go on, son," said Farther. "It won't hurt."

Hanny shook his head.

"Just a sip now, Andrew. That's all." Father Bernard tried to put the mug into Hanny's free hand, but Hanny panicked and knocked it away and the mug smashed against the stone wall.

He got up, threw the candle aside, and made for the steps. Miss Bunce squawked. David tried to stop him, but Hanny easily pushed him aside, and sent him sprawling onto the mossy floor.

Before I could go after him myself, Mummer was up the steps and I felt Father Bernard's hand on my arm.

"Let her fetch him," he said.

I could hear Mummer shouting at Hanny. She hadn't run after him. She didn't need to.

Farther and Miss Bunce helped David to his feet. His trousers were coated in filth and his lip was cut and bleeding where he had fallen against the wall. Miss Bunce felt around inside the pockets of her cagoule and brought out a tissue and dabbed at his mouth. I could see her face reddening and she was about to say something when Mummer appeared at the top of the steps gripping Hanny's elbow.

"He's going to try again," Mummer said.

"I don't know if now's the best time, Mrs Smith," said Father Bernard. "We're all a bit upset. Perhaps I should bring Andrew on his own tomorrow."

Mummer smiled thinly. "No, we can't do that, Father. We're going home tomorrow."

"Right enough," said Father Bernard. "But I can drive Andrew here before we go. I'm sure no one will mind me slipping away for a wee while."

The others shook their heads.

"I don't mind," said Mrs Belderboss.

"It might be better to bring the lad tomorrow," Mr Belderboss said. "Without everyone watching."

"We're here now," said Mummer, aware that Miss Bunce was glaring at her. "We've made a special effort to come and I'd like Andrew to take the water."

Farther put his hand on Mummer's back.

"Come on, Esther," he said. "Don't upset yourself."

"I'm not upset."

"Look," said Father Bernard. "Why don't we go back to the house? It looks like it's going to rain any minute."

"No," said Mummer. "I'm sorry, Father, but he is to take the water and that's that. He is not going to spoil the day."

"Ah, come on, Mrs Smith, he's hardly doing that now, is he?"

"Isn't he?"

"It's not his fault."

"Why? Because he's too stupid to know what he's doing?"

"I never said that."

"Not in so many words."

"Mrs Smith —"

She grabbed Hanny and took him over to the well, fending off Father Bernard's appeasements with a wave of her hand. She upturned a jam jar of dead stalks and knelt down and filled it from the well. The water spun with sediment and grime.

"Open your mouth," Mummer said sharply. "Look at me."

Hanny looked at up her and started to cry.

"Stop it," said Mummer. "What's the matter with you? Don't you want to get better?"

Hanny turned to get away again, but Mummer held his arm and looked over to Father Bernard.

"Well, help me," she said, but he looked away.

"Careful, Esther," said Mrs Belderboss. "You're hurting him."

Mummer tightened her grip and then more so again, as though she was bringing a wayward dog to heel. Slowly, Hanny opened his mouth.

"Wider," said Mummer, pinching his cheeks in so that his jaw opened.

"Esther, stop it," said Mr Belderboss.

"Please, Esther," Mrs Belderboss cried and then turned away, her eyes full of tears.

"Oh, for God's sake, just drink it," said Mummer.

Hanny closed his eyes and screwed up his face the way he did when he had to take Milk of Magnesia. Mummer carefully poured the water in, as though she was measuring it. Hanny coughed and choked and then spat the water into her eyes.

Mummer blinked and stretched her face, but said nothing. She found the lid of the jam jar on the ground, screwed it on tight and put the jar in her pocket. Father Bernard was leading everyone quietly out of the shrine. I took Hanny by the hand and followed them. Only Farther stayed behind, staring at his wife.

CHAPTER
TWENTY-THREE

Despite Father Bernard's best efforts to persuade them to stay, Miss Bunce and David packed their things and he drove them to the station in Lancaster to catch the sleeper train.

A heavy despondency filled Moorings to the brim and when I couldn't stand it any longer I went to bed, leaving Mummer and Farther and Mr and Mrs Belderboss to talk glumly in the sitting room.

Hanny was fast asleep, exhausted by what had happened at the shrine. I watched him for a while but must have dropped off quickly myself.

I had been asleep for about an hour when I heard someone coming into the room. It was Mummer. She was carrying a steaming cup on a tray. She looked at me and made a motion with her hand that I should lie back down.

"What are you doing?" I said.

"Giving Andrew a cup of tea."

"He's asleep."

Mummer shushed me and went and sat on the edge of Hanny's bed. She watched him sleeping for a minute and then took out the jam jar of water. She tipped some of it into the tea and set the cup on the bedside table.

The rest of the water she trickled into her hand and, using her finger, traced a cross very gently on Hanny's forehead.

He stirred a little and half woke. Mummer hushed him. Hanny settled again and went completely still, his consciousness sliding back down into the drains of sleep.

She ought to have left him alone. He was so worn out by what had happened at the shrine that he looked dead. His face had the same awful slackness as Father Wilfred's the day Mummer and the others went to wash his body in preparation for burial.

I had been made to go too, to help the visiting priest that had been sent by the bishop to oversee the ablutions. It would do no harm, said Mummer, for the bishop to know she had a capable son when the time came for me to be thinking of a career in the clergy.

They had Father Wilfred laid out in his coffin in the front room of the presbytery. It was a rarely used room and almost as cold as the January day that bristled against the window behind the curtains. A carriage clock futtered quietly on the mantelpiece next to the candles that would be kept lit until the funeral. Everyone stood around the coffin as the priest said a prayer and made the sign of the cross over the body.

Because it *was* a body now and not Father Wilfred at all. Death was a poor draughtsman and had rendered his likeness just a little off-centre, giving him the look of someone who was almost familiar but lacking the something that made him so. Like a waxwork, I suppose.

As a crop of white stubble had spread across his cheeks and chin, his face had taken on the texture of fake velvet. The skin on his arms and legs was like ancient parchment dotted with the ink of moles and liver spots, and beneath the skin lay stringy muscles that had been loosened by the funeral director to make the cleaning easier.

Mummer brought in basins of warm water and a bottle of Dettol and the ladies rolled up their sleeves and slowly opened the folds of linen and began to wash him, gently lifting his arms and turning his legs slightly to get around the backs of his knees. A swirl of a loincloth afforded him some modesty and spared our blushes.

I stood back and held a basin for Mummer. I noticed that there was a brown stain on the satin pillow as she cradled Father Wilfred's head so that she could run a flannel around his face and neck. Water and disinfectant trickled over the hard bow of his clavicle and down the grille of his ribs and when Mummer mopped his brow there remained little droplets among his eyelashes.

When it was done and the ladies were going in and out to sluice the water down the drains, Mummer opened up the newspaper parcel she had brought with her and took out a small bunch of white roses. She crossed Father Wilfred's shrivelled hands over his stomach and interlaced the fingers. Then, careful not to cut him, she lifted his hands and slotted the roses into his grasp one by one.

288

As they swaddled him again, there was an audible exhalation. Of pity, I thought, or relief. Relief that it was over. Relief that it wasn't them lying there on the table like meat.

Mummer crossed herself and then sat down on a wooden chair by the coffin with her rosary beads to take the first watch of the vigil. The other ladies said nothing and left one by one.

"Light the candles before you go," said Mummer as I was putting on my coat.

I did as she asked and watched the light flickering on Father Wilfred's face.

"Is Father in heaven?" I asked.

Mummer looked up and frowned. "Of course," she said. "Why wouldn't he be? All priests go straight to heaven."

"Do they?"

"Yes," she said. "It's their reward for serving God."

She looked at me a moment longer then went back to her rosary. I knew when Mummer was only half sure about something — like when I came home with algebra homework and Farther wasn't around, or she had to drive somewhere she hadn't been before, the confidence she feigned was tinged with irritation that she didn't actually know the right answer or the right way at all. What if Father Wilfred had gone to Purgatory?

As I cycled home in the snow I tried to imagine what it would be like. Father Wilfred had always described it as a place of closed doors, where sinners were shut off from God until their souls had been cleansed with fire.

What it felt like to have one's soul burnt to purity, I couldn't imagine. It couldn't be a physical pain now that his body was lying lifeless in a box, so was it then a mental torture? Were each of life's hidden sins illuminated and ignited one by one? Was one punished by being forced to live through them all again? All the fear and guilt?

Coming down Ballards Lane past the tube station, I surprised myself and prayed for him. After all, it wasn't his fault. He'd had a shock at the Loney. It was no wonder he went pieces. Anyone would have done the same.

"Andrew," said Mummer, touching him on the cheek with the back of her hand.

Hanny woke up and looked at her, then coming to consciousness he moved away from her on his elbows. He looked at me and Mummer put her hand on his shoulder.

"It's all right, Andrew," she said. "I've just brought you some tea."

She passed Hanny the cup and he held it like a bowl and sipped.

"That's it," said Mummer, standing up slightly so that she could check that its contents had all gone. When Hanny had drunk the lot, she put her hand on the back of his neck and kissed him on the forehead. Hanny beamed because she wasn't angry any more.

"Now," said Mummer. "Come and kneel down here with me."

She got off the bed and knelt down beside it.

"Come on, Andrew. Like this."

He smiled and got down on the floor with Mummer.

"Close your eyes," she said.

Hanny looked at me and I rubbed my fingers over my eyelids and then he understood.

"That's it," said Mummer. "Good lad."

She stroked his hair and once he was settled, she turned to me.

"Open the door," she whispered.

"What?"

"Open the door and let them in."

"Who?"

"The others."

I got out of bed and went to the door. Farther and Mr and Mrs Belderboss were waiting on the landing. They all turned to face me.

"Is he ready?" asked Mr Belderboss and as quietly as possible, they filed into the bedroom and stood looking at Hanny who had his hands pressed tightly together and his eyes squeezed shut.

"Shouldn't we wait for Father Bernard?" said Mrs Belderboss.

"We'd better start," said Mummer. "While Andrew's still settled."

Mrs Belderboss looked at him. "Yes, I suppose you're right," she said.

"You too," Mummer said to me, and pointed to the patch of floor to her right where she wanted me to kneel.

Farther and Mrs Belderboss knelt on the other side of the bed and Mr Belderboss lolloped over to the chair by the door and sat down heavily, his stick in between his legs and his forehead resting on the handle.

"Lord God," Mummer began. "We ask that your healing waters flow through Andrew and bring nourishment to his —"

She broke off as someone else came into the room. Father Bernard stood there in his coat and looked around at everyone. Mrs Belderboss pretended to inspect her fingers. Mr Belderboss smiled at him and then coughed and looked away.

"I thought I heard voices," said Father Bernard. "What's going on?"

"We're praying for Andrew," said Mrs Belderboss.

"Oh," said Father Bernard, looking at his wristwatch.

"Is that a problem, Father?" said Mummer.

"No, no," he said. "I'm just surprised you're all still up."

"Did Joan and David get off all right?" asked Mrs Belderboss.

"Aye," he said. "They caught the train on time. I did try to talk them out of it again on the way there, but they had their minds made up pretty tight about it. It's a shame."

"It is," said Mrs Belderboss, and there was a moment's silence before Farther spoke.

"Do you want to join us?" he said.

Father Bernard looked at Mummer.

"No," he said. "I'll leave you to it."

"Come on, Father," said Mr Belderboss. "I'm sure your prayers would be worth ten of ours."

292

He looked down at what he was wearing. Sodden raincoat. Sodden boots.

"I'm not sure I'm suitable, Reg," he said.

"It doesn't matter," said Mrs Belderboss. "God doesn't mind what you're wearing, so why should we?"

"No, really," he said. "I'll be away to my bed and pray for Andrew first thing in the morning when I'm more awake and I can concentrate on what I'm doing."

"Are you sure, Father?" said Mrs Belderboss, a little disappointed.

"Aye. Praying's like tuning a radio."

"Come again?"

"You have to be on the right frequency, otherwise all God hears is static."

"Yes, I see what you mean," said Mrs Belderboss, smiling sympathetically. "Well, as long as you're sure, Father."

"Aye. I'm fairly worn out, to be honest with you. And there's a long drive home tomorrow."

"Yes," said Mrs Belderboss with a sigh. "It has been a bit tiring all said, hasn't it? Nothing's gone quite right. It's all been so difficult. It's such a pity, Father, that you've not seen this place as it used to be."

"Places do change, Mary," Mr Belderboss chipped in.

"Oh I know that," she replied. "But it's been such a baptism of fire for Father. I mean, Wilfred knew us and he knew this place. He would have coped so much better with all these little problems we've had."

"True," said Mr Belderboss. "He was a firm hand on the tiller."

"It's no reflection of you, Father," Mrs Belderboss went on. "It's rather been our fault, I feel, asking you to take on too much too quickly. I mean, it's like anything, being a priest. It takes time to get things right, doesn't it, Esther?"

"Most definitely."

Mummer looked at Father Bernard who said nothing more and went out of the room. Mummer resettled herself and noticed that Farther was staring at her.

"What?" she said.

"What's the matter with you?"

"Nothing."

"Why did you speak to Father like that?"

"Like what?"

"You know what I mean."

"Do I?"

"Yes," he said. "You do."

Mummer looked at Mr and Mrs Belderboss.

"I'm sorry, Reg, Mary," she said. "My husband's obviously a little out of sorts."

"Out of sorts?" Farther raised his voice and Mr and Mrs Belderboss exchanged looks. "I think you're the one out of sorts, Esther," he said.

"And is it any wonder?" Mummer snapped. "Considering what we've been through since we got here? This whole thing has been an utter farce."

"Now steady on," Mr Belderboss said.

"Esther," said Mrs Belderboss, eyeing the door. "He'll hear you."

"I don't care," said Mummer, her colour rising in a way I'd rarely seen before. "I will have my say about

Father Bernard McGill. He's a mistake. He's not right for us. I've never met any priest so flippant and carefree with his authority. He makes a mockery of everything we do. I for one will be very glad when he's sent back to Ireland to his own kind."

Amid the angry voices, Hanny got up and went over to the window. He picked up the stuffed hare and smoothed his hand over its back.

"He's still a young man, Esther," said Mrs Belderboss. "He just needs time to mature into someone like Father Wilfred. He will one day. I'm convinced of it."

"Mary," said Mummer. "You were convinced that he wouldn't have gone drinking, but he did. And he invited those louts over."

"It was only a bit of fun," said Farther. "You said so yourself."

"Fun?" said Mummer. "You weren't the one being flung around the room like a rag doll."

"I didn't see you complaining too much," said Farther.

"And I didn't see you stepping in to stop it," said Mummer. "No, you were too busy egging them on with everyone else.

"Good God," she went on. "Just listen to what I'm saying. This was meant to be a pilgrimage, a chance for us all to find some peace after everything that's happened and I'm having to worry about strange, drunk men dancing around the sitting room at the invite of the priest who was supposed to be looking after us. What on earth did he think we'd come here for? Larks in the country? To trail around finding lost causes like Clement Parry and his mother? Bringing in every waif and stray he could find? Poking around in business that doesn't concern him or us? Everything's falling apart. I mean, he couldn't even keep us all together."

"It wasn't his fault that Joan and David went home," said Farther.

"It was," said Mummer. "And he knows it was. That's why he was so late back. Drowning his sorrows in the Bell and Anchor no doubt."

"Esther!" Farther raised his voice again. "You can't say things like that. Especially not about a priest. That's how rumours start."

"Yes, I know," said Mummer, looking pointedly at Mr Belderboss.

"What?" he said. "What have I done?"

"The other day you left Father Bernard with lots of questions that I don't really think we want him to be trying to answer."

"It's not Reg's fault, Esther," said Mrs Belderboss. "He was just upset, that's all. His emotions got the better of him."

"You let Father Bernard bully you," said Mummer.

"Oh, come on. It was hardly an interrogation," said Farther. "I'm sure he was only trying to help."

"We've got to be more careful," said Mummer. "None of us really knows what happened to Wilfred and we're probably never likely to. We can't give in to speculation. If we do that then we're handing over the

296

memory of Wilfred to those who don't care about him like we do."

"This is Reg's brother you're talking about," said Farther. "I think it's up to him what he says about Wilfred."

"No," said Mr Belderboss. "Esther's right. We must keep our suspicions to ourselves. We can't prove anything. I mean if I had his diary it might tell us once and for all."

"I agree," said Mrs Belderboss. "We can't let any rumours spread. It'd ruin Saint Jude's."

"Well, if there are rumours, I'm sure they're out there by now," said Farther. "You can't stop people talking. And anyway rumours come and go. They'll be talking about something else next week. You know what people are like."

"I'm not sure you've quite grasped how serious this is," said Mummer. "People might very well lose interest in gossip and move on, but it's left in their minds as fact. If people have it in their heads that Father Wilfred — you know — then it would turn everything he ever said into a lie. And what would that do to people's faith?"

"Faith's not an exact science, Esther," said Farther.

"Yes it is," said Mummer. "You either have it or you don't. It's quite simple."

"Esther's right," said Mr Belderboss.

Mrs Belderboss nodded in agreement.

"Listen," said Farther. "I think that if we have even the slightest suspicion that Wilfred took his own life then we ought to report it to the police."

"And what good would that do?" said Mummer.

"It would be the right thing to do."

"If we can't prove it, how would they?"

"I don't know. I don't think it matters if they do prove it. Wouldn't it at least take the burden off Reg a little?"

"Well, we can't say anything to the contrary now, can we?" said Mummer. "How would that look three months down the line?"

"Like we had something to hide," Mr Belderboss said.

"It sounds like we do," said Farther.

The apostle clock chimed for midnight. Everyone waited for it to stop.

"Well, Reg and I are a little tired," said Mrs Belderboss once the last ring had ended.

"It is quite late, I suppose," said Mr Belderboss. "We'll see you all in the morning."

Farther helped Mrs Belderboss to her feet and she held his arm as he led her to the door. Mr Belderboss used his stick to get himself out of the chair. Farther opened the door for them and they said goodnight and went off to their room along the corridor.

Once they were gone, Mummer said, "Aren't you going too?"

Farther sighed briefly and came and sat on the bed.

"I think you're the one who needs some rest," he said, taking her hand. "It's not doing you any good getting so worked up about everything. So things haven't gone all that smoothly, so what? Father Bernard likes a drink now and then, so what? It's really not the end of the world. Don't get so upset about everything."

"I'm not upset," she said. "In fact, in a funny way, I'm glad that I've seen Father Bernard for the inept he is. At least this trip's illustrated that much."

"Come on, love," said Farther softly and smiling at Hanny who was still by the window with the hare. "Leave Andrew be. Let him get some sleep. Come to bed."

"I haven't finished praying for him."

He took Mummer's hands in his.

"Esther," he said. "I think it's time that we accepted that he is the way he is, and that's how it's always going to be."

"I can't do that."

"We're going home tomorrow," he said. "And I think that's where we ought to stay. We shouldn't come here again. It's not a good place."

"What are you on about, not a good place? We've been coming here for years."

"I mean, I don't think Andrew's ever going to get better here."

"Why not?"

He looked at me and then down at his hands. "In that room next to the study . . ." he began and Mummer sighed. "No hear me out, Esther. It's important."

Mummer set her face and waited for him to go on.

"Before we went to the shrine, I went to lock it up and I found a name scratched into the plaster by the bed."

"So?"

"Well I think it was the name of the girl they put in there."

"It probably was."

"The thing is," he said. "I moved the bed away from the wall to get a better look and there were four other names there as well."

"So they were all ill," said Mummer. "What's that got to do with anything?"

"They all died, Esther."

"Don't be silly," said Mummer.

"It's true," said Farther. "Each name had a line scraped through it, and . . ."

"And what?"

"I know I've not said anything," he said. "And I wasn't going to. But I found some letters."

"Letters?"

"In a little box under the bed. From Gregson to the children's governess, asking her if the children were better, if they might be able to come home soon."

Mummer rubbed her eyes. "Why are you telling me all this?"

"Esther, it wasn't just that one room that was a quarantine," he said. "It was the whole house. Gregson didn't build it as a home, but a hospice."

"Of course it was a home," said Mummer.

Farther shook his head.

"Gregson never lived here himself; he only built it so the governess could take the children to the shrine."

Mummer looked at him irritably.

"I still don't know what this has to do with us," she said.

"Don't you see?" said Farther. "He kept on insisting that she take them even when it was obvious there was no hope of them getting any better."

"He had faith," said Mummer. "That's all that's obvious to me."

"It's not about faith," said Farther. "It's about knowing when to admit defeat."

"Defeat?"

"Before someone gets hurt."

"I'm not giving up on Andrew now. Where would that leave us?"

"Esther, it drove that poor man out of his mind in the end that he couldn't change anything."

"I know *I* can't change anything," Mummer snapped. "I'm not saying that *I* can do anything. I'm asking God."

Farther sighed and Mummer pushed his hands away.

"Leave me alone," she said.

"Esther."

"Leave me alone with my son."

"Don't do this to him any more. Don't do it to yourself. Let's go home as soon as we can tomorrow. It's not Bernard's fault that everything's gone wrong this week. It's this place. It's sick. It's not good for us."

"Listen," said Mummer, grabbing Farther's wrist suddenly. "Your faith might have crumbled along with Wilfred's but don't try and ruin mine as well."

Farther tried to prise off her fingers, but she gripped even tighter.

"Do you know what?" she said, smiling a little. "I think you're scared."

Farther stopped struggling.

"No," he said. "Not me." And he nodded to the corner of the room, where a gorilla sat under the shelves of pebbles and driftwood with his arms wrapped around his knees.

Hanny has changed beyond all recognition since then, but if I do see anything of the old him it is always through the eyes. There is an honesty of feeling there that betrays everyone, I suppose. And there in that room at Moorings, behind his silly mask, there was a fear that I was to see many years later when I was arrested that night outside his house. A fear that I was going to be taken away and I wouldn't be able to protect him. He has Caroline, of course, and the boys, but he still needs me. It's obvious. Not that Baxter agrees. He seems to think I was having some sort of breakdown.

"We're definitely getting somewhere, though," he said the last time I saw him.

It was a wet, blustery day at the beginning of November, a few days before they found the baby at Coldbarrow. The horse chestnut outside his office window was lumbering to and fro, sending its great yellow hands down onto the tennis courts below. They were closed for the winter now. The nets removed and the white lines buried under leaves and seeds. Baxter is a member there, as you might expect. It's that sort of place. Doctors, dentists, academics. He told me that his mixed-doubles partner was doing a postgrad in ancient Hebrew. Lovely girl. Very athletic. Yes, I could imagine

Baxter eyeing up her swaying rump as they waited for the serve.

He was standing by the window with a cup of Darjeeling, watching the tree moving in the rain. A clock ticked on the mantelpiece above the fire, which was feeding noisily on a stack of beechwood. He took a sip and set the cup back on the saucer.

"Do you feel the same?" he said.

"I suppose so."

He looked back outside and smiled to himself.

"Is that a polite *no*?"

"It's a polite *you tell me*."

He laughed gently and sat down on the leather chair that was facing me.

"You don't have to agree, old boy," he said. "Your brother's not paying me to make you jump through hoops. I just rather thought you'd turned a corner lately."

"In what way?"

"I think," he said, draining his cup and putting it down on his desk, "that you're beginning to genuinely understand your brother's concerns about you."

"Am I?"

"Mm," said Baxter. "I think you are. I think that if I asked you, you could explain them very eloquently now."

"*Are* you asking me?"

He interlaced his fingers and then opened his hands by way of prompting me to speak.

I told him what he wanted to hear and he dutifully jotted it down in his notebook. I told him that I understood Hanny and Caroline were worried about me. That sitting outside their house at all hours was unnecessary. That I shouldn't blame the neighbour who called the police. Hanny didn't need me to be his watchman. And the fact that I couldn't identify the particular threats I felt were ranged against him meant that they were unlikely to exist at all. I had invented them so that I still felt *essential* to Hanny, even though he was married and had a family of his own to look after him.

We'd never discussed that last point before but I added it in anyway, knowing that Baxter would be impressed with my self-perception. And I would be a step closer to making him think I was cured.

"Very good," he said, looking up briefly from his notebook. "You see, a corner turned. You're a different man to the one that came to me back in March."

"Is that right?"

"Indeed. I mean there's a way to go yet before you're . . ."

"Normal?"

"Happier, I was going to say. But it's all about little steps, Mr Smith. There's no point in trying to run and all that."

"I suppose not."

"And it's not about pressing you into some sort of societal mould either," he said. "It's about getting you to a level of understanding that will allow you to interact with others in a more fulfilling, less stressful way."

He looked down at his fingers and laughed quietly.

"I don't often admit this, Mr Smith, but I actually find myself envying my patients from time to time."

"How so?"

"It's the opportunity that a crisis can bring, I suppose," he said. "To really look at one's place in the grand scheme of things. To identify the things that really matter. It's so easy to bungle through life only experiencing a slender set of emotions and never thinking about why one does what one does. Who was it said, 'An unexamined life is not worth living'? Aristotle?"

"Socrates."

"Ah, yes, of course. Well, it's a sound philosophy whoever came up with it. And one that I'm afraid I cannot live by as well as you, Mr Smith. You are *living* life. You're engaging with the struggle. Not like me."

"Perhaps you ought to be telling Hanny all this. Then he might understand me."

Baxter smiled. "He will in time," he said. "You might feel like your relationship is broken, but we humans have an inbuilt urge to fix things. You'll work it out. Your brother is stronger than you think."

CHAPTER
TWENTY-FOUR

Hanny slipped away sometime in the night. His bed was empty and his boots and coat were gone. I always slept lightly at Moorings — even more so since Parkinson's visit — and I wondered how he had managed to leave without waking me. But as I got out of bed I realised that he'd laid towels down on the floorboards so that I didn't hear him go.

I felt his mattress. It was stone cold. Even the smell of him had vanished. I couldn't believe he had been so devious and dissembling. It wasn't like him at all.

In the middle of the room, the pink rug had been turned back and the loose floorboard lifted out. I felt around inside the cavity. The rifle was missing and he had taken the bullets from my coat pocket.

I knew where he had gone, of course. He had gone to Coldbarrow to see Else and his baby.

Downstairs in the kitchen, Monro lifted his head and pined when I came in. I stroked his neck to quieten him down and saw that the floor was littered with the treats Father Bernard had brought for him. Clever Hanny.

Monro sneezed and lay down and went back to chewing the bone-shaped biscuits that he discovered one by one in the folds of his blanket.

Outside, a light drizzle, briny and ripe, spread across the fields and its moisture grew on me like fur. The tandem was leaning against the wall, the tyres repaired. That was why Father Bernard had come in so late. He hadn't been at the Bell and Anchor as Mummer said, but out in the yard in the rain fixing the bike.

I pushed the tandem away from the house, manoeuvring it around the puddles and lifting it over the cattle grid so as not to wake anyone. Once I was around the front of the house, I set off down the lane, met the coast road, split the deep puddles that were standing there, and was soon passing through the marshes.

After days of rain they could become six or seven feet deep with no discernible bottom, only a jelly of mud and dead vegetation. I called Hanny's name, strangely hoping that he had stumbled into one of the pools. Better to go that way than whatever Parkinson had in mind.

But there was nothing. Only the hiss of the reeds and the slop of the ink-black water as the wind came across the marshes, bringing a flurry of white flakes.

For a moment I thought it was snowing — it wouldn't have been unheard of there, even in the late spring — but then as I got closer to the hawthorn tree I could see that it had burst into life well before it ought to have done, like the apple trees and the fresh green grass up at Moorings. Each gnarled limb held a garland of petals, the way Father Wilfred had held the white roses as he lay in his coffin.

At the dunes, I had to heave the tandem through the col as the wind had piled sand a foot thick over the road. Hanny's footprints were there, mixed with the impressions of car tyres. Leonard had passed this way and recently.

I called for Hanny again, thinking that he might be hiding in the marram somewhere. I waited and looked up at the grass bending in the wind, the grey clouds scudding overhead.

The tide was starting to come in. The sandflats were slowly sinking under the water, and way out, almost at Coldbarrow, was a figure leaning into the wind, his white shirt fluttering. It was Hanny. He had the rifle over his shoulder.

I made a cup with my hands and shouted, but he couldn't hear me, of course. And in the event I was glad. The last thing I wanted him to do was start to come back now that the tide was racing in. It was better that he went on and waited.

I left the tandem against the pillbox and began to run across the sand, following the posts as far as I could. In places there was no water at all, but further out in the full blast of the wind, the sand had collapsed into deep gutters, the edges of which fell apart alarmingly as I jumped over each that I came to.

The roar was all about me as the sea thrust itself towards the shore, breaking into foaming crowns when it smashed down into some hidden declivity. Driftwood and weed sped past, rising and falling on the grey swell, turning, breaking, and then sucked under by the currents.

To my right I could make out one of those temporary pathways the water and wind would conjure up at the Loney now and then; long backbones of sand that only became apparent when the high tide left them exposed above the water. I waded over and climbed up to the highest point and saw that it wound in a long, meandering ribbon towards Coldbarrow.

Yet, even that pathway ran out well before I got there. The ground broke and slipped away, and I was pitched forward into the sea, my legs suddenly kicking into nothingness.

The cold of it took my breath out like a punch and squeezed my scrotum into a walnut. I reached down, swiping my hands through the heavy, grey water, trying to hold on to something, anything, whatever unidentifiable thing of plastic or wood I could grasp — but the tide whipped everything away and there was nothing else to do but swim as hard as I could towards the shoreline of Coldbarrow.

I was a decent swimmer in those days. Quite hardy to the chill of open water and unafraid of the deeps. There weren't many brooks and pools around the Heath that I hadn't explored. But breast-stroking Highgate Ponds was one thing, the Loney was something else. The swell came at me from all sides and seemed determined to pull me under. There was a movement in the water that flowed and gripped and sucked at the same time. I swallowed mouthfuls of salt water and choked it out in bouts of desperate coughing, my throat and my nose burning.

I seemed to be getting no closer and after striking again and again towards land, it occurred to me that I was in the early stages of drowning; in that period of fighting, sinking, resurfacing. And a panic took hold of me. I could barely feel my body. My hands were locked into claws. I would soon get too tired to move. Then what? An ache in the lungs. Silence. Nothing.

Through a burst of blind splashing, the sky, Coldbarrow and the churning horizon were turned vertical first one way and then the other, but through the swing of the world I was aware of a blurred figure on the shoreline. Then, slipping down into the muffled darkness under the water and out again, they were suddenly closer. Something was being thrust out for me to hold. I made a grab for it and felt my fingers close on a frayed leather strap. I felt a pull that countered that of the tide, felt my thighs and knees eventually scraping against the cobbles of the slipway and then the clutch of the sea was gone and Hanny was standing over me. I let go of the rifle strap and he knelt down and touched my face. I could hardly breathe. Words came out juddering. Hanny cupped his hand to his ear, wanting me to repeat what I said, but I pushed him away and he went over to a rock and sat down with the rifle across his knees.

Still shivering, I took off my parka and then my sweater and twisted it into a thick knot to get some of the water out.

"Why did you go off like that?" I said. "Why didn't you tell me where you were going?"

Hanny looked at me.

"You're an idiot," I said, looking back across the sands which had now disappeared completely. "We're supposed to be going home this morning. How the hell are we going to get back? Everyone will be wondering where we are. Mummer will be cross, and it'll be me that gets it in the neck. It's always my fault when you do something stupid. You do know that, don't you, Hanny?"

Hanny patted his pockets. He took out his plastic dinosaur.

"You're always sorry, Hanny," I said. "Why can't you just think before you do things?"

Hanny looked at me. Then he bowed his head and fumbled in his pockets for the gorilla mask. I went over and took it off him before he could put it on.

"You're not frightened, Hanny," I said. "You weren't afraid to go sneaking off without me, were you? You weren't frightened of coming all the way here by yourself."

He didn't know any better, of course, but I was angry with him all the same. More than I should have been. I threw the mask into the sea. Hanny looked at me and then went to the edge of the water and tried to scrape it back towards him with the rifle. He made a few attempts but the mask filled with water and disappeared. He rounded on me and looked as if he was going to hit me. Then he stopped and looked in the direction of Thessaly and kissed the palm of his hand.

"No, Hanny," I said. "We can't go and see her. Not any more. We've got to stay away from that place."

He kissed his hand again and pointed.

"Jesus Christ, Hanny. Don't you understand? If they find us here they'll hurt us. We just need to keep out of sight until the tide turns. No one's going to come this way for now, not while they can't get across. If we stay here they'll never know that we've even been. Give me the rifle. Let me keep watch."

Hanny turned away from me and held it close to his chest.

"Give it to me, Hanny."

He shook his head.

"I can't trust you with it. You'll hurt yourself. Give it to me."

He turned his back to me completely. I took hold of one of his arms and twisted it. He struggled and easily got free and pushed me to the ground. He hesitated for a moment and then swung the butt of the rifle towards me and caught me sharply on the wrist when I put up my hand to protect myself.

Seeing me in pain, he looked momentarily concerned, but turned away and started walking across the heather.

I called him back. He ignored me. I put my sopping coat on and went after him, stumbling through the matted grass and the peat-haggs. I grabbed him by the sleeve, but he shrugged me off and carried on, more determined than I'd ever seen him before.

A dense fog was coming in off the sea now and I thought that he would be too frightened to go much further. But, despite the grey thickening and the silence that fell upon the place, Hanny went on, taking long strides, jumping across the bogs and pools of water, eventually coming to the remains of an old farmhouse or a barn, it was hard to tell what it had been. Only a few ruined walls remained, roughly forming a rectangle that was littered with other rocks and roof slates. Perhaps people had once lived here. Scavenged from the sea. Worshipped at the chapel and tried to pin God to the island like one of the butterflies in our room at Moorings.

Beneath the sound of Hanny's boots going through the debris I could hear something else. Voices, calls. I tried to make Hanny stop so that I could hear it properly and in the end had to kick away one of his feet so that he fell. He sprawled and the rifle clattered away. He went off on all fours to retrieve it and sat down on a rock to wipe off the mud.

I put my finger to my lips and Hanny stopped what he was doing and looked at me, breathing hard with anger.

"Listen," I said.

The sound of a dog barking came out of the mist, but it was hard to tell where it was coming from or how far away it was. I had no doubt it was Collier's. It was the same harsh barking that I'd heard in the field outside Moorings where the ewe had led her lamb to feed on the new grass.

"Hanny, we need to go back," I said. "We can't let them find us here. And I'm cold. Aren't you cold?"

I had started to shiver. My clothes seemed to be wrapped around my bones.

Hanny looked at me and although a flash of concern passed over his face, he turned and clambered over the broken-down wall he was sitting against without waiting for me. I didn't have the strength to hold him back any more. All I could do was follow him as best I could as his form slipped in and out of the fog.

I eventually caught up with him at the edge of a brook that came gushing milky-white down a gully of rocks and slid away through the limp bracken towards the sea.

Something was wrong.

I touched Hanny on the arm. He was staring straight ahead.

"What is it?" I said and, following his eyes, saw that there was a hare sitting on the other side looking back.

It turned its head to one side, sniffed the air, looked back at us, twitched one of its tall spoon ears, and then bolted just a little too late as a dog emerged from the fog, careered into it and tumbled it over in the mud. The hare kicked with its back legs, once, twice, trying to rake off the jaws that were clamped to its neck, but was limp a second later as the dog thrashed it from side to side and chewed out its throat.

This time I got a firm grip on Hanny's arm and tried to pull him back. If we went there and then I thought we could get away. But he stood rooted to the spot, still looking past me, over my shoulder, not at the hare or the dog but at the two men that had come out of the mist and were standing there watching us.

CHAPTER
TWENTY-FIVE

It was Parkinson and Collier. They were dressed in blue overalls and hard boots caked in mud. Scarves wound around their necks and mouths. Their flat caps dripped with the damp.

Collier had a chain over his shoulder. He lowered his scarf and called the dog to him and when it refused he went over and kicked it off the hare onto its side. He raised his hand to the dog and with a well-practised obedience it whined and cowered and Collier got a hold of its collar so that he could pass the chain through it. Parkinson continued to stare at us, cold breath misting around his face.

The brook cluttered over the rocks and bracken.

Still holding Hanny's arm I started to walk away, but Parkinson moved with an unexpected quickness. He sloshed through the water in a few steps and grabbed the hood of my parka, bringing me to heel like Collier had done with his dog. He turned me to face him and gently rearranged my coat so that it no longer strangled me.

"There's no need for thee to rush off," he said.

He took his hands off me and flicked the wetness from them.

"Hast tha been for a dip?" he said.

He smiled when I didn't respond, amused that I was drenched and shivering. Then he noticed the rifle Hanny was holding and took it off him. Hanny let the rifle slide out of his hands and looked down at his feet.

Parkinson fitted the stock against his shoulder and squinted through the sight.

"Where did you get this from?" he said.

"We found it," I said.

"It's a bit special is this, for a lad like thee," he said, glancing at Hanny.

Collier caught the frown I gave Parkinson.

"He means a retard," said Collier.

Parkinson took the rifle down and pulled back the bolt to open it up. Hanny had loaded it. I could see the top bullet of the clip pressed down inside the receiver.

Now that Parkinson had let go of me, I tried to lead Hanny back the way we'd come, thinking that they might settle for having the rifle off us. But Parkinson quickly held my shoulder again.

"Don't go just yet," he said.

"Everyone will be waiting for us," I said.

"Will they?"

"We're going today."

"Going? Where's tha going?"

"Back home to London."

"London?" he said. "Tha wouldn't make it back across to the mainland, never mind London."

"We can swim," I said, and Collier laughed.

"Nay," said Parkinson with mock concern. "I don't want thee drowned."

"Look," I said. "We're going home today. Do what you like at Moorings. Take what you want from the place. I don't care. No one will care."

It was bravado founded entirely on fear and went as quickly as it had arisen the moment Parkinson laughed and turned to Collier.

"I'm not sure I like that accusation. We're not thieves," he said. "Are we?"

"Nay," said Collier.

The sound of a baby crying came from the direction of the house. The dog looked up. Parkinson and Collier glanced at one another. The crying stopped.

"Here," said Parkinson, serious now. "It's nowt personal. But we can't let thee go. We're going to have to take out some insurance. You understand what I mean, don't you? By insurance?"

I looked at him and he put his hand on my shoulder again.

"It's the way it has to be. There's nowt you or I can do about it. You just fucked up, that's all. Wrong place, wrong time. Come to the house and we'll get everything sorted out."

Leonard was loading his car when we got to Thessaly. Clement was there too, fetching and carrying boxes. When he saw us he stopped and looked at us with — what was it? — pity, guilt?

"Carry on, Clement," said Leonard.

Clement nodded slowly and moved towards the Daimler and slotted the box he was carrying into the back.

Leonard came closer and lit a cigar. Collier's dog started barking loudly and straining on the chain. Leonard looked at Collier and, capitulating, he took out a frayed leather muzzle from his pocket and fitted it around the dog's face.

"You must love it here," said Leonard, turning to us. "You just can't stay away, can you?"

He took a drag on his cigar and looked at Parkinson.

"Are you sure this is necessary?" he said. "In an hour's time there'll be no trace that anyone's ever been here. If I were you, I'd send them back across when the tide goes out and leave it at that. They've already given their word to keep their mouths shut. What the hell are they going to say anyway? They don't know anything."

Parkinson answered him with a stare and Leonard sighed.

"Bring them inside then," he said.

I don't remember either of us trying to run or fight or do anything for that matter. I only remember the smell of the wet ferns, the sound of water churning out of a gutter, the feeling of numbness, knowing that no one was coming to help us and that we were surrounded by those people Father Wilfred had always warned us about but who we never thought we'd face, not really. Those people who existed in the realm of newspaper reports; dispatches from a completely different world where people had no capacity for guilt and trampled on the weak without a second thought.

We went into Thessaly by the back door that led into the empty kitchen we'd seen briefly the first time. On the floor was a metal dish of dog food that smelled as if

318

it had been there for months. Collier's dog nosed at some of the chunks of meat, trying to angle its mouth so that it could eat them through its muzzle.

From somewhere else in the house, the baby cried again. A desperate bawl that petered out into a whimper that seemed resigned to the fact that no one was going to come and give it comfort.

Parkinson opened the door that led out into the hallway.

"Go on," he said with a nod of the head.

I hesitated and felt Hanny's hand in mine. He was shaking.

"It's all right," I said. "We'll go home soon."

Collier let his dog out on the chain a little further. Under the grille of the muzzle it growled from its throat and bent its head to try and nip at our ankles.

"Go on," Parkinson said again.

"It'll be all right, Hanny," I said. "Don't worry."

Once we were in the hallway, Leonard, Parkinson and Collier stopped and looked at the door that led down to the cellar. The door was closed. From the other side came the sound of the baby screaming again. Hanny made kissing movements with his hand.

"What's the matter with him?" said Parkinson.

"He wants to see Else," I said.

"She's not here any more," said Leonard.

"Where is she?"

"How should I know? She's nothing to do with me now. She's not my daughter. Laura took her home yesterday. You don't need to worry about them. They both got paid. Everyone's got what they wanted."

"Apart from you two," said Parkinson.

"We don't want anything," I said. "Just let us go back home."

Leonard looked at Parkinson and then at us.

"If it were up to me," he said. "I'd trust you not to say anything. But I'm afraid Mr Parkinson here thinks otherwise. And as he's the one with the rifle I'd be inclined to trust his judgement."

"You know," Parkinson said to me. "I think that the problem is that tha doesn't believe that we can help him."

He nodded to Collier.

"Tell them what your dog did to your 'and."

Collier held up his hand — he was no longer wearing the black mitten — and drew a line slowly across the back of it with his finger.

"Every fuckin' tendon," he said. "Hanging off in rags it were."

"Five years without work," said Parkinson. "Int that right, Mr Collier?"

"Aye," said Collier. "There's not much call for a one-'anded drayman."

"And now?" Parkinson said.

Collier flexed his hand in and out of a fist and then grabbed hold of Hanny's arm, making him jump. He laughed, enjoyed Parkinson's approving grin, and let go.

"I had a cancer growing in the throat," said Parkinson, pressing a finger to his Adam's apple and then making a star with his hand to show that it had disappeared.

320

He put his arm around Leonard's shoulder.

"And my friend here looks a proper picture of health, dunt he? Not a sign of arthritis."

Leonard looked at me and smiled. I hadn't noticed, but Parkinson was right, Leonard's limp had gone.

"Hanny's fine," I said. "I don't want you to do anything to him."

Parkinson laughed and shook his head. "It's funny, int it?" he said. "How you church people can have more faith in something that can't be proved than something that's standing right in front of you? I suppose it comes down to seeing what you want to see, dunt it? But sometimes tha dunt get a choice. Sometimes the truth comes along whether tha wants it to or not. Int that right, Mr Collier?"

"Aye," he said.

Parkinson nodded and Collier grabbed Hanny's arm again. This time he didn't let go. Hanny struggled. I tried to prise Collier's hand away and was so intent on doing so that I only dimly registered Parkinson moving Leonard aside and taking the rifle down.

The shot brought little coughs of dust down from the ceiling and replaced all other sound with a high-pitched whining in my ears. A spent bullet casing skittered away down the hall and Hanny fell onto his side, clutching his thigh which had burst open all over the floorboards.

Parkinson put the rifle back over his shoulder and nodded at Hanny writhing in silent agony on the floor.

"Now tha'll have to have faith," he said. "Like it or not. Unless tha wants to take him home a cripple as well as a fuckin' retard."

Hearing the gun go off, Clement had come inside and was standing next to Leonard, looking on with horror at what had happened. Leonard noticed him gawping and gave him a nudge.

"Don't just stand there, Clement," he said. "Get him up."

Clement started to back away, but Parkinson pointed the rifle at his chest.

"Hey, tha's not delivered full payment quite yet, Clement."

"Let me go home," Clement pleaded. "I've done everything you've asked for."

"Aye, so far. But tha owes us a few more favours before we're done."

"Mother will be worrying where I am. I can't stay."

"I'm not sure tha's got a great deal of choice int matter, Clement. Not if tha dunt want to end up in Haverigg again. You know we could do it. It were easy enough last time. Tha didn't have the wit to get out of it then and I can't see that tha's found any more since. Moorings goes up in flames. Caretaker seen acting suspiciously by local men. What does tha get for arson these days, Clement?"

Clement looked at him and then knelt down at Hanny's side, rolling him gently onto his back so that he could get an arm under his shoulders. Hanny's face screwed up in pain. He was crying like the Hanny I knew as a little boy, his mouth opening and closing like a beached fish. It might have been the time he fell out of the apple tree in the back garden and broke his wrist, or when he came off his bike and left most of his chin on Hoop Lane. I'd always hated it when he cried. When he cried it meant I hadn't kept him safe. I had failed.

"Here," said Clement and showed me where to put my arm around Hanny's other shoulder.

Hanny opened his eyes and looked at me, completely bewildered, then he sagged and passed out. Between us, Clement and I got him up, snapped him back into consciousness and got him to take his weight on his good leg, while the other bent under him and dragged a trail of blood and fleshstrings along the hallway.

Leonard took a bunch of keys from his pocket and opened the door to the cellar. He went down, shaking them in his hand, turning the baby's cries to screams.

CHAPTER
TWENTY-SIX

It was the first of June and the street outside was breathless and hazy in a prelude to the punishing heat that summer was to bring. Hour by hour the day had been acquiring the tension that comes before a thunderstorm. Everything moved slowly, if it moved at all. The wood pigeons in the plane tree had been quiet and motionless for hours. On the window ledge a bumble bee sat in the sunlight and didn't stir even when I tapped the glass. The next-door neighbour's cats hunted for shade rather than the mice and finches they usually left on our doorstep.

I was revising *Hamlet* for an exam the following day. It was the final one. And once it was over, school would be done for good. Already the place had become different. Things had stopped mattering so much. No one, not even the teachers, seemed to care any more and I could see it for what it was: an intestinal factory line that was winding down at the end of a particular run of production. Though, what it had produced, I wasn't sure. I felt no different to when I started. Only a little soiled from having passed through its bowels.

What I was going to do next, I didn't know. I would be sixteen in a week's time, but the world didn't quite seem as open as I'd thought it might. When I looked at Farther I saw that work and school were really no different. One merely became qualified to pass from one system to the next, that was all. Routine was a fact of life. It was life, in fact.

She was leaving me alone at the moment, but I felt Mummer prowling around me, waiting for the day of my exam results when she could pounce and drag me away to the life she thought I ought to have. It'd be A levels in History, Latin and Religious Education, then a Theology degree before six years in seminary. I could fight back, of course, assert myself, but without knowing what I wanted to do I'd have little chance against her. I'd be like that hare in the mouth of Colliers dog.

Collier. Parkinson. I had thought about them every day since we'd come back from the Loney. It had been two months now but even with it fresh in my mind, as it were, I still wasn't sure what had happened at Thessaly. What they had done to Hanny for him to be able to walk back up the steps of the cellar by himself and then cross the heath, and go running over the sandflats to meet Father Bernard who had come looking for us in the minibus. How they mended his shattered leg down in that cellar.

When we got back to Moorings, I told Mummer what I'd told Father Bernard — that we'd been across to Coldbarrow to look at the birds and that Hanny had slipped on some rocks and torn his trousers open on a sharp corner. The lie came out easily, without any planning, without any guilt, because I didn't know what the truth was anyway.

Mummer didn't ask anything else. She seemed too exhausted with the worry of where we'd been and so drained by the whole trip that she was just glad to be leaving. Everyone quickly loaded their bags onto the minibus and didn't talk. The only sound was that of heavy fruit falling from the apple trees.

Mr and Mrs Belderboss were still keen to watch the beating of the bounds and although everybody else was tired and desperate to get away from the place, they agreed that they would stop at Little Hagby on the way. Yet when we got there, it was deserted. A warm wind blew across the uncut grass that thrummed with insects woken early from their cocoons. The priest was nowhere to be seen. The crowds that had in the past always gathered on the green with sticks of willow and birch ready to mark out the limits of the parish were shut away in their houses. We drove on.

When Hanny went back to Pinelands, I was glad. I didn't like what we'd brought home from the Loney. He had changed. He seemed not to notice I was there. He was distant and uncommunicative, more interested in everything else around him, which he seemed to examine as though he had never seen it before. He had regressed. Whatever they had done to him at Thessaly had reversed all his learning and turned him back into an ignorant child.

Now that he was back for the Whitsun holiday he seemed no different. Still the daft grinning all the time. Still the hours of just sitting and staring. I couldn't stand watching him like this, and had spent most of the time since he'd been back alone in my room. He hadn't come up to see me once.

Mummer and Farther were in denial about it all. They could see that something was wrong, that he had changed, but they made no mention of it. Mummer went back to work at the shop, Farther to his office in town. And neither of them could understand why I was so unhappy, why I couldn't just get on with things. Why did I brood so much?

The sun went in and the day became humid. I opened the window as far as the latch would allow, but still couldn't get any air into the room. I watched a car going down the road. One coming the other way. The postman in his shirt sleeves cycling through the shade of the plane trees.

I went back to *Hamlet* and read to the end of Act One. *The time is out of joint. O cursed spite, that ever I was born to set it right.* Then from downstairs I heard the sound of something smashing on the floor and Mummer crying out. I went down to the kitchen and she turned sharply and looked at me as I came in. Her eyes were wide. Her mouth slightly open. Her lips moving, making bits of words. The remains of her best fruit bowl lay around her feet. She looked back at Hanny who was sitting with his hands flat on the table, a cup of tea in front of him.

"What's the matter?" I said.

But before Mummer could reply Hanny said, "Nothing, brother."

Mummer called Farther and he came home at once, hot and flustered, thinking something terrible had happened. When he heard Hanny speak he cried.

Farther called Mr and Mrs Belderboss. Mr Belderboss called the presbytery and got Miss Bunce. The next-door neighbour came round to see what all the fuss was about and she cried too.

One by one they came and Mummer showed them into the kitchen where Hanny was still sitting. She hadn't let him move in case going into a different room might break the spell. They came in tentatively at first, as though they were sitting down with a lion, and took their turn to be with him and hold his hand and marvel.

Seeing that Mummer was still in shock and unsure of what was happening, Mrs Belderboss patted her hand and said, "It is a miracle, Esther. It ready is."

Mummer looked at her. "Yes," she said.

"What else can we call it?" Mr Belderboss said, smiling. "The Lord has blessed you."

"Yes, He has," said Mummer and clasped Hanny's hands in hers.

"It's like the story in Matthew, isn't it, David?" said Miss Bunce.

"Yes," said David. "Which one?"

"Nine, thirty-two," said Miss Bunce. "When Jesus heals the mute."

"All those prayers we said, Esther," said Mrs Belderboss. "All those years we asked for Andrew to be healed. God was listening all the time."

"Yes," Mummer said, looking into Hanny's eyes.

328

"And the holy water he drank," said Mr Belderboss.

"Oh, yes, the water too," said Mrs Belderboss. "That was the thing that really did it."

"I'm just sorry that Father Wilfred isn't here to see this," said Mummer.

"So am I," said Miss Bunce.

"He'd have been over the moon, wouldn't he, Reg?" said Mrs Belderboss.

Mr Belderboss was smiling and wiping away tears from his eyes.

"Whatever's the matter, Reg?" Mrs Belderboss said and got up to comfort him.

"I can feel him. Can't you feel him, Mary?"

"Yes," said Mrs Belderboss. "I can."

"God bless you, Andrew," said Mr Belderboss, reaching across the table and taking Hanny's hands. "It's you that's brought him here. He's with us now."

Hanny smiled. Mrs Belderboss crossed herself and began to pray. Everyone in the room joined hands and repeated the Our Father until the doorbell rang.

Father Bernard had been out on his rounds of the parish and had only found the note left by Miss Bunce on his return to the presbytery. I saw his form through the frosted glass of the front door as he rang the bell again and waited. When I opened it, he smiled, though he looked — how was it? — a little nervous, a little short-tempered even. I hadn't seen him look like that before.

"Hello, Tonto," he said. "How are you?"

"Fine, Father."

Farther came into the hallway and reached over my shoulder and shook Father Bernard's hand.

"Something wonderful's happened, Father," he said.

"So I hear, Mr Smith."

"He's in the kitchen."

Everyone stopped talking when Father Bernard came in. They all looked to him to verify the miracle, so that it could be theirs to enjoy properly.

"Father," said Mummer.

"Mrs Smith," Father Bernard replied.

The tension between them still hadn't quite dissipated in the months since we'd returned from Moorings.

"Well," said Farther, sitting down next to Hanny and putting his arm around him. "Aren't you going to say hello to Father Bernard?"

Hanny stood up and put out his hand. "Hello, Father," he said.

Word got around and before long the house was full of people. So many came that the front door was left propped open with a telephone directory.

The hesitancy that had been there earlier, when everyone had been worried that Hanny's speech might disappear as suddenly as it had come, was forgotten now. Hanny had been restored and they let themselves go in the praising of God. They sang around the piano and laughed like children.

Mummer took Hanny from person to person, showing off the gift that had been bestowed upon her, upon all of us. They passed Hanny amongst themselves like a chalice, everyone intoxicated by him. Everyone except Father Bernard who sat alone watching, a paper plate balanced on his knee, chewing the sandwiches I had helped Mummer to quickly prepare.

When I passed him with a tray of empty cups, he said, "Could I talk to you, Tonto?"

We went outside into the garden, where a few other people from church were standing about smoking and admiring Farthers dahlias. Father Bernard said hello to them and then we walked down to the end where there was a bench under the apple trees.

We sat for a minute listening to the swifts in the wasteground on the other side of the tube line and saw their black arrowheads whip through the garden now and then for the insects dancing over the greenhouses.

Father Bernard sat down and loosened his collar. The heat was making him sweat and there were rings of dried salt under the arms of his black shirt.

"So, now you know what a miracle looks like, eh Tonto?" he said, looking back towards the house.

"Yes, Father."

"Quite a thing, isn't it?"

"Yes, Father."

"How is he? Andrew?"

"I don't know."

"I mean how does he seem?"

"All right, I suppose. Happy."

He wafted away a bee that had droned towards him from the apple tree.

"What happened?" he said.

"How do you mean, Father?"

"You know what I mean."

"God cured him," I said. "Like in Matthew. Nine thirty-two."

He looked at me and frowned.

"When Jesus heals the mute," I said.

"Aye, I do know the story, Tonto."

"Well, that's what happened to Hanny, Father."

"Aye, but do you know the ending?"

"No, Father."

"You look it up then, Tonto. I have to say I'm with the Pharisees."

"How do you mean, Father?"

He set his eyes firmly on mine.

"Look, something happened to you and Andrew there at that house on Coldbarrow, and it wasn't anything to do with God."

I looked at him and then back at the house.

"Why did you go there?" he said. "I thought we'd agreed to steer well clear of the place."

"Hanny wanted to see the birds," I said.

He knew I was lying and couldn't conceal a look of hurt or even anger before he spoke softly again.

"Tonto," he said, edging forward. "If you've got yourself mixed up into something that you shouldn't have, I can help you, you know? You mustn't be afraid to tell me."

"There's nothing to tell," I replied.

"I don't mean the nonsense that Clement was talking about. There are certain tricks," he said, "that clever people can pull to make you believe all kinds of things."

"Hypnotists?"

"Not that exactly, but something like that. Whatever it is, it's not real, Tonto. It doesn't last. And I'd hate for all this happiness to be ruined."

"Is that what you think happened to Hanny? That he was hypnotised?"

"Of course not. But you give me a better answer."

"I don't know what to tell you, Father."

There was a sudden burst of laughter and we both looked. Hanny was outside now and trying to talk to the churchwardens who were sitting on the bench next to the greenhouse, but a gang of children were dragging him away to play football. Eventually, the children won and Hanny began dribbling the ball around the garden with them all chasing and harrying, trying to dig it out from his feet.

"*Can't* they believe it was God?" I said.

"You mean *let* them believe?" Father Bernard replied.

"Yes."

"That's called lying, Tonto."

"Or faith, Father."

"Don't be a smart arse."

He looked at me and then we turned to watch everyone up at the house. There was music drifting outside. Mr Belderboss was playing his harmonica. Mummer was dancing with Farther. I don't think I'd ever seen her so giddy with happiness, so much like she ought to be at her age. She wasn't quite forty.

When I think of Mummer and Farther now, I think of them that afternoon, her hands on his shoulders, his hands on her waist. I see the hem of Mummer's skirt playing about her thin ankles. She is wearing those shoes with the cork heels. Farther has his sleeves rolled up, his glasses in his shut pocket.

Mummer cried out and smacked Farther playfully on the arm as he dipped her.

"There's a different woman," said Father Bernard.

"Yes."

"It suits her."

"Yes. It does."

He looked down at his hands.

"I'm going be leaving soon," he said.

"Do you have to go back to the presbytery?"

"I mean the parish, Tonto."

"The parish? Why, Father?"

"I've decided to go back to Belfast. The bishop's not going to be all that enamoured, but I think it's best if I do. I'm not sure how much more I can do here. Not now, anyway."

"You can't leave," I said. "Who will we get instead?"

He smiled and gave me a sideways look. "I don't know, Tonto. Somebody."

He breathed out heavily

"Ah, look, I don't want to go," he said. "But I'm not what they want, or what they need. I'm no Wilfred Belderboss, am I?"

He bent down and picked up a fallen apple that lay by his feet. It was full of cinder-coloured holes where the wasps had chewed it. He turned it in his hand and tossed it into the long grass by the fence.

I thought for a moment, then said, "Father, will you wait here?"

"Aye," he said and sat back while I went over to the potting shed.

It was warm inside. A smell of old soil and creosote. Farther's tools hung up on rusty nails and above them at the back of some old cracked pots that he was always meaning to glue back together was a plastic bag under a seed tray. I brought it down and took it to where Father Bernard was waiting with one arm over the back of the bench, watching everyone milling around up at the house.

"What's this?" he said.

"I think you need to read it, Father."

He looked at me and took out the book that was in the bag. He opened it and then quickly shut it again.

"This is Father Wilfred's diary," he said, holding it out for me to take back. "You told me you didn't know where this was."

"I was keeping it safe."

"You mean you stole it."

"I didn't steal it, Father. I found it."

"Take it away, Tonto. Get rid of it."

"I want you to read it," I said. "I want you to know what happened to Father Wilfred. Then you might see that they're all wrong about him. That he wasn't ever the man they thought he was."

"What are you on about?"

"He stopped believing, Father. Here's the proof."

"I'm not going to read another man's diary, Tonto," he said. "And I'm surprised you have."

"It doesn't matter now," I said.

"All the more reason to let him be."

"Please, Father. Then they might stop comparing you with him."

He sighed, read for a half a minute and then closed his eyes.

"You need to read it all, Father," I said.

"I've read enough, Tonto."

"And?"

"And what? Look," he said. "This isn't going to change anything. I think everyone suspects that Father Wilfred stopped believing in God. If they choose to ignore it then there's not much I can do."

"Do you think he killed himself, Father?"

"Tonto . . ."

"Personally?"

"You know I can't answer that question."

"But you must have an opinion."

"It was an accidental death."

"But is that what you think?"

He put his fist under his nose and breathed in as he thought.

"If they recorded it as an accidental death, Tonto, that's how it was. And it's how it needs to stay if the rumours are to be kept to a minimum. Look, I know people will talk, and that's inevitable, but no one's going to beat their fists on a closed door forever. Sooner or later they'll just accept that he's gone. It won't matter how or why."

"But that's the truth in there, Father." I nodded to the book. "Oughtn't people to know what he was really like? Shouldn't Mr Belderboss know?"

Father Bernard brandished the book at me.

"And what would he know by reading this? How could the ramblings of some poor devil who's clearly lost his mind ever be anything to do with the truth? The best thing you can do is put it on the fire. I'm serious, Tonto. Wrap it in newspaper and burn the bloody thing."

"And leave Mr Belderboss in the dark?"

"And leave him happy. You saw him inside. He's certain his brother's in blissful peace. Why the hell would you want to try and convince him otherwise?"

He calmed his voice and then spoke again.

"Tonto, the truth isn't always set in stone. In fact it never is. There are just versions of it. And sometimes it's prudent to be selective about the version you choose to give to people."

"But that's lying, Father. You said so yourself."

"Then I was being as naive as you. Listen, I do have a bit of experience in these things. It's why I was sent to Saint Jude's in the first place."

"Experience of what?"

"Managing the truth. You see, that's what your mother didn't understand about me. I wasn't trying to expose anything about Wilfred, I was trying to help them keep the rumours on a short leash. But I couldn't do that if everyone was determined that I should be kept in the dark, could I?"

"Then you do think he killed himself?"

He thought for a moment.

"You remember you once asked me what Belfast was like?"

"Yes, Father."

"Well, I'll tell you. It's like an ants' nest," he said. "An ants' nest that's always being rattled with a stick. People scurry here and then they scurry there. Then the stick comes out again and everything changes.

"The Protestants move out of the Bone to Ballysillan and the Catholics in Ballysillan move back to the Bone. There are too many Catholics in the Bone but they'd rather sleep two to a bed than live in a Protestant street where there are empty houses. So they go across the Oldpark Road to Ballybone and the Protestants in Ballybone go back to the houses that the Catholics wouldn't take. And on the roads that are the fault lines between the estates, they pack up all their stuff, cross the road, swap houses and shout at each other from the other side of the street instead. A street that's probably changed its name half a dozen times, mind you. It's madness."

"What *is* the Bone, Father?"

It was strange, he'd mentioned the place so many times, and I'd never asked him where it was.

He made a rough shape with his fingers, something like a pentagram.

"Flax Street, Hooker Street, Chatham, Oakfield and Crumlin. But that's just my opinion. Ask someone else and they'd give you a different answer. No one knows where the hell they are in Belfast half the time."

He looked at me and when it was clear I didn't really understand what he was saying, he sighed and laughed a little.

"See," he said. "When you're a priest, you hear all kinds of things. And when you're a priest in Belfast you

338

get told all kinds of things. And when you're a priest in the Ardoyne you wish you didn't know anything. There's always rumours flying around about who's done what to whom and why. Who's an informer. Who's with the Provos. Who's not. Whose son's in the jail. Whose daddy keeps a pistol under his pillow. Who's your friend. Who's your enemy. And they'd look to me to give them the right answer. And that's the trick, Tonto. Making them believe that you know what the right answer is. God knows if I'd been honest about what I knew, the whole place would have gone up in flames. They shouldn't call us priests. Not when we're really firemen."

He looked back to Mummer and Farther and the others.

"I'm sure they know that you were only trying to help them," I said.

"Maybe, but it doesn't look as though they need it any more. I don't suppose anyone's going to think badly of Wilfred now this has happened."

"No?"

"You saw them in the kitchen, Tonto. He's come back and blessed them all. I don't think they really care how he died."

They couldn't say for certain. It may have been the loose handrail — after all it had come apart in the young policeman's hand when they'd gone up to the belfry. It might have been a simple misjudgement of the first step in the gloom — the bulb over the top of the stairs had blown. It might have been the old floorboards that had warped away from the joists. It might have been all three. It might have been none of these things. The only thing that seemed obvious, or easiest, was that it was a tragic accident.

While it was still dark, there was a phone call from Mrs Belderboss, and even before Mummer had finished speaking to her I knew that Father Wilfred was dead.

Everyone was at the church, she said. Something terrible had happened.

Mummer and Farther and I went and joined the group of people gathered around the doors in the snow. They had taken Father Wilfred away in an ambulance and there was no real reason for us to stand there. But no one knew what else to do.

A policeman was on the steps preventing anyone from going inside. He tried to look intimidating and sympathetic at the same time. A police car was parked at the side of the presbytery. I saw Miss Bunce sitting in the back seat with a policewoman. She was nodding and dabbing her eyes with a tissue.

"Poor Joan," one of the cleaning ladies said. "Finding him like that."

Mummer nodded with as much compassion as she could muster, but I knew she was put out by all the attention that was being lavished on Miss Bunce. And for what? The silly girl had gone to pieces.

She had come as usual at breakfast time and, worried that he was nowhere to be seen in the presbytery and that his bed was cold and unused, Miss Bunce had gone looking for Father Wilfred in the church. She searched the vestry and the sacristy and as she made for the book cupboard by the main doors — thinking his recent obsession for tidying and cataloguing might have taken him there — she came across him almost by accident at the foot of the belfry stairs. He was staring up at her, his head broken on the edge of the bottom step and an old sword lying a few feet away from his outstretched hand.

It was an open and shut case. It was, as they had first thought, an accidental death. An elderly priest had tripped and fallen. The sword? Had he been trying to defend himself against an intruder? There was no evidence of anyone else having been there. The church was locked from the inside. But then there was the bell that people had heard tolling around midnight. It was strange, certainly, but they had no grounds on which they could grant it any significance. Bells were often rung in churches. The sword and the bells proved nothing and were dismissed. They led nowhere useful.

The funeral took place the day the winter snow began to thaw. The parish turned out in black and stood under the dripping trees in the Great Northern Cemetery before heading back to the wake at the social centre.

Nobody stayed very long. Miss Bunce couldn't bring herself to eat anything. Mr and Mrs McCullough sat by the cardboard crib the Sunday School children had made, giving Henry accusatory looks between mouthfuls of pork pie, as though they suspected it was all his fault in some way. And the Belderbosses were worn out with the endless condolences offered by the other churchgoers who had turned up to pay their respects — not quite as grief-stricken as they but nervous and bewildered all the same about the ripple that had been sent across their pond. What would become of Saint Jude's now?

They shook Mr Belderboss's hand and kissed Mrs Belderboss on the cheek and went off to sit in huddles in their coats, eating their sandwiches quickly and letting their drinks go flat.

In the end, Mummer, Farther and I were the only ones left, and uncertain what else we could do, we started to clear away the plates of uneaten sandwiches and half-empty glasses of beer. Once the tables had been wiped clean, Mummer draped the dishcloth over the tap in the kitchen, Farther switched off the lights and we went out into the slush. It seemed an absurd ending to a life.

While the bishop was arranging Father Wilfred's replacement an ancient priest came to Saint Jude's for a few weeks to plug the gap. He was functional and nondescript. I can't even remember his name. Michael. Malcolm. Something like that. He had no responsibility other than to take Mass and receive confession, and perhaps feeling a little insignificant because of this he took his role as caretaker rather literally, sending us altar boys out to weed the beds in the presbytery garden or touch up the paint in the vestry.

After Mass one Sunday, he dispatched me to the belfry to check that there were no pigeons nesting there. He had had a great deal of bother with pigeons nesting in the belfry at a church in Gravesend, he said. Their muck played merry hell with the mortar on these old buildings. If pigeons were found, he would have to inform the bell-ringers to ring Erin Triples. Only Erin Triples would shift them. He was quite mad.

The belfry stairs had been made safe. The handrail had been replaced and a new bulb screwed into the light fitting. A heavy rug had been thrown down over the buckled floorboards while they waited on a carpenter.

There were no birds nesting there, of course. It was completely silent. The beds hung motionless in their frame. I went to look out through the small grimy window that faced south for the light. It was February. The snow had been washed away by the rain and the streets all around were slick with it. It being Sunday, the roads below were quiet. A car would occasionally go down the street with its lights on but that was all. Beyond, there were other streets, houses, low-rise flats, belts of diffused greenery and then the grey monoliths of the taller buddings in the city. I was struck by the sudden thought that my future lay amongst all that somewhere.

I was about to go back down when I noticed the stack of colour in the corner. Father Wilfred's robes. The purple that he wore at Lent, the red for Pentecost, the workaday green, and the white he had latterly put on for Christmas. The police hadn't noticed them. I suppose they looked like the kind of junk that ended up in belfries, which were only really loud attics when all said and done. But the robes hadn't been dumped. They had been neatly folded, the creases smoothed away. His crucifix was lying on the top along with his Bible and his white collar. And his diary.

CHAPTER
TWENTY-SEVEN

Everyone was starting to go inside the house. Farther came down the path to where Father Bernard and I were sitting.

"Will you come, Father?" he said. "Andrew's going to read for us."

"Aye, of course, Mr Smith," Father Bernard replied.

"Isn't it wonderful?" said Farther and shook Father Bernard's hand again before he went back to the house.

A train rushed past, leaving a skirl of litter and dust, and then the rails returned to their bright humming. In the scrubland beyond, the swifts were darting over the tufts of grass and the hard-baked soil with its beetroot-coloured weeds. We watched them turning on their hairpins deftly as bats.

"You will get rid of that book, won't you, Tonto?" said Father Bernard.

"Yes, Father."

"Then we'd be all square, won't we?"

"Yes, Father."

"We'd better go," he said and waved back to Farther who was beckoning us to hurry.

★   ★   ★

I knew that Father Bernard was right and that I ought to get rid of the diary for Mr Belderboss's sake, but I didn't, and I never have.

I've read it so many times that it has become inked onto my brain like a well-known fairy tale, especially the day that everything changed for him.

It began like any other at Moorings. There was the usual carnival of weather. The gathering for prayers in the sitting room. The various shades of gloom moving about the house like extra guests. But after supper, an unexpected burst of evening sunshine had drawn him out of the house and he had been taken by a sudden urge to go down to the sea.

For a number of reasons, he noted, he had never been there before. He had always been rather put off by the local stories about the vagaries of the tides, and in any case, to reach the sea meant traversing the marshland by a road that seemed to be barely there, inundated as it was by overspill from the rain-swollen pools. And when he got to the shoreline, what would he find? Surely there would be little of interest. Only sludge and what the sea had left behind. He feared it would be a waste of time, which led him to consider the other main reason why he had never gone. Time was his gift to his parishioners when they stayed at Moorings and it wouldn't be fair of him to take it back. It was important that he was on call, so to speak.

But, the compulsion to go to the sea wouldn't leave him. It felt as strong as any demand he had ever had from God. There was no option, then, but to put on his coat, take his notebook and go and answer Him. It was, he supposed, the mere fact that he had never been there before that made the call so powerful. For wasn't it the responsibility of Christians to seek, to move forward, to be missionaries? Not to take God with them to new lands like a trading commodity, but to make Him manifest there. To raise Him out of the land. God was already everywhere. People needed only to notice Him.

He was sure that God would walk with him on the sand, give him His guidance and explain the lessons he needed to take back to Saint Jude's. He would tell him what he needed to put into the spiritual alms boxes of those who hadn't been able to come on the pilgrimage and had missed out on the special attention God had conferred upon those who had made the effort. Surely for the good of the parish, his fellow pilgrims wouldn't begrudge him an hour alone. They would understand the importance.

He thought of himself as a shepherd in one of those pre-Raphaelite paintings, drowsing under the dapple of an ancient tree, his thoughts taken away by the flowers and the dancing insects to higher things or nothing. His sheep down the hillside out of his immediate protection but safe enough to roam the pastures for a time unattended. Yes, they would understand.

But if it was God's will that he should go to the sea, what was that apprehension that still dogged him as he started off across the marsh road? It was the feeling that he had disturbed something. The growing unease that the marshes were somehow aware of his presence. It was, he wrote, a dark and watchful place that seemed to have become adept at keeping grim secrets; secrets that were half heard in the whispered shibboleths that passed from one bank of dry reeds to the other.

It reminded him of an illustration of the Styx in the book of Greek history and legend he had had as a boy — his only book, fatter than the family Bible on the mantelpiece. And what stories he had found between the pasteboard covers. Perseus, Theseus, Icarus. What about Xerxes the Persian king, who had tried to bridge the Hellespont in order to crush the Greeks? Or Narcissus, kneeling by his woodland pool? Or Charon, the pilot of Hades? He would have felt at home here, old Charon. Drifting through the marshes in his coracle.

He inspected his feelings again — that was, after all, why he had come — and found that he was not actually afraid, nor was he really apprehensive. It was more a nervous excitement. Whatever lay in wait here, watching him, was nothing so malevolent. It was evidence of God. He scribbled down a quote from Psalms that came to mind: *Let the heavens be glad, and let the earth rejoice; let the sea roar, and all that fills it.*

There was nothing here that should make him wary, only glad. This corner of England was theirs, something they alone had discovered and had been blessed in the finding. In the springtime God was in the wheat fields and the pasturelands; He was in the rain and in the sunlight that followed and glossed every dripping leaf and branch. He was in the cry of the lambs and in the little cups of life the swifts built in the eaves of old barns. And down here on the beach, even though it was bleak and deserted, God was still at work. Here was the wild God who made nature heave and bellow. The violent shadow that followed Jesus through his tender ministry and could test men in an instant with water and wind. But if the weather should turn, there was nothing to be afraid of. There would be a goodness in His purging. A better world made from the wreck of the old.

Once he realised this, the marshes seemed to let down their guard. He noted the birds that he would not normally have seen up at Moorings, and never in London. Coots. Shelducks. An egret, brilliantly white, dipping for the water snails he had seen clinging to the bullrushes.

Further out over the marsh, he saw a cuckoo being mobbed by a squabble of little brown birds. Reed buntings, most likely. He had read that cuckoos liked to use their nests most of all for their arch deception, secluded as they were and woven so beautifully into soft chalices that kept the eggs from the worst of the weather.

As it turned out, the road was not nearly so flooded as it had looked from the house. The water had only washed across the surface and it was clear and still, like a thin mirror reflecting the icy horseheads of cumulus above him, their edges crisp against the blue. If he stood still long enough, he observed, one had the sensation of looking down into the sky, with infinity under one's feet. A strange sense of vertigo that he disturbed after a moment by breaking the puddle with his toe and moving on.

The shadow cast by the dunes was lengthening and he found himself walking in shade well before the tarmac give way to sand.

There must be something about sand that invites a person to put themselves directly into contact with it. To walk on it in boots or shoes seems a waste almost. He saw fit anyway to make a note of the fact that he had taken off his shoes and turned up the bottoms of his trousers.

Picking a route that wound through the sprouts of marram grass, he climbed up the slope, feeling the wonderful collapse of it under his feet. The burn it put into his thighs. The coldness of the sand when he broke the surface. He was seventy-three years old, but he felt like a child again.

When he reached the top, he was quite worn out with the effort and stood catching his breath and taking in the panorama. He recalled the instruction given to him years before by his tutor at Saint Edmund's College — a keen amateur naturalist, like him.

"Look first," he had told him. "And then see. Be patient and you will notice the workings of nature that most people miss."

It was a piece of advice that he had taken as it was meant — as a metaphor for focusing on the interdependencies of God's world, yes, but also one that he could apply practically in his role as a priest.

He had learnt to watch his parishioners closely, to monitor their progression through the sacraments so that he was better able to correct any deviation from the road that would lead them to heaven. It was his duty. It was the fulfilment of his calling. Their road was his road also. If they found peace at last, then so would he.

He watched and waited and began to see the way the grass moved in the wind, the way the wind came with all the subtleties of a voice. He started to see how the colours of the sea changed as light followed shadow across its vast surface. Turquoise, cobalt, slate, steel. It was quite beautiful. As was the natural geometry of the horizon as it bisected the sea and the sky and invited the eye to be drawn along its length — from the distant industry spiking out of the Fylde peninsula to the south, across to Coldbarrow with its empty heath and its empty house — across to the Furness shipyards faint and grey.

There were the genteel seaside towns full of white houses further away up the coast, and beyond them the Cumbrian mountains rose in severe crags that bared their teeth in the lowering sun.

It was the gulls that made him look back to the beach. He hadn't noticed their noise before. In fact he hadn't been aware of them at all. He had startled them away, perhaps, as he blundered up the sand dune and now that he had been standing there for a few minutes and they knew he was no threat they had returned to feed on the stuff that had rolled in with the seaweed and driftwood and marked the stretch of the tide. It was going out now. Little by little. With each break and foam and hiss it lost its grip on the land and slipped further back. It had been a high tide, he noticed. It had come as far as the old pillbox and left a skirt of wetness around its base.

They were stupid creatures, seagulls. There was something vile about them. As there was with brattish children. The way they screeched and fought over the same scraps, even though the place was an embarrassment of riches.

They were like the people who lived in that esurient underworld, from which he had separated Saint Jude's and its congregation successfully enough for it to seem a place of vivid contrast. The people of that Other world were not the same. They walked in darkness. They were to be pitied. And shunned, if they would not change.

He carried no guilt about such defensiveness. In Romans, Paul talked about associating with the lowly, but it seemed like idealistic nonsense now. Paul's world had gone for good and had been replaced by a vacuum. The sinful no longer worried that they would be punished by God, because God to them did not exist. And how could they be punished by an absence? Wrath and fury, when they came, were no longer attributed to any kind of divine retribution but to natural freakishness and bad luck — and so it was up to him to interpret and judge the world as it truly was. Not to play God — never to do that — but to make it clear for his parishioners by drawing divisions between their world and the Other that God was still present and in authority.

In their world, cause and effect continued. If they sinned, they confessed and were absolved. If they performed good deeds they would be rewarded in heaven. In the Other world there was nothing but inconsequence. Oh, there were people jailed and so on — he had, in his younger days visited them all: rapists and murderers and incorrigible thieves — but for most it was only a temporary withdrawal of their liberty. They cared little, if at all, about their eternal freedom or incarceration. A manila file of forms in an office somewhere to be pulled out at the next offence was the only legacy of their sins. No heed did they pay to the entry that had been added to the greater book of reckoning.

It had been Paul's decree that neighbour should love neighbour and this he stuck to — but only within the world he had created at Saint Jude's. The people of the Other world would care little if he loved them or not, if he rejoiced with them or wept with them or pitied them. Paul had warned of the dangers of judging others — that only God was fit for the task — but those in the Other world needed to be shown up for what they were. And he felt qualified to judge them; they had made it easy for him to do so. Despite what Paul said, his sins — such as they were — were not like theirs. Their sins came from a greater depth entirely.

He had never left a child to die in its own filth as a mother had done in one of the high-rise estates not long ago. He had never poured petrol through a pensioner's letterbox and tossed in a match for fun. He had never come stumbling out of a vice club at four in the morning. He had never stolen anything, destroyed anything. Nor had any of his flock. He had never lusted after anything or anyone, as people in that Other world seemed to encourage and applaud.

He knew what such people would think of his relationship with Miss Bunce. She couldn't be his housekeeper without being his lover also. It was impossible that he would have no carnal desire for her, she being so much younger than he and at his beck and call. He loved her, yes, but not in the way that the Other people understood it, for whom love could not be separated from intercourse.

Galatians, Ephesians, Peter and John. He could have picked a weapon from a vast arsenal to defend himself and show them that it was possible, an act of devotion in fact, to express God's love in the loving of a brother or sister in Christ.

She was the most pious girl he knew. She was a beacon of light in the presbytery. She was untainted by the world that lay outside, and the proof that he had made a difference.

Indeed, all his parishioners deserved to feel like Miss Bunce. Different, loved, guided and judged. It was their reward for being held to ransom by a world that demanded the right to engage in moral brinkmanship whenever it pleased.

People talked about a permissive society, but, as he knew it, permission was something one asked for. No, this was what it was — an assault. They were being beaten into submission by morals that were the reverse of their own. He had lived a long time and had seen the world regressing. With each year that went by it seemed that people were no better than children in their petulant demands.

And children themselves were changing. Youth still had the natural rebelliousness that had been there since the time of Moses, but it seemed to have had something added to it, or forced into it — a fearlessness. No, more a detachment. He had seen it in the youngsters he had caught one evening smashing gravestones with bricks they had knocked out of the churchyard wall, a kind of emptiness in their eyes. They had looked at him as though he wasn't quite real, or what he was saying wasn't quite real. They had been no more than eight years old.

These weren't just the jittery fears of an ageing priest, it was a genuine feeling that all goodness and simple humility — for who on earth was humble nowadays? — had been excised from the hearts of men. He alone, it seemed, had noticed the apparent descent from depravity to depravity that had taken that Other world to a place that was unique and irreversible. There was no darkness now that couldn't be explored or expressed.

Only a few weeks ago had he watched them all coming out of the Curzon at midnight from some horror film that the paper said involved jack hammers and acid. They were laughing. The girls with their hands in the back pockets of the men.

It had been the same night a homeless lady had been kicked to death under Waterloo Bridge. And while the two things weren't connected in any literal sense, he felt certain that they occupied the same pool that had formed when the wall between sick imagination and the real world came down.

It was against this potent mixture that they protected themselves at Saint Jude's and could, ironically, practise the very freedoms the Other people claimed to enjoy, the freedoms that were bandied around as being somehow the looked-for end result of millennia of social cultivation. At Saint Jude's they were free to think; they were free to examine the meanings of love or happiness, unlike the Other people, for whom happiness was the accumulation of objects and experiences that satisfied the simplest of desires.

The Other world had equality now, they said, but what they meant was that everyone had the means to exhibit their own particular unpleasantness. There had been people shot dead in Londonderry and women blown to shreds in Aldershot in the name of equality. And they were always marching. He had seen men marching for the right to sleep with other men. He had seen women marching for the right to rid themselves of their unborn children without reproach. He had seen them marching to Trafalgar Square with their heavy boots and their Union Jacks. Oh, the black shirts might have been hidden under suits and donkey jackets but they were the same men who had infected the place where he had grown up.

Equality. It was laughable. It wasn't equality at all. Not what he understood by the word. Only in the eyes of God were people equal. In the eyes of God each person had the same opportunity to be rewarded with everlasting peace, even the most hardened sinners.

They could all walk the same path together if the people of the Other world would only repent. But they never would.

He detested leaving Saint Jude's or the presbytery and dreaded any meeting that would necessitate the use of the tube, which at rush hour really did seem to be a place from Hell.

The only way to cope was to think of himself as Dante, documenting evidence of this Other world's iniquities to share with his flock on his return. That way as he was swept along in its currents, he might lift himself out of the tide of filth that pressed up against the doors of the train, the way the gulls were pressing against one another now to get at whatever it was that had become such a prized catch.

At first it was an old fishing net rolled up by the sea into a cocoon; no, a beached seal, he decided, when a gull lifted off and he caught a glimpse of pale skin.

But then he saw the boots tumbling in the edge of the water.

He went down the dune, slipping and almost falling, grasping the marram and feeling it hold firm for a moment before it came loose in his hand. At the bottom he took his shoes from around his neck and started across the sand, running for the first time in years, shouting and waving his hands, scattering the gulls.

It was as he had feared. The man was drowned. The thought that he might yet be saved had crossed his mind as he ran towards him, but it was far too late for that. The gulls had pecked deep holes in his neck and slit the tattoos there, but had drawn no blood.

The man's hair was half covering his face, but when he knelt down and bent his head close to the sand he could see that it was the old tramp they had been talking about at the dinner table. The wretch he had seen asleep in bus shelters and leaning against the gates of cattle fields, his body limp with drink, his eyes slow to follow what was passing. Well, now his eyes were as blank as mushrooms.

A fresh wave broke and surged up the beach and washed under the body, leaving little bubbles in the tramp's hair and in his beard as it ebbed away.

Dying was so easy. A brief, salty sousing and it was done.

The next wave came soon after and as it retreated again the sand gave way and broke into little runnels, the grains pouring down into the gouges.

He looked around, but there was no use in calling for help. Not here. There was no one. He thought about going back up the dune and waving his arms to try and attract their attention back at Moorings, but it was unlikely they would see him. He would seem a tiny figure to them, obscured to shadow by the sun. And if they did see him what would they think? Would they come? If they came, what use would they be? There was nothing they could do now. And was it fair to compel them to see what he had found? The women especially. It would cast a shadow over the whole trip.

Faster and faster the sand was liquefying around the tramp's body, running away from under him and making him turn slowly on to his side. A larger crack appeared, running out of the top of his head to where Father Wilfred was kneeling. The water filled it on the next wave and widened it so that a great cake of sand broke and the body suddenly rolled and fed and floated. He hadn't realised it until now, but the tramp had been lying at the very edge of a deep trench.

What made him reach out and grab the shirt, he wasn't sure. It was instinctive, he supposed. He caught a sleeve and taking it firmly in his grip he dragged the body towards him, feeling for the first time — and with a shock that made him take hold with his other hand as well — the strength of the sea as it was pulling away from the land.

As the water in the trench lowered, the walls became apparent. They were made of a grey substance that was neither sand nor mud. He slipped down, dug in his feet, and slipped further. The outgoing water was moving apace, its speed increasing as it neared the narrowing bottom of the gulley, where he now found himself up to his knees. A section under his foot gave way and disappeared and he fell and ran the side of his face down the wall, tasting the gritty sulphur of the sludge. He let go, floundered, felt the water sucking him, tried to regain his grip, but the body was hurried away. He pushed himself upright and waded after the body a few paces before it was clear that it was pointless and although it was washed back towards him a few times as the tide engaged in its last ebb and flow, it was with the same mockery as a child who holds out a ball for its playmate only to snatch it away. Eventually the body sank out of sight.

He got out of the water and went up the beach and crossed the line of weed. He leant against the pillbox and wiped the mess off his face and stared at the sea, wondering if anything might reappear. But already it seemed that what had happened was unreal. That only minutes before he had been clinging to the sleeve of a corpse. There was no evidence of the old tramp at all now. Even his boots had gone.

It was shock, he supposed, the cold that was making him shiver, but he was terrified. He had almost been dragged into the sea, yes, but it wasn't the sea that he was afraid of.

He felt alone.

More alone than he had ever felt in his life. It was a kind of nakedness, an instant disrobing. His skin prickled. A cold eel slithered in his stomach. Feelings that he thought he had left behind in childhood on those nights he had cried himself to sleep over another dead brother or sister surfaced and spread and overwhelmed him.

Was it pity? No, he felt nothing for the tramp. He was from the Other world and had got what he deserved. Wasn't that so?

Why, then, did he feel so altered? So abandoned?

It was the place itself.

What was it about this place?

And then it came to him.

He had been wrong about everything.

God was missing. He had never been here. And if He had never been here, in this their special place, then He was nowhere at all.

He tried to dismiss the thought as quickly as it had come, but it returned immediately and with more insistence as he stood there watching the gulls flocking for the crustaceans left behind, and the clouds slowly knotting into new shapes, and the parasites swarming in the carcass of some thing.

It was all just machinery.

Here there was only existence coming and going with an indifference that left him cold. Life here arose of its own accord and for no particular reason. It went unexamined, and died unremembered.

He had fought with the sea for the dead drunk's body with the same futility with which Xerxes had flogged the Dardanelles with chains. The sea had no concept of quarrel or possession — he had only been a witness to its power. He had been shown the perfect religion. One that required no faith. Nor were there any parables to communicate its lessons, because there were none to be taught. Only this: that death was blank. Not a doorway, but a wall, against which the whole human race was mounded like jetsam.

He felt like a drowning man himself, flailing about for something to hold on to. Just one thing that might help him stay afloat a little longer, even if it was bound to sink in the end.

After what seemed like an age, he put on his shoes, and walked for an hour back and forth, as the dusk settled, from one end of the beach to the other, searching the dunes, the rock pools, the deep channels.

Finding nothing.

CHAPTER
TWENTY-EIGHT

Mummer had corralled everyone into the sitting room to listen to Hanny read. The elderly folk sat on the sofa. The rest stood behind them. The armchair that Father Bernard had been given that rainy night when we'd first decided to go back to Moorings, was now set out for Hanny instead. He sat down and Mummer kissed his face and handed him our Bible.

Hanny smiled and looked around the room. He opened the Bible and Mummer knelt down at his side.

"There," she said, turning a few pages and pointing.

Hanny looked around at everyone again. They were all waiting for him to begin.

He stared down and put his finger on the page and began to read. It was from the end of Mark — the passage that Father Wilfred often branded onto our mortal souls as we sat in the vestry after Mass.

The disciples had refused to believe that Jesus had risen from the dead, but we were not to be like them. We could not be afraid to see Him in all his glory.

"'These signs will accompany those who believe,'" Hanny read. "'In my name they will drive out demons; they will speak in new tongues; they will pick up snakes with their hands; they will place their hands on sick people, and they will get well.'"

As Hanny spoke, a murmur of excitement ran through the room, and they knew that God was among them. Mummer was sobbing. Farther went over and put his arms around her. Mr and Mrs Belderboss had their heads bowed and were praying quietly, encouraging others to do the same. Miss Bunce and David stared as Hanny read slowly and carefully, but never once faltered on a single word.

Father Bernard glanced over at me. One day I thought I might be able to explain to him, to everyone, what had happened, or have to, but what I would say I didn't know. I would only be able to give them the facts as I remembered them, as I'm writing them now.

I've left this part until last, but it must be set down as well as everything else. When they come asking questions, as they surely will, I'd need to have things straight, no matter the horror.

Doctor Baxter says I ought to worry less about the minutiae of life and look at the bigger picture, but I have no choice and the details are important now. Details are truth. And in any case, I don't care what Baxter says. I saw what he scrawled on my notes. It was only a few words that I glimpsed before he closed the file, but it was enough. *Some improvement, but continues to exhibit childlike worldview. Classic fantasist.* What the hell does he know anyway? He wouldn't understand. He doesn't know what it means to protect someone.

I've walked down those cellar steps again and again for the last thirty years, in bad dreams and small-hours insomnia. I know every footfall, every creak of wood. I can feel the damp plaster under my hand as I did on that foggy afternoon as Clement and I inched down in the dark, holding the wall, holding Hanny.

He had lost consciousness by the time we reached the bottom and we had to drag his full weight to a mattress in the middle of the floor that had been freshly stained around the buttons. He slithered from our grip and fell heavily. Clement knelt down and placed a grubby pillow under his head.

There was a smell of burning. A table by the mattress was covered in a black cloth, and the bunches of mistletoe hanging from the ceiling were turning in the heat from the candles. The air was thick and stagnant and the walls glistened with condensation. Here and there, thin stalactites had formed and roots of weeds sprigged through where the mortar had dissolved. It was nothing more than a cave clad with white bricks. It was the place Elizabeth Percy had taken all those sea-weary sailors to be bludgeoned and eaten.

By the mattress was a heap of dirty towels and an enamel bowl of instruments coated in blood that had turned dark and resinous: a scalpel, scissors, a pair of forceps. Else had given birth down here. The child had never seen the daylight.

At the end of the room was a wicker basket, which shook as the baby kicked and screamed itself hoarse. Clement put his hands over his ears. In the low room, the noise was terrible. Parkinson and Collier stood against the wall. The dog lay with its chin on its paws, its frightened eyes looking up for some comfort. It whimpered once and was silent.

Under the screaming there was another sound, a soft thudding coming from somewhere, something like thunder heard from a distance. It rolled and scattered and returned. And I realised that it was the sea pounding the rocks under Thessaly.

"You can go back upstairs now," Leonard said to me as he went over to the basket and took out the baby which was wrapped in a white sheet.

"No," I said. "I want to be with Hanny."

I bent down and squeezed Hanny's hand, but he couldn't open his eyes. He had been sick down his new white shirt. His whole body was shaking as his leg seeped blood. He was dying moment by moment.

"Clement," said Leonard.

Clement put his hand gently on my shoulder.

"Come on," he said. "Tha'd better do as they say. There's nothing tha can do for him now."

"I want to stay."

"Nay," said Clement, his voice almost at a whisper now. "Tha doesn't. Believe me."

I knew Clement was right and that I had to go with him, but I didn't want to leave Hanny alone with them.

Leonard came past me with the bundle. The baby was still screaming in a ferocious way, terrified and violent, like a trapped animal. It was so strong that Leonard had to hold it close to his chest.

"Go on," said Leonard, raising his voice. "You can't stay."

I felt myself being pulled out of the room as Clement dragged me up the stairs and out into the hallway where he stood against the door so that I couldn't go back down.

"They'll tell you when it's been done," he said.

"When what's been done?"

"When he's better."

"What will they do to him?"

"Them?" said Clement. "*They* don't do anything."

"I don't understand."

Clement looked at me in a way that suggested he didn't either.

How long I waited there, I don't know. An hour, two maybe. The fog pressed close to the house and the hallway was filled with a pallid light. All the while Clement stood with his back to the door, eyeing me nervously, until finally we heard Leonard calling us down.

Clement stood aside as I went down the steps two at a time into the darkness. The main bulb had been turned off and the cellar was lit only by the candles placed around the rim of a chalk circle that had been drawn on the floor. Leonard, Parkinson and Collier were standing inside the circle. Collier's dog lay by his feet shivering.

Outside the ring, Hanny was lying on the mattress, the baby next to him. Both of them were motionless — Hanny curled up with his hands around his knees as he had been when I left him, the baby half wrapped in a sheet.

The swaddling clothes had come apart, and although Leonard quickly stepped out of the ring to draw the sheets back over the child, he wasn't quick enough. I saw the baby's blind grey eyes. Its shrivelled yellow face. The grotesque swellings on its neck. The mangled claw of a hand.

I say baby. I'm not sure that it was human.

Leonard knelt down by Hanny and shook him gently by the shoulder. Hanny woke blearily. He rubbed his face with the backs of his hands and sat up. After a moment he seemed to recognise me, though his eyes were still half closed and drooping, and Leonard helped him to his feet. The bleeding had stopped and he came to me without a limp.

"Now what dost tha think?" said Parkinson from the gloom beyond the candlelight.

I felt Hanny put his hand into mine. It was warm and heavy.

Parkinson laughed quietly to himself. Seeing my expression of disbelief, Collier laughed too. The dog barked once and shook its collar.

Still the baby didn't stir. It lay there with its eyes half open staring at the ceiling.

The sea thumped against the rocks and faded and returned but more faintly now than it had been before.

"The tide's going out," said Leonard.

"The sands will be clear by two," said Parkinson.

"The fog won't lift though," said Collier.

"No?" said Leonard.

"It's cold as you like out there," said Collier. "Especially with all t'flood water. Frets will sit well inland all afternoon."

"Good," said Leonard. "Then there should be fewer people on the roads."

He looked past me at Clement, who had come down the steps without me noticing.

"Is everything ready?" he said.

"Aye," replied Clement.

"Well then," said Leonard. "I think we ought to conclude our business here."

"Gladly," said Parkinson and he took a candle to the end of the room, returning with the palm leaves Mummer had used on Easter Sunday. He had evidently stolen them from the kitchen when he'd come to Moorings with the Pace Eggers.

Setting the candle down, he pushed the leaves into his fist and offered the first draw to Leonard.

"Oh no," said Leonard with a quiet laugh. "You know full well I was never part of the disposal, Parkinson. We agreed that from the start."

Parkinson looked at him and then moved on to Collier, who took a leaf and glanced sidelong at Clement.

"Go on," said Parkinson.

Clement shook his head and Parkinson smiled and drew one for him anyway, placing it into his hand and closing his fingers around it.

Clement began to cry, and I was so taken aback to hear him sobbing like a child that I didn't realise that Hanny and I had been given a leaf each until Parkinson was ready to draw the lot.

"Let's see then," he said and everyone showed their leaves.

Parkinson smiled and Collier let out a breath of relief.

"The best result eh, Parkinson?" said Leonard.

"Aye," he said, grinning at me. "Couldn't've been better."

Clement sniffed and wiped his nose on his arm.

"You can't do this," he said, holding Hanny by the shoulder. "He's only a lad."

"Nay," said Parkinson, holding out the rifle for Hanny to hold. "Fair's fair. He drewt shortest straw."

"Come on," said Clement. "Tha knows tha tricked him."

"You sawt straws, Clement. There was nowt amiss."

Still dazed, Hanny took the rifle and looked at it curiously before he slipped his hand around the small of the butt and placed his finger lightly on the trigger.

"Draw it again then," said Clement, turning to Leonard, thinking that out of the three of them he might have some pity.

"Fuck that," said Collier anxiously. "It's been done. It's not right to do it again."

"Don't worry," said Parkinson, reaching into his jacket and taking out one of his butcher's knives — a cleaver that looked as though it could split a pig in one blow. "The lad's not going anywhere until everything's been cleared away."

"Leave him alone," said Clement. "Look at him. He's still out of it. He dunt understand what tha wants him to do."

"Oh, he will," said Parkinson.

Clement swallowed hard and after hesitating for a moment, he took the rifle out of Hanny's hands.

"Go home," he said. "Go on."

Collier looked at Parkinson again. Parkinson dismissed his worries with a little shake of his head and put the knife away.

"Such nobility, Clement," he said. "I never knew tha had it in thee."

"It can be something of a false victory, though, nobility," said Leonard, who came out of the gloom wiping his brow with a handkerchief. "Wouldn't you say?"

He slowly folded the handkerchief and put it back in his pocket as he looked down at the baby on the mattress.

"I mean it might seem as though Clement's relieved your brother of an awful task, but I'm afraid it doesn't really matter who drew the short straw. And I'd hate you to think that his graciousness has somehow taken the pair of you out of the equation. You're down here with us like it or not. We could lay the blame at your door whenever we wanted to. But I think you know that."

"And they wouldn't like prison much, would they, Clement?" said Parkinson.

Clement looked down at his feet and Leonard went over to him and held him by the shoulder.

"No one's going to prison," he said, looking from one person to the next. "Not if everything that's happened here is buried away for good. Right, Clement?"

Clement looked at Leonard and then extracted himself from his hand and took Hanny and I by the arms towards the stairs.

"Don't listen to them," he said. "None of this has owt to do with you. You don't belong down here."

He gave Hanny and me a shove.

"Go on," he said, fretful that we were taking so long to leave. "You'll be able to cross now. Go home."

He nodded up the stairs and then went back over to Leonard who was waiting for him by the mattress. Leonard clapped him on the shoulder and Parkinson gripped him playfully round the back of the head.

"Don't worry, Clement," he said. "Dog'll eat whatever's left."

Clement closed his eyes and began to pray and his voice followed us up the stairs as he begged God for mercy and forgiveness.

But there was no one listening.

CHAPTER
TWENTY-NINE

Coldbarrow is still all over the television.

I saw yesterday morning that they had erected a tent on the sands close to where I almost drowned all those years ago. They were working quickly to collect as much forensic evidence as possible before the tide turned, though there can't have been much left. Not now.

The reporter was standing on the mainland, shouting over the driving gales and sleet. The police had now launched a murder inquiry, he said. Two elderly local men had been taken in for questioning, and they were searching for a third.

Things were gathering apace. But I was prepared. All those evenings I'd spent writing everything down hadn't been wasted. Everything was clear now. Everything was straight. Hanny was safe. It didn't matter what anyone said to the contrary. Leonard, Parkinson and Collier wouldn't have had the wit to plan as I had. They had been too reliant on each other's silence and hadn't reckoned on the Loney revealing everything they'd done.

I waited for as long as I possibly could before I had to leave for work, with one eye on the news and the other on the weather outside. A blizzard had been raging since the dark of the early morning and the street outside was becoming lost under heavy drifts of snow. It was starting to come light but only just. A grey colour spilled across the sky, pale as dishwater.

Walking down to the station I outpaced the cars that were waiting to get onto the North Circular in a long line of exhaust fumes and brake lights. People stood huddled at bus stops or in shop doorways which were still shuttered and dark. Even the Christmas lights they had strewn along the high street were out. The city was grinding to a standstill, it seemed, and the crib outside the church on the corner was the only thing of brightness.

They set it up every year — a kind of garden shed crammed with life-sized shepherds and wise men and Mary and Joseph kneeling before the plump little Christ in the hay. Music plays on a loop all day and night, and as I paused to cross the road, I caught the tinny trickle of "Joy to the World" before the lights changed.

The tube was packed, of course. Everyone steamed and sneezed. Coldbarrow was headline news on most of the papers. Each had the same syndicated photograph of Thessaly tumbled to ruins on the beach. Some had grainy images of people in white boiler suits stooped over the rubble. I wondered how long it would be before I saw Parkinson or Collier or even Clement blazoned across the front page. They would be in their seventies now, perhaps their eighties. About to be jolted out of the complacency of old age.

At the museum, I let myself in through the back door. It was so quiet that I wondered if there was

374

anyone else there, but going through the staff kitchen there were a few others standing around in their coats drinking tea, in a kind of holiday mood, thinking that it was very likely the museum would be closed for the day. And they were probably right. I mean, who was going to risk life and limb or a bout of the flu to come and see an exhibition of pewter or Edwardian millinery?

"Hey, I wouldn't get settled," said Helen jovially, as I gave them all a cursory good-morning nod and headed to the basement.

I know they think me rather odd and talk about me when I'm not there. But I don't really care. I know who I am and I've worked out all my failings by myself a long time ago. If they think I'm fastidious or reclusive then they'd be right. I am. And so where do we go from there? You've worked me out. Well done. Have a prize.

Helen gave me a frowned smile as I undid the security grille. She looked as though she was going to come over and speak to me but she didn't, and I pulled the shutters aside and went down the stairs, unlocking the door at the bottom that, once closed behind me, meant that no one was likely to bother me for the rest of the day. There is a phone but if I get any correspondence it's through email. They understand that I need quiet to work. They've learnt that much about me at least.

A waft of warm air met me. It's always warm in the basement. A dry heat to stop the damp getting to the books. It can be a bit oppressive in the summer but that morning I was more than thankful for it.

I switched on the strip lights and they pinked and flickered and lit up the long rows of bookshelves and cabinets. The homes of many old friends. Ones I've got to know intimately over the last two decades.

When I have a moment, which is becoming rarer these days, I like to visit Vertot's *History of the Knights of Malta* or Barrett's *Theorike and Practike of Moderne Warres*. There's no better way to spend an hour or two once the museum has closed than reading these volumes as they were written — in quiet reflection and study. Any other way is worthless. Having them spread open in a display case upstairs for people to glance at in passing is an insult if you ask me.

I generally work at the far end of the basement where there's a computer I use for research and a wide desk where I can keep all the bookbinding equipment and still have plenty of elbow room.

I don't know why I felt the urge to do it, and it makes me feel like someone out of a Dickens novel, one of Scrooge's clerks perhaps, but a while ago I moved the desk under one of those glass grids they have at street level where I could look up and watch the shadows of feet going past. I suppose there was something comforting about it. I was down there warm and dry and they were out in the rain with people and places to hurry to and be late for.

But today the glass was opaque with snow, making the basement even gloomier. The strip lights don't do much apart from create shadows, if I'm honest, and so I switched on the anglepoise lamp and sat down.

For the past few weeks, I had been working on a set of Victorian wildlife books that had been donated from the sale of some laird's estate up in Scotland.

Encyclopaedias of flora and fauna. Manuals of veterinary science. Copious volumes about badgers and foxes and eagles and other reprehensible predators. Their habits and breeding patterns and the many ways to cull them. They were in a reasonable condition, given that they had been languishing in a gillie's hut for years, but the leather covers would have to be replaced and the pages re-sewn if anyone was ever going to read them again. Someone would. There was always someone who would find such things fascinating. Academics might take pains to go through all the details, but what was of interest to the museum, the bit of social history they could sell to the public, was the handwritten marginalia. The little insights of the anonymous game-keeper who had stalked the moors of the estate and kept his master's animals safe for nigh on fifty years.

Notes about the weather and nesting sites were strewn around the sketches he had made of the things he had had to kill in order to protect the deer and the grouse. A fox caught in a snare. An osprey spread-eagled by shotgun pellets. They seemed at first glance, gruesome, boastful things, no better than hanging trophy heads along a hallway, or rats along a fence, but the detail of feathers and fur and eyes that he had taken time to render with his fine pencil made it clear that he loved them dearly.

It was, to him, no different to pruning a garden, I suppose. The gillie hadn't hated these animals for following their instincts of survival any more than a gardener hates his plants for growing. It was a necessary mastery that he exercised over the estate. Without him, there would have been nothing but chaos, and I suspect that it's reverted back to wilderness now that there's no one looking after it any more.

I worked for an hour or more until I heard the doors at the other end of the basement opening. I put my glasses down on the desk (I have become short-sighted in recent years) and looked around the shelves. Helen appeared, her coat over her arm.

"Are you there?" she called, making a visor with her mittened hand and peering through the shadows.

I got up from the desk.

"Yes? What is it?"

"Good news. We can go home," she said.

"Home?"

"They're going to close the museum because of the snow."

"I've got work to finish off."

"You don't have to do it," said Helen. "Everyone else is leaving."

"All the same. I'd like to get it done."

"It's really coming down out there," she said. "I'd get going if I were you. Otherwise you might be stuck here all night. If you need a lift, I can take you as far as Paddington."

She had come further towards me now and stood at the end of the 990s: *history of New Zealand* to *extraterrestrial worlds*.

"I don't mind," she said.

"It's out of your way," I replied.

"It doesn't have to be."

I looked back at the book on the desk.

"I've too much to do to go home," I said. "Haven't you?"

She looked at me, gave me that frown-smile again and zipped up her coat.

"I'll see you on Monday," she said and went back towards the door. The basement became silent again apart from the steady tick of the central heating.

I returned to the book and gently removed the stitching from the spine of McKay's *Prevention of Galliforme Diseases* with a pair of tweezers before dropping the brittle strands of thread into the bin. No, it was better that I stayed here. It wasn't fair to ask Helen to drive a mile out of her way in this weather. And they would only start gossiping again if they saw us together in her car.

I didn't stop working until hours later. It was three in the afternoon. I hadn't eaten any lunch, but I wasn't hungry, and I often lose track of time down there in the basement anyway, separated as I am from the world of scurrying feet above. A day could sometimes easily pass without me once looking up from what I was doing.

I switched on the kettle to make tea and as it boiled I looked up at the glass panel. It glowed with a buttery light and I wondered if it had stopped snowing at last and the sun had come out. Whatever, it would be going dark before long.

I sat back down at the desk but hadn't taken a sip before there was someone knocking at the door. It wasn't Helen come back to rescue me, I knew that. She had keys. Most likely it was Jim, the caretaker, who I'd fought tooth and nail to keep out of the basement with his anti-bacterial sprays and his polish and his propensity for throwing things away. He'd always been a little abrupt with me since I'd had his key off him, and rattled the ones he had left in a plaintive way, it seemed, as though without the full set he felt somehow emasculated.

Don't get me wrong. I don't dislike him. I'd just rather it was me who kept the place clean and tidy. Jim doesn't really get the idea of an archive, keeping things. I quite admire him in many ways and had half-expected him to have stuck around that afternoon. He's a stubborn old sod like me and wouldn't have gone home just because it was snowing.

I put the cup down and went to open the door. Jim stood there — brown overcoat and navy tattoos — his mace-head of keys hanging from his belt.

"Yes?"

"Visitor for you," he said, stepping aside.

"Hanny?" I tried to sound surprised, but I knew with all this business at Coldbarrow that he would come to see me sooner or later.

"Hello, brother," he said as he sidled past Jim and shook my hand.

"I'm locking up at four," said Jim pointedly and wandered off up the stairs, jangling his keys.

"What are you doing here?" I said and gestured for Hanny to go down to my desk as I closed the door. He was damp with snow and his scarf was caked in ice.

"I rang the flat, but there was no answer," he said. "I must admit I thought you'd be at home today."

"I've too much to do," I replied.

"You work too hard."

"Pot. Kettle."

"Well, you do."

"Is there any other way to work?"

He laughed. "No, I suppose not, brother."

"Tea?"

"If you're having one."

I made Hanny a cup as he draped his wet things over the radiator.

"Don't you get lonely down here, brother?" he said, looking up at the glass panel.

"Not at all."

"But you do work alone?"

"Oh yes."

"You said that with some conviction."

"Well, there was someone else once."

"What happened to them?"

"She wasn't quite suited."

"To what?"

"To detail."

"I see."

"It's important, Hanny."

"It must be."

"It's not easy staying focused all day," I said. "It takes a particular type of mind."

"Like yours."

"Evidently."

Hanny took the cup of tea off me and pressed the back of his thighs against the radiator. He looked up at me, went to say something, but stopped short and changed tack.

"How are things going with Doctor Baxter?" he asked.

"Baxter? All right, I suppose."

"He said you were making progress last time I spoke to him."

"I thought our sessions were meant to be confidential."

"They are, you fool," said Hanny dismissively "He didn't give me any details. He just said you'd turned a corner."

"That's what he seems to think."

"And have you?"

"I don't know."

"You seem happier."

"Do I?"

"Less anxious."

"You can tell that about me in just a few minutes?"

"I do *know* you, brother. I can see it, even if you can't."

"Am I that transparent?"

"I didn't mean that. I meant that it's hard to perceive things about yourself sometimes."

"Such as?"

"Well, I can see that Baxter's making a difference. And that our prayers are too."

"Oh yes, how are things at the church?" I said.

"Couldn't be better," he replied.

"Still packing them in every Sunday?"

"Sunday, Monday, Tuesday . . . We've been very blessed, brother. We light a candle for you every day."

"That's good of you."

Hanny laughed quietly. "God loves you, brother," he said. "Even if you don't believe in Him, He believes in you. It will end. This sickness will leave you. He will take it away."

Perhaps it was the light down there, but he looked old suddenly. His black hair was still thick enough to have been tousled into a nest by his woollen hat, but his eyes were starting to sink into the soft cushions of the sockets and there were liver spots on the backs of his hands. My brother was slowly slipping towards pension age and I was following like his shadow.

He embraced me and I felt his hand on my back. We sat down at the desk and finished the tea in silence.

Having circled around what concerned him and run dry of small talk, he looked troubled now, frightened even.

"What is it, Hanny?" I said. "I'm sure you didn't come all this way to ask me about Doctor Baxter."

He breathed out slowly and ran his hand over his face.

"No, brother, I didn't."

"What then?"

"You've heard the news about Coldbarrow, I take it?" he said.

"I could hardly have missed it, could I?"

"But have you heard what they're saying now?"

"What's that?"

"That this poor child was shot."

"It was on the news this morning, yes."

"And they reckon it was some time ago. Thirty or forty years. Back in the seventies."

"Yes?"

"When we were there."

"So?"

His hands were trembling slightly as he brought them to his face again.

"I've been having this memory," he said. "They sometimes come back to me out of the blue but I don't always know what they mean."

"Memories about the pilgrimage?"

"I suppose they must be."

"Like what?"

"A beach. A girl. An old house with ravens."

"Rooks. That was Moorings."

"Moorings, yes that's right. And I vaguely recall going to the shrine, but that might just have been Mummer putting things into my head. She was always talking about it, wasn't she?"

"Yes."

It was all she talked about.

"And there are other things, brother, things that are just feelings or images. A door. A tower. Being trapped and frightened. And . . ."

"And what, Hanny?"

He looked at me, blinked back a few tears.

"Well, this is it. This is the memory I've been having since I saw Coldbarrow on the news."

"A memory of what?"

"A noise close and loud. And something thumping against my shoulder."

He looked at me.

"Like a gunshot, brother. Like I'd fired a gun."

"What are you saying, Hanny? That you think you did it? That you killed this child?"

"I don't know."

"Why would you? It makes no sense."

"I know it doesn't."

"It's a trick of the mind, Hanny," I said. "We were always playing soldiers on the beach. That's what you're remembering."

"But it seems so real."

"Well it isn't. It can't be."

His head sagged.

"What happened to me, brother? I've prayed so many times for Him to show me, but there's nothing but shadows."

"You were healed by God. Isn't that what you believe?"

"Yes, but . . ."

"Isn't that what everyone believes?"

"Of course . . ."

"Isn't that what brings them to the church every day, Hanny?"

"No, no," he said, raising his voice a little. "Something else happened that Easter."

"What?"

He breathed out and sat back in the chair, nervously thumbing his bottom lip.

"I've never really talked about it, brother, not even with Caroline, and I suppose I've tried to push it down inside me, but if I ever think about the pilgrimage, there's always something else there in the background."

"Something else?"

"Behind all the euphoria."

"What?"

"A terrible guilt, brother."

I shook my head and touched him on the shoulder.

"I feel as though I'm going to drown in it sometimes," he said and his eyes glistened again.

"It's not real, Hanny."

"But why would I feel like that, brother, unless I'd done something wrong?"

"I don't know. Perhaps you don't feel as though you deserved to be cured. I understand it's quite common in people who have been saved or rescued from something. Don't they call it survivor guilt?"

"Maybe."

"Look, I may not believe in what you believe, Hanny, and perhaps that's my loss, but wherever it's come from, even I can see that you've not wasted the opportunity you've been given. You're important to people. You've brought so much happiness into their lives. Mummer, Farther. Everyone at the church. If anyone deserved to be released from the prison they were in, it was you, Hanny. Don't throw all that away now. You're a good man."

"If only Mummer and Farther were still around."

"I know."

"I just wish I could remember more," he said.

"You don't need to. I can remember everything as it was. I'll speak for you if the police come."

"Will you?"

"Of course."

"I'm sorry to have to rely on you, brother, but I just can't remember anything clearly."

"Do you trust me?"

"Yes, yes of course I do."

"Then you needn't be troubled any more."

He wept now and I put my arms around him.

"Those nights I spent outside the house," I said. "I didn't mean to scare you or worry you. I just wanted you to know that I was there."

"I'm sorry."

"I'm not ill."

"No, no, I know that now."

Jim knocked on the door again. I heard him coughing and rattling his keys.

"We'd better go," I said.

"Yes, all right."

"Once Jim sets his mind on something there's no getting around it."

He looked me square in the eyes. "Thank you, brother."

"What for?"

"Watching over me."

"That's all I've ever wanted to do, Hanny."

"I'm sorry that I didn't let you."

"It doesn't matter now," I said.

Jim let us out and then closed the main doors behind us.

"Did you come in the car?" I asked as we wound scarves and fitted gloves at the top of the steps.

"No, I couldn't face the traffic. I got the tube."

"I'll come with you some of the way then."

Hanny looked at me.

"Why not stay on and come back to the house?" he said.

"Are you sure?"

"Yes," he said. "I'm sure."

"What about Caroline?"

"I'll talk to her. She'll understand."

It had stopped snowing and had gone dark. The sky was clear and full of hard stars. Everything had been whitened and thickened and there was a crust of ice over the drifts. Road signs were buried and street edges dissolved. Hanny went down the steps and hesitated at the bottom.

"I think I've lost my bearings, brother," he said, looking back up at me with a smile.

"This way," I said and took his arm and led him along the road to the station.

We sat opposite one another on the tube, my faint reflection hanging next to his face. We couldn't have looked more different (I have become a little gaunt around the cheeks these last few years, a little thin on top) but we were brothers nonetheless. Bonded by the business of security and survival.

Like Father Bernard said, there are only versions of the truth. And it's the strong, the better strategists who manage them.

Who were the police going to believe fired the rifle? Hanny? Pastor Smith? The dumb boy healed by God? My gentle, middle-aged brother sitting across from me, swaying with the rhythm of the train?

No, they would believe what I would tell them. That we were nowhere near Thessaly when it happened. That we were running back across to the mainland, stumbling through the water channels in the fog, when a single gunshot echoed around the Loney, and was lost in the silence of the sands.